# THE FOURTH DEADLY SIN

# THE
# FOURTH
# DEADLY SIN

*Lawrence Sanders*

G. P. PUTNAM'S SONS/NEW YORK

G. P. Putnam's Sons
*Publishers Since 1838*
200 Madison Avenue
New York, NY 10016

# THE FOURTH DEADLY SIN

# 1.

The November sky over Manhattan was chain mail, raveling into steely rain. A black night with coughs of thunder, lightning stabs that made abrupt days. Dr. Simon Ellerbee, standing at his office window, peered out to look at life on the street below. He saw only the reflection of his own haunted face.

He could not have said how it started, or why. He, who had always been so certain, now buffeted and trembling . . .

All hearts have dark corners, where the death of a loved one is occasionally wished, laughter offends, and even beauty becomes a rebuke.

He turned back to his desk. It was strewn with files and tape cassettes: records of his analysands. He stared at that litter of fears, angers, passions, dreads. Now his own life belonged there, part of the untidiness, where once it had been ordered and serene.

He stalked about, hands thrust deep into pockets, head bowed. He pondered his predicament and dwindling choices. Mordant thought: How does one seek "professional help" when one is a professional?

The soul longs for purity, but we are all hungry for the spiced and exotic. Evil is just a word, and what no one sees, no one knows. Unless God truly is a busybody.

He lay full-length on the couch some of his patients insisted on using, though he thought this classic prop of psychiatry was flimflam and often counterproductive. But there he was, stretched out tautly, trying to still his churning thoughts and succeeding no better than all the agitated who had occupied that same procrustean bed.

Groaning, he rose from the couch to resume his pacing. He paused again to stare through the front window. He saw only a rain-whipped darkness.

The problem, he decided, was learning to acknowledge uncertainty. He, the most rational of men, must adjust to the variableness of a world in which nothing is sure, and the chuckles belong to chance and accident. There could be satisfaction in living with that—fumbling toward a dimly glimpsed end. For if that isn't art, what is?

The downstairs bell rang three times—the agreed-upon signal for all late-night visitors. He started, then hurried into the receptionist's office to press the buzzer unlocking the entrance from the street. He then unchained and unbolted the door leading from the office suite to the corridor.

He ducked into the bathroom to look in the mirror, adjust his tie, smooth his sandy hair with damp palms. He came back to stand before the outer door and greet his guest with a smile.

But when the door opened, and he saw who it was, he made a thick, strangled sound deep in his throat. His hands flew to cover his face and hide his dismay. He turned away, shoulders slumping.

The first heavy blow landed high on the crown of his head. It sent him stumbling forward, knees buckling. A second blow put him down, biting at the thick pile carpeting.

The weapon continued to rise and fall, crushing his skull. But by that time Dr. Simon Ellerbee was dead, all dreams gone, doubts fled, all questions answered.

# 2.

By Monday morning the sky had been rinsed; a casaba sun loomed; and pedestrians strode with opened coats flapping. A chill breeze nipped, but New York had the lift of early winter, with stores preparing for Christmas, and street vendors hawking hot pretzels and roasted chestnuts.

Former Chief of Detectives Edward X. Delaney sensed the acceleration. The city, *his* city, was moving faster, tempo changing from andante to con anima. The scent of money was in the air. It was the spending season—and if the boosters didn't make it in the next six weeks, they never would.

He lumbered down Second Avenue, heavy overcoat hanging from his machine-gunner's shoulders. Hard homburg set solidly, squarely, atop his head. Big, flat feet encased in ankle-high shoes of black kangaroo leather. A serious man who looked more like a monsignor than an ex-cop. Except that cops are never ex-.

The sharp weather delighted him, and so did all the food shops opening so rapidly in Manhattan. Every day seemed to bring a new Korean greengrocer, a French patisserie, a Japanese take-out. And good stuff, too—delicate mushrooms, tangy fruits, spicy meats.

And the breads! That's what Edward X. Delaney appreciated most. He suffered, as his wife, Monica, said, from "sandwich senility," and this sudden bonanza of freshly baked breads was a challenge to his inventiveness.

Pita, brioche, muffins, light challah and heavy pumpernickel. Loaves no larger than your fist, and loaves of coarse German rye as big as a five-inch shell. Flaky stuff that dissolved on the tongue, and some grainy doughs that hit the stomach with a thud.

He stopped in a half-dozen shops, buying this and that, filling his net shopping bag. Then, fearful of his wife's reaction to his spree, he trundled his way homeward. He had a vision of something new: smoked chub tucked into a split croissant—with maybe a thin slice of Vidalia onion and a dab of mayonnaise, for fun.

This hunched, ponderous man, weighty shoes thumping the pavement, seemed to look at nothing, but saw everything. As he passed the 251st Precinct house—*his* old precinct—and came to his brownstone, he noted the unmarked black Buick illegally parked in front. Two uniformed cops in the front seat. They glanced at him without interest.

Monica was perched on a stool at the kitchen counter, going through her recipe file.

"You have a visitor," she said.

"Ivar," he said. "I saw his car. Where'd you put him?"

"In the study. I offered a drink or coffee, but he didn't want anything. Said he'd wait for you."

"He might have called first," Delaney grumbled, hoisting his shopping bag onto the counter.

"What's all that stuff?" she demanded.

"Odds and ends. Little things."

She leaned forward to sniff. "Phew! What's that smell?"

"Maybe the blood sausage."

"Blood sausage? Yuck!"

"Don't knock it unless you've tried it."

He bent to kiss the back of her neck. "Put this stuff away, will you, hon? I'll go in and see what Ivar wants."

"How do you know he wants anything?"

"He didn't come by just to say hello—that I know."

He hung his hat and coat in the hall closet, then went through the living room to the study at the rear of the house. He opened and closed the door quietly, and for a moment thought that First Deputy Commissioner Ivar Thorsen might be dozing.

"Ivar," Delaney said loudly, "good to see you."

The Deputy—known in the Department as the "Admiral"—opened his eyes and rose from the club chair alongside the desk. He smiled wanly and held out his hand.

"Edward," he said, "you're looking well."

"I wish I could say the same about you," Delaney said, eyeing the other man critically. "You look like something the cat dragged in."

"I suppose," Thorsen said, sighing. "You know what it's like downtown, and I haven't been sleeping all that much lately."

"Take a glass of stout or port before you go to bed. Best thing in the
world for insomnia. And speaking of the old nasty—it's past noon, and
you could use some plasma."

"Thank you, Edward," Thorsen said gratefully. "A small scotch
would do me fine."

Delaney brought two glasses and a bottle of Glenfiddich from the
cellarette. He sat in the swivel chair behind his desk and poured them
both tots of the single malt. They tinked glass rims and sipped.

"Ahh," the Admiral said, settling into his armchair. "I could get
hooked on this."

He was a neat, precise man. Fine, silvery hair was brushed sideways.
Ice-blue eyes pierced the world from under white brows. Ordinarily he
had a baby's complexion and a sharp nose and jaw that could have been
snipped from sheet metal. But now there were stress lines, sags,
pouches.

"Monica had lunch with Karen the other day," Delaney mentioned.
"Said she's looking fine."

"What?" Thorsen said, looking up distractedly.

"Karen," Delaney said gently. "Your wife."

"Oh . . . yes," Thorsen said with a confused laugh. "I'm sorry; I
wasn't listening."

Delaney leaned toward his guest, concerned. "Ivar, is everything all
right?"

"Between Karen and me? Couldn't be better. Downtown? Couldn't
be worse."

"More political bullshit?"

"Yes. But this time it's not from the Mayor's office; it's the Department's own bullshit. Want to hear about it?"

Delaney really didn't want to. Political infight in the upper echelons
of the New York Police Department was the reason he had filed for
early retirement. He could cope with thieves and killers; he wasn't interested in threading the Byzantine maze of Departmental cliques and
cabals. All those intrigues. All those naked ambitions and steamy hatreds.

In the lower, civil service ranks of sergeant, lieutenant, captain, he
had known the stress of political pressure—from inside and outside the
Department. He had been able to live with it, rejecting it when he
could, compromising when he had to.

But nothing had prepared him for the hardball games they played in the appointive ranks. When he got his oak leaves as a Deputy Inspector, he was thrown into a cockpit where the competition was fierce, a single, minor misstep could mean the end of a twenty-year career, and combatants swigged Maalox like fine Beaujolais.

And as he went up the ladder to the two stars of an Assistant Chief, the tension increased with the responsibility. You not only had to do your work, and do it superbly well, but you had constantly to look over your shoulder to see who stood close behind you with a knife and a smirk.

Then he had the three stars of Chief of Detectives, and wanted only to be left alone to do the job he knew he could do. But he was forced to spend too much time soothing his nervous superiors and civilian politicos with enough clout to make life miserable for him if he didn't find out who mugged their nephew.

He couldn't take that kind of constraint, and so Edward X. Delaney turned in his badge. The fault, he acknowledged later, was probably his. He was mentally and emotionally incapable of "going along." He had a hair-trigger temper, a strong sense of his own dignity, and absolute faith in his detective talents and methods of working a case.

He couldn't change himself, and he couldn't change the Department. So he got out before the ulcers popped up, and tried to keep busy, tried to forget what might have been. But still . . .

"Sure, Ivar," he said with a set smile, "I'd like to hear about it."

Thorsen took a sip of his scotch. "You know Chief of Detectives Murphy?"

"Bill Murphy? Of course I know him. We came through the Academy together. Good man. A little plodding maybe, but he thinks straight."

"He's put in his papers. As of the first of the year. He's got cancer of the prostate."

"Ahh, Jesus," Delaney said. "That's a crying shame. I'll have to go see him."

"Well . . ." the Admiral said, peering down at his drink, "Bill thought he could last until the first of the year, but I don't think he's going to make it. He's been out so much we've had to put in an Acting Chief of Detectives to keep the bureau running. The Commish says he'll appoint a permanent late in December."

"Who's the Acting Chief?" Delaney asked, beginning to get interested.

Thorsen looked up at him. "Edward, you remember when they used to say that in New York, the Irish had the cops, the Jews had the schools, and the Italians had the Sanitation Department? Well, things have changed—but not all that much. There's still an Old Guard of the Irish in the Department, and they take care of their own. They just refuse to accept the demographic changes that have taken place in this city—the numbers of blacks, Hispanics, Orientals. When it came to getting the PC to appoint an Acting Chief of Detectives, I wanted a two-star named Michael Ramon Suarez, figuring it would help community relations. Suarez is a Puerto Rican, and he's been running five precincts in the Bronx and doing a hell of a job. The Chief of Operations, Jimmy Conklin, wanted the Commissioner to pick Terence J. Riordan, who's got nine Brooklyn precincts. So we had quite a tussle."

"I can imagine," Delaney said, pouring them more whiskey. "Who won?"

"I did," Thorsen said. "I got Suarez in as Acting Chief. I figured he'd do a good job, and when the time came, the PC would give him his third star and appoint him permanent Chief of Detectives. A big boost for the Hispanics. And the Mayor would love it."

"Ivar, you should have gone into politics."

"I did," Thorsen said with a crooked grin.

"So? You didn't stop by just to tell me how you creamed the Irish. What's the problem?"

"Edward, did you read the papers over the weekend? Or watch local TV? That psychiatrist who got wasted—Dr. Ellerbee?"

Delaney looked at him. "I read about it. Got snuffed in his own office, didn't he? And not too far from here. I figured it was a junkie looking for drugs."

"Sure," Thorsen said, nodding. "That was everyone's guess. God knows it happens often enough. But Ellerbee didn't keep any drugs in his office. And there was no sign of forced entry, either at the street entrance or his office door. I don't know all the details, but it looks like he let someone in he knew and expected."

Delaney leaned forward, staring at the other man. "Ivar, what's this all about—your interest in the Ellerbee homicide? It happens four or five times a day in the Big Apple. I didn't think you got all that concerned about one kill."

Thorsen rose and began to pace nervously about the room. "It isn't just another kill, Edward. It could be big trouble. For many reasons. Ellerbee was a wealthy, educated man who had a lot of friends in what they call 'high places.' He was civic-minded—did free work in clinics, for example. His wife—who's a practicing psychologist, by the way—is one of the most beautiful women I've ever seen, and she's been raising holy hell with us. And to top that, Ellerbee's father is Henry Ellerbee, the guy who built Ellerbee Towers on Fifth Avenue and owns more Manhattan real estate than you and I own socks. He's been screaming his head off to everyone from the Governor on down."

"Yes, I'd say you have a few problems."

"And the clincher," Thorsen went on, still pacing, "the clincher is that this is the first big homicide Acting Chief of Detectives Michael Ramon Suarez has had to handle."

"Oh-ho," Delaney said, leaning back in his swivel chair and swinging gently back and forth. "Now we get down to the nitty-gritty."

"Right," the Admiral said, almost angrily. "The nitty-gritty. If Suarez muffs this one, there is no way on God's green earth he's going to get a third star and permanent appointment."

"And you'll look like a shithead for backing him in the first place."

"Right," Thorsen said again. "He better clear this one fast or he's in the soup, and I'm in there with him."

"All very interesting," Delaney said. "So?"

The Admiral groaned, slumped into the armchair again. "Edward, you're not making this any easier for me."

"Making what easier?" Delaney said innocently.

Then it all came out in a rush.

"I want you to get involved in the Ellerbee case," the First Deputy Commissioner said. "I haven't even thought about how it can be worked; I wanted to discuss it with you first. Edward, you've saved my ass before—at least twice. I know I gave you a lot of bullshit about doing it for the Department, or doing it just to keep active and not becoming a wet-brained retiree. But this time I'm asking you on the basis of our friendship. I'm asking for a favor—one old friend to another."

"You're calling in your chits, Ivar," Delaney said slowly. "I would never have gone as far as I did without your clout. I know that, and you know I know it."

Thorsen made a waving gesture. "Put it any way you like. The bottom line is that I need your help, and I'm asking for it."

Delaney was silent a moment, looking down at his big hands spread on the desk top.

"I'm getting liver spots," he said absently. "Ivar, have you talked to Suarez about this?"

"Yes, I talked to him. He'll cooperate one hundred percent. He's out of his depth on this case and he knows it. He's got some good men, but no one with your experience and know-how. He'll take help anywhere he can get it."

"Is he working the Ellerbee case personally?"

"After the flak started, he got personally involved. He had to. But from what he told me, so far they've got a dead body, and that's all they've got."

"It happened Friday night?"

"Yes. He was killed about nine P.M. Approximately. According to the ME."

"More than forty-eight hours ago," Delaney said reflectively. "And getting colder by the minute. That means the solution probability is going down."

"I know."

"What was the murder weapon?"

"Some kind of a hammer."

"A hammer?" Delaney said, surprised. "Not a knife, not a gun? Someone brought a hammer to his office?"

"Looks like it. And crushed his skull."

"A hammer is usually a man's weapon," Delaney said. "Women prefer knives or poison. But you never know."

"Well, Edward? Will you help us?"

Delaney shifted his heavy bulk uncomfortably. "If I do—and you notice I say *if*—I don't know how it could be done. I don't have a shield. I can't go around questioning people or rousting them. For God's sake, Ivar, I'm a lousy *civilian.*"

"It can be worked out," Thorsen said stubbornly. "The first thing is to persuade you to take the case."

Delaney drew a deep breath, then blew it out. "Tell you what," he said. "Before I give you a yes or no, let me talk to Suarez. If we can't get along, then forget about it. If we hit it off, then I'll consider it. I know that's not the answer you want, but it's all you're going to get at the moment."

"It's good enough for me," the Deputy said promptly. "I'll call Suarez, set up the meet, and get back to you. Thank you, Edward."

"For what?"

"For the scotch," Thorsen said. "What else?"

After the Admiral left, Delaney went back into the kitchen. Monica had gone, but there was a note on the refrigerator door, held in place with a little magnetic pig. "Roast duck with walnuts and cassis for dinner. Be back in two hours. Don't eat too many sandwiches."

He smiled at that. But they usually dined at 7:00 P.M., and it was then barely 1:30. One sandwich was certainly not going to spoil his appetite for roast duck. Or even two sandwiches, for that matter.

But he settled for one—which he called his U.N. Special: Norwegian brisling sardines in Italian olive oil heaped on German schwarzbrot, with a layer of thinly sliced Spanish onion and a dollop of French dressing.

He ate this construction while leaning over the sink so it would be easy to rinse the drippings away. And with the sandwich, to preserve the international flavor, he had a bottle of Canadian Molson ale. Finished, the kitchen restored to neatness, he went down into the basement to find the newspapers of the last two days and read again about the murder of Dr. Simon Ellerbee.

Shortly after midnight, Monica went up to their second-floor bedroom. Delaney made his customary rounds, turning off lights and checking window and door locks. Even those in the empty bedrooms where his children by his first wife, Barbara (now deceased), had slept— rooms later occupied by Monica's two daughters.

Then he returned to the master bedroom. Monica, naked, was seated at the dresser, brushing her thick black hair. Delaney perched on the edge of his bed, finished his cigar, and watched her, smiling with pleasure. They conversed in an intimate shorthand:

"Hear from the girls?" he asked.

"Maybe tomorrow."

"Should we call?"

"Not yet."

"We've got to start thinking about Christmas."

"I'll buy the cards if you'll write the notes."

"You want to shower first?"

"Go ahead."

"Rub my back?"

"Later. Leave me a dry towel."

The only light in the room came from a lamp on the bedside table. The tinted silk shade gave the illumination a rosy glow. Delaney watched the play of light on his wife's strong back as she raised her arms to brush, religiously, one hundred times.

She was a stalwart woman with a no-nonsense body: wide shoulders and hips, heavy bosom, and a respectable waist. Muscular legs tapered to slender ankles. There was a warm solidity about her that Delaney cherished. He reflected, not for the first time, how lucky he had been with women: first Barbara and now Monica—two joys.

She took up her flannel robe and went into the bathroom, pausing to glance over her shoulder and wink at him. When he heard the shower start, he began to undress, slowly. He unlaced his high shoes, peeled off the white cotton socks. He removed the heavy gold chain and hunter from his vest. The chunky chain had been his grandfather's, the pocket watch his father's. It had stopped fifty years ago; Delaney had no desire to have it started again.

Off came the dark suit of cheviot as coarse as an army blanket. White shirt with starched collar. Silk rep tie in a muted purple, like a dusty stained-glass window. He hung everything carefully away, moving about the bedroom in underdrawers as long as Bermuda shorts and balbriggan undershirt with cap sleeves.

Monica called him a mastodon, and he supposed he was. There was a belly now—not big, but it was there. There was a layer of new fat over old muscle. But the legs were still strong enough to run, and the shoulders and arms powerful enough to deal a killing blow.

He had come to an acceptance of age. Not what it did to his mind, for he was convinced that was as sharp as ever. Sharper. Honed by experience and reflection. But the body, undeniably, was going. Still, it was no good remembering when he was a young cop and could scamper up a fire escape, leap an airshaft, or punch out some gorilla who wanted to remake his face.

His face . . . The lines were deeper now, the features ruder—everything beginning to look like it had been hacked from an oak stump with a dull hatchet. But the gray hair, cut *en brosse,* was still thick, and Doc Hagstrom assured him once a year that the ticker was still pumping away sturdily.

Monica came out of the bathroom in her robe, sat again at the dresser, and began to cream her face. He headed for the shower, pausing to touch her shoulder with one finger. Just a touch.

He bathed swiftly, shampooed his stiff hair. Then he put on his pajamas—light cotton flannel, the pants with a drawstring waist, the coat buttoned as precisely as a Norfolk jacket.

When he came out, Monica was already in her bed, sitting up, back propped with pillows. She had taken the bottle of Rémy from the bedside table and poured them each a whack of the cognac in small crystal snifters.

"Bless you," he said.

"You smell nice," she said.

"Nothing but soap."

He turned down the thermostat, opened the window a few inches. Then he got into his own bed, propping himself up as she had done.

"So tell me," she said.

"Tell you what?" he asked, wide-eyed.

"Bastard," she said. "You know very well. What did Ivar Thorsen want?"

He told her. She listened intently.

"Ivar's done a lot for me," he concluded.

"And you've done a lot for him."

"We're friends," he said. "Who keeps score?"

"Diane Ellerbee," she said. "The wife—the widow of the man who was killed—I know her."

"You *know* her?" he said, astonished.

"Well, maybe not know—but I met her. She addressed one of my groups. Her subject was the attraction between young girls and horses."

*"Horses?"*

"Edward, it's not a joke. Young girls *are* attracted to horses. They love to ride and groom them."

"And how did Mrs. Diane Ellerbee explain this?"

*"Dr.* Diane Ellerbee. There was a lot of Freud in it—and other things. I'll dig out my notes if you're interested."

"Not really. What did you think of her?"

"Very intelligent, very eloquent. And possibly the most beautiful woman I've ever seen. Breathtaking."

"That's what Ivar said."

They were silent a few moments, sipping their cognacs, reflecting.

"You're going to do it?" she asked finally.

"Well, as I said, I want to talk to Suarez first. If we can get along, and work out a way I can act like a, uh, consultant, maybe I will. It might be interesting. What do you think?"

She turned onto her side to look at him. "Edward, if it was a poor nobody who got murdered, would Ivar and the Department be going to all this trouble?"

"Probably not," he admitted. "The victim was a white male Wasp. Wealthy, educated, influential. His widow has been raising hell with the

Department, and his father, who has mucho clout, has been raising double-hell. So the Department is calling up all the troops."

"Do you think that's fair?"

"Monica," he said patiently, "suppose a junkie with a snootful of shit is found murdered in an alley. The clunk has a sheet as long as your arm, and he's a prime suspect in muggings, robberies, rapes, and God knows what else. Do you really want the Department to spend valuable man-hours trying to find out who burned him? Come on! They're delighted that garbage like that is off the streets."

"I suppose . . ." she said slowly. "But it just doesn't seem right that the rich and influential get all the attention."

"Go change the world," he said. "It's always been like that, and always will. I know you think everyone is equal. Maybe we all are—in God's eyes and under the law. But it's not as clear-cut as that. Some people try to be good, decent human beings, and some are evil scum. The cops, with limited budgets and limited personnel, recognize that. Is it so unusual or outrageous that they'll spend more time and effort protecting the angels than the devils?"

"I don't know," she said, troubled. "It sounds like elitism to me. Besides, how do you know Dr. Simon Ellerbee was an angel?"

"I don't. But he doesn't sound like a devil, either."

"You're really fascinated by all this, aren't you?"

"Just something to do," he said casually.

"I have a better idea of something to do," she said, fluttering her eyes.

"I'm game," he said, smiling.

# 3.

The small, narrow townhouse on East 84th Street, between York and East End Avenue, was jointly owned by Drs. Diane and Simon Ellerbee. After its purchase in 1976, they had spent more than $100,000 in renovations, stripping the pine paneling of eleven layers of paint, restoring the handsome staircase, and redesigning the interior to provide four useful floor-throughs.

The first level, up three stone steps from the sidewalk, was occupied by the Piedmont Gallery. It exhibited and sold handwoven fabrics, quilts, and primitive American pottery. It was not a profitable enterprise, but was operated almost as a hobby by two prim, elderly ladies who obviously didn't need income from this commercial venture.

The offices of Dr. Diane Ellerbee were on the second floor, and those of Dr. Simon Ellerbee on the third. Both floors had been remodeled to include living quarters. Living room, dining room, and kitchen were on the second; two bedrooms and sitting room on the third. Each floor had two bathrooms.

The professional suites on both floors were almost identical: a small outer office for a receptionist and a large, roomy inner office for the doctor. The offices of Drs. Diane and Simon Ellerbee were connected by intercom.

The fourth and top floor of the townhouse was a private apartment, leased as a pied-à-terre by a West Coast filmmaker who was rarely in residence.

In addition to the townhouse, the Ellerbees owned a country home near Brewster, New York. It was a brick and stucco Tudor on 4.5 wooded acres bisected by a swift-running stream. The main house had two master bedrooms on the ground floor and two guest bedrooms on the second. A three-car garage was attached. In the rear of the house was a tiled patio and heated swimming pool.

Both the Ellerbees were avid gardeners, and their English garden was one of the showplaces of the neighborhood. They employed a married couple, Polish immigrants, who lived out. The husband served as groundsman and did maintenance. The wife worked as housekeeper and, occasionally, cook.

It was the Ellerbees' custom to stay in their East 84th Street townhouse weekdays—and, on rare occasions, on Saturday. They usually left for Brewster on Friday evening and returned to Manhattan on Sunday night. Both spent the entire month of August at their country home.

The Ellerbees owned three cars. Dr. Simon drove a new bottle-green Jaguar XJ6 sedan, Dr. Diane a 1971 silver and black Mercedes-Benz SEL 3.5. Both these cars were customarily garaged in Manhattan. The third vehicle, a Jeep station wagon, was kept at their Brewster home.

On the Friday Dr. Simon Ellerbee was murdered, he told his wife—according to her statement to the police—that he had scheduled an evening patient. He suggested she drive back to Brewster as soon as she was free, and he would follow later. He said he planned to leave by 9:00 P.M. at the latest.

Dr. Diane said she left Manhattan at approximately 6:30 P.M. She described the drive north as "ferocious" because of the 40 mph wind and heavy rain. She arrived at their country home about 8:00 P.M. Because of the storm, she guessed her husband would be delayed, but expected him by 10:30 or 11:00.

By 11:30, she stated she was concerned by his absence and called his office. There was no reply. She called two more times with the same result. Around midnight, she called the Brewster police station, asking if they had any report of a car accident involving a Jaguar XJ6 sedan. They had not.

Becoming increasingly worried, she phoned the Manhattan garage where the Ellerbees kept their cars. After a wait of several minutes, the night attendant reported that Dr. Simon Ellerbee's Jaguar had not been taken out; it was still in its slot.

"I was getting frantic," she later told detectives. "I thought he might have been mugged walking to the garage. It happened once before."

So, at approximately 1:15 A.M., Dr. Diane called Dr. Julius K. Samuelson. He was also a psychiatrist, a widower, and close friend and frequent houseguest of the Ellerbees. Dr. Samuelson was also president of the Greater New York Psychiatric Association. He lived in a cooperative apartment at 79th Street and Madison Avenue.

Samuelson was not awakened by Diane Ellerbee's phone call, having recently returned from a concert by the Stuttgart String Ensemble at Carnegie Hall. When Dr. Diane explained the situation, he immediately agreed to taxi to the Ellerbees' house and try to find Dr. Simon or see if anything was amiss.

Samuelson stated he arrived at the East 84th Street townhouse at about 1:45 A.M. He asked the cabdriver to wait. It was still raining heavily. He stepped from the cab into a streaming gutter, then hurried across the sidewalk and up the three steps to the front entrance. He found the door ajar.

"Not wide open," he told detectives. "Maybe two or three inches."

Samuelson was fifty-six, a short, slender man, but not lacking in physical courage. He tramped determinedly up the dimly lighted, carpeted staircase to the offices of Dr. Simon on the third floor. He found the office door wide open. Within, he found the battered body.

He checked first to make certain that Ellerbee was indeed dead. Then, using the phone on the receptionist's desk, he dialed 911. The call was logged in at 1:54 A.M.

All the above facts were included in New York City newspaper reports and on local TV newscasts following the murder.

# 4.

Delaney planted himself across the street from Acting Chief Suarez's house on East 87th, off Lexington Avenue. He squinted at it, knowing exactly how it was laid out; he had grown up in a building much like that one.

It was a six-story brownstone, with a flight of eight stone steps, called a stoop, leading up to the front entrance. Originally, such a building was an old-law tenement with two railroad flats on each floor, running front to back, with almost every room opening onto a long hallway.

"Cold-water flats," they were sometimes called. Not because there was no hot water; there was if you had a humane landlord. But the covered bathtub was in a corner of the kitchen, and the toilet was out in the hall, serving the two apartments.

Not too many brownstones like that left in Manhattan. They were being demolished for glass and concrete high-rise co-ops or being purchased at horrendous prices in the process called "gentrification," and converted into something that would warrant a six-page, four-color spread in *Architectural Digest.*

Edward X. Delaney wasn't certain that was progress—but it sure as hell was change. And if you were against change, you had to mourn for the dear, departed days when all of Manhattan was a cow pasture. Still, he allowed himself a small pang of nostalgia, remembering his boyhood in a building much like the one across the street.

He saw immediately that the people who lived there were waging a valiant battle against the city's blight. No graffiti. Washed windows and clean curtains. Potted ivy at the top of the stoop (the pots chained to the railing). The plastic garbage cans in the areaway were clean and had lids. All in all, a neat, snug building with an air of modest prosperity.

Delaney lumbered across the street, thinking it was an offbeat home for an Acting Chief of the NYPD. Most of the Department's brass lived in Queens, or maybe Staten Island.

The bell plate was polished and the intercom actually worked. When he pressed the 3-B button alongside the neatly typed name, M.R. SUAREZ, a childish voice piped, "Who is it?"

"Edward X. Delaney here," he said, leaning forward to speak into the little round grille.

There was static, the sound of thumps, then the inner door lock buzzed, and he pushed his way in. He tramped up to the third floor.

The man waiting for him at the opened apartment door was a Don Quixote figure: tall, thin, splintery, with an expression at once shy, deprecatory, rueful.

"Mr. Delaney?" he said, holding out a bony hand. "I am Michael Ramon Suarez."

"Chief," Delaney said. "Happy to make your acquaintance. I appreciate your letting me stop by; I know how busy you must be."

"It is an honor to have you visit my home, sir," Suarez said with formal courtesy. "I hope it is no inconvenience for you. I would have come to you gladly."

Delaney knew that; in fact, Deputy Commissioner Thorsen had suggested it. But Delaney wanted to meet with the Acting Chief in his own home and get an idea of his life outside the Department: as good a way to judge a man as any.

The apartment seemed mobbed with children—five of them ranging in age from three to ten. Delaney was introduced to them all: Michael, Jr., Maria, Joseph, Carlo, and Vita. And when Mrs. Rosa Suarez entered, she was carrying a baby, Thomas, in her arms.

"Your own basketball team," Delaney said, smiling. "With one substitute."

"Rosa wishes to try for a football team," Suarez said dryly. "But there I draw the line."

They made their guest sit in the best chair, and, despite his protests that he had just dined, brought coffee and a platter of crisp pastries dusted with powdered sugar. The entire family, baby included, had coffee laced with condensed milk. Delaney took his black.

"Delicious," he pronounced after his first cup. "Chicory, Mrs. Suarez?"

"A little," she said faintly, lowering her eyes and blushing at his praise.

"And these," he said, raising one of the sweetmeats aloft. "Home-made?"

She nodded.

"I love them," he said. "You know, the Italians and French and Polish make things very similar."

"Just fried dough," Suarez said. "But Rosa makes the best."

"I concur," Delaney said, reaching for another.

He got the kids talking about their schools, and while they chattered away he had a chance to look around.

Not a luxurious apartment—but spotless. Walls a tenement green. A large crucifix. One hanging of black velvet painted with what appeared to be a view of Waikiki Beach. Patterned linoleum on the floor. Furniture of orange maple that had obviously been purchased as a five-piece set.

None of it to Delaney's taste, but that was neither here nor there. Any honest cop with six children wasn't about to buy Louis Quatorze chairs or Aubusson carpets. The important thing was that the home was warm and clean, the kids were well fed and well dressed. Delaney's initial impression was of a happy family with love enough to go around.

The kids begged to watch an hour of TV—a comedy special—and then promised to go to their rooms, the younger to sleep, the older to do their homework. Suarez gave his permission, then led his visitor to the large kitchen at the rear of the apartment and closed the door.

"We shall have a little peace and quiet in here," he said.

"Kids don't bother me," Delaney said. "I have two of my own and two stepdaughters. I like kids."

"Yes," the Chief said, "I could see that. Please sit here."

The kitchen was large enough to accommodate a long trestle table that could seat the entire family. Delaney noted a big gas range and microwave oven, a food processor, and enough pots, pans, and utensils to handle a company of Marines. He figured good food ranked high on the Suarez family's priority list.

He sat on one of the sturdy wooden chairs. The Chief suddenly turned.

"I called you Mr. Delaney," he said. "Did I offend?"

"Of course not. That's what I am—a mister. No title."

"Well . . . you know," Suarez said with his wry smile, "some re-tired cops prefer to be addressed by their former rank—captain, chief, deputy . . . whatever."

"Mister will do me fine," Delaney said cheerfully. "I'm just another civilian."

"Not quite."

They sat across the table from each other. Delaney saw a long-faced man with coarse black hair combed back from a high forehead. A thick mustache drooped. Olive skin and eyes as dark and shiny as washed coal. A mouthful of strong white teeth.

He also saw the sad, troubled smile and the signs of stress: an occasional tic at the left of the mouth, bagged shadows under the eyes, furrows etched in the brow. Suarez was a man under pressure—and beginning to show it. Delaney wondered how he was sleeping—or if he was sleeping.

"Chief," he said, "when I was on active duty, they used to call me Iron Balls. I never could figure out exactly what that meant, except maybe I was a hard-nosed, blunt-talking bastard. I insisted on doing things my way. I made a lot of enemies."

"So I have heard," Suarez said softly.

"But I always tried to be up-front in what I said and what I did. So now I want to tell you this: On the Ellerbee case, forget what Deputy Commissioner Thorsen told you. I don't know how heavily he's been leaning on you, but if you don't want me in, just say so right now. I won't be offended. I won't be insulted. Just tell me you want to work the case yourself, and I'll thank you for a pleasant evening and the chance to meet you and your beautiful family. Then I'll get out of your hair."

"Deputy Thorsen has been very kind to me," he said. "Kinder than you can ever know."

"Bullshit!" Delaney said angrily. "Thorsen is trying to save his own ass and you know it."

"Yes," Suarez said earnestly, "that is true. But there is more to it than that. How long has it been since you turned in your tin, Mr. Delaney—five years?"

"A little more than that."

"Then you cannot be completely aware of the changes that have taken place in the Department, and are taking place. A third of all the cops on duty today have less than five years' experience. The old height requirement has been junked. Now we have short cops, black cops, female cops, Hispanic cops, Oriental cops, gay cops. At the same time we have more and more cops with a college education. And men and women who speak foreign languages. It is a revolution, and I am all for it."

Delaney was silent.

"These kids are motivated," Suarez went on. "They study law and take courses in sociology and psychology and human relations. It has to help the Department—don't you think?"

"It can't hurt," Delaney said. "The city is changing. If the Department doesn't change along with it, the Department will go down the tube."

"Yes," the Chief said, leaning back. "Exactly. Thorsen realizes that also. So he has been doing whatever he can whenever he can to remake the Department so that it reflects the new city. He has been pushing for more minority cops on the street and for advancement of minorities to higher ranks. Especially appointive ranks. You think I would have two stars today if it was not for Thorsen's clout? No way! So when you tell me he is trying to save his own ass by bringing you in on the Ellerbee case, I say yes, that is true. But it is also to protect something in which he believes deeply."

"Thorsen is a survivor," Delaney said harshly. "And a shrewd in-fighter. Don't worry about Thorsen. I owe him as much as you do. I know damned well what he's up against. He's fighting the Irish Mafia every day he goes downtown. Those guys remember the way the Department was thirty years ago, and that's the way they want it to be today—an Irish kingdom. I can say that because I'm a mick myself, but I had my own fights with harps in high places. I agree with everything you've said. I'm just telling you to be your own man. Screw Thorsen and screw me. If you want to work the Ellerbee case on your own, say so. You'll break it or you won't. Either way, it'll be *your* way. And God knows if I do come in, there's absolutely no guarantee that I can do a damned bit of good—for you, for Thorsen, or for the Department."

There was silence, then Suarez said in a low voice, "I admit that when Deputy Thorsen first suggested that he bring you into the investigation, I was insulted. I know your reputation, of course. Your record of closed files. Still, I thought Thorsen was saying, in effect, that he did not trust me. I almost told him right off that I wanted no help from you or anyone else; I would handle the Ellerbee homicide by myself. Fortunately, I held my tongue, came home, thought about it, and talked it over with Rosa."

"That was smart," Delaney said. "Women may know shit-all about

Department politics, but they sure know a hell of a lot about people—and that's what the Department is."

"Well . . ." Suarez said, sighing, "Rosa made me see that it was an ego thing for me. She said that if I failed on the Ellerbee case, everyone in the city would say, 'See, the spic can't cut the mustard.' She said I should accept help anywhere I could get it. Also, there is another thing. If the Ellerbee crime is solved, Thorsen will try to get me a third star and permanent appointment as Chief of Detectives when Murphy retires. Did you know that?"

"Yes. Thorsen told me."

"So there are a lot of motives involved—political, ethnic, personal. I cannot honestly tell you which is the strongest. So I gave the whole matter many hours of very heavy thought."

"I'll bet you did," Delaney said. "It's a tough decision to make."

"Another factor . . ." Suarez said. "I have some very good men in my bureau."

"I trained a lot of them myself."

"I know that. But none have your talent and experience. I don't say that to butter you up; it is the truth. I spoke to several detectives who worked with you on various cases. They all said the same thing: If you can get Delaney, *get him!* So that finally made up my mind. If you would be willing to help me on the Ellerbee homicide, I will welcome your help with deep gratitude and give you all the cooperation I possibly can."

Delaney leaned forward to look at him. "You're sure about this?"

"Absolutely sure."

"You realize I might strike out? Believe me, it wouldn't be the first time I failed. Far from it."

"I realize that."

"All right, let's get down to nuts and bolts. I've been following the case in the papers. Reading between the lines, I'd say you haven't got much."

"Much?" Suarez cried. "We have nothing!"

"Let me tell you what I know about it. Then you tell me what I've got wrong."

Speaking rapidly, Delaney summarized what he had read in newspaper accounts and heard on TV newscasts. Suarez listened intently, not interrupting. When Delaney finished, the Chief said, "Yes, that is about it. Some of the times you mentioned are a little off, but not enough to make any big difference."

Delaney nodded. "Now tell me what you *didn't* give to the reporters."

"Several things," Suarez said. "They may or may not mean anything. First of all, the victim told his wife he was staying in Manhattan because he was expecting a patient late on Friday evening. We found his appointment book on his desk. The last patient listed was for five P.M. No one listed after five. The receptionist says that was not unusual. Sometimes the doctor got what they called 'crisis screams.' A patient who is really disturbed phones and says he must see the shrink immediately. The doctor makes the appointment and neglects to tell the receptionist. She left at five o'clock anyway, right after the last patient listed in the appointment book arrived."

"Uh-huh," Delaney said. "Could happen . . ."

"The second thing is this. The Medical Examiner thinks the murder weapon was a ball peen hammer. You know what that is?"

"A ball peen? Sure. It's got a little rounded knob on one side of the head."

"Correct. I asked, and found that such a hammer is used to shape metal—like taking a dent out of a fender. Ellerbee was struck multiple blows on the top and back of his skull with the ball peen. They found many round wounds, like punctures."

"Multiple blows? Someone hammering away even after he was a clunk?"

"Yes. The ME calls the attack 'frenzied.' Many more blows than were needed to kill him. But that is not all. After Ellerbee was dead, the killer apparently rolled him over onto his back and struck him two more times. In his eyes. One blow to each eye."

"That's nice," Delaney said. "Was the rounded knob of the ball peen used on the eyes?"

"It was. When Dr. Samuelson found the corpse, it was on its back, the eyes a mess."

"All right," Delaney said. "Anything else you didn't give the press?"

"Yes. When Samuelson discovered the body, he called nine-eleven, then went back downstairs to wait for the cops. A car with two uniforms responded. Here is where we got a little lucky—I think. Because those two blues, first on the scene, did everything by the book. One of them hung on to Samuelson and his cabdriver, making sure they would not take off. Meanwhile, he called in for backup, saying they had a reported homicide. The second blue went upstairs to confirm the kill. You remember how hard it was raining Friday night? Well, the uniform who went upstairs saw soaked tracks on the carpet of the hall and the staircase leading to the third floor. So he was careful to step as close to the wall as he could to preserve the prints."

"That was smart," Delaney said. "Who was he?"

"A big, big black," Suarez said. "I talked with him, and he made me feel like a midget."

"My God!" Delaney said, astonished. "Don't tell me his name is Jason T. Jason?"

It was Suarez's turn to be astonished. "That is who it was. You know him?"

"Oh, hell yes. We worked together. They call him Jason Two. A brainy lad. There's detective material if ever I saw it. He'd never go trampling over everything."

"Well, he did not. So when the Crime Scene Unit arrived, they were able to eliminate his wet prints on the carpet of the staircase and in the receptionist's office where the body was found. A day later, they had also eliminated Dr. Samuelson's footprints. He was wearing street shoes and has very small feet. The kicker is this: That left *two* sets of unidentified wet prints on the carpet."

"*Two* sets?"

"Absolutely. The photos prove it. Ellerbee had two visitors that night. Both were wearing rubbers or galoshes. Indistinct blots, but there is no doubt they were made by two different people."

"Son of a bitch," Delaney said. "Male or female?"

Suarez shrugged. "With rubbers or boots, who knows? But there were two sets of prints left after Samuelson's and Jason's were eliminated."

"Two sets of prints," Delaney repeated thoughtfully. "How do you figure that?"

"I do not. Do you?"

"No."

"Well," Suarez said, "that's all the information that has not yet been released. Now let us discuss how we are going to manage your assistance in this investigation. You tell me what you would like and I will make every effort to provide what I can."

They talked for another half-hour. They agreed it would be counterproductive to run two separate investigations of the same crime.

"We'd be walking up each other's heels," Delaney said.

So they would try to coordinate their efforts, with Suarez in command and Delaney offering suggestions and consulting with Suarez as frequently as developments warranted.

"Here's what I'll need," Delaney said. "First of all, a Department car, unmarked. Then I want Sergeant Abner Boone as an assistant to serve as liaison officer with you and your crew. Right now he's heading a Major Crime Unit in Manhattan North. I want him."

"No problem," Suarez said. "I know Boone. Good man. But he . . ."

His voice trailed away. Delaney looked at him steadily.

"Yes," he said, "Boone was on the sauce. But he straightened himself out. Getting married helped. He hasn't had a drink in more than two years. My wife and I see him and his wife two or three times a month, and believe me, I know: the man is clean."

"If you say so," Suarez said apologetically. "Then by all means let us have Sergeant Boone."

"And Jason Two," Delaney said. "I want to give that guy a chance; he deserves it."

"In uniform?"

Delaney thought a moment. "No. Plainclothes. I need Boone and Jason because they've got shields. They can flash their potzies and get me in places I couldn't go as a civilian. Also, I'll want to see copies of everything you've got on the case—reports, memos, photos, the PM, fake confessions, tips, the whole schmear."

"It can be done," Suarez said, nodding. "But you realize of course I will have to clear all this with Deputy Thorsen."

"Sure. Keep him in the picture. That'll keep him off my back."

"Yes," Suarez said sadly, "and on mine."

Delaney laughed. "It comes with the territory," he said.

They sat back and relaxed.

"Tell me, Chief, what have you done so far?"

"At first," Suarez said, "we thought it was a junkie looking to score. So we leaned on all our snitches. No results. We searched every garbage can and sewer basin in a ten-block area for the murder weapon. Nothing. We canvassed every house on the street, and then spread out to the whole area. No one had seen anything—they said. We checked out the license plates of all parked cars near the scene of the crime and contacted the owners. Again, nothing. We have more or less eliminated the wife and Dr. Samuelson; their alibis hold up. Now we are attempting to question every one of his patients. And former patients. Almost a hundred of them. It is a long, hard job."

"It's got to be done," Delaney said grimly. "And his friends and professional associates?"

"Yes, them also. So far we have drawn a blank. You will see all this from the reports. Sometimes I think it is hopeless."

"No," Delaney said, "it's never hopeless. Occasionally you get a break when you least expect it. I remember a case I worked when I was a dick two. This young woman got offed in Central Park. The crazy thing was that she was almost bald. We couldn't figure it until we talked to her friends and found out she had cancer and was on chemotherapy. The friends said she usually wore a blond wig. We were nowhere with the case, but three weeks later the One-oh Precinct raided an after-hours joint and picked up a transvestite wearing a blond wig. One of the arresting cops remembered the Central Park killing and called up. Same wig. It had the maker's name on a tiny label inside. So we leaned on the transvestite. He hadn't chilled the woman, but he told us who he had bought the wig from, and eventually we got the perp. It was luck—just dumb luck. All I'm saying is that the same thing could happen on this Ellerbee kill."

"Let us pray," Michael Ramon Suarez said mournfully.

After a while Delaney rose to leave. The two men shook hands. Suarez said he would check everything with Deputy Thorsen immediately and call Delaney the following morning.

"I thank you," he said solemnly. "For your honesty and for your kindness. I believe we can work well together."

"Sure we can," Delaney said heartily. "We may scream at one another now and then, but we both want the same thing."

In the living room, Mrs. Rosa Suarez was seated before the darkened television set, placidly knitting. Delaney thanked her for her hospitality, and suggested that she and her husband might like to visit his home.

"That would be nice," she said, smiling shyly. "But with the children and the baby . . . Well, perhaps we can arrange it."

"Try," he urged. "I have a feeling you and my wife would hit it off."

She looked at her husband. If a signal passed between them, Delaney didn't catch it.

At the door, she put a hand on his arm. "Thank you for helping," she said in a low voice. "You are a good man."

"I'm not so sure about that," he said.

"I am," she said softly.

# 5.

They were having a breakfast of eggs scrambled with onions and lox. Delaney was chomping a buttered bagel.

"What are your plans for today?" he asked idly.

"Shopping," Monica said promptly. "With Rebecca. All day. We'll have lunch somewhere. I'll buy the Christmas cards and gifts for the children."

"Good."

"What would you like for Christmas?"

"Me? I'm the man who's got everything."

"That's what *you* think, buster. How about a nice cigar case from Dunhill?"

He considered that. "Not bad," he admitted. "That old one I've got is falling apart. A dark morocco would be nice. What would you like?"

"Please," she said, "no more drugstore perfume. Surprise me. Are you going shopping?"

"No, I'll hang around awhile. Suarez said he'd call, and I want to be here."

"What would you like for dinner?"

"You know what we haven't had for a long time? Creamed chicken on buttermilk biscuits with—"

"With mashed potatoes and peas," she finished, laughing. "A real goyish meal. A good Jew wouldn't be caught dead eating that stuff."

"Force yourself," he told her. "I just suffered through a Jewish breakfast, didn't I?"

"Some suffering," she jeered. "You gobbled that—"

But then the phone rang, and he rose to answer it.

"Edward X. Delaney here," he said. "Yes, Chief . . . Good morning

. . . You did? And what was his reaction? Fine. Fine. I thought he'd go
for it. Yes, I'll wait for them. Thank you, Chief. I'll be in touch."

He hung up and turned to Monica.

"Thorsen okayed everything. I'm getting the car, and Boone and
Jason T. Jason will be delegated to me, through Suarez, on temporary
assignment. They're copying the files now and will probably be here
before noon."

"Can I tell Rebecca about Abner?"

"Sure. He's probably told her already."

"Are you happy about this, Edward?"

"Happy?" he said, surprised at the word. "Well, I'm satisfied. Yes, I
guess I'm happy. It's nice to be asked to do a job."

"They need you," she said stoutly.

"No guarantees. I warned Thorsen and I warned Suarez."

"But the challenge really excites you."

He shrugged.

"You'll crack it," she assured him.

*"Crack* it?" he said, smiling. "You're showing your age, dear. Cops
don't crack cases anymore, and reporters don't get scoops. That was all
long ago."

"Goodbye then," she said, "if I'm so dated. You clean up. I'm going
shopping."

"Spend money," he said. "Enjoy."

He did clean up, scraps and dishes and coffeemaker. He shouted a
farewell to Monica when she departed, then went into the study to read
the morning *Times* and smoke a cigar. But then he put the paper aside a
moment to reflect.

You just couldn't call it a challenge—as Monica had; there was more
to it than that.

Every day hundreds—thousands—of people were dying in wars, rev-
olutions, terrorist bombings, religious feuds; on highways, in their
homes, walking down the street, in their beds. Unavoidable deaths,
some of them—just accidents. But too many the result of deliberate
violence.

So why be so concerned with the killing of a single human being? Just
another cipher in a long parade of ciphers. Not so. Edward X. Delaney
could do little about wars; he could not end mass slaughter. His particular talent was individual homicide. Event and avenger were evenly
matched.

A life should not be stopped before its time by murder. That's what it came down to.

He took up his newspaper again, wondering if he was spinning fantastical reasons that had no relation to the truth. His motives might be as complex as those of Michael Ramon Suarez in seeking his help.

Finally, common sense made him mistrust all these soft philosophical musings and he came back to essentials: A guy had been chilled, Delaney was a cop, his job was to find the killer. That defined his role as something of value: hard, simple, and understandable. He could be content with that.

He finished his newspaper and cigar at about the same time, and put both aside. The *Times* carried a one-column story on the Ellerbee homicide in the Metropolitan Section. It was mostly indignant tirades from Henry Ellerbee and Dr. Diane Ellerbee, denouncing the NYPD for lack of progress in solving the murder.

Acting Chief of Detectives Suarez was quoted as saying that the Department was investigating several "promising leads," and "significant developments" were expected shortly. Which was, as Delaney well knew, police horseshit for "We ain't got a thing and don't know where to turn next."

The two officers arrived a little after noon, lugging four cartons tied with twine. Delaney led them directly into the study, where they piled the boxes in a high stack. Then they all had a chance to shake hands, grinning at each other. The two cops were wearing mufti, and Delaney took their anoraks and caps to the hall closet. They were still standing when he returned to the study.

"Sit down, for God's sake," he said. "Sergeant, I saw you ten days ago, so I know how *you* are. Monica's out with Rebecca today, by the way, spending our money. Jason, I haven't seen you in—what's it been? —almost two years. Don't tell me you've lost some weight?"

"Maybe a few pounds, sir. I didn't think it showed."

"Well, you're looking great. Family okay?"

"Couldn't be better, thank you. My two boys are sprouting up like weeds. All they talk about is basketball."

"Don't knock it," Delaney advised. "Good bucks there."

The two officers didn't ask any questions about what the deal was and what they were doing there—and Delaney knew they wouldn't. But he felt he owed them a reason for their presence.

Briefly, he told them that Acting Chief of Detectives Suarez had more on his plate than he could handle, and Deputy Commissioner Thorsen had asked Delaney to help out on the Ellerbee homicide because the Department was getting so much flak from the victim's widow and father—both people of influence.

Delaney said nothing about the cutthroat ethnic and political wars being waged in the top ranks of the NYPD. Boone and Jason seemed to accept his censored explanation readily enough.

"Sergeant," Delaney said, "you'll assist in my investigation and liaise with Suarez's crew. Remember, he's in command; I'm just a civilian consultant. Jason, you'll be here, there, everywhere you're needed. These are temporary assignments. If the case is cleared, or I get bounced, the two of you go back to your regular duties. Okay?"

"Suits me just fine," Jason Two said.

"It'll be a vacation," Sergeant Boone said. "Working just one case."

"Vacation, hell!" Delaney said. "I'm going to run your ass off. Now the first thing the three of us are going to do is go through all the paper on the Ellerbee kill. We'll read every scrap, look at every photo. We'll take a break in an hour or so. I've got some sandwiches and drinks. Then we'll get back to it until we've emptied the cartons. Then we'll sit around and gas and decide what we do first."

They set to work, opening the cartons, piling the photocopied documents on Delaney's desk. He read each statement first, then handed it to Boone, who scanned it and passed it along to Officer Jason. Most of the stuff was short memos, and those went swiftly. But the Medical Examiner's postmortem and the reports of the Crime Scene Unit were longer and took time to digest.

Delaney smoked another cigar, and the two cops chain-smoked cigarettes. The study fogged up, and Delaney rose to switch on an exhaust fan set in the back window. But there was no conversation; they worked steadily for more than an hour. Then they broke for lunch. Delaney brought in a platter of sandwiches he'd prepared earlier and cans of Heineken for Jason and himself. Abner Boone had a bottle of club soda.

Delaney parked his feet up on his desk.

"Jason," he said, "you did a hell of a job keeping clear of those wet tracks on the carpet."

"Thank you, sir."

"I think your report covered just about everything. Nothing you left out, was there?"

"Nooo," the officer said slowly, "not to my remembrance."

"When you went up the stairs," Delaney persisted, "and into the receptionist's office, did you smell anything?"

"Smell? Well, that was a damned wet night. The inside of that house smelled damp. Almost moldy."

"But nothing unusual? Perfume, incense, cooking odors—something like that?"

The big black frowned. "Can't recall anything unusual. Just the wet."

"That art gallery on the first floor—the door was locked?"

"Yes, sir. And so was the door to Dr. Diane Ellerbee's office on the second floor. And so was that private apartment on the fourth. The victim's office was the only one open."

"He was lying on his back?"

"Yes, sir. Not a pretty sight."

"Sergeant," Delaney said, swinging his swivel chair to face Boone, "how do you figure those two hammer blows to the eyes? After the poor guy was dead."

"That seems plain enough. Symbolic stuff. The killer wanted to blind him."

"Sure," Delaney agreed. "But after he was dead? That's heavy."

"Well, Ellerbee was a psychiatrist dealing with a lot of crazies. It could have been a patient who thought the doctor was seeing too much."

Delaney stared at him. "That's interesting—and plausible. Listen, there are three sandwiches left, and I've got more beer and soda. Why don't we finish eating and work at the same time?"

They were done a little after 3:00 P.M., and stuffed everything back in the cartons. Then they all sat back and stared at each other.

"Well?" Delaney demanded. "What do you think of the investigation so far?"

Boone drew a deep breath. "I don't like to put the knock on anyone," he said hesitantly, "but it appears to me that Chief Suarez hasn't been riding herd on his guys. For instance, in her statement Dr. Diane Ellerbee says she called Dr. Julius Samuelson about one-fifteen in the morning. The guy who's supposed to check it out goes to Samuelson and asks, 'Did Dr. Diane call you at one-fifteen?' And Samuelson says, 'Yes, she did.' Now what kind of garbage is that? Maybe the two of them were in it together and protecting each other's ass. She says she called from their Brewster home. That's a toll call to Manhattan. So why didn't someone check phone company records to make sure the call was actually made?"

"Right!" Jason T. Jason said loudly. "Ditto her call to the Ellerbees' garage. The night attendant says, 'Yeah, she called,' but no one checked to make sure the call was made from Brewster. Sloppy, sloppy work."

"I concur," Delaney said approvingly. "And Samuelson said he was at a concert in Carnegie Hall when Ellerbee was offed. But I didn't see a damned thing in those four cartons that shows anyone checked that out. Was he at the concert with someone or was he alone? And if he was alone, did anyone see him there? Does he have a ticket stub? Can the Carnegie Hall people place him there that night? Chief Suarez said he had more or less eliminated the widow and Samuelson as suspects. *Bullshit!* We've got a way to go before I'll clear them. Don't blame Suarez; he's got a zillion other things on his mind besides this Ellerbee kill. But I agree; so far it's been a half-ass investigation."

"So?" Boone said. "Where do we go from here?"

"Jason," Delaney said, pointing a thick forefinger at him, "you take the widow. Check out those two calls she says she made from Brewster. And while you're at it, talk to the Brewster cop she says she phoned to ask if there was a highway accident. Make sure she *did* call, and ask the cop how she sounded. Was she hysterical, cool, angry—whatever. Boone, you take Samuelson and his alibi. See if you can find out if anyone can actually place him at Carnegie Hall at the time Ellerbee was killed."

"You think the widow and Samuelson might be lying?" Jason said.

"Oh, Jesus," Delaney said. "I lie, you lie, Boone lies, everyone lies. It's part of the human condition. Mostly it's innocent stuff—just to help us all get through life a little easier. But in this case we've got a stiff on our hands. Yes, the widow and Samuelson might be lying—even if they're not the perps. Maybe they have other reasons. Let's find out."

"What do *you* plan on doing, sir?" Sergeant Boone asked curiously.

"Me? I want to study those statements about the hassle Dr. Samuelson had with the Department's legal eagles. The argument was about the doctor-patient relationship, which is supposed to be sacred under the law. Ha-ha. But here we have a case where a doctor has been knocked off and the Crime Scene Unit guys grabbed his appointment book. So now we know the names of his patients, but Samuelson claimed the files were confidential. The Department's attorneys said not so; a murder was committed and the public good required that patients be questioned. As I understand it, they came to a compromise. The patients can be investigated, but they cannot be *questioned* unless they agree to it, because the questioning might involve their illness—the reason they were consulting Ellerbee in the first place. It's a nice legal point, and could keep a platoon of lawyers busy for a year. But as things stand now, we can check the whereabouts of every patient at the time of Ellerbee's death, but we can't question the patients or examine their files unless they agree to it. Now isn't that as fucked up as a Chinese fire drill?"

"You think the patients will agree to answer questions?" Boone said.

"I think if one of his patients chilled Ellerbee, he or she will agree to be questioned, figuring that if they refuse, they'll be automatically suspected by the cops."

"Oh, wow," Jason Two said, laughing. "You figure crazies can reason like that?"

"First of all we don't know yet just how nutty his patients are. Second, you can be a complete whacko and still be able to think as rationally as any so-called normal man or woman. I remember a guy we racked up who was a computer whiz. I mean a genius. All his work involved mathematical logic. But he had one quirk: He liked to rape little girls. Except for that, he was an intellectual giant. So don't get the idea that all of Ellerbee's patients are dummies."

"When are we going to get started on the patient list, sir?" Jason asked.

"Another thing," Delaney said, ignoring Jason's question. "I saw nothing in those cartons to indicate that anyone had thought to run the victim, his widow, his father, and Dr. Samuelson through Records."

"My God," Boone said, "you don't think people like that have jackets, do you?"

"No, I don't—but you never know, do you, and it's got to be done. Ditto the Ellerbees' two receptionists, the old ladies who own the art gallery, and the guy who leases the apartment on the top floor. Sergeant, you do that. Run them all through Records. For the time being let's concentrate on the people who live and work in that townhouse. Plus Samuelson and Ellerbee's father. After we've cleared them, we'll spread out to friends, acquaintances, and Ellerbee's patients."

They talked awhile longer, discussing how they'd divide up use of the Department car and how they'd keep in touch with each other. Delaney urged both men to call him any hour of the day or night if they had any problems or anything to report.

Then the two officers left, and Delaney returned to his study. He called Deputy Commissioner Thorsen and was put through immediately.

"All right, Ivar," Delaney said. "We've started."

"Thank God," the Admiral said. "If there's anything I can do to help, just let me know."

"There is something," Delaney said. "The Department has a house shrink, doesn't it?"

"Sure," Thorsen said. "Dr. Murray Walden. He set up alcohol and drug rehabilitation programs. And he's got a family counseling service. A very active, innovative man."

"Dr. Murray Walden," Delaney repeated, jotting the name on his desk calendar. "Would you phone him and tell him to expect a call from me?"

"Of course."

"He'll cooperate?"

"Absolutely. Did you go through the files, Edward?"

"I did. Once."

"See anything?"

"A lot of holes."

"That's what I was afraid of. You'll plug them, won't you?"

"That's what I'm getting paid for. By the way, Ivar, what *am* I getting paid?"

"A case of Glenfiddich," Thorsen said. "And maybe a medal from the Mayor."

"Screw the medal," Delaney said. "I'll take the scotch."

He hung up after promising the Deputy he'd keep him informed of any developments. Then he tidied up, returning the emptied sandwich platter, beer cans, and soda bottles to the kitchen.

Back in the study, he eyed the cartons of Ellerbee records with some distaste. He knew that eventually all that bumf would have to be divided logically and neatly into separate file folders. He could have told Boone or Jason to do it, but it was donkey labor, and he didn't want their enthusiasm dulled by paperwork.

It took him five minutes to find the two documents he was looking for: the exchange of correspondence and memos between Dr. Julius K. Samuelson and the Department's attorneys regarding the issue of doctor-patient confidentiality, and the photocopies of Dr. Simon Ellerbee's appointment book.

After rereading the papers, Delaney was definitely convinced that their so-called compromise was ridiculous and unworkable. No way could a detective investigate a possible suspect without direct questioning. He decided to ignore the whole muddle, and if he stepped on toes and someone screamed, he'd face that problem when it arose.

What interested him was that Samuelson had made his argument for the inviolability of Ellerbee's files as president of the Greater New York Psychiatric Association. He was, in effect, a professional upholding professional ethics.

But Samuelson was also a witness involved in a murder case and a friend of the victim. Nowhere in his correspondence did he state his personal views about investigating Ellerbee's patients to find the killer.

Even more intriguing, the opinions of Dr. Diane Ellerbee on the subject were never mentioned. Granted that the lady was a psychologist, not a psychiatrist, still the absence of her objection suggested that she was willing to see her husband's patients interrogated.

Delaney pushed the papers away and leaned back in his swivel chair, hands clasped behind his head. He admitted to an unreasonable impatience with lawyers and doctors. In his long career as a detective, they had too often obstructed, sometimes stymied, his investigations. He recalled he had spoken about it to his first wife, Barbara.

"Goddamn it! How can a guy become a lawyer, doctor—or even an undertaker, for that matter. All three are making a living on other people's miseries—isn't that so? I mean, they only get paid when other people are in a legal bind, sick, or dead."

She had looked at him steadily. "You're a cop, Edward," she said. "That's the way you make your living, isn't it?"

He stared at her, then laughed contritely. "You're so right," he said, "and I'm an idiot."

But still, lawyers and doctors weren't his favorite people. "Carrion birds," he called them.

Closer inspection of Ellerbee's appointment book proved more rewarding. It was an annual ledger, and, starting at the first of the year, Delaney attempted to list the name of every patient who had consulted the doctor. He used a long, yellow legal pad which he ruled into neat columns, writing in names, frequency of visits, and canceled appointments.

It was an arduous task, and when he finished, more than an hour later, he peered at the yellow pages through his reading glasses and wasn't sure what in hell he had.

Some patients consulted Ellerbee at irregular intervals. Some every two or three months. Some once a month. Some every two weeks. Some weekly. Many twice or thrice a week. Two patients five times a week!

In addition, a few patients' names appeared in the appointment book one or two times and then disappeared. And there were entries that read simply: "Clinic." The doctor's hours were generally from 7:00 A.M. to 6:00 P.M., five days a week. But sometimes he worked later, and sometimes he worked Saturdays.

No wonder the whole month of August was lined through and marked exultantly: VACATION!

Delaney knew from other reports that Dr. Simon had charged a hundred dollars for a forty-five-minute session. A break of fifteen minutes to recuperate, then on to the next patient. Dr. Diane Ellerbee charged seventy-five dollars for the same period.

He did some rough figuring. Assuming fifty consultations a week for both Dr. Simon and Dr. Diane Ellerbee, the two were hauling in an annual take of about $420,000. A sweet sum, but it didn't completely explain the townhouse, the Brewster country home, the three cars.

But the victim had been the son of Henry Ellerbee, who owned a nice chunk of Manhattan. Maybe Daddy was coming up with an allowance or there was a trust involved. And maybe Dr. Diane was independently wealthy. Delaney knew nothing about her background.

He remembered an old detective, Alberto Di Lucca, a pasta fiend, who had taught him a lot. That was years ago, and Big Al and he were working Little Italy. One day they were strolling up Mott Street, picking their teeth after too much linguine with white clam sauce at Umberto's, and Delaney expressed sympathy for the shabbily dressed people he saw around him.

"They look like they haven't got a pot to piss in," he said.

Big Al laughed. "You think so, do you? See the old gink leaning in the doorway of that bakery across the street? You could read the *News* through his pants, they're so thin. Well, he owns that bakery, which just shits money. I also happen to know he owns three mil of AT&T."

"You're kidding!"

"I'm not," Di Lucca said, shaking his head. "Don't judge by appearances, kiddo. You never know."

Big Al had been right. When it came to money, you never knew. A beggar could be a millionaire, and a dude hosting a party of eight at Lutèce could be teetering on the edge of bankruptcy.

So maybe the Drs. Ellerbee had sources of income Suarez's men hadn't gotten around to investigating. Another hole that had to be plugged.

Edward X. Delaney liked Michael Ramon Suarez, liked his wife, liked his children and his home. But so far the Acting Chief of Detectives's investigation had been a disaster.

It offended Delaney's sense of order. He realized that he and his two assistants would really have to start from scratch.

He finished the warm dregs of his ale, then went into the kitchen to set the table. He hoped Monica wouldn't forget the buttermilk biscuits.

# 6.

"Edward X. Delaney here," he said.

There was an amused grunt. "And Doctor Murray Walden here," a raspy voice said. "Thorsen told me you'd be calling. What can I do for you, Delaney?"

"An hour of your time?"

"I'd rather lend you money—and I don't even *know* you. I suppose you want it today?"

"If possible, doctor."

There was a silence for a moment, then: "Tell you what—I've got to come uptown for a hearing. It's supposed to adjourn at one o'clock, which means it'll break up around two, which means I'll be so hungry I won't be able to see straight. This business of yours—can we talk about it over lunch?"

"Sure we can," Delaney said, preferring not to.

"Delaney—that's Irish. Right?"

"Yes."

"You like Irish food?" the psychiatrist asked.

"Some of it," Delaney said cautiously. "I'm allergic to corned beef and cabbage."

"Who isn't?" Walden said. "There's an Irish pub on the East Side—Eamonn Doran's. You know it?"

"Know it and love it. They've got J.C. ale and Bushmill's Black Label—if the bartender knows you."

"Well, can you meet me there at two-thirty? I figure the lunch crowd will be cleared out by then and we'll be able to get a table and talk."

"Sounds fine. Thank you, doctor."

"You'll have no trouble spotting me," Walden said cheerfully. "I'll be the only guy in the place with no hair."

He wasn't joking. When Delaney walked through the bar into the back room of Eamonn Doran's and looked around, he spotted a lean man seated alone at a table for two. The guy's pate was completely naked. A black mustache, no larger than a typewriter brush, didn't make up for it.

"Doctor Walden?" he asked.

"Edward X. Delaney?" the man said, rising and holding out a hand. "Pleasure to meet you. Sit. I just ordered two of those J.C. ales you mentioned. Okay?"

"Couldn't be better."

Seated, they inspected each other. Walden suddenly grinned, displaying a mouthful of teeth too good to be true. Then he ran a palm over his shiny scalp.

"Yul Brynner or Telly Savalas I'm not," he said. "But I had so little fringe left, I figured the hell with it and shaved it all off."

"A rug?" Delaney suggested.

"Nah, who needs it? A sign of insecurity. I'm happy with a head of skin. People remember me."

The waitress brought their ales and menus. The police psychiatrist peered at his digital wristwatch, bringing it up close to his eyes.

"I promised you an hour," he said, "and that's what you're going to get; no more, no less. So let's order right now and start talking."

"Suits me," Delaney said. "I'll have the sliced steak rare with homefries and a side order of tomatoes and onions."

"Make that two, please," Walden told the waitress. "Now then," he said to Delaney, "what's this all about? Thorsen sounded antsy."

"It's about the murder of Doctor Simon Ellerbee. Did you know the man?"

"We weren't personal friends, but I met him two or three times professionally."

"What was your take?"

"Very, very talented. A gifted man. Heavy thinker. The last time I met him, I got the feeling he had problems—but who hasn't?"

"Problems? Any idea what kind?"

"No. But he was quiet and broody. Not as outgoing as the other times I met him. But maybe he'd just had a bad day. We all do."

"It must be a strain dealing with, uh, disturbed people every day."

"Disturbed people?" Dr. Walden said, showing his teeth again. "You weren't about to say 'nuts,' or 'crazies,' or 'whackos,' were you?"

"Yes," Delaney admitted, "I was."

"Tell me something," Walden said as the waitress set down their food, "have you ever felt guilt, depression, grief, panic, fear, or hatred?"

Delaney looked at him. "Sure I have."

The psychiatrist nodded. "You have, I have, everyone has. Laymen think psychotherapists deal with raving lunatics. Actually, the huge majority of our patients are very ordinary people who are experiencing those same emotions you've felt—but to an exaggerated degree. So exaggerated that they can't cope. That's why, if they've got the money, they go to a therapist. But nuts and crazies and whackos they're not."

"You think most of Ellerbee's patients were like that—essentially ordinary people?"

"Well, I haven't seen his files," Dr. Walden said cautiously, "but I'd almost bet on it. Oh, sure, he might have had some heavy cases—schizoids, patients with psychosexual dysfunctions, multiple personalities: exotic stuff like that. But I'd guess that most of his caseload consisted of the kind of people I just described: the ones with emotional traumata they couldn't handle by themselves."

"Tell me something, doctor," Delaney said. "Simon Ellerbee was a psychiatrist, and his wife—his widow—is a psychologist. What's the difference?"

"He had an MD degree; his widow doesn't. And I expect their education and training were different. As I understand it, she specializes in children's problems and runs group therapy sessions for parents. He was your classical analyst. Not strictly Freudian, but analytically oriented. You've got to understand that there are dozens of therapeutic techniques. The psychiatrist may select one and never deviate or he may gradually develop a mix of his own that he feels yields the best results. This is a very personal business. I really don't know exactly how Ellerbee worked."

"By the way," Delaney said when the waitress presented the bill, "this lunch is on me."

"Never doubted it for a minute," Walden said cheerily.

"You said before that most of Ellerbee's patients were probably ordinary people. You think any of them are capable of violence? I mean against the analyst."

Dr. Walden sat back, took a silver cigarette case from his inside jacket pocket, and snapped it open.

"It doesn't happen too often," he said, "but it does happen. The threat is always there. Back in 1981 four psychiatrists were murdered by their patients in a six-week period. Scary. There are a lot of reasons for it. Psychoanalysis can be a very painful experience—worse than a root canal job, believe me! The therapist probes and probes. The patient resists. That guy behind the desk is trying to get him to reveal awful things that have been kept buried for years. Sometimes the patient attacks the doctor for hurting him. That's one reason. Another is that the patient fears the therapist is learning too much, peering into the patient's secret soul."

"I'm telling you this in confidence," Delaney said sternly, "because it hasn't been released to the press. After Ellerbee was dead, the killer rolled him over and hit him two or more times in the eyes with a ball peen hammer. One of my assistants suggested it might have been an attempt to blind the doctor because he saw, or was seeing, too much. What do you think of that theory?"

"Very perceptive. And quite possible. I think that most assaults on therapists are made by out-and-out psychotics. In fact, most of the attacks are made in prisons and hospital wards for the criminally insane. Still, a number do occur in the offices of high-priced Park Avenue shrinks. What's worse, the psychiatrist's family is sometimes threatened and occasionally attacked."

"Could you estimate the percentage of therapists who have been assaulted by patients?"

"I can give you a guess. Between one-quarter and one-third. Just a guess."

"Have you ever been attacked, doctor?"

"Once. A man came at me with a hunting knife."

"How do you handle something like that?"

"I pack a handgun. You'd be surprised at how many psychiatrists do. Or keep it in the top drawer of their desk. Usually slow, soft talk can defuse a dangerous situation—but not always."

"Why did the guy come at you with a knife?"

"We were at the breaking point in his therapy. He had a lech for his fifteen-year-old daughter and couldn't or wouldn't acknowledge it. But he was taking her clothes to prostitutes and making them dress like the daughter. Sad, sad, sad."

"Did he finally admit it?" Delaney asked, fascinated.

"Eventually. I thought he was coming along fine; we were talking it out. But then, about three weeks later, he left my office, went home, and

blew his brains out with a shotgun. I don't think of that case very often
—not more than two or three times a day."

"Jesus," Delaney said wonderingly. "How can you stand that kind of
pressure?"

"How can a man do open-heart surgery? You go in, pray, and hope
for the best. Oh, there's another reason patients sometimes assault their
therapists. It involves a type of transference. The analysand may have
been an abused child or hate his parents for one reason or another. He
transfers his hostility to the therapist, who is making him dredge up his
anger and talk about it. The doctor becomes the abusive parent. Con-
versely, the patient may identify with the aggressive parent and try to
treat the psychiatrist as a helpless child. As I told you, there are many
reasons patients might attack their therapists. And to confuse you further, I should add that some assaults have been made for no discernible
reason at all."

"But the main point," Delaney insisted, "is that murderous attacks
on psychiatrists are not all that uncommon, and it's very possible that
Doctor Ellerbee was killed by one of his patients."

"It's possible," Walden agreed.

Then, when Delaney saw the doctor glance at his watch, he said, "I
should warn you, I may bother you again if I need the benefit of your
advice."

"Anytime. You keep buying me steak and I'm all yours."

They rose from the table and shook hands.

"Thank you," Delaney said. "You've been a big help."

"I have?" Dr. Murray Walden said, stroking his bald pate. "That's
nice. One final word of caution: If you're thinking of questioning Ellerbee's patients, don't come on strong. Play it very low-key. Speak
softly. These people feel threatened enough without being leaned on by
a stranger."

"I'll remember that."

"Of course," Walden said thoughtfully, "there may be some from
whom you'll get the best results by coming on strong, shouting and
browbeating them."

"My God!" Edward X. Delaney cried. "Isn't there anything definite
in your business?"

"Definitely not," Walden said.

# 7.

The three sat in the study, hunched forward, intent.

"All right, Jason," Delaney said, "you go first."

The black officer flipped through his pocket notebook to find the pages he wanted. "The widow lady is clean as far as those Brewster calls go. She did phone the Manhattan garage at the time she says she did. Ditto the call later to Doctor Samuelson. The phone company's got a record. I talked to the Brewster cop who took her call when she asked about an accident involving her husband's car. He says she wasn't hysterical, but she sounded worried and anxious. So much for that. Then, just for fun, I dropped by that Manhattan garage to ask when the lady claimed her car on that Friday night."

"Smart," Delaney said, nodding.

"Well, she checked her car out at six twenty-two in the evening, which fits pretty close to her statement. No holes that I could find."

"Nice job," Delaney said. "Sergeant?"

Boone peered down at his own notebook. "Samuelson seems to be clean, too. Before the concert he had dinner with two friends at the Russian Tea Room. They swear he was there. He picked up the tab and paid with a credit card. I got a look at his signed check and the restaurant's copy of his credit card bill. Everything looks kosher. Then Samuelson and his friends went to the concert. They say he never left, which is probably true because after the concert was over, the three of them dropped by the St. Moritz for a nightcap. All this covers Ellerbee's time of death, so I guess we can scratch Doctor Samuelson."

Delaney didn't say anything.

"Now, about Records . . ." the Sergeant continued. "I checked out Ellerbee, his widow, his father, the two receptionists, the two old dames who own the art gallery on the first floor, the part-time super who takes care of the building, and the guy who leases the top floor. The only one with a jacket is the last—the West Coast movie producer who keeps that fourth-floor apartment to use when he's in town. His name is J. Scott Hergetson, and his sheet is minor stuff: traffic violations, committing a public nuisance—he peed on the sidewalk while drunk—and one drug bust. This disco was raided and he was pulled in with fifty other people. No big deal. Charges dropped."

"So that's it?" Delaney asked.

"Not all of it," Boone said, flipping his notebook. "The ME says Ellerbee died about nine P.M. This is where all these people claim they were at that time . . .

"Doctor Diane Ellerbee was up in Brewster, waiting for her husband to arrive.

"Henry Ellerbee was at a charity dinner at the Plaza Hotel. I confirmed his presence there at nine o'clock.

"Doctor Samuelson was at the Carnegie Hall concert. Confirmed.

"One of the receptionists was home watching television with her mother. Mommy says yes, she was. Who knows?

"The other receptionist says she was shacked up with her boyfriend in his apartment. He says yes, she was. Who knows?

"The super was playing pinochle at his basement social club. The other guys in the game say yeah, he was there.

"The two ladies who run the art gallery were at a private dinner with eight other people of the Medicare set. Their presence is confirmed. Besides, the two of them are so frail I don't think they could *lift* a ball peen hammer.

"The top-floor movie producer was at a film festival in the south of France. His presence there is confirmed by news reports and photographs. Scratch him.

"And that's it."

Delaney looked admiringly from Boone to Jason and back again. "What the hell does Suarez need me for? You two guys can break this thing on your own. Well, here's what I've got. It isn't much."

He gave them a précis of his conversation with the police psychiatrist and told them what Dr. Walden had said about the incidence of attacks on therapists by their patients.

"He guessed about one-quarter to one-third of all psychiatrists have been assaulted. Those percentages look good. After what you've just told me, I'm beginning to think Ellerbee's patient list may be our best bet."

Then he said that Walden had agreed with Boone's theory about those hammer blows to the eyes: It could be a symbolic effort to blind the doctor.

"After he was dead?" Jason said.

"Well, Walden thinks most attacks on therapists are made by psychotics. I didn't tell him about the two sets of unidentified footprints. That could mean there were two psychotics working together, or Ellerbee had two visitors that night at different times. Any ideas?"

Jason and Boone looked at each other, then shook their heads.

"All right," Delaney said briskly. "Here's where we go from here. I want to see that townhouse and I want to meet Doctor Diane Ellerbee. Maybe we can do both at the same time. Sergeant, suppose you call her right now. Tell her you'd like to see her as soon as possible, as part of the investigation into her husband's death. Don't mention that I'll be with you."

Rather than dig through the records in the cartons for Diane Ellerbee's phone number, Boone looked it up in the Manhattan directory. He identified himself and asked to speak to the doctor. He ended by giving Delaney's phone number. Then he hung up.

"She's with a patient," he reported. "The receptionist said she'll give the doctor my message and she'll probably call back as soon as she's free."

"We'll wait," Delaney said. "It shouldn't be more than forty-five minutes. Meanwhile, there's something else I want to know more about. Boone, do you know a dick one named Parnell? I think his first name is Charles."

"Oh, hell, yes," the Sergeant said, smiling. "I know him. They call him Daddy Warbucks. He's still on active duty."

"That's the guy," Delaney said. He turned to Jason. "You've got to realize that some detectives make a good career for themselves by specializing. Now this Parnell, he's a financial whiz. You want a money picture on someone and he can come up with it. He's got good contacts with banks, stockbrokers, credit agencies, accountants, and, for all I know, the IRS. He knows how to read wills, trusts, and reports of probate. He's just the guy we need to get a rundown on the financial status of the deceased and his widow. Sergeant, tell Chief Suarez everything we've done so far—don't leave anything out—and then ask him to have Daddy Warbucks check out the net worth of the dead guy and

Doctor Diane Ellerbee." He paused a moment, pondering. Then: "And throw in Doctor Julius K. Samuelson for good measure. Let's find out how fat his bank account is."

"Will do," Boone said, making some quick jottings in his notebook.

"Sir," Jason T. Jason said hesitantly, "would you mind telling me the reason for this?"

*"Cui bono,"* Delaney said promptly. "Who benefits? In this case, who stands to gain from the death of Simon Ellerbee? I'm not saying money was the motive here, but it might have been. It sure as hell has been in a lot of homicides where the perp turns out to be a member of the family or a beneficiary. It's something that's got to be checked out."

"I'll get on it right—" Boone started to say, but then the phone rang.

"That may be Doctor Diane," Delaney said. "You better answer, Sergeant."

He talked briefly, then hung up and turned to them.

"Six o'clock tonight," he said. "She'll be finished with her patients by then."

"How did she sound?" Delaney asked.

"Furious. Trying to keep her cool. I'm not looking forward to that meeting, sir."

"Has to be done," Delaney said stubbornly. "The lady is said to be a real beauty—if that's any consolation. Well, we've got about eight hours. Boone, why don't you contact Suarez and get Charlie Parnell working on the financial reports. Jason, you take the car and go up to Brewster. The Ellerbees have a married couple who take care of their place. The man does maintenance and works around the grounds. Talk to him. He may have a toolshed or workshop on the premises."

"Oh-ho," Jason T. Jason said. "You want to know if he owns a ball peen hammer—right?"

"Right. And if he does, has he still got it? And if he has, you grab it."

"Oh, yeah," Jason said.

"And while you're at it, get a look at the house and grounds. I'd like your take on it."

"I'm on my way."

"And so am I," Boone said, as both officers rose.

"Sergeant, I'll meet you at the Ellerbees' townhouse at five-thirty. It'll give us a chance to look around the neighborhood before we brace the widow."

"I'll be there," Abner Boone promised.

After they left, Delaney returned to his study and looked at the cartons of files with dread. It had to be done, but he didn't relish the task.

He set to work, dividing the records into separate folders: the victim, Dr. Diane Ellerbee, Dr. Julius Samuelson, the ME's reports and photographs, the reports, photos, and map of the Crime Scene Unit, statements of everyone questioned. Then he added notes of his conversation with Dr. Murray Walden, and what Sergeant Boone and Jason T. Jason had just told him.

It went faster than he had anticipated, and by 12:30 he had a satisfyingly neat stack of labeled file folders that included all the known facts concerning the murder of Dr. Simon Ellerbee. It was time, he decided, for a sandwich.

He went into the kitchen, opened the refrigerator, and inspected the possibilities. There was a single onion roll in there, hard as a rock, but it could be toasted. And there were a few slices of pork left over from a roast loin. Some German potato salad. Scallions he could slice. Maybe a wee bit of horseradish.

He slapped it all together and ate it leaning over the sink. Monica would have been outraged, but she was gone, doing volunteer work at a local hospital. She kept nagging him about his addiction, and she was right; he was too heavy in the gut. It was hard to convince her that the Earl of Sandwich had been one of civilization's great benefactors.

He returned to the study and stared at the stack of Ellerbee file folders.

He had a disturbing hunch that this was going to be a "loose-ends case." That's what he called investigations in which nothing was certain, nothing could be pinned down. A hundred suspects, a hundred alibis, and no one could say yes or no.

You had to live with that confusion and, if you were lucky, discard the meaningless and zero in on the significant. But how to tell one from the other? False trails and time wasted chasing leads that dribbled away. Meanwhile, Thorsen was sweating to have a murder cleaned up, neat and clean, by the holidays. So his man could be promoted.

Two sets of unidentified footprints and two blows to the victim's eyes. Was there any meaning in that? Or in Ellerbee telling his wife he had scheduled a late patient, presumably meaning someone after 6:00 P.M. But he had died at approximately nine o'clock. Would he have waited that long for a late patient? Someone who would arrive, say, at 8:00 P.M.

No signs of forced entry. So Ellerbee buzzed someone in, someone he was expecting. One person or two? And why leave that street door open when they left?

"The butler did it," Delaney said aloud, and then pulled his yellow legal pad toward him, put on his reading glasses, and began making notes on how much he didn't know. It was a long, depressing list. He stared at it and had an uneasy feeling that he might be missing the obvious.

He remembered a case he had worked years ago. There had been a string of armed robberies on Amsterdam Avenue; six small stores had been hit in a period of two months. Apparently the same cowboy was pulling all of them—a young punk with a Fu Manchu mustache, waving a nickel-plated pistol.

One of the six places allegedly robbed at gunpoint was a mom-and-pop grocery store near 78th Street. The owners lived in a rear apartment. The old lady opened the store every morning at 7:30. Her husband, who had a weakness for slivovitz, usually joined her behind the counter a half-hour or hour later.

On this particular morning, the old man said, his wife had gone into the store to open up as usual. He was dressing when he heard a gunshot, rushed out, and found her lying behind the counter. The cash register was open, he said, and about thirty dollars' worth of bills and coin were gone.

The old lady was dead, hit in the chest with what turned out to be a .38 slug. Delaney and his partner, a Detective second grade named Loren Pierce, chalked it up to the Fu Manchu punk with the shiny pistol. They couldn't stake out every little shop on Amsterdam Avenue, but they haunted the neighborhood, spending a lot of their off-hours walking the streets and eyeballing every guy with a mustache.

They finally got lucky. The robber tried to rip off a deli, not knowing the owner's son was on his knees, out of sight behind a pile of cartons, putting stock on the shelves. The son rose up and hit Fu Manchu over the head with a five-pound canned ham. That was the end of that crime wave.

It turned out the punk was snorting coke and robbing to support a $500-a-day habit. Even more interesting, his nickel-plated weapon was a .22, the barrel so dirty it would have blown his hand off if he had ever fired it.

Detectives Delaney and Pierce looked at each other and cursed. Then they went back to the mom-and-pop grocery store, but only after they had checked and discovered that Pop had a permit to keep a .38 hand-gun in his store. They leaned on him and he caved almost immediately.

"She was always nagging at me," he complained.

That was what Delaney meant when he worried about missing the obvious. He and Pierce should have checked immediately to see if the old man had a gun. It never hurt to get the simple, evident things out of the way first. It was a mistake to think all criminals were great brains; most of them were stupes.

He pondered all the known facts in the Ellerbee homicide and couldn't see anything simple and obvious that he had missed. He thought the case probably hinged on the character of the dead man and his relationship with his patients.

He reflected awhile and admitted he had an irrational contempt for people who sought aid for emotional problems. He would never do it; he was convinced of that. The death of Barbara, his first wife, had left him numb for a long time. But he had bulled his way out of that funk—by himself.

Still, he had no hesitation in seeking help for physical ills. A virus, a twinge of the liver, a skin lesion that wouldn't heal—and off he went to consult a physician. So why this disdain for people who took their inner torments to a trained practitioner?

Because, Delaney supposed, there was an element of fear in his preju-dice. Psychologists and psychiatrists were dealing with something you couldn't see. There was a mystery there, and dread. It was like taking your brain to a witch doctor. Still, Delaney knew that if he was going to get anywhere on the Ellerbee case he'd have to cultivate and evince sympathy for those who fled to the witch doctor.

He left the house early, deciding to walk to the Ellerbees' townhouse to meet Abner Boone. It was a dull day with a cloud cover as rough as an elephant hide. The air smelled of snow, and a hard northwest wind made him grab for his homburg more than once.

On impulse, he stopped in at a First Avenue hardware store. All the clerks were busy, for which he was thankful. He found a display of hammers and picked up a ball peen. He hefted it in his hand, swinging it gently in a downward chop. So many useful tools made lethal weap-ons. He wondered which came first. If he had to guess, he'd say weap-ons evolved into tools.

That shiny round knob could puncture a man's skull if swung with sufficient force—no doubt about that. A man could do it easily, but then so could a woman if she were strong and determined. He replaced the hammer in the display, having learned absolutely nothing.

Boone was waiting for him across the street from the townhouse. He was huddling in his parka, hands in his pockets, shoulders hunched.

"That wind's a bitch," he observed. "My ears feel like tin."

"I feel the cold in my feet," Delaney said. "An old cop's complaint. The feet are the first to go. Did you talk to Suarez?"

"Yes, sir, I did. On the phone. He was tied up with a million other things."

"I imagine."

"He sounds like a patient man. Very polite. Said to thank you for keeping in touch, and he's grateful for what we've done so far."

"What about Parnell?"

"He'll get him going on the financial reports immediately. I think he was a little embarrassed that he hadn't thought of it himself."

"He's got enough to think about," Delaney said absently, staring across the street. "That's the place—the gray stone building?"

"That's the one, sir."

"Smaller than I thought it would be. Let's wander around a little first."

They walked over to East End Avenue, inspecting buildings on both sides of 84th Street. The block contained a mix of apartment houses with marbled lobbies, crumbling brownstones, a school, smart town-houses, dilapidated tenements, and a few commercial establishments on the avenue corners.

They looked at the East River, turned, and walked back to York.

"Plenty of areaways," Boone observed. "Open lobbies and vestibules with the outer door unlocked. The perp could have gone into any of them to get out of the rain."

"Could have," Delaney agreed. "But then how did he get into the Ellerbees' building? No signs of forced entry. What I'm wondering about is what the killer did afterwards. Walk away in the rain, leaving the front door open? Or did the killer have a car parked nearby? Or maybe stroll over to York or East End and take a cab? Both avenues are two-way."

"My God, sir," the Sergeant said, "you're not thinking of checking taxi trip-sheets for that night, are you? What a job!"

"We won't do it right now, but it may become necessary. Besides, there couldn't have been so many cabs working that Friday night. It wasn't just raining; it was a flood. Well, this street isn't going to tell us anything; let's go talk to the widow; it's almost six."

The outer door of the Ellerbee townhouse was unlocked, leading to a lighted vestibule with mailboxes and a bell plate of polished brass. Boone tried the inner door.

"Locked," he reported. "This is the inner door Doctor Samuelson found open when he arrived."

"Fine door," Delaney said. "Bleached oak with beveled glass. You can ring now, Sergeant."

Boone pressed the button alongside the neatly printed nameplate: DR. DIANE ELLERBEE. The female voice that answered was unexpectedly loud:

"Who is it?"

"Sergeant Abner Boone, New York Police Department. I spoke to you earlier today."

The buzzer sounded and they pushed in. They stood a brief moment in the entranceway. Delaney tried the door of the Piedmont Gallery. It was locked.

They looked about curiously. The hall and stairway were heavily carpeted. Illumination came from a small crystal chandelier hung from a high ceiling.

"Very nice," Delaney said. "And look at that banister. Someone did a great restoration job. Well, let's go up. Sergeant, you do the talking."

"Don't let me miss anything," Boone said anxiously.

Delaney grunted.

The woman who greeted them at an opened door on the second floor was tall, stiff. Braided flaxen hair, coiled atop her head, made her appear even taller.

A Valkyrie, was Delaney's initial reaction.

"May I see your identification, please?" she said crisply.

"Of course," Boone said, and handed over his case with shield and ID card.

She inspected both closely, returned the folder, then turned to Delaney.

"And who are you?" she demanded.

He was not put off by her loud, assertive voice. In fact, he admired her caution; most people would have accepted Boone's credentials and not questioned anyone accompanying him.

"Edward X. Delaney, ma'am," he said in a quiet voice. "I am a civilian consultant assisting the New York Police Department in the

investigation of your husband's death. If you have any questions about
my presence here—any doubts at all—I suggest you telephone First
Deputy Commissioner Ivar Thorsen or Acting Chief of Detectives Michael Ramon Suarez. Both will vouch for me. Sergeant Boone and I can
wait out here in the hall while you make the call."

She stared at him fixedly. Then: "No," she said, "that won't be necessary; I believe you. It's just that since—since it happened, I've been
extra careful."

"Very wise," Delaney said.

They stepped into the receptionist's office, and both men noted that
Dr. Diane Ellerbee double-locked and chained the door behind them.

"Ma'am," Boone said, "is the floor plan of this office the same as—
uh, the one upstairs?"

"You haven't seen it?" she asked, surprised. "Yes, my husband's and
my office are identical. Not in decorations or furnishings, of course, but
the layout of the rooms is the same."

She ushered them into her private office, leaving open the connecting
door to the receptionist's office. She got them seated in two cretonne-
covered armchairs with low backs.

"Not too comfortable, are they?" she said—the first time she had
smiled: a shadow of a smile. "Deliberately so. I don't want my young
patients nodding off. Those chairs keep them twisting and shifting. I
think it's productive."

"Doctor Ellerbee," Boone said solemnly, leaning forward, "I'd like to
express the condolences of Mr. Delaney and myself on the tragic death
of your husband. From all accounts he was a remarkable man. We
sympathize with you on your loss."

"Thank you," she said, sitting behind her desk like a queen. "I appreciate your sympathy. I would appreciate even more your finding the
person who killed my husband."

During this exchange, Delaney had been examining the office, trying
not to make his inspection too obvious.

The room seemed to him excessively neat, almost to the point of
sterility. Walls were painted a cream color, the carpet a light beige.
There was one ficus tree (which looked artificial) in a rattan basket. The
only wall decorations were two framed enlargements of Rorschach blots
that looked as abstract as Japanese calligraphy.

"Both of us," Boone continued, "have read your statement to the
investigating officers several times. We don't want to ask you to go over
it again. But I would like to say that occasionally, after a shocking event

like this, witnesses recall additional details days or even months later. If you are able to add anything to your statement, it would help if you'd contact us immediately."

"I certainly hope it's not going to take months to find my husband's killer," she said sharply.

They looked at her expressionlessly, and she gave a short cough of laughter without mirth.

"I know I've been a pain in the ass to the police," she said. "And so has Henry—my father-in-law, Henry Ellerbee. But I have not been able to restrain my anger. All my professional life I have been counseling patients on how to cope with the injustices of this world. But now that they have struck me, I find it difficult to endure. Perhaps this experience will make me a better therapist. But I must tell you in all honesty that at the moment I feel nothing but rage and a desire for vengeance— emotions I have never felt before and which I seem unable to control."

"That's very understandable, ma'am," Boone said. "Believe me, we're just as anxious as you to identify the killer. That's why we asked for this meeting, hoping we might learn something from you that will aid our investigation. First of all, would it hurt too much to talk about your husband?"

"No," she said decisively. "I'll be thinking about Simon and talking about Simon for the rest of my life."

"What kind of a man was he?"

"A very superior human being. Kind, gentle, with a marvelous sympathy for other people's unhappiness. I think everyone in the profession who knew him or met him recognized how gifted he was. In addition to that, he had a first-class mind. He could get to the cause of a psychiatric problem so fast that many of his associates called it instinct."

As she spoke, Delaney, while listening, observed her closely. Ivar Thorsen and Monica had been right: Diane Ellerbee was a regal beauty.

A softly sharp profile suitable for a coin. Sky-blue eyes that seemed to change hue with her temper. A direct, challenging gaze. A porcelain complexion. A generous mouth that promised smiles and kisses.

She was wearing a severely tailored suit of pin-striped flannel, but a tent couldn't have concealed her figure. She didn't move; she flowed.

What was so disconcerting, almost frightening, was the woman's completeness. She wasn't a Valkyrie, he decided; she was a Brancusi sculpture—something serene that wooed the eye with its form and soothed with its surface. "Marvelous" was the word that came to his mind—meaning something of wonder. Supernatural.

"Don't get me wrong," she said, fiddling with a ballpoint pen on her desk and looking down at it. "I don't want to make Simon sound like the perfect man. He wasn't, of course. He had his moods. Fits of silence. Rare but occasional outbursts of anger. Most of the time he was a sunny, placable man. When he was depressed, it was usually because he felt he was failing a patient. He set for himself very high goals indeed, and when he felt he was falling short of his potential, it bothered him."

"Did you notice any change in him in, say, the last six months or a year?" Boone asked.

"Change?"

"In his manner, his personality. Did he act like a man with worries or, maybe, like a man who had received serious threats against his life?"

She pondered that for a moment. "No," she said finally, "I noticed no change."

"Doctor Ellerbee," Boone said earnestly, "we are currently investigating your husband's patients, under the terms of an agreement negotiated between Doctor Samuelson and the NYPD. Are you familiar with that compromise?"

"Oh, yes," she said. "Julie told me about it."

"Do you think it possible that one of the patients may have been the assailant?"

"Yes, it's possible."

"Have you yourself ever been attacked by one of *your* patients?"

"Occasionally."

"And how do you handle that?"

"You must realize," she said with a wry smile, "that most of my patients are children. Still, my first reaction is to protect myself. And I am a strong woman. I refuse to let myself be bullied or suffer injury."

"You fight back?"

"Exactly. You'd be surprised at how effective that technique can be."

"Did you and your husband talk business when you were alone together?"

"Business?" she said, and the smile became broader and more charming. "Yes, we talked business—if you mean discussing our cases. We did it constantly. He sought my reactions and advice and I sought his. Sergeant, this is not a profession that ends when you lock your office door for the night."

"The reason I asked, ma'am, is this: Your husband had a great number of patients, particularly if you include all he'd discharged. It's going to take a lot of time and a lot of work to investigate them all. We were hoping you might be able to help us speed up the process. If your husband discussed his cases with you—as you say he did—would you be willing to pick out those patients you feel might be violent?"

She was silent, staring at them both, while her long, tapered fingers played with the pen on the desk top.

"I don't know," she said worriedly. "It's a troublesome question, involving medical ethics. I'm not sure how far I should go on this. Sergeant, I'm not going to say yes or no at this moment. I think I better get some other opinions. Julie Samuelson's, for one. If I acted on impulse, I'd say, hell, yes, I'll do anything I can to help. But I don't want to do the wrong thing. Can I get back to you? It shouldn't take more than a day or so."

"The sooner the better," Boone said, then glanced swiftly at Delaney, signaling that he was finished.

Delaney, who was pleased with the way the Sergeant had conducted the interrogation, hunched forward in his chair, hands clasped between spread knees, and stared at Diane Ellerbee.

"Doctor," he said, "I have a question—a very personal question you may find offensive. But it's got to be asked. Was your husband faithful to you?"

She threw the ballpoint pen across the desk. It fell to the floor, and she didn't bother to retrieve it. They saw her spine stiffen, jaw tighten. Those sky-blue eyes seemed to darken. She glared at Edward X. Delaney.

"My husband was faithful," she said loudly. "Faithful from the day we were married. I realize people say that the wife is always the last to know, but I swear to you I *know* my husband was faithful. We worked at our marriage, and it was a happy one. I was faithful to Simon, and he was faithful to me."

"No children?" Delaney said.

She gave a slight grimace—pain, distaste?

"You go for the jugular, don't you?" she said harshly. "No, no children. I'm incapable. Is that going to help you find my husband's killer?"

Delaney rose to his feet, and a second later, Sergeant Boone jumped up.

"Doctor Ellerbee," Delaney said, "I want to thank you for your cooperation. I can't promise that what you've told us will aid our investigation—but you never know. It would help a great deal if you'd be willing to name those of your husband's patients you feel might be capable of homicidal violence."

"I'll talk to Julie," she said, nodding. "If he approves, I'll do it. Either way, I'll be in touch as soon as I can."

Boone handed over his card. "I can be reached at this number, Doctor Ellerbee, or you can leave a message. Thank you for your help, ma'am."

Outside, they walked west to York Avenue, fists jammed into their pockets, shoulders hunched against the cutting wind.

"Nice job," Delaney said. "You handled that just right."

"A beautiful, beautiful woman," Boone said. "But what did we get? Zilch."

"I'm not so sure. It was interesting. And yes, she's a beautiful woman."

"You think she was telling the truth, sir? About her husband being faithful?"

"Why not? You're faithful to Rebecca, aren't you? And I know I'm faithful to Monica. Not all husbands sleep around. Sergeant, I think you better make an appointment for us with Doctor Samuelson as soon as possible. Maybe we can convince him to tell her to pick out the crazies from her husband's patient list."

"She sure seems to rely a hell of a lot on his opinion."

"Oh, you noticed that too, did you?"

They parted on York. Boone headed uptown to his apartment; Delaney walked down to his brownstone.

He had left a note for Monica, telling her that he might be late and to go ahead and have dinner if she was hungry. But she had waited for him, keeping a casserole of veal and onions warm in the oven.

While they ate, he told her about the interview with Dr. Diane Ellerbee. He wanted to get her reaction.

"She sounds like a woman under very heavy pressure," Monica said when Delaney finished describing the interview.

"Oh, hell, yes. The death of her husband has gotten to her—no doubt of that. That's why she's been leaning on the Department; at least it gives her the feeling that she's doing something. Both Abner and I thought she put unusual reliance on Doctor Samuelson. Granted that he's the president of an important professional association, still it sounded like she doesn't want to make a move without consulting him. A curious relationship. Abner is going to set up a meet with Samuelson. Maybe we'll learn more."

"Do you believe her about her husband being faithful?"

"I have no reason not to believe," he said cautiously.

"I've never heard even a whisper of gossip about them," Monica said. "Things like that usually get out—one way or another."

"I suppose so. But I think Diane Ellerbee is a very complex woman. She's going to take a lot of study."

"You don't suspect her, do you, Edward?"

He sighed. "Oh, hell—I suspect everyone. You know I go by percentages, and most homicides are committed by relatives or close friends. So, sure—the widow has got to be a suspect. But up to now, I admit, there isn't an iota of evidence to make me doubt her innocence. Well, we're just beginning."

He helped Monica clean up and put the dishes in the washer. Then he went into the study, poured himself a small Rémy, and put on his reading glasses. He wrote out a complete report of the interrogation of Dr. Diane Ellerbee and slid it into the file folder neatly labeled with her name.

He was interrupted twice. The first phone call came from Boone, who said that he had made an appointment with Samuelson for 7:00 A.M. the following morning.

"Seven o'clock! I'm just dragging myself out of bed at that hour."

"Me, too," Boone said mournfully. "But these psychiatrists apparently start the day early—to take patients before they go off to work."

"Well, all right, we'll make it at seven. What's the address?"

The second call was from Jason, who had just returned to the city from Brewster.

"No ball peen hammer, sir," he reported. "The handyman says he doesn't own one and never has. I think he's telling the truth."

"Probably," Delaney agreed. "It was just a gamble and had to be checked out."

"And the victim wasn't very mechanical," Jason went on. "He owned maybe a tack hammer and a screwdriver—five-and-ten tools like that. Whenever any repairs had to be done, even like changing a washer, the caretaker was called in."

"You got to see the house?"

"Oh, yes, sir. Not as big as I thought it would be, but really beautiful. Even with all the trees bare, you can imagine what that place must look like in spring and summer. Plenty of land with a sweet little brook running through. Patio, garden, swimming pool—the whole bit."

"It sure sounds great," Delaney said. "I've got to get up there and take a look. Jason, we've got Parnell working on the financial backgrounds of the two Ellerbees and Doctor Samuelson. What I'd like you to do is dig into their personal backgrounds. Ages, where born, living relatives, education, professional careers, and so forth. You can get most of that stuff from *Who's Who,* records of colleges, universities and hospitals, yearbooks of professional societies, and any other sources you can think of. Dig as deep as you think necessary."

"Well . . . sure," Jason said hesitantly. "But I've never done anything like that before, sir."

"Then it's time you learned. Don't lean on anyone too hard, but don't let them fluff you off either. It'll be a good chance to make contacts. You never know when you might be needing them again."

"Get started on it in the morning. When do you want this stuff, sir?"

"Yesterday," Delaney said. "Get a good night's sleep."

A little after midnight, in the upstairs bedroom, he went in to shower first, leaving Monica brushing her hair at the dressing table. She came into the open bathroom after he finished, catching him sucking in his gut and examining his body in the full-length mirror.

"Now I know you met Diane Ellerbee today," she said.

He gave her a sour grin. "You really know how to hurt a guy, don't you?"

She laughed and patted his bare shoulder. "You'll do for me, pops."

"Pops?" he said in mock outrage. "I'll pop you!"

They giggled, wrestled a moment, kissed.

Later, when they were in their beds, he said, "Well, she is a beautiful woman. Incredible. Correct me if I'm wrong, but can't great physical beauty be a curse?"

"How so?"

"It seems to me that a young woman who starts out tremendously lovely would have no incentive to develop her mind or talents or skills. I mean people worship her automatically. Some rich guy grabs her off and buys her everything she wants—so where's her ambition to be anything? She thinks she deserves her good fortune, and her looks will last forever."

"Well, that obviously didn't happen to Diane Ellerbee. She's a respected professional and she's got brains to spare. Maybe some beautiful women go the route you said, but not her. She's made her own good fortune. I told you I heard her speak, and the woman is brilliant."

"You don't think there's something cold and detached about her?"

"Cold and detached? No, I didn't get that impression at all."

"Maybe it was a poor choice of words. Forceful and self-assured. Will you agree to that?"

"Yes," Monica said slowly, "I think that's fair. But of course a psychotherapist has to be self-assured—or at least give that impression. You're not going to get many patients if you seem as neurotic as they are."

"You're probably right," he admitted. "But something about her disturbs me. It's the same feeling I get when I see a great painting or sculpture at the Met. It's pleasing visually, but there's something mysterious there. I've never been able to figure it out. I can look at a painting and really admire it, but sometimes it saddens me, too. It makes me think of death."

"Great beauty makes you think of death?"

"Sometimes."

"Did you ever consider seeking professional help?"

"Never," he said, laughing. "You're my therapist."

"Do you think Diane Ellerbee is more beautiful than I am?"

"Absolutely not," he said immediately. "To me, you're the most beautiful woman in the world."

"You really know what's good for you, don't you, buster?"

"You better believe it," he said, reaching out for her.

# 8.

Dr. Samuelson's apartment was on the 18th floor of the co-op at 79th Street and Madison Avenue. His office was on the ground floor of the same building. It was not unusual for him to descend to work in the automatic elevator, wearing a holey wool cardigan and worn carpet slippers.

Delaney and Boone huddled under the marquee of the building for a moment, trying to keep out of a sleety rain that had been falling all night.

"Just for the fun of it," Delaney said, "let's both of us go after this guy. Short, punchy questions with no logical sequence. Biff, bang, pow! We'll come at him from all angles."

"So he won't be able to get set?" Boone asked.

"Partly that. But mostly because he got me up so early on a miserable morning."

Dr. Samuelson opened the door to his office himself; there was no visible evidence that he employed a receptionist. He took their wet coats and hats and hung them away. He ushered them into a cluttered inner office in which all the furnishings seemed accumulated rather than selected. The place had a fusty air, and the few good antiques were in need of restoration. A stuffed barn owl moldered atop a bookcase.

In addition to an old horsehair patient's couch, covered with an Indian blanket, there were two creaky morris chairs in the office. These Samuelson pulled up facing his massive desk. He sat behind it in a wing chair upholstered in worn maroon leather.

Sergeant Boone displayed his ID, introduced Delaney, and explained his role in the investigation.

"Oh, yes," Samuelson said in a high-pitched voice, "after you called last night I thought it best to make some inquiries. You both are highly recommended. I am willing to cooperate, of course, but I have already told the police everything I know."

"About the events of that Friday night," Delaney said, "when Ellerbee was killed. But there are things we need that are not included in your statement."

"For instance," Boone said, "how well did you know the victim?"

"Very well. Ever since he was my student in Boston."

Delaney: "Did you know his wife as well?"

"Of course. We visited frequently here in New York, and I was often their houseguest up in Brewster."

Boone: "Do you think a patient could have killed Ellerbee?"

"It's possible. Unfortunately, assaults on psychiatrists are not all that uncommon."

Delaney: "Was it a happy marriage?"

"The Ellerbees'? Yes, a very happy, successful marriage. They loved each other and, of course, had an additional link in their work."

Boone: "What kind of patient would attack Ellerbee?"

"A psychopath, obviously. Or someone temporarily deranged by the trauma of his analysis. It is sometimes an extremely painful process."

Delaney: "You said *his* analysis. You believe the killer was a man?"

"The nature of the crime would seem to indicate it. But it could have been a woman."

Boone: "Was Diane Ellerbee also your student?"

"No, she was Simon's student. That's how they met—when he was teaching."

Delaney: "Did he convince her to start her own practice?"

"He persuaded her, yes. We often joked about their Pygmalion-Galatea relationship."

Boone: "You mean he created her?"

"Of course not. But he recognized her gifts, her talents as a therapist. Before she met him, I understand, she was somewhat of a dilettante. But he saw something in her he thought should be encouraged. He was right. She has done—is doing—fine work."

Delaney: "How do you account for those two hammer blows to the victim's eyes?"

Samuelson exhibited the first signs of unease at this fusillade of rapid questions. He fiddled with some papers and they noted his hand trembled slightly.

He was a wisp of a man with narrow shoulders and a disproportionately large head balanced on a stalky neck. His complexion was grayish, and he wore wire-rimmed spectacles set with thick, curved lens that magnified his eyes. Surprisingly, he had wavy russet hair that appeared to have been carefully blown dry.

He sipped his coffee and seemed to regain his poise.

"What was your question?" he asked.

Boone: "Those two hammer blows to the victim's eyes—could they have been a symbolic attempt to blind the dead man?"

"It is a possibility."

Delaney: "Do you think Simon Ellerbee was faithful to his wife?"

"Of course he was faithful! And she to him. I told you it was a happy, successful marriage. There are such things. I really don't see how all this is going to help you find the person who committed this despicable act."

Boone: "Diane Ellerbee was younger than her husband?"

"By about eight years. Not such a great gap."

Delaney: "She's a very beautiful woman. But you're certain she was faithful?"

"Of course I'm certain. There was never any gossip about them, never a rumor. And I was their closest friend. I would have heard or noticed something."

Boone: "Did you notice any change in Simon Ellerbee in the last six months or a year?"

"No, no change."

Delaney: "Nervousness? Fear? Sudden fits of silence or outbursts of anger? Anything like that?"

"No, nothing."

Boone: "Did he ever say he had been threatened by any of his patients?"

"No. He was an extremely competent man. I'm sure he would have known how to handle such threats—if any had been made."

Delaney: "Have you ever been married?"

"Once. My wife died of cancer twenty years ago. I never remarried."

Boone: "Children?"

"One son killed in an automobile accident."

Delaney: "So the Ellerbees were the only family you had?"

"I have brothers and sisters. But the Ellerbees were very close friends. Two beautiful people. I loved them both."

Boone: "They never fought?"

"Of course they fought occasionally. What married couple doesn't? But always with good humor."

Delaney: "When you went over to the Ellerbees' townhouse that Friday night and went upstairs, did you hear anything? Like someone might still be in the house, moving around?"

"No, I heard nothing."

Boone: "Did you smell anything unusual? Perfume, incense, a strong body odor—anything like that?"

"No. Just the damp. It was a very wet night."

Delaney: "There were no signs of forced entry, so we assume the victim buzzed the door open for someone he was expecting or knew. Now we're back to the possibility of one of Ellerbee's patients putting him down. We want Doctor Diane to go through her husband's caseload and select those she thinks might be capable of the murder."

"Yes, she told me that. Last night."

Boone: "She relies on your opinion. Will you advise her to cooperate?"

"I have already so advised her. The law prevents her from giving you her husband's files, but I think that here the public good demands she at least name those parties she thinks might be capable of violence. You have the complete list and I assume will run a basic check on them all."

Delaney: "Checking that many alibis is almost impossible, so I'm glad you've encouraged Mrs. Ellerbee to cooperate. She obviously respects your opinions. Are you a father figure?"

Dr. Samuelson, confidence regained, relaxed. His enlarged eyes glittered behind the heavy glasses.

"Oh, I doubt that," he said softly. "Diane is a very independent woman. Her beauty warms the heart. But she is very intelligent and capable. Simon was a lucky man. I told him that often, and he agreed."

"Thank you for your help," Delaney said, rising abruptly. "I hope we may consult you again if we need more information."

"Of course. Anytime. You think you will find the person who did this thing?"

"If we're lucky," Delaney said.

Outside, they dashed across Madison to a luncheonette that had not yet filled up with the breakfast crowd. They both ordered black coffee and jelly doughnuts and took them to a small, Formica-topped table alongside the tiled wall.

"I'm proud of you," Delaney said.

"How so?"

"You knew about Pygmalion and Galatea."

Boone laughed. "Blame it on crossword puzzles. You pick up a lot of useless information."

"Funny thing," Delaney said, "but just last night I was talking to Monica about the fact that so many beautiful women make a career out of just being beautiful. But from what Samuelson said, Simon was the one who convinced Diane she had a brain in addition to looks."

"I think the good doctor is in love with her."

"That wouldn't be hard. But what chance would he have? Did you see the photos of Ellerbee in the file? A big, handsome guy. Samuelson looks like a gnome compared to him."

"Maybe that's why he snuffed him," Boone said.

"You really think that?"

"No. Do you?"

"I can't see it," Delaney said. "But there's a hell of a lot I can't see about this thing. For instance, I asked Samuelson if Simon had fits of silence or outbursts of anger. Now that was an almost word-for-word quote from Diane. She said her husband was a lovely man, but occasionally had fits of silence and outbursts of anger. Samuelson, supposedly a close friend, says he never noticed anything like that."

"Maybe he thought it was of no consequence, or maybe he was trying to protect the memory of a dead friend."

"Right now, I'd say we can scratch Diane and Samuelson," Delaney said, "unless Parnell or Jason can come up with something. That leaves the victim's patients as our best bet. Will you call the widow and set up a meet to get the list of possibles from her?"

"Sure. I also better check in with Suarez's crew and find out how many of the patients they've already tossed."

"Right. You know, so far this whole thing is smoke—you realize that, don't you?"

"No doubt about that."

"Nothing hard," Delaney said fretfully, "nothing definite. It's really the worst part of a case—the opening, when everything is mush."

"No great hurry to clear it," the Sergeant said. "Is there?"

Delaney didn't want to tell him there was—that it had to be closed by the end of the year if Deputy Thorsen wanted that third star for Michael Suarez, but the Sergeant was a sharp man and probably aware of the Departmental politics involved.

"I'd just like to tidy it up fast," he said casually, "or admit failure and get back to my routine. Can you drop me?"

"Of course," Boone said, "if I can get that clunker started."

The Sergeant was driving his personal car, an old, spavined Buick he had bought at a city auction of towed-away cars. But the wheels turned, and he delivered Delaney to his brownstone.

"Give you a call, sir," he said, "as soon as I set up something with Doctor Diane."

"Good enough," Delaney said. "And brief Suarez on our talk with Samuelson. I promised to keep him in the picture."

Monica was in the living room, watching a women's talk show on television.

"What's the topic this morning?" Delaney inquired pleasantly. "Premature ejaculation?"

"Very funny," Monica said. "How did you make out with Samuelson?"

He was tempted to tell her about the doctor's comments about the Ellerbees' Pygmalion-Galatea relationship, but he didn't mention it, fearing it would sound like gloating.

"We got nothing you can hang your hat on," he said. "Just general background stuff. I'll tell you about it tonight."

He went into the study, sat at his desk, and wrote out a full report on the interrogation of Dr. Julius K. Samuelson, doing his best to recall the psychiatrist's exact words.

There was something in that interview that disturbed him, but he could not for the life of him think of what it was. He read over his report of the questioning, and still could not pinpoint it. But he was convinced something was there.

His vague disquiet was characteristic of the entire case, he decided. So far, the investigation of the murder of Dr. Simon Ellerbee was all obscure overtones and subtle shadings. The damned case was a watercolor.

Most homicides were oils—great, bold slashings of pigment laid on with a wide brush or palette knife. Killings were generally stark, brutal affairs, the result of outsize passions or capital sins.

But this killing had the whiff of the library about it, something literary and genteel, as if plotted by Henry James.

Perhaps, Delaney admitted, he felt that way because the scene of the crime was an elegant townhouse rather than a roach-infested tenement. Or maybe because the people involved were obviously educated, intelligent, and with the wit to lie smoothly if it would serve their purpose.

But murder was murder. And maybe a delicate, polite case like this needed a lumbering, mulish old cop to strip away all the la-di-dah pretense and pin an artful, perceptive, refined killer to the goddamned wall.

# 9.

"We ought to start thinking about Thanksgiving," Monica said at breakfast. "It'll be here before you know it. A turkey, I suppose . . ."

"Oh . . . I don't know," Delaney said slowly.

"How about a goose?"

"A roast goose," he said dreamily. "Maybe with wild rice and brandied apples. Sounds good. You do the goose and I'll do the apples. Okay?"

"It's a deal."

"Are the girls coming down?"

"No, they're going to a friend's home. But they'll be here for Christmas."

"Good. Would you like to invite Rebecca and Abner for Thanksgiving dinner? We can't eat a whole goose by ourselves."

"That would be fun. I think they'd like it. How about Jason and his family?"

"That guy could demolish a roast goose by himself. But if I ask Boone, I'll have to ask Jason. I suspect he'll want to have Thanksgiving dinner at home with his family, but I'll check and let you know."

"What are your plans for today, Edward?"

"I want to stick around in case Abner calls to tell me when we're going to meet with Doctor Diane. Where are you off to?"

"More Christmas shopping. I want to get it all done and out of the way so I can relax and enjoy the holiday season."

"Until the bills come in," he said. "Have fun."

He went into the study to read the morning *Times* and smoke his breakfast cigar. He was halfway through both when the phone rang. He expected it to be Boone, but it was not.

"Edward X. Delaney here," he said.

"Good morning. This is Detective Charles Parnell."

"Oh, yes. How are you?"

"Fine, sir. And you?"

"Surviving," Delaney said. "You probably don't remember, but you and I have met. It was at the retirement party for Sergeant Schlossman."

"Sure," Parnell said, laughing. "I remember. I tried to chug-a-lug a quart bottle of Schaefer and upchucked all over Captain Rogers' new uniform. I haven't had a promotion since! Listen, Abner Boone said you wanted these financial reports on the people in the Ellerbee case as soon as possible."

"Don't tell me you've got them already?"

"Well, I may not be good, but I'm fast. I've got a single typed page on each of them. It's not Dun & Bradstreet, but it should give you what you want. I was wondering if I could bring them by and go over them with you. Then if there's anything else you need, you can steer me in the right direction."

"Of course," Delaney said promptly. "I'll be in all morning. You have my address?"

"Yep. Be there in half an hour."

Delaney relighted his cigar and finished the *Times.* It was perfect timing; he had put the newspaper together neatly and was taking it into the living room to leave for Monica when the front door bell chimed.

The detective they called Daddy Warbucks was wearing a black bowler with a rolled brim, and a double-breasted topcoat of taupe gabardine. He carried an attaché case of polished calfskin.

Seeing Delaney blink, Parnell grinned. "It's my uniform," he explained. "I work with bankers and stockbrokers. It helps if I look like I belong to the club. Off duty, I wear cord jeans and a ratty sweatshirt."

"Haven't seen a derby in years," Delaney said admiringly. "On you it looks good."

After his hat and coat had been hung away in the hall closet, the detective was revealed in all his conservative elegance: a three-piece suit of navy flannel with muted pin-stripe, light blue shirt with starched white collar and cuffs, a richly tapestried cravat, and black shoes with a dull gloss—wingtips, of course.

"Sometimes I feel like a clown in this getup," he said, following Delaney back to the study, "but it seems to impress the people I deal with. Beautiful home you've got here."

"Thank you."

"You own the whole house?"

"That's right."

"If you ever want to rent out a floor, let me know. The wife and I and two kids are jammed into a West Side walk-up."

But his comments were without bitterness, and Delaney pegged him for a cheerful, good-natured man.

"Tell me something," he asked Parnell, "that suit fits so snugly, where do you carry your piece?"

"Here," Daddy Warbucks said. He turned, lifted the tail of his jacket, and revealed a snub-nosed revolver in a belt holster at the small of his back. "Not so great for a quick draw, but it's a security blanket. Do you carry?"

"Only on special occasions," Delaney said. "Listen, can I get you anything—coffee, a cola?"

"No, but thanks. I'm up to my eyeballs in coffee this morning."

"Well, then," Delaney said, "why don't you sit in that armchair and make yourself comfortable."

"I smell cigar smoke," Parnell said, "so I guess it's okay if I light a cigarette."

"Of course."

While the detective lit up, Delaney studied the man.

Crew-cut pepper-and-salt hair. A horsey face with deep furrows and laugh crinkles at the corners of the eyes. A good set of strong choppers. A blandly innocent expression. A rugged ugliness there, but not without charm. He looked like a good man to invite to a party.

"Well . . ." Parnell said, leaning over to snap open his attaché case, "how do you want to do this? Want to read the stuff first or should I give you the gist of it?"

"Suppose you summarize first," Delaney said. "Then I'll ask questions if I've got any."

"Okay," Parnell said. "We'll start with Doctor Julius K. Samuelson. His net worth is about one mil, give or take. Moneywise, he's a very cautious gentleman. CDs, Treasury bonds, and tax-free municipals. He owns his co-op apartment and office. Keeps too much in his checking account, but like I said, he's a mossback financewise. No stocks, no tax shelters, no high-fliers. He's made three irrevocable charitable trusts—all to hospitals with major psychiatric research departments. Nothing unusual. Nothing exciting. Any questions?"

"I guess not," Delaney said. "I don't suppose you got a look at his will?"

"No, I can't do that. I was lucky to learn about those charitable trusts. I really don't think there's anything in Samuelson for you, sir—lootwise. I mean, he's not rich-rich, but he's not hurting either."

"You're probably right," Delaney said, sighing. "What about the Ellerbees?"

"Ah," Charles Parnell said, "now it gets mildly interesting. If you were thinking maybe the wife knocked off the husband for his assets, it just doesn't work. He was doing okay, but she's got megabucks of her own."

"No kidding?" Delaney said, surprised. "How did she do that?"

"Her father died, leaving a modest pile to her mother. Two years later, her mother died. She had some money of her own as well. Diane Ellerbee inherited the whole bundle. Then, a year after that, a spinster aunt conked, and Diane *really* hit the jackpot—almost three mil from the aunt alone."

"Diane was an only child?"

"She had a younger brother who got scragged in Vietnam. He had no family of his own—no wife or kids, I mean—so she picked up all the marbles."

"How many marbles?" Delaney asked.

"Her husband's will hasn't been filed for probate yet, but even without her take from him, I estimate the lady tips the scales at close to five mil."

"Wow!" Delaney said. "Beautiful *and* rich."

"Yeah," Parnell said, "and she handles it all herself. No business manager or investment counselor for her. She's been doing great, too. She's smart enough to diversify, so she's into everything: stocks, bonds, real estate, tax shelters, mutual funds, municipals, commercial paper—you name it."

Delaney shook his head in wonder. "Beautiful *and* rich *and* shrewd."

"You better believe it. And she's got nerve. Some of her investments are chancy stuff, but I've got to admit she's had more winners than losers."

"What about the victim?" Delaney asked. "How was he fixed?"

"Like Samuelson, he wasn't hurting. But nothing like his wife. I'd guess his estate at maybe a half-mil, after taxes. Here's something interesting: She handled his investments for him."

"Really?" Delaney said thoughtfully. "Yes, that *is* interesting."

"Maybe he didn't have the time, or just had no great desire to pile it up buckwise. Anyway, she did as well for him as she did for herself. They have no joint accounts. Everything is separate. They don't even file a joint return."

"What about his father?" Delaney asked. "Was he giving Simon anything?"

Daddy Warbucks smiled. "Henry Ellerbee, the great real estate tycoon? That's a laugh. I had to do a money profile on the guy about six months ago. He's a real cowboy. Got a million deals working and he hasn't got two nickels to rub together. He lost control of Ellerbee Towers and he's mortgaged to the hilt. If everyone calls in his paper at once, the only place he'll be sleeping will be in bankruptcy court. I'll bet you and I have more hard cash than he does. Help out Simon? No way! More likely he was leaning on his son. Well, that's about all I've got. Do you have any more questions?"

Delaney pondered a moment. "I don't think so. Not right now. If you'll leave me your typed reports, I'll go over them. Then I may need your help on some details."

"Sure," Parnell said. "Anytime. When Simon Ellerbee's will is filed for probate, I'll be able to get the details for you."

"Good," Delaney said. "I'd appreciate that." He looked at the detective narrowly. "You like this kind of work?" he asked.

"Love it," the other man said immediately. "You know what I drag down per year. Snooping into other people's private money affairs is a kind of fantasy life for me. I'm fascinated by their wealth, and I imagine how I'd handle it—if I had it!"

"You working on anything interesting right now?"

"Oh, yeah," Daddy Warbucks said. "It's lovely—a computerized check-kiting scam. This guy worked in the computer section of a big Manhattan bank. He knows banking and he knows computers—right? So he starts out kiting checks, opening accounts at three or four New York City banks under phony names with fake ID he bought on the street. He started out small with a ten-G investment. Within six months, taking advantage of the float, he's shuffling deposits and transfers up to a quarter of a mil."

"Good God!" Delaney said. "I thought there were safeguards against that."

"It's the float!" Parnell cried. "That wonderful, marvelous, goddamned float! You can't safeguard against that. Anyway, like most check-kiters, this guy couldn't stop. He could have cashed in, grabbed his profits, and taken off for Brazil. But the scam was working so well, he decided to go for broke. He starts opening accounts in New Jersey, Connecticut, and so forth. Longer float, more profits. Then he realizes that if he had accounts in California, he'll have maybe a ten-day or two-week float. So, on his vacation, he flies out to the West Coast and opens a dozen accounts, using the same phony names as in New York and giving the New York banks as references! How do you like that?"

"As you said, it's lovely."

"The kicker is this," the detective said. "By this time the nut has got so many accounts and so many names, with checks flying all over the country, that he can't keep track of it all. So he writes his own program and fits it into one of the computers at the bank where he works. His personal program that can only be tapped by a code word, and he's the only one who knows that. So now his bank's computer is running this guy's check-kiting con. Can you believe that he had run his total up to more than two mil before the roof fell in?"

"How did they catch up with him?"

"It was an accident. Some smart lady in an Arizona bank was supposed to monitor heavy out-of-state deposits and transfers. She was out sick for a week, and when she got back to work, she found her desk piled high. She began to wade through the stuff, dividing it up by account numbers. She spotted all these deposits and transfers made by the same person, gradually increasing in size. She knew what that probably meant, and blew the whistle. It'll take at least a year to straighten out the mess. Meanwhile the guy is languishing in durance vile because he can't make bail. And a few months ago he could have cashed in and skipped with two mil. I figure it wasn't just greed that kept him going. I think he was absolutely mesmerized by the game. He just wanted to see how far he could go."

"A fascinating case," Delaney agreed.

"Yeah, but right now it's a mess. I mean, every state where he operated wants a piece of this guy, plus the Feds, plus the banks, and God knows who else. The funniest thing is that nobody lost any money. In fact, practically everyone *made* money because they were putting his fake deposits to work until he transferred the funds. The only one who lost was the perp. And all he lost was his original ten grand. There's a moral there somewhere, but I don't know what it is."

Delaney offered Parnell a beer, but the detective reluctantly declined, saying he had to get down to Wall Street for lunch with two hotshot arbitragers.

He handed over three typewritten reports and his card in case more information was needed. They went out into the hallway and Delaney helped Daddy Warbucks on with his natty coat.

"Really a great home," Parnell said, looking around. "I'd like one exactly like it. Well, maybe someday."

"Just don't start kiting checks," Delaney warned.

"Not me," the detective said, laughing. "I haven't got the chutzpah. Besides, I can't work a computer."

They shook hands and Delaney thanked the other man for his help. Parnell departed, bowler cocked at a jaunty angle, attaché case swinging.

Delaney went back to the kitchen, smiling. He had enjoyed the company of Daddy Warbucks. He was always interested in other dicks' cases—especially new scams and innovative criminal techniques.

He made a "wet" sandwich, leaning over the sink to eat it. Slices of canned Argentine corned beef with a layer of sauerkraut and a few potato chips for crunch. And Dijon mustard. All on thick slabs of sour rye. Washed down with dark Heineken.

Finished, he cleaned up the kitchen and returned to the study. He put on his reading glasses and went over the three financial statements Parnell had given him. He saw nothing of importance that Daddy Warbucks hadn't covered in his oral report.

The detective was right: The idea that Diane Ellerbee might have chilled her husband for his gelt just didn't wash; she had ten times his wealth and Delaney couldn't see her as an inordinately avaricious woman.

So that, he supposed, was that. Unless Jason T. Jason came up with something in the biographies, the only way to go was investigation of Simon Ellerbee's patients.

And right on cue, the telephone rang. This time it *was* Abner Boone. He said Dr. Diane Ellerbee would see them that evening at nine o'clock.

"Suppose I pick you up about fifteen minutes early," Boone suggested.

"Make it a half-hour early," Delaney said. "Charlie Parnell stopped by, and I want to bring you up to date on what he found out."

# *10.*

Delaney turned sideways on the front passenger seat, looking at Abner Boone as he filled him in on Charlie Parnell's report. They were parked near the East 84th Street townhouse.

Boone was a tall, gawky man who walked with a shambling lope, wrists and ankles protruding a little too far from his cuffs. He had short, gingery hair, lightly freckled complexion, big, horsey teeth. There was a lot of "country boy" in his appearance and manner, but Delaney knew that masked a sharp mind and occasionally painful sensitivity.

"Well, sir," the Sergeant said when Delaney had finished, "the lady sure sounds like a powerhouse. All that money to manage, two houses, and a successful career. But you know who interests me most in this thing?"

"The victim?" Delaney guessed.

"That's right. I can't get a handle on him. Everyone says how brilliant he was. Maybe that's so, but I can't get a mental picture of him—how he dressed, talked, what he did on his time off. From what Doctor Diane and Samuelson told us, he seems almost too good to be true."

"Well, you can't expect his widow and best friend to put him down. I'm hoping his patients will open up and tell us a little more about him. I guess it's about time; we don't want to keep the doctor waiting."

On the lobby intercom, Dr. Diane Ellerbee told them to come up to the third floor, then buzzed them in. They tramped up the stairway, carrying their hats. She met them in the hallway and shook hands firmly with both of them.

"This may take a little time," she said briskly, "so I thought we'd be more comfortable in the sitting room."

She was wearing a long-sleeved jumpsuit of black silk, zipped from high collar to shirred waist. Her wheaten hair was down, splaying about her shoulders in a silken skein. As she led the way toward the rear of the house, Delaney admired again her erect carriage and the flowing grace of her movements.

She ushered them into a brightly lighted chamber, comfortably cluttered with bibelots, framed photos, bric-a-brac. One wall was a ceiling-high bookcase jammed with leather-bound sets, paperbacks, magazines.

"The rooms downstairs are more formal than this," she said with a half-smile. "And neater. But Simon and I spent most of our evenings here. It's a good place to unwind. Let me have your coats, gentlemen. May I bring you something—coffee, a drink?"

They both politely declined.

She seated them in soft armchairs, then pulled up a ladder-back chair with a cane seat to face them. She sat primly, spine straight, chin lifted, head held high.

"Julie—" she started, then: "Doctor Samuelson approves of my cooperating with you, but I must say I am not absolutely certain I am doing the right thing. The conflict is between my desire to see my husband's murderer caught and at the same time protect the confidentiality of his patients."

"Doctor Ellerbee," Delaney said, "I assure you that anything you tell us will be top secret as far as we're concerned."

"Well . . ." she said, "I suppose that's as much as I can hope for. One other thing: The patients I have selected as potential assailants are only six out of a great many more."

"We've got to start somewhere, ma'am," Boone said. "It's impossible for us to run alibi checks on them all."

"I realize that," she said sharply. "I'm just warning you that my judgment may be faulty. After all, they were my *husband's* patients, not mine. So I'm going by his files and what he told me. It's quite possible— probable, in fact—that the six people I've selected are completely innocent, and the guilty person is the one I've passed over."

"Believe me," Delaney said, "we're not immediately and automatically going to consider your selections to be suspects. They'll be thoroughly investigated, and if we believe them to be innocent, we'll move on to others in your husband's caseload. Don't feel you are condemning these people simply by giving us their names. There's more to a homicide investigation than that."

"Well, that makes me feel a little better. Remember, psychotherapy is not an exact science—it is an uncertain art. Two skilled, experienced therapists examining the same patient could very likely come up with two opposing diagnoses. You have only to read the opinions of psychiatrists testifying in court cases to realize that."

"We used to call them alienists," Delaney said. "Usually they confused a trial more than they helped."

"I'm afraid you're right," she said with a wan smile. "Objective criteria are hard to recognize in this field. Well, having said all that, let me show you what I've done."

She rose, went over to a small Sheraton-styled desk, came back with two pages of typescript.

"Six patients," she told them. "Four men, two women. I've given you their names, ages, addresses. I've written a short paragraph on each, using my husband's notes and what he told me about them. Although I've listed their major problems, I haven't given you definitive labels—schizoid, psychotic, manic-depressive, or whatever. They were not my patients, and I refuse to attempt a diagnosis. Now let me get started."

She donned a pair of wire-rimmed reading glasses. Curiously, these old-fashioned spectacles softened her chiseled features, gave her face a whimsical charm.

"I should warn you," she said, "I have listed these people in no particular order. That is, the first mentioned is not, in my opinion, necessarily the most dangerous. All six, I believe, have the potential for violence. I won't read everything I've written—just give you a very brief synopsis. . . .

"Number One: Ronald J. Bellsey, forty-three. He saw my husband three times a week. Apparently a violent man with a history of uncontrollable outbursts of anger. Ronald first consulted my husband after injuring his wife in a brutal attack. At least he had sense enough to realize he was ill and needed help.

"Number Two: Isaac Kane, twenty-eight. He was one of my husband's charity patients, treated once a week at a free clinic. Isaac is what they call an idiot savant, although I hate that term. He is far from being an idiot, but he is retarded. Isaac does absolutely wonderful landscapes in pastel chalk. Very professional work. But he has, on occasion, attacked workers and other patients at the clinic.

"Number Three: Sylvia Mae Otherton, forty-six. She saw my husband twice a week, but frequently made panic calls. Sylvia suffers from heavy anxieties, ranging from agoraphobia to a hatred of bearded men. On the few occasions when she ventured out in public, she made vicious and unprovoked attacks against men with beards."

"Was your husband bearded, ma'am?" Boone asked.

"No, he was not. Number Four: L. Vincent Symington, fifty-one. Apparently his problem is a very deep and pervasive paranoia. Vince frequently struck back at people he believed were persecuting him, including his aged mother and father. He saw my husband three times a week.

"Number Five: Joan Yesell, thirty-five. She is a very withdrawn, depressed young woman who lives with her widowed mother. Joan has a history of three suicide attempts, which is one of the reasons I have included her. Suicide, when tried unsuccessfully so often, often develops into homicidal mania.

"And finally, Harold Gerber, thirty-seven. He served in Vietnam and won several medals for exceptional valor. Harold apparently suffers intensely from guilt—not only for those he killed in the war, but because he came back alive when so many of his friends died. His guilt is manifested in barroom brawls and physical attacks on strangers he thinks have insulted him.

"And that's all I have. You'll find more details in this typed report. Do you have any questions?"

Delaney and Boone looked at each other.

"Just one thing, doctor," Delaney said. "Could you tell us if any of the six was being treated with drugs."

"No," she said immediately. "None of them. My husband did not believe in psychotropic drugs. He said they only masked symptoms but did nothing to reveal or treat the cause of the illness. Incidentally, I hold the same opinion, but I am not a fanatic on the subject as my husband was. I occasionally use drugs in my practice—but only when the physical health of the patient warrants it."

"Are you licensed to prescribe drugs?" Delaney asked.

She gave him a hard stare. "No," she said, "but my husband was."

"But of course," Boone said hastily, "it's possible that any of the six could be using drugs on their own."

"It's possible," Dr. Ellerbee said in her loud, assertive voice. "It's possible of anyone. Which of you gets this report?"

"Ma'am," Delaney said softly, "you have just the one copy?"

"That's correct. I made no carbon."

"You wouldn't happen to have a copying machine in your office, would you? It would help a great deal if both Sergeant Boone and I had copies. Speed things up."

"There's a copier in my husband's outer office," she said, rising. "It'll just take a minute."

"We'll come along if you don't mind," Delaney said, and both men stood up.

She looked at them. "If you're thinking about my safety, I thank you —but there's no need, I assure you. I have lived in this house since Simon died. There are people here during the day, but I'm alone at night. It doesn't frighten me. I won't let it frighten me. This is my *home.*"

"If you'll allow us," Delaney said stubbornly, "we'll still come along. It'll give us a chance to see the scene—to see where it happened."

"If you wish," she said tonelessly.

She took a ring of keys from the desk drawer, then led the way along the hall. She unlocked the door of her husband's office and turned on the light. The floor of the receptionist's room was bare boards.

"I had the carpeting taken up and thrown out," she said. "It was stained, and I didn't wish to have it cleaned."

"Have you decided what to do with this space, ma'am?" Boone asked.

"No," she said shortly. "I haven't thought about it."

She went over to the copier in the corner and switched it on. While she was making a duplicate of her report, they looked about.

There was little to see. The outer office was identical in size and shape to the one on the second floor. It was aseptically furnished with steel desk, chairs, filing cabinet. There was no indication it had been the scene of murderous frenzy.

Dr. Ellerbee turned off the copier, handed each of them her two-page report.

"I wouldn't care to have this circulated," she said sternly.

"It won't be," Delaney assured her. "Doctor, would you mind if we took a quick look into your husband's office?"

"What for?"

"Standard operating procedure," he said. "To try to learn more about your husband. Sometimes seeing where a victim lived and where he worked gives a good indication of the kind of man he was."

She shrugged, obviously not believing him, but not caring.

"Help yourself," she said, gesturing toward the inner door.

She sat at the receptionist's desk while they went into Dr. Simon Ellerbee's private office. Boone switched on the overhead light.

A severe, rigorous room, almost austere. No pictures on the white walls. No decorations. No objets d'art, memorabilia, or personal touches. The room was defined by its lacks. Even the black leather patient's couch was as sterile as a hospital gurney.

"Cold," Boone said in a low voice.

"You wanted a handle on the guy," Delaney said. "Here's a piece of it: He was organized, logical, emotionless. Notice how all the straight edges are parallel or at right angles? A very precise, disciplined man. Can you imagine spending maybe twelve hours a day in a cell like this? Let's go; it gives me the willies."

They reclaimed their coats and hats from the sitting room, thanked Dr. Diane Ellerbee for her assistance, and said they'd keep her informed of the progress of the investigation.

"I warn you," Delaney said, smiling, "we may call on you for more help."

"Of course," she said. "Anytime." She seemed tired.

Out on the street, walking slowly to the car, Boone said, "Ballsy lady. Most women would have gone somewhere else to live or asked a friend to stay awhile after something like that happened."

"Mmm," Delaney said. "She claims she's not frightened and I believe her. By the way, did you notice how she referred to those patients by their first names? I wonder if all shrinks do that. It reminds me of the way cops talk to suspects to bring them down."

"I thought it was just to—you know—to show how sympathetic you are."

"Maybe. But using a suspect's first name diminishes him, robs him of his dignity. It proves that you're in a position of authority. You call a Mafia chief Tony when he's used to being called Mr. Anthony Gelesco and it makes him feel like a two-bit punk or a pushcart peddler. Well, all that's smoke and getting us nowhere. Tomorrow morning check to see if Chief Suarez's men have talked to any of those six patients. We better start with their whereabouts at the time of the homicide."

"Even if Suarez's guys have talked to them, you'll still want them double-checked, won't you, sir?"

"Of course. As far as I'm concerned, this investigation is just starting. And get hold of Jason Two; see how he's coming along on the biographies. I'd like him to finish up as soon as possible; we're going to need his help knocking on doors."

Sergeant Boone drove Delaney home. Outside the brownstone, before Delaney got out of the car, Boone said, "What did you think of Doctor Diane's selections, sir? They all seem like possibles to me."

"Could be. You know, when I talked to Doc Walden, he tried to convince me that most people who go to psychotherapists aren't nuts or crazies or weirdos; they're just poor unfortunates with king-size emotional hangups. But all these people on Doctor Diane's list sound like half-decks. Good night, Sergeant."

Monica was in the living room, working the *Times* crossword puzzle. She looked up as Delaney came in, peering at him over the top of her Ben Franklin glasses.

"How did it go?" she asked.

"I need something," he said. "Maybe a tall scotch with a lot of ice and a lot of soda."

He mixed the drinks in the kitchen and brought them back to the living room. Monica held her glass up to the light.

"You have a heavy hand with that scotch bottle, kiddo," she said. She tried a sip. "But I forgive you. Now tell me—how did it go?"

Delaney slumped in his high wing chair covered with bottle-green leather worn glassy smooth. He loosened his tie, unbuttoned his collar, and sighed.

"It went all right. She gave us a list of six possibles."

"Then what are you so grumpy about?"

"Who says I'm grumpy?"

"I do. You've got that squinchy look around the eyes, and you're gritting your teeth."

"I am? Well, it's not going to work."

"What's not going to work?"

"The investigation. *My* investigation. Now we've got six people to check out, and I have only Boone and Jason. I can't do any legwork myself without a tin to flash. So, in effect, there are two men to investigate six suspects. Oh, it could be done if we had all the time in the world, but Thorsen wants this thing cleared up by the end of the year."

"Only one answer to that, isn't there? Ask Ivar for more help."

"I don't know how Chief Suarez would take that. He said he'd cooperate in any way he could, but I have a hunch he still sees me as competition."

"Then instead of asking Ivar for more men, ask Suarez. That makes him part of the team, doesn't it? Gives him a chance to share the success if you find out who killed Simon Ellerbee."

He stared at her reflectively. "I knew I married a great beauty," he said. "Now I realize I also married a great brain."

She sniffed. "You're just finding that out? Why don't you call Suarez right now."

"Too late," Delaney said. "I'll wake up that family of his. I'll get hold of him first thing in the morning. Meanwhile I've got a little work to do. Don't wait up for me; go to bed whenever you like."

He rose, lumbered over to her, swooped to kiss her cheek. Then he took his drink into the study. He closed the connecting door to the living room in case Monica wanted to watch the Johnny Carson show.

He sat at the desk, put on his heavy black-rimmed glasses, and slowly read through Dr. Diane's two-page report. Then he read it again.

There was more there than she had given them in her oral summary. The six paragraphs described very disturbed people who showed every evidence of being out of control. Any one of them seemed to have the potential for ungovernable violence.

Delaney sat back and gently tinked the rim of his highball glass against his teeth. He thought about Simon Ellerbee. What was it like, he wondered, to spend your life working with people whose thought processes were so chaotic?

It was, he supposed, like being in a foreign country where all the natives were hostile, spoke a strange language, and even the geography of their world was terra incognita.

He imagined that any man who deliberately ventured into the alien land might suffer from bewilderment and disorientation. He'd have to clamp a tight hold on his own feelings to keep from being swept away by disorder.

Delaney remembered that cold, disciplined office of Dr. Simon Ellerbee. Now he could understand why a psychiatrist would want to work in rigidly geometric surroundings where parallel lines never met and hard edges reminded that arrangement and sequence did exist, and logic was not dead.

# *11.*

Isaac Kane had been going to the clinic every Wednesday. He was given endless tests. Sometimes, with the permission of his mother, he was handed pills or liquids to swallow. They made him do things with wooden blocks and photographed him on videotape. Then he would spend an hour with Dr. Simon.

Kane didn't mind talking to the doctor. He was a nice, quiet man and really seemed interested in what Isaac had to say. In fact, Dr. Simon was about the only one who listened to Isaac; his mother wouldn't listen, and other people made fun of the way he talked. There was so much Kane wanted to say, and sometimes he couldn't get it out fast enough. Then he went, "Bub-bub-bub," and people laughed.

But Dr. Simon stopped coming to the clinic, so Kane stopped, too. They tried to get him to continue coming in every Wednesday, but he just wouldn't do it. They kept at him, and finally he had to hit some of them. That did the trick, all right, and they didn't bother him anymore.

So now he could spend all his days at the Harriet J. Raskob Community Center on West 79th Street. The clinic had been painted all white—Isaac didn't like that—but the Center was pink and green and blue and yellow. It was warm in there, and they let him work on his pastel landscapes.

The head of the Center, Mrs. Freylinghausen, sold some of Kane's landscapes and gave the money to his mother. But she kept enough to buy him a wonderful box of at least a hundred pastel crayons in all colors and hues, an easel, paper, and panels. When he ran out of supplies, Mrs. Freylinghausen bought him more—Isaac wasn't very good at shopping—and locked up all his property when the Center closed at 9:00 P.M.

Most of the people who came to the Center were very old, some in wheelchairs or on walkers. They were as nice to Isaac Kane as Mrs. Freylinghausen. But there were younger people, too, and some of them weren't so nice. They mimicked Isaac's "Bub-bub-bub" and they tripped him or pushed his elbow when he was working or tried to steal his chalks. One girl liked to touch him all over.

Sometimes they got him so mad that he had to hit them. He was strong, and he could really hurt someone if he wanted to.

One afternoon—Kane didn't know what day it was—Mrs. Freylinghausen came out of her office with two men and headed for the corner where Isaac had set up his easel under a skylight. Both the men were big. The older wore a black overcoat and the other a dark green parka. Both carried their hats.

"Isaac," Mrs. Freylinghausen said, "I'd like you to meet two friends of mine who are interested in your work. This gentleman is Mr. Delaney, and here is Mr. Boone."

Isaac shook hands with both of them, leaving their palms smeared with colored chalk. They both smiled and looked nice. Mrs. Freylinghausen moved away.

"Mr. Kane," Delaney said, "we just saw some of your landscapes, and we think they're beautiful."

"They're okay, I guess," Isaac said modestly. "Sometimes they're not, you know, what I want. I can't always get the colors just right."

"Have you ever seen Turner's paintings?" Delaney asked.

"Turner? No. Who is he?"

"An English painter. He worked in oil and watercolor. He did a lot of landscapes. The way you handle light reminds me of Turner."

"Light!" Isaac Kane cried. "That's very hard to do." And then, because he wanted to say so much about light, he began to go "Bub-bub-bub . . ."

They waited patiently, not laughing at him, and when he got out what he wanted to say, they nodded understandingly.

"Mr. Kane," Boone said, "I think we may have a mutual friend. Did you know Doctor Ellerbee?"

"No, I don't know him."

"Doctor Simon Ellerbee?"

"Oh, Doctor Simon! Sure, I know him. He stopped coming to the clinic. What happened to him?"

Boone glanced at Delaney.

"I'm afraid I have bad news for you, Mr. Kane," Delaney said. "Doctor Simon is dead. Someone killed him."

"Gee, that's too bad," Isaac said. "He was a nice man. I liked to talk to him."

He turned back to his easel, where a sheet of grainy paper had been pinned to a square of cardboard. He was working on an idyllic farm scene with a windmill, thatched cottage, a running brook. There were plump white clouds in the foreground and, beyond, dark menacing rain clouds. The rendition of shadows and the changing light saved the work from mawkishness.

"What did you talk to Doctor Simon about?" Delaney asked.

"Oh . . . everything," Isaac said, working with a white chalk to get a little more glitter on the water's surface. "He asked me a lot of questions."

"Mr. Kane," Boone said, "can you think of anyone who might have wanted to hurt Doctor Simon?"

He turned to face them. They saw a rudely handsome young man clad in stained denim overalls, a red plaid shirt, tattered running shoes. His brown hair was cut short enough to show pink scalp. Dark eyes revealed nothing, but there was a sweet innocence in his expression.

"That's the way some people are," he said sadly. "They want to hurt you."

"Do people hurt you, Mr. Kane?" Delaney asked.

"Sometimes they try, but I don't let them. I hit them and then they stop. I don't like mean people."

"But Doctor Simon never hurt you, did he?"

"Oh, no—he was a nice man! I never—he would—we talked and—" But then there was so much he wanted to say about Dr. Simon that he began to stutter again. They waited, but he had nothing intelligible to add.

"Well, we've got to get going," Delaney said. "Thank you for giving us so much time." He looked down at Kane's ragged running shoes. "I hope you have boots or galoshes," he said, smiling. "It's snowing outside."

"I don't care," Isaac said. "I just live around the corner. I don't need boots."

They all shook hands. Delaney and Boone headed for the doorway. A young girl with disheveled hair was propped up against the wall of the vestibule. She looked at them with glazed eyes and said, "Oink, oink."

Out on the sidewalk, Boone said, "She had us pegged."

"Stoned out of her skull," Delaney said grimly.

They were double-parked on 80th Street. Boone had propped a PO-
LICE OFFICER ON DUTY card inside the windshield, and for once it had
worked: He still had his hubcaps. They got in, started the engine,
turned on the wheezy heater, sat a few moments, shivering, and
watched the wet snow drift down.

"Poor guy," Boone observed. "Not much there."

"No," Delaney agreed. "But you never know. He seems to be quick
with his fists when he thinks someone is out to hurt him."

"How could Simon Ellerbee hurt him?"

"Maybe he asked one question too many. It's possible."

"What was the business about the boots and galoshes?" Boone said.

"Those two sets of unidentified tracks on the Ellerbees' carpet."

"Jesus!" the Sergeant said disgustedly. "I forgot all about them."

"Well, we still don't know if Kane *owns* boots. All he said was that he
wasn't wearing them today. I think we better get back to my place,
Sergeant. Chief Suarez said he'd call at noon, and I have a feeling he's a
very prompt man."

"You think he's checking with Thorsen, sir?"

"Of course. If I was in Suarez's place I'd say something like this:
'Deputy, Delaney wants six more detectives. That's okay with me, but I
don't want to give him any of the people working the case for me. It
would hobble what we're doing. So I'd like to assign six new bodies to
Delaney.' "

"You think Thorsen will go for that?"

"Sure he will. He's got no choice."

With the holiday traffic getting heavier and the snow beginning to
pile up, it took them almost a half-hour to get over to the East Side.
Boone parked in front of the 251st Precinct house, leaving his ON DUTY
card on display. Then they trudged next door to Delaney's brownstone.

"How about a sandwich?" Delaney suggested. "We've got some cold
roast beef, sweet pickle relish, sliced onions. Maybe a little pink horseradish. How does that sound?"

"Just right," Boone said. "A hot coffee wouldn't go bad either."

Delaney spread old newspapers on the kitchen table and they ate
their lunch hunched over that.

"Now let's see . . ." Delaney said. "You told me that Suarez's men
have checked out four of the names on our list?"

"That's right, sir. Just their whereabouts at the time of the homicide.
As of this morning, they hadn't gotten around to Otherton or Gerber."

"We'll have to double-check them all anyway. If we get the six new people, I want to assign one to each possible. But I want to question each of the patients personally. That means you or Jason Two will have to come with me to show your ID."

"I talked to Jason. He says he'll be finished with the biogs by tonight. He'll call you."

"Good. I want you there when he makes his report. We'll hit Otherton this afternoon. We won't call her first; just barge in. The other four we'll have to brace in the evening or over the weekend. Sergeant, can you think of anything we should be doing that we're not?"

Boone had finished his sandwich. He sat back, lighted a cigarette.

"I'd like to get a lead on that ball peen hammer," he said. "We didn't ask Isaac Kane if he had one."

"Don't worry," Delaney said. "We'll be getting back to that lad again. I can't see the two women owning a hammer like that—but you never know. We'll have to lean on the four men. Maybe one of them is a do-it-yourself nut or does his own car repairs or something like that."

"How do you get rid of a hammer?" Boone said. "You can't burn it. The handle maybe, but not the head. And the first crew on the scene checked every sewer, catch basin, and garbage can in a ten-block area."

"If I was the killer," Delaney said, "I'd throw it in the river. Chances are good it'd never be found."

"Still," Boone said, "the perp might have—"

But just then the phone rang, and Delaney rose to answer it. "I hope that's Suarez," he said.

"Edward X. Delaney here . . . Yes, Chief . . . Uh-huh. That's fine . . . Monday will be just right . . . Of course. Maybe you and I can get together next week . . . Whenever you say . . . Thank you for your help, Chief."

He hung up and turned to Boone. "He didn't sound too happy about it, but six warm bodies are coming in Monday morning. I'll want you there; maybe you know some of those guys. More coffee?"

"Please. I'm just getting thawed."

"Well, drink up. Then we'll descend on Sylvia Mae Otherton. Sure as hell no woman with agoraphobia is going out on a day like this."

She lived in an old battleship of an apartment house on East 72nd Street between Park and Lexington avenues. Boone drove around the block twice, trying to find a parking space, then gave up. He parked in front of the marquee, and when an indignant doorman rushed out, the Sergeant flashed his shield and quieted him down.

The cavernous lobby was lined with brownish marble that needed cleaning, and the steel Art Deco elevator doors obviously hadn't been polished in years. The carpeting was fretted, and the whole place had a musty odor.

"A mausoleum," Delaney muttered.

There was a marble-topped counter manned by an ancient wearing an old-fashioned hearing aid with a black wire that disappeared into the front of his alpaca jacket. Boone asked for Miss Sylvia Mae Otherton.

"And who shall I say is calling?" the gaffer asked in sepulchral tones.

The Sergeant showed his ID again, and the white eyebrows slowly rose.

The lobby attendant picked up the house phone and punched a three-digit number with a trembling forefinger. He turned his back to them; all they could hear was murmurs. Then he turned back to them.

"Miss Otherton would like to know the purpose of your visit."

"Tell her we want to ask a few questions," Boone said. "It won't take long."

More murmurs.

"Miss Otherton says she is not feeling well and wonders if you can come back another time."

"No, we cannot come back another time," Boone said, beginning to steam. "Ask her if she prefers to see us in her home or should we take her down to the station house and ask the questions there."

The white eyebrows rose even farther. More murmurs. Then he hung up the phone.

"Miss Otherton will see you now," he said. "Apartment twelve-C." Then, his bleary eyes glistening, he leaned over the counter. "Is it about that doctor who got killed?" he asked in a conspiratorial whisper.

They turned away.

"She was devastated," he called after them. "Just devastated."

"Damned old gossip," the Sergeant said angrily in the elevator. "By tonight everyone in the building will know Otherton had a call from the cops."

"Calm down," Delaney said. "Everyone loves a gruesome murder—especially an unsolved one. They'd like to think the perp will get away with it."

Boone looked at him curiously. "You really believe that, sir?"

"Sure," Delaney said cheerfully. "It feeds their fantasies. They can dream of knocking off wife, husband, boss, lover, or that pain in the ass next door—and walking away from it scot-free."

Boonc pushed the buzzer at the door of apartment 12-C. They waited. And waited. Finally they heard sounds of bolts being withdrawn, and the door opened a few inches, held by a chain still in place.

A muffled voice said, "Let me see your identification."

Obediently, the Sergeant passed his ID wallet through the chink. They waited. Then the door closed, the chain came off, and the door was opened wide.

"Wipe your feet on the mat," the woman said, "before you come in." They obeyed.

The apartment was so dimly lighted—heavy drapes drawn across all the windows—that it was difficult to make out much of anything. Heavy furniture loomed along the walls, and they had a muddled impression of an enormous overstuffed couch and two armchairs placed about a round cocktail table.

Delaney smelled sandalwood incense, and, as his eyes became accustomed to the gloom, he saw vaguely Oriental wall hangings, a torn shoji used as a room divider.

The woman who faced them, head bowed, wadded tissue clutched in one hand, seemed as outlandish as her overheated apartment. She wore a loose garment of black lace over a lining of deep purple satin. The pointed hem came to her ankles, and her small feet were shod in glittery evening slippers.

She wore a torrent of necklaces: pearls and rhinestones and shells and wooden beads. Some were chokers and some hung to her shapeless waist. Her plump fingers were equally adorned: rings on every finger, and some with two and three rings. And as if that weren't enough, stacks of bracelets climbed both arms from wrists to elbows.

"Miss Sylvia Mae Otherton?" Sergeant Boone asked.

The bowed head bobbed.

"I wonder if we might take off our coats, ma'am. We won't stay long, but it is warm in here."

"Do what you like," she said dully.

They took off their coats, and, holding them folded, hats on top, took seats on the couch. It was down-filled, and unexpectedly they sank until they were almost swaddled.

The only illumination in the room came from a weak, blue-tinted bulb in an ornate floor lamp of cast bronze shaped like a striking cobra. In this watery light they strained to see the features of Sylvia Mae Otherton when she folded herself slowly into one of the armchairs opposite them. They could smell her perfume; it was stronger than the incense.

"Miss Otherton," Boone said gently, "as I suppose you've guessed, this concerns the murder of Doctor Simon Ellerbee. We're talking to all his patients as part of our investigation. I know you'll want to help us find the person responsible for Doctor Ellerbee's death."

"He was a saint," she cried. "A saint!"

She raised her head at this last, and they got a clear look at her for the first time.

A fleshy face, now riddled with grief. Chalky makeup, round patches of rouge, and lips so caked with lipstick that they were cracked. Her black hair hung limply, uncombed, and long glass pendants dangled from her ears. Under brows plucked into thin carets her eyes were swollen and brimming.

"Miss Otherton," Boone continued, "it's necessary that we establish the whereabouts of Ellerbee's patients on the night of the crime. Where were you that Friday evening?"

"I was right here," she said. "I very, very rarely go out."

"Did you have any visitors that night?"

"No."

"Did you see any neighbors—in the lobby or the hallways?"

"No."

"Did you receive any phone calls?"

"No."

Boone gave up; Delaney took over.

"How did you spend that evening, Miss Otherton?" he asked. "Read? Watch television?"

"I worked on my autobiography," she said. "Doctor Simon got me started. He said it would help if I tried to recall everything and write it down."

"And did you then show what you had written to Ellerbee?"

"Yes. And we'd discuss it. He was so sympathetic, so understanding. Oh, what a beautiful man!"

"You saw him twice a week?"

"Usually. Sometimes more when I—when I had to."

"How long had you been seeing Doctor Ellerbee?"

"Four years. Four years and three months."

"Did you feel he was helping you?"

"Oh, yes! My panic attacks are much less frequent now. And I don't do those—those things as often. I don't know what's going to happen to me with Doctor Simon gone. His wife—his widow—is trying to find another therapist for me, but it won't be the same."

"What things?" Boone said sharply. "You said you don't do those things as often. What were you referring to?"

She raised her soft chin. "Sometimes when I go out, I hit people."

"Have they done anything to you?"

"No."

"Just anyone?" Delaney said. "Someone on the street or in a restaurant?"

"Men with beards," she said in a husky voice, her head slowly bowing again. "Only men with beards. When I was eleven years old, I was raped by my uncle."

"And he had a beard?"

She raised her head and stared at him defiantly. "No, but it happened in his office, and he had an old engraving of Ulysses Grant on the wall."

It's Looney Tunes time, Delaney thought, and was vaguely ashamed they had dragged that confession from this hapless woman.

"But your assaults on bearded men became less frequent after you started seeing Doctor Ellerbee?"

"Oh, yes! He was the one who made the connection between bearded men and the rape."

"When was the last time you made an attack on a stranger?"

"Oh . . . months ago."

"How many months?"

"One or two."

"It must have been very painful for you—when Doctor Ellerbee told you the reason for your hostility toward bearded men."

"He didn't *tell* me. He never did that. He just let me discover it for myself."

"But that was painful?"

"Yes," she said in a whisper. "Very. I hated him then, for making me remember."

"Was this a recent discovery?"

"Months ago."

"How many months?"

"One or two," she said again.

"But earlier you called Doctor Simon a saint. So your hatred of him didn't last."

"No. I knew he was trying to help me."

Delaney glanced at the Sergeant.

"Miss Otherton," Boone said, "did you know any of Doctor Simon's other patients?"

"No. I rarely saw them, and we never spoke."

"Do you know Doctor Diane Ellerbee?"

"I met her twice and spoke to her once on the phone."

"What do you think of her?" Boone asked.

"She's all right, I guess. Awfully skinny. And cold. She doesn't have Doctor Simon's personality. He was a very warm man."

"Do you know of anyone who might have wanted to harm him? Anyone who threatened him?"

"No. Who would want to kill a *doctor?* He was trying to help everyone."

"Did you ever attack Doctor Simon?"

"Once," she said and sobbed. "I slapped him."

"Why did you do that?"

"I don't remember."

"How did he react?"

"He slapped me back, not hard. Then we hugged each other, laughing, and it was all right."

She seemed willing enough to continue talking—eager in fact. But the sandalwood incense, her perfume, and the steamy heat were getting to them.

"Thank you, Miss Otherton," Delaney said, struggling out of the depths of the couch. "You've been very cooperative. Please try to recall anything about Doctor Simon that might help us. Perhaps a name he mentioned, or an incident. For instance, do you think his manner or personality changed in, say, the last six months or year?"

"Strange you should ask that," she said. "I thought he was becoming a little quieter, more thoughtful. Not depressed, you understand, but a little subdued. I asked him if anything was worrying him, and he said no."

"You've been very helpful," Boone said. "We may find it necessary to come back and ask you more questions. I hope you won't mind."

"I won't mind," she said forlornly. "I don't have many visitors."

"I'll leave my card," the Sergeant said, "in case you remember something you think might help us."

In the elevator, going down, Delaney said, "Odd. She says he was such a warm guy. That's not the feeling I got from that private office of his."

"I wonder what was bothering him," Boone said. "If anything was."

"The question is," Delaney said, "did she hate him enough to dust him? She says she hated him after he made her recall the rape. Maybe he dredged up something else out of her past that really set her off."

"You think she's strong enough to bash in his skull?"

"When the adrenaline is flowing, a flyweight could do that, and she's a hefty woman."

"Yeah. That's why I'm going home and shave. I don't want to take any chances!"


That night, after dinner, Delaney told Monica about his day. She listened intently, fascinated.

"Those poor people," she mourned when he had finished.

"Yes. They're not exactly demented, but neither Isaac Kane nor Sylvia Mae has both oars in the water. And there are four more patients I want to meet."

"It depresses you, Edward?"

"It's not exactly a million laughs."

He had started a small fire in the grate and turned off the living room lamps. They sat on the couch, close together, staring into the flames. Suddenly he put his arm about her shoulders.

"You okay?" she asked.

"Yes," he said. "But it's cold out there, and dark."

# 12.

"It's going to be a mixed-up weekend," he warned Monica on Saturday morning. "I want to brace the other four patients before the new boys report in on Monday morning. And Jason called; he's coming by this afternoon."

"Don't forget to ask Boone and Jason about Thanksgiving dinner."

"I'll remember," he promised.

He went into the study to scribble a rough schedule, consulting the patients' addresses on Dr. Diane Ellerbee's list. He decided to hit Ronald J. Bellsey and L. Vincent Symington on Saturday and Joan Yesell and Harold Gerber on Sunday.

He and Boone would have to return to the brownstone to hear Jason's report, and it was possible some of the patients wouldn't be home. But if all went well, Delaney could spend Sunday evening bringing his files up to date in preparation for briefing the six new detectives.

By the time Boone arrived, Delaney had the weekend organized. Everything but the weather. It was a miserable day, with lowering clouds, sharp gusts of rain, and a mean wind that came out of the northwest, whipping coattails and snatching at hats.

Bellsey lived on East 28th Street. They drove south on Second Avenue, windshield wipers working in fits and starts, and the ancient heater fighting a losing battle against the windchill factor.

"I keep hoping someone will steal this heap," the Sergeant said. "But I guess even the chop shops don't want it. One of these days I'll hit the lottery and get a decent set of wheels. By the way, I talked to the dick who checked out Bellsey. The subject claims he was home on the night Ellerbee got snuffed. His wife confirms. Not much of an alibi."

"Not much," Delaney agreed. "Did you find out what Bellsey does for a living?"

"Yeah. He's manager of a big wholesale butcher on West Eighteenth Street. They handle high-class meats and poultry, and sell only to restaurants and hotels."

"That reminds me," Delaney said. "Would you and Rebecca like to come over for Thanksgiving Day dinner? We're having roast goose."

"Sounds good to me," Boone said. "Thank you, sir. But I'll have to check with Rebecca first in case she's made other plans."

"Sure. Either way, why don't you ask her to give Monica a call."

Ronald J. Bellsey lived in a new high-rise on the corner of Third Avenue. They found a parking space on 29th Street and walked back through the windswept rain, holding on to their hats. They were then told by the lobby attendant that Mr. and Mrs. Bellsey were not at home, having gone shopping no more than fifteen minutes earlier.

"Shit," the Sergeant said as they plodded back to the car. "Well, I guess we can't expect to win them all."

"We'll try him again this afternoon," Delaney said. "No one's going to spend all day shopping in this weather. Let's give L. Vincent Symington a go. He lives in Murray Hill; Thirty-eighth Street east of Park. Did you get any skinny on him?"

"He's a bachelor. Works for an investment counseling outfit on Wall Street. On the night of the murder, he says he was at a big dinner-dance at the Hilton. Some of the other guests remember seeing him there, but it was such a mob scene, he could easily have ducked out, murdered Ellerbee, and gotten back to the Hilton without anyone noticing he was gone. It's never neat and tidy—is it, sir?"

"Never," Delaney said. "Always loose ends. You know what they call them in the navy? Irish pennants. That's what this case is—all Irish pennants."

Symington lived in an elegant townhouse with bay windows on the first two floors, fanlights over the upper windows, and a mansard roof of greened copper. A lantern of what appeared to be Tiffany glass hung suspended over the front door.

"Money," Delaney pronounced, surveying the building. "Probably all floor-throughs."

He was right; there were only five names listed on the gleaming brass bell plate. L. VINCENT SYMINGTON, printed in a chaste script, was opposite the numeral 3. Boone pressed the button and leaned down to the intercom grille.

"Who is it?" a fluty voice asked.

"Sergeant Abner Boone, New York Police Department. Is this Mr. Symington?"

"Yes."

"Could we speak to you for a few minutes, sir?"

"What precinct are you from?"

"Manhattan North."

"Just a minute, please."

"Cautious bastard," Boone whispered to Delaney. "He's calling the precinct to see if I exist."

Delaney shrugged. "He's entitled."

They waited almost three minutes before the buzzer sounded. They pushed inside and climbed the carpeted stairs. The man waiting for them on the third-floor landing might have been wary enough to check with Manhattan North, but he nullified that prudence by failing to ask for their ID.

"I suppose this is about Dr. Ellerbee," he said nervously, retreating to his doorway. "I've already talked to the police about that."

"Yes, sir, we know," the Sergeant said. "But there are some additional questions we wanted to ask."

Symington sighed. "Oh, very well," he said petulantly. "I hope this will be the end of it."

"That," Boone said, "I can't guarantee."

The apartment was meticulously decorated and looked, Delaney thought, about as warm and lived-in as a model room in a department store. Everything was just so: color-coordinated, dusted, polished, shining with newness. No butts in the porcelain ashtrays. No stains on the velvet upholstery. No signs of human habitation anywhere.

"Beautiful room," he said to Symington.

"Do you *really* think so? Thank you so much. You know, everyone thinks I had a decorator, but I did it myself. I can't tell you how *long* it took. I knew exactly what I wanted, but it was *ages* before it all came together."

"You did a great job," Boone assured him. "By the way, I'm Sergeant Boone and this is Edward Delaney."

"Pleased, I'm sure," Symington said. "Forgive me for not shaking hands. I'm afraid I've got a thing about that."

He took their damp hats and coats, handling them with fingertips as if they might be infected. He motioned them to director's chairs: blond cowhide on stainless-steel frames. He stood lounging against an antique brick fireplace with a mantel of distressed oak.

He was wearing a jumpsuit of cherry velour that did nothing to conceal his paunch. A gold medallion hung on his chest, and a loose bracelet of chunky gold links flopped on his wrist when he gestured. His feet were bare.

"Well," he said with a trill of empty laughter, "I suppose you know *all* about me."

"Beg pardon, sir?" Boone said, puzzled.

"I mean, I suppose you've been digging into Doctor Simon's files, and you know all my dirty little secrets."

"Oh, no, Mr. Symington," Delaney said. "Nothing like that. We have the names and addresses of patients—and that's about it."

"That's hard to believe. I'm sure you have ways . . . Well, I have nothing to hide, I assure you. I've been seeing Doctor Simon for six years, three times a week. If it hadn't been for him, I'm sure I would have been a *raving* maniac by now. When I heard of his death, I was devastated. Just devastated."

And, Delaney recalled, the lobby attendant at Sylvia Mae Otherton's apartment house had said she was devastated. Perhaps all of Ellerbee's patients were devastated. But not as much as the doctor . . .

"Mr. Symington," Boone said, "were your relations with Doctor Simon friendly?"

*"Friendly?"* he said with a theatrical grimace. "My God, no! How can you be friendly with your shrink? He hurt me. Continually. He made me uncover things I had kept hidden all my life. It was *very* painful."

"Let me try to understand," Delaney said. "Your relations with him were kind of a duel?"

"Something like that," Symington said hesitantly. "I mean, it's not all fun and games. Yes, I guess you could say it was a kind of duel."

"Did you ever attack Doctor Simon?" Boone asked suddenly. "Physically attack him?"

The gold chain clinked as Symington threw out his arm in a gesture of bravura. *"Never!* I never touched him, though God knows I was tempted more than once. You must understand that most people under analysis have a love-hate relationship with their therapist. I mean, intellectually you realize the psychiatrist is trying to help you. But emotionally you feel he's trying to hurt you, and you resent it. You begin to suspect him. You think he may have an ulterior motive for making you confess. Perhaps he's going to blackmail you."

"Did you really believe that Doctor Simon might blackmail you?" Delaney asked.

"I thought about it sometimes," Symington said, stirring restlessly. "It wouldn't have surprised me. People are such shits, you know. You trust them, you even love them, and then they turn on you. I could tell you stories . . ."

"But you stuck with him for six years," Boone said.

"Of course I did. I *needed* the man. I was really dependent on him. And, of course, that made me resent him even more. But kill him? Is that what you're thinking? I'd never do that. I loved Doctor Simon. We were very close. He knew so much about me."

"Did you know any of his other patients?"

"I knew a few other people who were going to him. Not friends, just acquaintances or people I'd meet at parties, and it would turn out that they were his patients or former patients."

"To your knowledge," Boone said, "was he ever threatened by a patient?"

"No. And if he was, he'd never mention it to another patient."

"Did you notice any changes in his manner?" Delaney asked. "In the past year or six months."

L. Vincent Symington didn't answer at once. He came over to the long sectional couch opposite their chairs and stretched out. He stuffed a raw silk cushion under his head and stared at them.

He had a doughy face, set with raisin eyes. His lips were unexpectedly full and rosy. He was balding, and the naked scalp was sprinkled with brown freckles. Delaney thought he looked like an aged Kewpie doll, and imagined his arms and legs would be sausages, plump and boneless.

"I loved him," Symington said dully. "Really loved him. He was almost Christlike. Nothing shocked him. He could forgive you anything. Once, years ago, I went off the deep end and punished my parents. Really hurt them. Doctor Simon got me to face that. But he didn't condemn. He never condemned. Oh, Jesus, what's going to happen to me?"

"You haven't answered my question," Delaney said sternly. "Did you notice any change in him recently?"

"No. No change."

Suddenly, without warning, Symington began weeping. Tears ran down his fat cheeks, dripped off, stained the cushion. He cried silently for several minutes.

Delaney looked at Boone and the two rose simultaneously.

"Thank you for your help, Mr. Symington," Delaney said.

"Thank you, sir," Boone said.

They left him there, lying on his velvet couch in his cherry jumpsuit, wet face now turned to the ceiling.

Outside, they ran for the car, splashing through puddles. They sat for a moment while Boone lighted a cigarette.

"A butterfly?" he said. "Do you think?"

"Who the hell knows?" Delaney said roughly. "But he's a real squirrel. Listen, I'm hungry. There's a Jewish deli on Lex, not too far from here. Great corned beef and pastrami. Plenty of pickles. Want to try it?"

"Hell, yes," the Sergeant said. "With about a quart of hot coffee."

The delicatessen was a steamy, bustling place, fragrant with spicy odors. The decibel level was high, and they shouted their orders to one of the rushing waiters.

"Good scoff," Boone said to Delaney when their sandwiches came. "How did you happen to find this place?"

"Not one of my happier moments. I was a dick two, and I was tailing a guy who was a close pal of a bent-nose we wanted for homicide in a liquor store holdup. The guy I was hoping would lead us to the perp came in here for lunch, so I came in, too. The guy ordered his meal, and when it was served, he got up and headed for the rear of the place. The john is back there, so I figured he was going to take a leak, then come back and eat his lunch. But when he didn't return in five minutes, I thought, Oh-oh, and went looking. That's when I found out there's a back door, and he was long gone. I guess he spotted me and took off. So I came back and finished my lunch. The food was so good, I kept coming here every time I was in the neighborhood."

"Did you get the perp?"

"Eventually. He made the mistake of belting his wife once too often, and she sang. He plea-bargained it down to second degree. That was years ago; he's probably out of the clink by now."

"Robbing more liquor stores."

"Wouldn't doubt it for a minute," Delaney said with heavy good humor. "It was the only trade he knew."

"You know," said Boone, "that Symington didn't strike me as the kind of guy who'd own a ball peen hammer."

"Or galoshes either. But it wouldn't surprise me if he owned a pair of cowboy boots. These people we're dealing with are something. They hold down good jobs and make enough loot to see a therapist three times a week. I mean they *function.* But then they get talking, and you realize their gears don't quite mesh. They think that if A equals B, and B equals C, then X equals Y. We've got to start thinking like that, Sergeant, if we expect to get anywhere on this thing. No use looking for logic."

They were silent awhile, looking idly at the action in the deli as customers arrived and departed, the sweating waiters screamed orders, and the guys behind the hot-meat counter wielded their long carving knives like demented samurai.

"I think," Boone said, "that maybe Symington really was in love with Ellerbee. Sexually, I mean."

"It's possible," Delaney said. "It's even possible that Ellerbee responded. Maybe the good doctor was iced because of a lover's quarrel. But that just shows how this warped world is getting to me. Finished? I think we better get back; Jason said he'd be there at one o'clock."

"I hope he's found something heavy."

"Don't hold your breath," Delaney advised.

Monica had been out doing volunteer work at a local hospital. When she returned home, she had found Jason T. Jason sitting outside the brownstone in the unmarked police car. She brought him into the kitchen and they were having a coffee when Delaney and Boone walked in. The three men went into the study, Jason carrying a manila envelope.

"So," Delaney said to Jason, "how did you make out?"

The black cop was a boulder of a man: six-four, 250—and very little of that suet. His skin was a ruddy cordovan that always seemed polished to a high gloss. He wore his hair clipped short, like a knitted helmet, but his sharply trimmed mustache stretched from cheek to cheek. His hands were hams and his feet bigger than Delaney's.

Jason Two lived with his wife, Juanita, and two young sons in Hicksville, Long Island. He had been six years in the Department and had two citations, a number of solid busts and some good assists. He was hoping for a detective's shield—but so were twenty thousand other cops.

"I don't know how I did," he confessed, opening the manila envelope. "First time I looked for a perp in a *library.* I got three reports here, on the two Ellerbees and Doc Samuelson. I did them up on my older boy's typewriter. I'm a two-fingered typist, both thumbs, so there's a lot of marking out and corrections, but I think you'll be able to read them. Anyway, they're mostly cut-and-dried stuff: dates, ages, education, family background, their college degrees, and so forth. To be honest, sir, I don't think it all amounts to diddley-squat. I mean, I can't see any of it helping us find Ellerbee's killer."

"Nothing unusual?" Delaney asked. "Nothing that struck you as being out of the ordinary or worth taking a second look at?"

"Not really," Jason said slowly. "About the most unusual thing was that Samuelson had a breakdown some years ago. That seemed odd to me: a psychiatrist cracking up. They said it was exhaustion from overwork. He was out of action for about six months. But then he went back to his office and took up his caseload again."

Delaney turned to Boone. "He said his wife died of cancer, didn't he, and his son was killed in an automobile accident? That would be enough to knock anyone for a loop. Anything else, Jason?"

"Well, sir, I collected all the facts and figures I could in the time I had. All that's in my reports. Most of it came from books, newspapers, and professional journals. But I talked to a lot of people, too. Friends and associates of all three doctors. And after I got the factual stuff I wanted, I'd bullshit awhile with them. Funny how people run off at the mouth when they hear it's a murder investigation. Anyway, I heard some stuff that may or may not mean anything. I didn't put it in my reports because it was just hearsay. I mean, none of it is hard evidence."

"You did just right, Jase," Sergeant Boone said. "We need every scrap we can get. What did you hear?"

"First of all, practically every guy I talked to mentioned how beautiful Diane is. They all sounded like they were in love with her. I've never seen her, but she must be some foxy lady."

"She is," Delaney and Boone said simultaneously, and they all laughed.

"Well, everyone said how lucky Doc Simon was to hook on to someone like her: a looker with plenty of the green. But one guy swears Ellerbee wasn't all that anxious to marry, but she had her mind set on it. I told you I heard a lot of rumors. Some of the guys admitted they made a play for her, even after she was married, but it was no dice; she was straight."

"Any gossip about Doctor Simon playing around?" Delaney asked.

*"Nada,"* Jason said. "Apparently he was a cold, controlled kind of guy. I mean, he was pleasant enough, good company and all that, but a secret man; he didn't reveal much. At least that's what most people

said. But I talked to one woman—she's the secretary of that association he belonged to—and she said she saw Ellerbee at a dinner about a month before he was iced. She said she was surprised at how he had changed since she saw him last. She said he was smiling, and a lot more outgoing than he had been. Seemed really happy, she said."

Delaney and Boone stared at each other.

"Crazy," the Sergeant said, shaking his head.

Delaney explained to Jason why they were puzzled. He told him that Sylvia Mae Otherton had claimed Ellerbee had become quieter, more thoughtful, not depressed but subdued.

"It doesn't jibe," Jason said. "One of those ladies must be wrong."

"Not necessarily," Delaney said. "Maybe they just caught him in different moods. But what's interesting is that they both noticed a recent change in his disposition. I'd like to know what brought that on. It's probably nothing, but still . . . Sergeant, why don't you tell Jason about the patients we've seen."

When Boone finished, Jason said, "Whoo-ee! Those people—doesn't sound like their elevators go to the top floor."

"They're a little meshugenah," Delaney admitted. "Sometimes they make sense and sometimes they're way out in left field. Our problem is going to be separating what's real from what's part of their never-never world. I don't see how we can do anything but let them blabber and then try to figure the meaning later. I'll have to warn the new people about that when they come in Monday morning."

"Sir," Boone said, "how are you going to handle those guys—assign one to each of the patients?"

"That was my first plan, and maybe it would work if we were covering punks and small-time hoods. But these subjects are mostly educated and intelligent, even if their brains rattle a little. I think we'll get better results if each detective has a chance to talk to three or four of the patients. And then select the one he feels he can work with best. You know how sometimes a witness with clam up with one dick and then spill his guts to another because he feels the second guy is more simpatico. We'll try to pair detective and subject so it'll do us the most good."

They talked for another hour, discussing how they would organize the investigation so detectives wouldn't be duplicating each other's work unless a double-check was deemed necessary.

Delaney decided that Boone and Jason would each be responsible for scheduling and supervising three detectives. The two of them would then submit daily reports to Delaney on the activities of their squads.

"I expect a certain amount of confusion at first," he told them, "but I want the two of you to coordinate your planning as much as possible. I'll keep the files, which will be open to all of you. Just tell your guys to put *everything* in their reports, no matter how stupid or meaningless they might think it. And the first thing I want done is to have these six patients run through Records. If they're as violent as Doctor Diane seems to think, some of them should have sheets."

They traded ideas awhile longer, then Delaney glanced up at the walnut-cased regulator on the wall, a relic from a demolished railroad station.

"Getting late," he said. "Why don't the three of us try Ronald J. Bellsey again—just walk in on him without warning. He should be home by now. Jason, we'll take your car and you can drop us back here."

On the drive south, Delaney remembered to ask Jason Two if he and his family would like to come for Thanksgiving Day dinner.

"Thank you, sir," the officer said, "but we've already signed on with Juanita's parents. They're making a big deal out of it, and the kids and the old folks would kill me if I canceled."

"Don't even consider it," Delaney said. "We'll make it another time. Your boys should see their grandparents as often as possible. I wish I could see more of my grandchildren."

They double-parked in front of Bellsey's high-rise. Boone flashed his ID and asked the doorman to keep an eye on their car. There was no house phone; the lobby attendant explained they'd have to use the intercom. In addition, they were told to stand in front of a small, ceiling-mounted television camera that would relay their picture via closed circuit to a monitor in Bellsey's foyer.

"Cute gimmick," Delaney said.

"First time I've been on TV," Jason said, grinning. "Should I do a buck-and-wing or something?"

Boone spoke softly to Bellsey on the intercom, then held up his shield before the camera's eye.

"Apartment 2407," he reported to the others. "He said to come up, but he didn't sound too happy about it."

In the elevator, Delaney said to Jason, "Don't be bashful about chiming in when we question this guy. Let's overwhelm him with muscle."

The door of Apartment 2407 was jerked open by a stocky, red-faced man wearing a rugged sport jacket and whipcord slacks. Behind him, a smallish, graying woman stood in the foyer archway, hands clasped, peering at them timidly.

"I suppose this is about Ellerbee," Bellsey burst out angrily. "I already talked to the cops about that."

"We know you did, Mr. Bellsey," Boone said. "That was just a preliminary questioning. Unfortunately, you're involved in a murder investigation, and we—"

"What do you mean I'm *involved?*" Bellsey demanded, his voice rising. "Jesus Christ, I was just one of his patients! I don't know a damned thing about how he got killed."

"Mr. Bellsey," Delaney said stonily, "are you going to keep us standing out here in the hallway while you shout at us and the neighbors get an earful?"

"Screw the neighbors! I don't see why I have to be harassed like this."

Jason T. Jason shoved his big bulk forward. "No one's harassing you," he said quietly. "Just a few questions and we'll be out of your hair."

Bellsey looked up at the big cop. "Shit!" he said disgustedly. "Well, come on in then. I want you to know you're interrupting our dinner." He turned to the woman.

"Lorna, you get back to the kitchen; this has nothing to do with you."

The woman scurried away.

"Your wife?" Delaney asked as the three men entered the apartment.

"Yeah," Bellsey said. "Leave her out of this."

He didn't offer to take their coats and made no effort to get them seated. So they all remained standing in a tight little group.

"I'm Sergeant Boone and these men are Delaney and Jason. Your full name is Ronald J. Bellsey?"

"That's right. The J. is for James in case you're interested."

"When was the last time you saw Doctor Ellerbee?"

"On Thursday afternoon, the day before he was killed. Don't tell me you didn't get that from his appointment book. Or is that expecting too much brains from cops?"

"Be nice, Mr. Bellsey," Delaney said softly. "You get snotty with us and you'll be answering our questions at the precinct house and waiting a long, long time for your dinner. Is that what you want?"

He glowered at them.

Bellsey was heavy through the shoulders and chest. His neck was short and thick, supporting a squarish head topped with an ill-fitting toupee. He stood leaning belligerently forward, pugnacious jaw thrust out, hands balled into fists.

"Mr. Bellsey," Boone said, "you claim you were home on the night Ellerbee was killed."

"That's right."

"All night?"

"Yeah. I got home around seven and didn't go out of the house until Saturday. Ask my wife; she'll tell you."

"Did you have any visitors Friday evening? See any neighbors? Make or receive any phone calls?"

"No."

"Do you have a police record, Mr. Bellsey?" Delaney asked. "We'll check, of course, but it would be smart if you told us first."

Bellsey opened his mouth to speak, then shut it with a click of teeth. He hesitated, then tried again.

"I was never really arrested," he said grudgingly. "Not formally, I mean. But I got into trouble a few times. I don't know what's on my record."

"What kind of trouble?" Jason asked.

"Fights. I was defending myself."

"How many times?"

"Once. Or twice."

"Or maybe more?"

"Maybe. I don't remember."

"Ever get in a fight with Doctor Ellerbee?" Boone asked. "Ever attack him?"

"Shit, no! He was my doctor. A decent guy. I liked him."

"How long had you been seeing him?"

"About two years."

"You own a car?" Delaney asked suddenly.

Bellsey looked at him, puzzled. "Sure."

"What kind?"

"Last year's Cadillac."

"Where do you keep it?"

"In the basement. We have an underground garage."

"You ever do any repairs on it yourself?"

"Sometimes. Minor stuff."

"You own tools?"

"Some."

"Where do you keep those?"

"In the trunk of the car."

Delaney glanced at Boone.

"Mr. Bellsey," the Sergeant said, "did Ellerbee ever mention to you that he had been attacked or threatened by a patient?"

"No."

"Did you know any of his other patients?"

"No."

"Did you notice any change recently in his manner or personality?"

"No, he was just the same."

"What's 'the same'?" Jason asked. "What kind of a man was he?"

"Calm, cool, and collected. Never blew his stack. Never raised his voice. A real put-together guy. I cursed him out once, and he never held it against me."

"Why did you curse him out?"

"I don't remember."

"When you went out shopping today," Boone said, "what did you wear?"

"What did I wear?" Bellsey said, bewildered. "I wore a rainhat and a lined trenchcoat."

"Galoshes? Boots?"

"No. A pair of rubbers."

"You work for a wholesale butcher?" Delaney said.

"That's right."

"What do you do—slice salami?"

"Christ, no! I'm the manager. Production manager."

"You oversee the butchers, loaders, drivers—is that it?"

"Yes."

"You must deal with some rough guys."

"They think they are," Bellsey said grimly. "But they shape up or ship out."

"You ever do any boxing?" Jason Two asked.

"Some. When I was in the navy. Middleweight."

"Never professionally?"

"No."

"You keep in shape?"

"I sure do," Bellsey boasted. "Jog five miles twice a week. Lift iron. Go to a health club once a week for a three-hour workout on the machines. What the hell has all this got to do with Ellerbee's murder?"

"Just asking," Jason said equably.

"You're wasting my time," Bellsey said. "Anything else?"

"I think that's all," Delaney said. "For now. Have a nice dinner, Mr. Bellsey."

There were other people in the elevator; they didn't talk. But when they got into Jason's car, Sergeant Boone said, "A real sweetheart. How did you pick up on the boxing, Jase?"

"He looks like a pug. The way he stands and moves."

"We'll have to get into the trunk of that Cadillac," Delaney said. "The ball peen. And let's try to talk to the wife when he's not around."

"You think he could be it?" Boone asked.

"Our best bet yet," Delaney said. "A guy with a sheet, a short fuse, and he's a brawler. I think we better take a very close look at Mr. Bellsey."

That night, after dinner, he wanted to write out reports of the questioning of L. Vincent Symington and Ronald J. Bellsey. But Monica said firmly that she had to make a start on addressing Christmas cards, so he deferred to her wishes.

She sat in his swivel chair behind his desk in the study. As she worked, adding a short personal note to each card, he slumped in one of the worn club chairs, nursing a small Rémy. He told her about Symington and Bellsey.

When he finished, she said definitely, "It was Bellsey. He's the one who did it."

Delaney laughed softly. "Why do you say that?"

"He sounds like a dreadful man."

"Oh, he is a dreadful man—but that doesn't make him a killer."

She went back to her Christmas cards. A soft cone of light shone down from a green student lamp on the desk. Delaney sat in dimness, staring with love and gratitude at the woman who brightened his life.

He saw her pursed lips as she wrote out her holiday greetings, dark eyes gleaming. Her glossy black hair was gathered in back with a gold barrette. Strong face, strong woman. He thought of what his life would be like, sitting alone in that shadowed room, without her warm presence, and a small groan escaped him.

"What are you thinking?" she asked, without looking up.

He didn't tell her. Instead, he said, "Did you ever work a jigsaw puzzle?"

"When I was a kid."

"Me, too. Remember how you spilled all the pieces out of the box onto a tabletop, hoping none of them was missing. Then you turned all the pieces picture-side up and looked for the four pieces with two straight edges. Those were the corners of the picture. After you had those, you put together all the pieces with one straight edge to form the frame. Then you gradually filled in the picture."

She looked up at him. "The Ellerbee case is a jigsaw puzzle?"

"Sort of."

"And you know what the picture is going to be?"

"No," he said with a tight smile, "but I see some straight edges."

# 13.

Sunday was the best day of the week for Harold Gerber. He didn't have to see anyone; he didn't have to talk to anyone. He bought his Sunday *Times* on Saturday night, along with a couple of six-packs. The paper, the beer, and two pro football games on TV filled up his Sundays. He never left the house.

Gerber had lost a lot of weight in Vietnam and never put it back on. He had lost a lot of things there, including his appetite. So on Sunday morning he usually had some juice, a piece of toast, and two cups of coffee with sugar and cream. That carried him through to evening, when he might heat up a frozen dinner that came in a cardboard box and tasted like the container.

For some reason, on Sundays he never got out the photographs and looked at them again. All those guys—grinning, scowling, laughing, mugging it up for the camera. Some of the photos were autographed, just like Gerber had autographed some of the shots they took of him. A family album . . . It fed his fury.

Since he couldn't comprehend it himself, Gerber could appreciate why other people were unable to understand the way he felt and why he did the things he did. Gerber couldn't figure it out, and no one else could either.

Doc Simon was coming close, really beginning to pin it down, but now Ellerbee was dead, and Gerber wasn't about to start all over again with another therapist. He had tried two before he found Ellerbee, but they had turned out to be bullshit artists, and Gerber knew after a few sessions that they weren't going to do him a damned bit of good.

Dr. Simon Ellerbee was different. No bullshit there. He went right in with a sharp scalpel, and all that blood didn't daunt him. He was tear-ing Harold Gerber apart and putting him back together again. But then Doc Simon got himself scragged and Gerber was alone again, with no one but ghosts for company.

The checks from his parents came regularly, every month, and he was on partial disability, so he wasn't hurting for money. Harold Gerber was just hurting for life, wondering if he was fated to drag his corpse through the world for maybe another fifty years, acting like a goddamn maniac and really wanting the whole fucking globe to blow up—the sooner the better.

That Sunday morning, driving down to Gerber's place in Greenwich Village, Delaney said to Boone, "I feel guilty about making you work this weekend. Rebecca probably thinks I'm a slave driver."

"Nah," Boone said. "She's used to my working crazy hours. I guess every detective's wife is."

"Jason volunteered to come along, but weekends are the only chance he gets to spend some time with his sons. That's important, so I told him to stay home today. When the new guys come in, we should all be able to keep reasonable hours. Did you find out anything about this Gerber?"

"Nothing. Suarez's men hadn't gotten around to him yet. So all we have is what Doctor Diane put in her report: He's thirty-seven, a Vietnam veteran with a lot of medals and a lot of problems. Gets into fights."

"Another Ronald Bellsey?"

"Not exactly," Boone said. "This Gerber sometimes attacks strangers for no apparent reason. And once he put his fist through a plate-glass window and ended up in St. Vincent's Emergency where they stitched him up."

"That's nice," Delaney said. "An angry young man."

"Something like that," Boone agreed.

Harold Gerber lived in a run-down tenement on Seventh Avenue South, around the corner from Carmine Street. The windows of the first two floors were covered with tin, and the stoop was clotted with garbage. The façade of the six-story building was chipped, stained with rust, defaced with graffiti.

Inspecting this dump, Delaney and Boone had the same reaction: How could anyone living there afford an uptown shrink?

"Maybe he doesn't pay rent," Delaney suggested. "See that empty lot next door? Some developer's assembling a parcel. Once he gets the remaining tenants out, he'll demolish that wreck and have enough spare feet to put up a luxury high-rise."

"Could be," Boone said. "Right now it looks like a Roach Motel."

In the littered vestibule they discovered all the mailboxes had been jimmied open. The intercom had been wrenched from the wall to dangle suspended from its wires. The front door had been pried open so often that now it couldn't be closed. The odor of rot and urine was gagging.

"Jesus!" Boone said. "Let's get in and out of here fast."

"Have we got an apartment number for him?"

"No. We'll have to bang on doors."

They cautiously climbed a tilted wooden stairway, the loose banister carved and hacked. More graffiti on the damp plaster walls. The doors on the first two floors were nailed shut. They began knocking on third-floor doors. No answers. No sounds of habitation.

They got an answer on the fourth floor.

"Go away," a woman screamed, "or I'll call the cops."

"Lady, we *are* the cops," Boone shouted back. "We're looking for Harold Gerber. What apartment?"

"Never heard of him."

They went up to the fifth, stepping over piles of broken laths and crumbling plaster. They found two more occupied apartments, but no doors were unlocked, and no one knew Harold Gerber—they said.

Finally, on the sixth floor, they banged on the chipped door of the rear apartment.

"Who is it?" a man yelled.

"New York Police Department. We're looking for Harold Gerber."

"What for?"

Delaney and Boone looked at each other.

"It's about Doctor Simon Ellerbee," Boone said. "A few questions."

They heard the sounds of bolts sliding back. The door was opened on a thick chain. They saw a slice of a man clad in a turtleneck sweater and plaid mackinaw.

"ID?" he said in a hoarse voice.

The Sergeant held up his shield. The chain was slipped, the door opened.

"Welcome to the Taj Mahal," the man said. "Keep your coats on if you don't want to freeze your ass off."

They stepped in and looked around.

It was a slough, and obviously the occupant had done nothing to make it even marginally livable. Clothing and possessions were piled helter-skelter on the cot, a single rickety bureau, on the floor. The scummy sink was piled with unwashed dishes, the two-burner stove thick with grease. It was so cold that the inside of the window was coated with a skim of ice.

"The toilet's in the hall," the man said, grinning. "But I wouldn't recommend it."

"Harold Gerber?" Boone asked.

"Yeah."

"May we sit down, please?" Delaney asked. "I'm worn out from that climb. My name is Delaney and this is Sergeant Abner Boone."

"Sergeant . . ." Gerber said in his gravelly voice. "I was a sergeant once. Then I got busted."

He threw clothing off the cot, removed a six-pack from one spindly chair, and lifted a small black-and-white TV set from another.

"We still got electricity and water," he said, "but no heat. The fucking landlord is freezing us out. Take it easy when you sit down; the legs are loose."

They gingerly eased onto the chairs. Gerber sat on the cot.

"You think I did it?" he said with a cracked grin.

"Did what?" Boone said.

"Fragged Doc Ellerbee."

"Did you?" Delaney asked.

"Shit, no. But I could have."

"Why?" Boone said. "Why would you want to kill him?"

"Who needs a reason? You like my home?"

"It's a shithouse," Delaney told him.

Gerber laughed. "Yeah, just the way I want it. When they tear this joint down, I'm going to look for another place just like it. A buddy of mine—he lives in Idaho—came back from Nam and tried to pick up his life. He gave it six months and couldn't hack it. So he took off all his clothes, every stitch, and walked bare-ass naked into the woods without a thing—no weapons, no watch, no matches—absolutely nothing. Well, Manhattan is my woods. I like living like this."

"What happened to him?" Delaney said. "Your buddy."

"A ranger came across him a couple of years later. He was wearing clothes and moccasins made out of animal skins. His hair and beard were long and matted. He had built himself a lean-to and planted some wild stuff he found growing in the woods that he could eat. Made a bow and arrows. Set traps. Had plenty of meat. He was doing great. Never saw anyone, never talked to anyone. I wish I had the balls to do something like that."

They stared him, seeing a lean, hollowed face shadowed by a three-day beard. The skin was pasty white, nose bony, eyes brightly wild. Uncombed hair spiked out from under a black beret. Gerber moved jerkily, gestures short and broken.

The sweater and mackinaw hung loosely on his lank frame. Even his fingers seemed skeletal, the nails gnawed away. And on his feet, heavy boots.

"You wear those boots all the time?" Boone said.

"These? Sure. They're fleece-lined. I even sleep in them. I'd lose toes if I didn't."

"How long did you know Doctor Ellerbee?" Delaney asked.

"I don't want to talk about that," Gerber said.

"You don't want to help us find his killer?" Boone said.

"So he's dead," Gerber said, shrugging. "Half the guys I've known in my life are dead."

"He didn't die of old age," Delaney said grimly. "And he didn't die in an accident or in a war. Someone deliberately bashed in his skull."

"Big deal," Gerber said.

Delaney looked at him steadily. "You goddamned cocksucking son of a bitch," he said tonelessly. "You motherfucking piece of shit. You wallow in your pigsty here, feeling sorry for yourself and, gosh, life is unfair, and gee, you got a raw deal, and no one knows how sensitive you are and how it all hurts, you lousy scumbag. And meanwhile, a good and decent man—worth ten of the likes of you—gets burned, and you won't lift a finger to help find his murderer because you want the whole world to be as miserable as you are. Ellerbee's biggest mistake was trying to help a turd like you. Come on, Sergeant, let's go; we don't need any help from this asshole."

There was cold silence as they began to rise warily from their chairs. But then Harold Gerber held out a hand to stop them.

"You—what's your name? Delehanty?"

"Delaney."

"I like you, Delaney; you're a no-bullshit guy. Doc Simon was like that, but he didn't have your gift of gab. All right, I'll play your little game. What do you want to know?"

They eased back onto the fragile chairs.

"When was the last time you saw Ellerbee?" Boone asked.

"The papers said he was killed around nine o'clock. Right? I saw him five hours earlier, at four o'clock that Friday afternoon. My usual time. It'll be in the appointment book."

"Was he acting normally?"

"Sure."

"Notice any change in him in the last six months or a year?"

"What kind of change?"

"In his manner, the way he acted."

"No," Gerber said, "I didn't notice anything."

"Do you know any of his other patients?" Delaney asked.

"No."

"Did Ellerbee ever mention that he had been attacked or threatened by anyone?"

"No."

"Did you ever attack him?" Boone said. "Or threaten him?"

"Now why would I want to do anything like that? The guy was trying to help me."

"Analysis is supposed to be painful," Delaney said. "Weren't there times when you hated him?"

"Sure there were. But those were temporary things. I never hated him enough to off him. He was my only lifeline."

"What are you going to do now? Find another lifeline?"

"No," Gerber said, then grinned: a death's-head. "I'll just go on wallowing in my pigsty."

"Do you own a ball peen hammer?" Boone asked abruptly.

"No, I do not own a ball peen hammer. Okay? I'm going to have a beer. Anyone want one?"

They both declined. Gerber popped the tab on a can of Pabst and settled back on the cot, leaning against the clammy wall.

"How often did you see Ellerbee?" Delaney said.

"Twice a week. I'd have gone more often if I could have afforded it. He was helping me."

"When was the last time you got in trouble?"

"Ah-ha," Gerber said, showing his teeth. "You know about that, do you? Well, I haven't acted up in the last six months or so. Doc Simon told me if I got the urge—felt real out, you know—I could call him any hour of the day or night. I never did, but just knowing he was there was a big help."

"Where were you the Friday night he got killed?"

"Bar-hopping around the Village."

"In the rain?"

"That's right. I didn't get home until after midnight. I was in the bag."

"Do you remember where you went?"

"I have some favorite hangouts. I guess I went there."

"See anyone you know? Talk to anyone?"

"The bartenders. They'll probably remember me; I'm the world's smallest tipper—if I tip at all. Usually I stiff them. Bartenders and waiters tend to remember things like that."

"Can you recall where you were from, say, eight o'clock to ten?"

"No, I can't."

"You better try," Boone advised. "Make out a list of your hangouts—the ones you hit that Friday night. There'll be another cop coming around asking questions."

"Shit," Gerber said, "I've told you guys all I know."

"I don't think so," Delaney said coldly. "I think you're holding out on us."

"Sure I am," Gerber said in his hoarse voice. "My deep, dark secret is that I once met Doc Simon's wife and I wanted to jump her. She's some sweet piece. Now are you satisfied?"

"You think this is all a big, fat joke, don't you?" Delaney said. "Let me tell you what we're going to do about you, Mr. Gerber. We're going to check you out from the day you were popped to this minute. We're going to talk to your family, relatives, friends. We'll go into your military record from A to Z. We'll even find out why you got busted from sergeant. Then we'll talk to people in this building, your women, the bartenders, anyone you deal with. We'll question the strangers you assaulted and the doctors at St. Vincent's who stitched you up. By the time we're through, we'll know more about you than you know about yourself. So don't play cute with us, Mr. Gerber; you haven't got a secret in the world. Come on, Boone, let's go; I need some fresh air."

While they were picking their way carefully down the filthy staircase, Boone said in a low voice, "Are we really going to do all that, sir? What you told him?"

"Hell, no," Delaney said grumpily. "We haven't got the time."

They sat in the car a few moments, the heater coughing away, while Boone lighted a cigarette.

"You really think he's holding out?" Boone asked.

"I don't know," Delaney said, troubled. "That session was nutsville. His moods shifted around so often and so quickly. One minute he's cooperating, and the next he's a wiseass cracking jokes. But remember, the man was in a dirty war and probably did his share of killing. For some guys—not all, but some—once they've killed, the others come easier until it doesn't mean a goddamn thing to them. The first is the hard one. Then it's just as mechanical as a habit. A life? What's that?"

"I feel sorry for him," Boone said.

"Sure. I do, too. But I feel sorrier for Simon Ellerbee. We've got to ration our sympathy in this world, Sergeant; we only have so much. Listen, it's still early; why don't we skip lunch and drive up to Chelsea. Maybe we can catch Joan Yesell at home. Then we'll be finished and can take the rest of the day off."

"Sounds good to me. Let's go."

Joan Yesell lived on West 24th Street, in a staid block of almost identical brownstones. It was a pleasingly clean street, garbage tucked away in lidded cans, the gutters swept. Windows were washed, façades free of graffiti, and a line of naked ginkgo trees waited for spring.

"Now this is something like," Delaney said approvingly, "Little Old New York. O. Henry lived somewhere around here, didn't he?"

"East of here, sir," Boone said. "In the Gramercy Park area. The bar where he drank is still in business."

"In your drinking days, Sergeant, did you ever fall into McSorley's Old Ale House?"

"I fell into every bar in the city."

"Miss it?" Delaney asked curiously.

"Oh, God, yes! Every day of my life. You remember the highs; you don't remember wetting the bed."

"How long have you been dry now—four years?"

"About. But dipsos don't count years; you take it day by day."

"I guess," Delaney said, sighing. "My old man owned a saloon on Third Avenue—did you know that?"

"No, I didn't," Boone said, interested. "When was this?"

"Oh, hell, a long time ago. I worked behind the stick on afternoons when I was going to night school. I saw my share of boozers. Maybe that's why I never went off the deep end—although I do my share, as you well know. Enough of this. What have you got on Joan Yesell?"

"One of Suarez's boys checked her out. Lives with her widowed mother. Works as a legal secretary in a big law firm up on Park. Takes home a nice buck. Never been married. Those three suicide attempts Doctor Diane mentioned proved out in emergency room records. She claims that on the evening Ellerbee was killed she was home all night.

Got back from work around six o'clock and never went out. Her mother confirms."

"All right," Delaney said, "let's go through the drill again. The last time—I hope."

The ornate wood molding in the vestibule had been painted a hellish orange.

"Look at this," Delaney said, rapping it with a knuckle. "Probably eighteen coats of paint on there. You strip it down and there's beautiful walnut or cherry underneath. You can't buy molding like that anymore. Someone did a lousy restoration job."

There were two names opposite the bell for apartment 3-C: Mrs. Blanche Yesell and J. Yesell.

"The mother gets the title and full first name," Delaney noted. "The daughter rates an initial."

Boone identified himself on the intercom. A moment later the door lock buzzed and they entered. The interior was clean, smelling faintly of disinfectant, but the colors of the walls and carpeting were garish. The only decorative touch was a plastic dwarf palm in a rattan planter.

The ponderous woman waiting outside the closed door of apartment 3-C eyed them suspiciously.

"I am Mrs. Blanche Yesell," she announced in a hard voice, "and you don't look like policemen to me."

Sergeant Boone silently proffered his ID. She had wire-rimmed pince-nez hanging from her thick neck on a black silk cord. She clamped the spectacles onto her heavy nose and inspected the shield and identification card carefully while they inspected her.

The blue-rinsed hair was pyramided like a beehive. Her features were coarse and masculine. (Later, Boone was to say, "She looks like a truck driver in drag.") She had wide shoulders, a deep bosom, and awesome hips. All in all, a formidable woman with meaty hands and big feet shod in no-nonsense shoes.

"Is this about Doctor Ellerbee?" she demanded, handing Boone's ID back to him.

"Yes, ma'am. This gentleman is Edward Delaney, and we'd like to—"

"I don't want my Joan bothered," Mrs. Yesell interrupted. "Hasn't the poor girl been through enough? She's already told you everything she knows. More questions will just upset her. I won't stand for it."

"Mrs. Yesell," Delaney said mildly, "I assure you we have no desire to upset your daughter. But we are investigating a brutal murder, and I know that you and your daughter want to do everything you can to help bring the vile perpetrator to justice."

Bemused by this flossy language, the Sergeant shot Delaney an amazed glance, but the plushy rhetoric seemed to mollify Mrs. Yesell.

"Well, of course," she said, sniffing, "I and my Joan want to do everything we can to aid the forces of law and order."

"Splendid," Delaney said, beaming. "Just a few questions then, and we'll be finished and gone before you can say Jack Robinson."

"I used to know a man named Jack Robinson," she said with a girlish titter.

A certified nut, Sergeant Boone thought.

She opened the door and led the way into the apartment. As overstuffed as she was: velvets and chintz and tassels and lace and ormolu, and whatnots, all in stunning profusion. Plus two sleepy black cats as plump as hassocks.

"Perky and Yum-Yum," Mrs. Yesell said, gesturing proudly. "Aren't they cunning? Let me have your coats, gentlemen, and you make yourselves comfortable."

They perched gingerly on the edge of an ornate, pseudo-Victorian loveseat and waited until Mrs. Yesell had seated herself opposite them in a heavily brocaded tub chair complete with antimacassar.

"Now then," she said, leaning forward, "how may I help you?"

They looked at each other, then back at her.

"Ma'am," Sergeant Boone said softly, "it's your daughter we came to talk to. She's home?"

"Well, she's home, but she's lying down right now, resting, and I wouldn't care to disturb her. Besides, I'm sure I can answer all your questions."

"I'm afraid not," Delaney said brusquely. "Your daughter is the one we came to see. If we can't question her today, we'll have to return again until we can."

She glared at him, but he would not be cowed.

"Oh, very well," she said. "But it's really quite unnecessary. Oh, Joan!" she caroled. "Visitors!"

Right on cue, and much too promptly for one who had been lying down, resting, Joan Yesell entered from the bedroom with a timid smile. The men stood to be introduced. Then the daughter took a straight-back chair and sat with hands clasped in her lap, ankles demurely crossed.

"Miss Yesell," Boone started, "we know how the murder of Doctor Simon Ellerbee must have shocked you."

"My Joan was devastated," Mrs. Yesell said. "Just devastated."

Another one! Delaney thought.

Boone continued: "But I'm sure you appreciate our need to talk to all his patients in the investigation of his death. Could you tell us the last time you saw Doctor Simon?"

"On Wednesday afternoon," the mother said promptly. "The Wednesday before he died. At one o'clock."

The Sergeant sighed. "Mrs. Yesell, these questions are addressed to your daughter. It would be best if she answered."

"On Wednesday afternoon," Joan Yesell said. "The Wednesday before he died. At one o'clock."

Her voice was so low, tentative, that they strained to hear. She kept her head down, staring at her clasped hands.

"That was the usual time for your appointment?"

"Yes."

"How often did you see Doctor Simon?"

"Twice a week."

"And how long had you been consulting him?"

"Four years."

"Three," Mrs. Yesell said firmly. "It's been three years, dear."

"Three years," the daughter said faintly. "About."

"Did Doctor Ellerbee ever mention to you that he had been attacked or threatened by any of his patients?"

"No." Then she raised her head to look at them with faraway eyes. "Once he was mugged while he was walking to his garage late at night, but that happened years ago."

"Miss Yesell," Delaney said, "I have a question you may feel is too personal to answer. If you prefer not to reply, we'll understand completely. Why were you going to Doctor Ellerbee?"

She didn't answer at once. The clasped hands began to twist.

"I don't see—" Mrs. Yesell began, but then her daughter spoke.

"I was depressed," she said slowly. "Very depressed. I attempted suicide. You probably know about that."

"And you feel Doctor Simon was helping you?"

She came briefly alive. "Oh, yes! So much!"

She could not, in all kindness, be called an attractive young woman. Not ugly, but grayly plain. Mousy hair and a pinched face devoid of makeup. She lacked her mother's bold presence and seemed daunted by the older woman's assertiveness.

Her clothing was monochromatic: sweater, skirt, hose, shoes—all of a dull beige. Her complexion had the same cast. She looked, if not unwell, sluggish and beaten. Even her movements had an invalid's languor; her thin body was without shape or vigor.

"Miss Yesell," Boone said, "did you notice any change in Doctor Simon recently? In his manner toward you or in his personality?"

"No," Mrs. Blanche Yesell said. "No change."

"Madam," Delaney thundered, "will you allow your daughter to answer our questions—*please.*"

Joan Yesell hesitated. "Perhaps," she said finally. "The last year or so. He seemed—oh, I don't know exactly. Happier, I think. Yes, he seemed happier. More—more lighthearted. He joked."

"And he had never joked before?"

"No."

"You have stated," Boone said, "that on the night Ellerbee was killed, you returned home directly from work and never went out again until the following day. Is that correct?"

"Yes."

Delaney turned to Mrs. Yesell with a bleak smile. "Now is your chance, ma'am," he said. "Can you confirm your daughter's presence here that night?"

"Of course."

"Did you have any visitors, see any neighbors, make or receive any phone calls that night?"

"No, we did not," she said decisively. "Just the two of us were here."

"Read? Watched television?"

"We played two-handed bridge."

"Oh?" Delaney said, rising to his feet. "And who won?"

"Mama," Joan Yesell said in her wispy voice. "Mama always wins."

They thanked the ladies politely for their help, reclaimed coats and hats, and left. They didn't speak until they were back in the car.

"I can understand why the daughter's depressed," Delaney remarked.

"Yeah," Boone said. "The old lady's a dragon."

"She is that," Delaney agreed. "The only time the daughter contradicted her was about Ellerbee's manner changing. The mother said no."

"How the hell would she know?" Boone said. "She wasn't seeing him twice a week."

"Exactly," Delaney said. "Could you drop me uptown, Sergeant? Let's call it a day."

Just before Delaney got out of the car in front of his brownstone, Boone said, "If you had to make a wild guess, sir, which of the six would you pick as the perp?"

"Oh, I don't know," Delaney said thoughtfully. "Maybe Ronald Bellsey. But only because I don't like the guy. Who's your choice?"

"Harold Gerber—for the same reason. We're probably both wrong."

Delaney grunted. "Probably. Too bad there's not a butler involved. See you tomorrow morning, Sergeant. Give my best to Rebecca."

Monica was in the kitchen, cutting up chicken wings. She had four prepared bowls before her: Dijon mustard, Worchestershire sauce, chicken broth, flavored bread crumbs. She looked up when he came in, and he bent to kiss her cheek.

"Just one sandwich," he pleaded. "I haven't had a thing all day, and we're not eating for hours. One sandwich won't spoil my appetite."

"All right, Edward. Just one."

He rummaged through the refrigerator, saying, "I really deserve this. I've had a hard day. Did you know that psychiatrists have a very high suicide rate? The highest of all doctors except ophthalmologists."

He was standing at the sink, but turned to face her, sandwich clamped in one big hand, a glass of beer in the other.

"Don't tell me you think Doctor Ellerbee crushed in his own skull with a hammer?"

"No, I just mentioned it because I'm beginning to understand what shrinks go through. No wonder they need a month a year to recharge their batteries. These patients of Ellerbee's are wild ones. It's hard to get a handle on them. They don't live in my world."

Monica nodded.

"Do you think women are more sensitive than men?" he asked her.

"Sensitive?" Monica said. "Physically, you mean? Like ticklish?"

"No, not that. Sensitive to emotions, feelings, the way people behave. We've been asking everyone if they noticed any change recently in Doctor Ellerbee's manner. The reason is to find out if he was being threatened or blackmailed or anything like that. All the men we asked said they saw no change. But so far, three women have said yes, they noticed a change. They don't agree on *how* he changed, but all three said there was a difference in his manner in the last six months. That's why I asked you if women are more sensitive to that sort of thing than men."

"Yes," Monica said, "we are."

Five hours later, when Delaney had finished bringing his files up to the minute and Monica had long since cleaned up the dinner dishes, he came out of his study and asked, "Do you know anyone who's under analysis?"

She looked up at him. "Yes, Edward, I know two or three women who are in therapy."

"Well, will you ask them how they pay? I mean, do they fork over cash or a check after every session or does the doctor bill them by the month? I'm just curious about how the shrink's money comes in."

"You think that has something to do with Ellerbee's murder?"

"I don't know. There's so much I don't know about this case. Like how does a psychiatrist get patients? Referrals from other doctors? Or do patients walk in off the street or use the Yellow Pages? I just don't know."

"I'll ask around," Monica promised. "I suspect every case is different."

"I suspect the same thing," he grumbled. "Makes it hard to figure percentages."

And, four hours later, when they were in their upstairs bedroom preparing for sleep, he said, "I haven't even looked at the Sunday *Times.* Was there anything on the Ellerbee case?"

"I didn't notice anything. But there's an interesting article in the magazine section about new colors for women's hair. Would you like me to get pink streaks, Edward?"

"I'd prefer kelly green," he said. "But suit yourself."

"Monster," she said affably and crawled into her bed.

"You know what I think?" he said. "I think absolute craziness and absolute normality are extremes, and very few people fit into either category. Most of us suffer varying degrees of abnormality that can range from mild eccentricity to outright psychosis. Look at that article on hair coloring. I'll bet a lot of women are going to dye their hair pink or orange or purple. That doesn't make them all whackos."

"What's your point, Edward?"

"This afternoon I said those patients we've been questioning don't live in my world. But that's not true; they do live in my world. They're just a little farther along toward craziness than I am, so I find it difficult to understand them."

"What you're saying is that we're all loonies, some more, some less."

"Yes," he said gratefully. "That's what I mean. I've got to keep in mind that I share the patients' queerness, but to a milder degree."

She turned her head to stare at him.

"Don't be so sure of that, buster," she said, and he gave a great hoot of laughter and climbed into her bed.

# 14.

"I stopped at the precinct on my way over," Boone said on Monday morning. "Talked to the Sergeant handling paperwork for Suarez's investigation. He says the new people will be here by nine o'clock. Gave me a copy of the roster. He wasn't happy about losing them."

"No," Delaney said, "I don't imagine he would be."

"You don't think Chief Suarez will send us six dummies, do you, sir?" Jason T. Jason asked.

"Sabotage?" Delaney said, smiling. "No, I don't think he'll do that. Not with Deputy Thorsen looking over his shoulder. But if any of these men don't work out, we'll ask for replacements."

"They're not all men, sir," Boone said. "Five men and a woman. And one of the guys is a black—Robert Keisman. You know him, Jase?"

"Oh, sure. He's a sharp cat; you won't need a replacement for him. They call him the Spoiler because for a time there he was assigned to busting bunco artists and three-card-monte games in the Times Square area. One of the guys he grabbed screamed, 'You're spoiling all our fun!' and the name stuck. You know any of the others, Sergeant?"

"I've worked with two of them. Not much flash, but they're solid enough. Benny Calazo has been around a hundred years. He's slowing down some, but he still makes all the right moves. The other guy I know is Ross Konigsbacher. He's a dick two. They call him Kraut. He's built like a dumpster, and maybe he likes to use his hands too much. But he's thorough; I'll say that for him. The other people I don't know."

"All right," Delaney said. "Let's get set up for this. We're going to need more chairs in here—five more should do it."

They carried in chairs from the living room and kitchen and arranged them in a rough semicircle facing the desk in the study. They also brought in extra ashtrays.

"I was going to let them read my reports on the six patients," Delaney said, "but I decided not to. I don't want them prejudiced by my reactions to those people. We'll just give them a brief introduction, hand them their assignments, and turn them loose. I'm hoping we can get them out on the street by noon. You two decide who you want to partner first, then switch around from day to day."

The new recruits began arriving a little before 9:00 A.M. Sergeant Boone served as doorman, showing them where to hang their coats and bringing them back to the study to introduce them to Delaney and Jason Two.

By 9:15, everyone was present and Boone closed the doors. Delaney had hidden his glasses away, firmly believing that wearing spectacles while issuing orders was counterproductive, being a sign of physical infirmity in a commanding officer.

"My name is Edward X. Delaney," he said in a loud, forceful voice. "Former Captain, Commander of the Two-Five-One Precinct, and former Chief of Detectives prior to my retirement several years ago. As you probably know, I am assisting Chief Suarez in his investigation of the Ellerbee homicide. Are you all familiar with that case?"

They nodded.

"Good," he said. "Then I won't have to repeat the details. By the way, you can smoke if you like."

He waited while a few of them lighted cigarettes. Detective Brian Estrella, a string bean of a man, took pipe and pouch from his jacket pockets and started slowly packing the tobacco.

Delaney told them that the first job of this "task force," as he called it, was to investigate six of the victim's patients who had a history of violence. He emphasized that these people were not yet considered suspects, just subjects worth checking out in depth. Later they might have to investigate other of Ellerbee's patients.

"The first thing you'll want to do," he said, "is to run them through Records and see if any of them have sheets."

He said that eventually each detective would be assigned to one patient. But for the first few days, they'd be moved around, meeting the patients, questioning them, digging into their backgrounds and personal lives.

"We're hoping," he continued, "you will each find one subject who will think you simpatico and talk a little more freely. Now let me give you a rundown on the people we're dealing with."

He was gratified to see all the detectives take out their notebooks and ballpoints.

He delivered brief summaries of the six patients.

When he finished, he turned to Boone. "Anything to add, Sergeant?"

"Not about the people, sir; I think you've covered what we know. But the hammer . . ."

"I was getting to that."

Delaney told them that the murder weapon was apparently a ball peen hammer. It had not been found, and none of the six subjects had admitted owning such a tool. He urged them to make a search for the hammer an important part of their investigation.

He also reminded them of the two sets of footprints and suggested they query the subjects as to ownership of rubbers, galoshes, boots, or any other type of foul-weather footwear.

"If you can get their shoe size," he told them, "so much the better. We have photos of the footprints. Anything else, Boone?"

"No, sir."

"Anything you want to add, Jason?"

"No, sir."

"All right," Delaney said to the others. "Any questions?"

The female detective, Helen K. Venable, raised her hand. "Sir," she said, "are these people all crackpots?"

There was some amused laughter, but Delaney didn't smile. "This job is going to take patience and understanding. Your first impression might be of a bunch of whackos, but don't underestimate them because of that. Remember, quite possibly one of them had the intelligence, resolve, and cunning to zap Doctor Ellerbee and, so far, get away with it."

Benjamin Calazo, the old gumshoe, raised a meaty hand. "I'd like to take Isaac Kane. My brother's kid is retarded. A sweet boy, no harm in him, but like you said, he needs patience and understanding. I've learned to deal with him, so if it's okay with you, I'd like to take on Isaac Kane."

"Fine with me," Delaney said. "Anyone else got a preference?"

Robert Keisman, the Spoiler, spoke up: "If no one else wants him, I'll start with the Vietnam vet—what's his name? Gerber? I can jive with those guys."

"He's all yours," Delaney said. "Just watch your back; I think the kid can be dangerous. Any other preferences?"

There were none, so they set to work making assignments, arranging schedules, exchanging phone numbers so any of them could be reached at any hour, either directly or by leaving a message.

Boone selected Detectives Konigsbacher, Calazo, and Venable for his squad. Jason had Estrella, the pipe smoker; Keisman; and Timothy (Big Tim) Hogan, a short, blunt man as bald as a peeled egg.

Delaney impressed on all of them the need for daily reports, as complete as they could make them.

"Include everything," he told them. "Even if it seems silly or insignificant. If you think it's important, contact Boone or Jason immediately. If you can't get hold of them, call me any hour of the day or night. Now let's get moving. The trail is getting colder by the day, and the Department wants to close out this file as soon as possible. If you need cars, backup, special equipment, or the cooperation of technical squads, just let me know."

They all shook his hand and tramped out, along with Boone and Jason. Delaney returned the extra chairs to their proper place and emptied the ashtrays. Then he called Suarez, but the Chief was in a meeting and not available. Delaney left his name and asked that Suarez call him back.

He sat at his desk, put on his reading glasses, lighted a cigar. Working from the duty roster, from what Boone and Jason had told him, and from his own observations, he made a list of the newly assigned detectives on a pad of yellow legal paper. It went like this:

Boone's squad—

1. Ross (Kraut) Konigsbacher. Heavy. Muscular. Blond mustache. Likes to use fists. Faint scar over left eyebrow.
2. Benjamin Calazo. Old flatfoot. White hair. Heavy hands, keratosis on backs. Picked Isaac Kane.
3. Helen K. Venable. Short. Chubby. Reddish brown hair. Very intense. Deep voice.

Jason's squad—

1. Brian Estrella. Tall. Stringy. Smokes pipe. Left-handed. Prominent Adam's apple.
2. Robert (Spoiler) Keisman. Black. Slender. Elegant. Packs shoulder holster. Picked Harold Gerber.

3. Timothy (Big Tim) Hogan. Stubby. Bald. Big ears. Nicotine-stained fingers. Whiny voice.

Finished, Delaney read over the list and could visualize the new people, recognize them as individuals. He put his notes in the back of the top drawer of his desk. Comments on their performance would be added later. Some of them might earn citations out of this.

Pushing aside the yellow pad, he searched through his file cabinet and dug out a wide worksheet pad designed for accountants. It had fourteen ruled columns and provided enough horizontal lines for what he proposed to devise: a time schedule for the night Dr. Simon Ellerbee was murdered.

He listed the names of individuals at the tops of columns. Down the left margin of the page he noted times from 4:00 P.M. on the fatal day to 1:54 A.M., when the body was discovered.

This was donkeywork, he knew, but it had to be done. It would require constant reference to the reports, statements, and Dr. Ellerbee's records in his file cabinet. And all the times would be approximate. Even the time of death, estimated at nine o'clock by the ME, could be off by an hour or more. Still, you had to start somewhere.

He started with the first column:

*Dr. Simon Ellerbee:*
   4:00 P.M.—Appointment with Harold Gerber.
   5:00—Appointment with Mrs. Lola Brizio. Who is she? Check.
   6:00—Tells wife he expects late patient, but doesn't tell her who or when. Appointment not listed in book. Receptionist doesn't know who or when. Tells wife he will leave N.Y. for Brewster at 9:00. That suggests late patient at 7:00 or 8:00.
   9:00—Dead.
*Dr. Diane Ellerbee:*
   6:00—Leaves office after speaking to husband.
   6:30—Departs Manhattan, driving.
   8:00—Arrives Brewster home.
   11:30—Calls Manhattan office. No answer. Calls twice more, times not stated.
   12:00—Calls Brewster police. No report of highway accident.
   Calls Manhattan garage, time not stated, learns Simon's car is still in slot.
   1:15—Calls Dr. Samuelson.
*Dr. Julius K. Samuelson:*

> 7:00 P.M.–?—Dinner with friends at Russian Tea Room.
> 8:30–11:30—Concert at Carnegie Hall.
> 11:30–12:30(?)—Nightcap at St. Moritz.
> 1:15 A.M.—Receives Diane's call.
> 1:45—Arrives 84th Street townhouse.
> 1:54—Finds body, calls 911.

When the phone rang, Delaney was startled and jagged his pen across the page.

"Chief Suarez is calling," a voice announced.

"How are you doing, Chief," Delaney asked.

"Surviving," Suarez said with a sigh. "I hope you have some good news for me."

"I'm afraid not, Chief, but I would like to get together with you—just to keep you informed of what we're doing."

"Yes," Suarez said, "I would appreciate that."

"Would you care to drop by here, Chief? I'll be in all day and it shouldn't take long."

A hesitation. "A bad day. So much to do. I do not expect to get uptown until this evening. Will eight or nine o'clock be too late for you?"

"Not at all. I'll be here."

"Suppose I stop at your place on my way home. I will call you first to tell you when I am leaving. Will that be satisfactory?"

"That's fine," Delaney said. "See you tonight."

He put down the receiver, and went back to the time schedule.

*Henry Ellerbee:*
    9:00—Charity dinner at Plaza. Presence confirmed.
*Receptionist:*
    5:00 or 6:00?—When did she leave. Check.
*Isaac Kane:*
    9:00—Leaves Community Center when it closes. Goes home?
*Sylvia Mae Otherton:*
    9:00—At home alone. No confirmation.
*L. Vincent Symington:*
    9:00—Dinner-dance at Hilton. Could have left, gone back.
*Ronald J. Bellsey:*
    9:00—Home all night. Wife confirms.
*Harold Gerber:*
    9:00—Bar-hopping, no recollection of where. No confirmation.

*Joan Yesell:*
9:00—Home all night. Mother confirms.

Delaney had just started reading over what he had written when the phone rang again. It was Boone.

"I'm in Ronald Bellsey's garage with the Kraut," he reported. "Bellsey's Cadillac is here. I called his meat market, and he's at work all right. There's no one around. I can get into that Cadillac trunk. I've got my picks."

He paused. Delaney thought it over.

"Where are you calling from, Sergeant?"

"A public phone in the garage."

"All right, go into the trunk. Just look it over, then call me back. If there's any trouble, I authorized you to make the break-in, and Chief Suarez and Deputy Thorsen authorized me. Don't put *your* ass on the line."

"There won't be any trouble," Boone assured him. "Right now the place is deserted, and the Kraut will stand lookout."

"Call me back," Delaney repeated, and hung up.

He tried to concentrate on the time schedule, but couldn't. When the phone rang again, he grabbed it.

"Boone again," the Sergeant said in an excited voice. "I got in! There's ball peen hammer in there, an old one, all greasy."

"Glom on to it," Delaney said at once. "Get it to the techs as soon as possible. Can you relock the trunk?"

"No strain."

"Good. Bellsey will never miss his hammer for a day or two."

He hung up, smiling, and went back to the schedule, satisfied that things were beginning to happen. They were *making* them happen.

He read over the timetable twice, paying attention to every word. Then he pushed the pad away, leaned back in his swivel chair, lighted a cigar.

What interested him even more than those half-confirmed and unconfirmed alibis was what Dr. Simon Ellerbee did the last three hours of his life.

Did the mystery patient show up and stay longer than usual? Not likely; every patient got the forty-five-minute hour. Did Ellerbee work at his caseload while waiting for the patient to arrive? Did he read, listen to music, watch television?

Delaney looked at his watch and thought of a sandwich. *Eat!* When did the bastard eat? He told his wife he'd be leaving New York about nine o'clock. Even if he were planning on a late supper in Brewster at 10:30, that was a long time to go without food. Delaney didn't think it was humanly possible.

He retrieved the autopsy report from the file and flipped through the pages until he found what he sought. The victim had eaten about an hour before his death. Stomach contents included boiled ham, Swiss cheese, rye bread, mustard. Ellerbee had been a man after his own heart.

So part of those three hours had been spent consuming a sandwich. Did Ellerbee go out for it? In that weather? Doubtful. He probably went down one floor to the kitchen and made himself a snack. But that wouldn't use up many minutes of that three-hour period.

The gap in the victim's time schedule bothered Delaney. It was not neat, ordered, logical—the way he liked things. Too many unanswered questions:

1. Why didn't Ellerbee tell his wife the name of the late patient and when he or she was expected?

2. Why didn't he tell his receptionist?

3. If the late patient was expected at, say, seven o'clock, then Ellerbee could have left for Brewster at eight. But he told his wife he'd be leaving at nine. Ergo, the patient was expected at eight o'clock. But if that was so, how come the autopsy showed he had eaten an hour before death? It was ridiculous to suppose he munched on a sandwich while listening to a troubled patient.

4. How did Ellerbee spend the time from six to eight o'clock, assuming the late patient *was* scheduled for eight?

5. Those two sets of tracks—did the doctor expect *two* late patients that night?

It was, Delaney acknowledged, probably much ado about nothing. But it gnawed at him, and he suddenly decided he'd take on this puzzle himself. He couldn't sit in his study all day, waiting for phone calls and reports from his task force. He'd hit the street and do a little personal sleuthing.

He started by searching through the records for the name and address of Doctor Simon's receptionist. He finally found them: Carol Judd, living on East 73rd Street. Clipped to her card was Boone's report on her alibi for the night of the murder: She said she had been shacked up with her boyfriend in his apartment. He confirmed.

Delaney looked up her phone number in the Manhattan directory.

He called, mentally keeping his fingers crossed. It rang seven times and he was about to hang up when suddenly the receiver was lifted.

"Hello?" A breathless voice.

"Miss Carol Judd?"

"Yes. Who is this?"

"My name is Edward X. Delaney," he said, speaking slowly and distinctly. "I am a civilian consultant with the New York Police Department, assisting in the investigation of the death of Doctor Simon Ellerbee. I was hoping you—"

"Hey," she said, "wait a minute, let me put these groceries down. I just walked through the door."

He waited patiently until she came on the line again.

"Now," she said, "who are you?"

He went through it again. "I was hoping you might give me a few minutes of your time. Some questions have come up that only you can answer."

"Gee, I don't know," she said hesitantly. "Ever since my name was in the papers, I've been getting crazy calls. Real weirdos—you know?"

"I can imagine. Miss Judd, may I suggest you call Doctor Diane Ellerbee and tell her that you have received a call from me and that I'd like to ask you a few questions. I'm sure she'll tell you that I am not a weirdo. I'll give you my number and you can call me back. Will you do that, please?"

"Well . . . I guess so. It may take some time getting through to her if she has a patient."

"I'll wait," Delaney said and gave her his phone number.

He cleared the clutter from his desk, replacing all the records back in their proper file folders. He kept out the time schedule and read it over again. That three-hour gap in Ellerbee's activities still intrigued him, and he hoped Carol Judd could supply some answers.

It was almost twenty minutes before she called back.

"Doctor Diane says you're okay," she reported.

"Fine," he said. "I wonder if I could come over now; I'm not too far from where you live."

"Right this minute? Gee, you better give me some time to straighten up this place; it's a mess. How about half an hour?"

"I'll be there. Thank you."

That gave him time for a Michelob and a "wet" sandwich, eaten while leaning over the kitchen sink. It consisted of meat scraped off the bones of leftover chicken wings, with sliced tomatoes and onions and Russian dressing—all jammed into an onion roll as big as a Frisbee.

Then, donning his hard black homburg and heavy overcoat, he set out to walk down to East 73rd Street.

It was the kind of day that made pedestrians step out: cold, clear, brilliant, with sharp light dazzling the eyes and a wind that stung. The city seemed renewed and glowing.

He strode down Third Avenue, mourning the passing of all those familiar Irish bars, including his father's saloon. There was now a health food store where that had been. It was change all right, but whether it was progress, Delaney was not prepared to say.

Carol Judd lived in a fourteen-story apartment house that had glass doors, marble walls in vestibule and lobby, and a pervasive odor of boiled cabbage. Delaney identified himself on the intercom and was buzzed in immediately. He rode up to apartment 9-H in an automatic elevator that squeaked alarmingly.

If she had spent the last half-hour tidying up, Delaney hated to think of what her tiny studio apartment had been before she started. It looked like a twister had just blown through, leaving a higgledy-piggledy jumble of clothing, books, records, cassettes, and what appeared to be a collection of Japanese windup toys: dancing bears, rabbits clashing cymbals, and somersaulting clowns.

"Pardon the stew," she said, smiling brightly.

"Not at all," he said. "It looks lived-in."

"Yeah," she said, laughing, "it is that. Would you believe I've had a party for twenty people in here?"

"I'd believe it," he assured her, and thought, The poor neighbors!

She lifted a stack of fashion magazines out of a canvas sling chair, and he lowered himself cautiously into it, still wearing his overcoat, his homburg on his lap. Unexpectedly, she crossed her ankles and scissored down onto the floor without a bump, an athletic feat he admired.

In fact, he admired her. She was tall, lanky, and in tight denim jeans seemed to be 90 percent legs. She was not beautiful, but her perky features were vivacious, and her mop of blond curls—an Orphan Annie hairdo—had an outlandish charm. She wore a T-shirt that had a portrait of Beethoven printed on the front.

"Miss Judd," he started, "I'll try to make this as brief as possible; I don't want to take up too much of your time."

"I've got plenty," she told him. "I've been looking for a job, but no luck yet. When I spoke to Doctor Diane before, she said she's looking for me, too, and thinks she may be able to get me something with a shrink she knows who's opening a clinic for rich alcoholics."

"How long did you work for Doctor Simon Ellerbee?"

"Almost five years. Gee, that was a dreamy job. Good hours and very little work. No pressure—you know?"

"I assume you handled his appointments, took care of the billing, and things of that nature?"

"That's right. And I could use their kitchen for lunch. They even invited me and Edith Crawley—she's Doctor Diane's receptionist—up to their Brewster home for a weekend every summer. That's a dreamy place. And, of course, I got the whole month of August off every year."

"Did you like Doctor Simon?"

"A wonderful, wonderful man. Swell to work for. I really had eyes for him, but I knew that would get me nowhere. You've seen Doctor Diane? Too much competition!" She laughed merrily, clasping her knees with her arms and rocking back and forth on the floor.

"What hours did you work?"

"Nine to five. Usually. Sometimes he would ask me to come in a little earlier or stay a little later if an hysterical woman was scheduled. You know, some of those crazy ladies could scream rape—it's possible."

"Did it ever happen—that a woman patient screamed rape?"

"It never happened to Doctor Simon, but it happened to a friend of his, so he was very careful."

"Let's talk about the Friday he was killed. Did anything unusual happen that day?"

She thought a moment. "Noo," she said finally, "it was ordinary. Lousy weather; it poured all day. But nothing unusual happened in the office."

"What time did you leave?"

"A few minutes after five. Right after Mrs. Brizio arrived."

"Ah," he said, "Mrs. Lola Brizio . . . She was the last patient listed in his appointment book."

"That's right. She came in once a week, every Friday, five to six."

"Tell me about her."

"Mrs. Brizio? Gee, she must be sixty—at least. And very, very rich. That dreamy chinchilla coat she wears—I could live five years on what she paid for that. But a very nice lady. I mean, not stuck-up or anything like that. Real friendly. She was always telling me the cute things her grandchildren said."

"What was her problem?"

"Kleptomania. Can you believe it? With all her loot. She'd go in these stores, like Henri Bendel, and stuff silk scarves and costume jewelry in her handbag. Been doing it for years. The stores knew about it, of course, and kept an eye on her. They never arrested her or anything because she was such a good customer. I mean, she bought a lot of stuff in addition to what she stole. So they'd let her swipe what she wanted and just add it to her bill. She always paid. She came to Doctor Simon about three years ago." Carol Judd burst out laughing. "The first session she had, she stole a crystal ashtray off Doctor Simon's desk, and he didn't even notice until she was gone. Can you imagine?"

"Sixty years old, you say?"

"At least. Probably more."

"A big woman?"

"Oh, no! A little bitty thing. Not even five feet tall. And fat. A roly-poly."

"All right," Delaney said, tentatively eliminating Mrs. Lola Brizio as a possible suspect, "after she arrived at five o'clock, you left a few minutes later. Is that correct?"

"Right."

"Did Doctor Simon tell you he was expecting a late patient?"

"No, he didn't."

"Wasn't that unusual?"

"Oh, no, it happened all the time. Like maybe in the evening he'd get a panic call from some patient who had to see him right away. The next morning he'd just leave a note on my desk telling me to bill so-and-so for a session."

"Did Doctor Diane ever have late patients?"

"Oh, sure. They both did, all the time."

"Apparently, after six o'clock, when Mrs. Lola Brizio was gone, Doctor Simon told his wife that he was expecting a late patient, but didn't tell her who or when. Isn't that a little surprising?"

"Not really. Like I said, it happened frequently. They'd tell each other so it wouldn't interfere with their plans for the night—dinner or the theater, you know—but I don't think they'd mention who it was that was coming in. There was just no need for it."

Delaney sat silently, brooding, and somewhat depressed. As explained by Carol Judd, the mystery patient now seemed no mystery at all. It was just routine.

"And you have no idea who the late patient was on that Friday night?" he asked her.

"No, I don't."

"Well, whoever had the appointment," he said, trying to salvage something from his inquiries, "was probably the last person to see Doctor Simon alive. And may have been the killer. But let's suppose the late patient arrived at seven and left at eight. Would it—"

"Fifteen minutes to eight. Patients got forty-five minutes."

"What did the doctor do in those fifteen minutes between patients?"

"Relax. Return phone calls. Look over the files of the next patient. Maybe have a cup of coffee."

"All right," he said, "let's suppose the late patient arrived at seven and left at fifteen minutes to eight. Do you think it's possible that sometime during the evening Doctor Simon got a phone call from *another* patient who wanted to see him? A second late patient?"

"Of course it's possible," she said. "Things like that happened all the time."

Which left him, he thought, nowhere.

"Thank you very much, Miss Judd," he said, heaving himself out of the silly canvas sling and putting on his hat. "You've been very cooperative and very helpful."

She rose from her folded position on the floor without using her hands—just unflexed her limber body and floated up.

"I hope you catch the person who did it," she said, suddenly solemn and vengeful. "I wish we had the death penalty. Doctor Simon was a dear, sweet man, and no one deserves to die like that. I cried for forty-eight hours after it happened. I still can't believe he's gone."

Delaney nodded and started for the door. Then he stopped and turned.

"One more thing," he said. "Did Doctor Simon ever mention to you that he had been attacked or threatened by a patient?"

"No, he never did."

"In the past year or six months, did you notice any change in him? Did he act differently?"

She stared at him. "Funny you should ask that. Yes, he changed. In the last year or so. I even mentioned it to my boyfriend. Doctor Simon became, uh, moodier. He used to be so steady. The same every day: pleasant and kind to everyone. Then, in the last year or so, he became moodier. Some days he'd really be up, laughing and joking. And other days he'd be down, like he had the weight of the world on his shoulders."

"I see."

"About a month ago," she added, "he wore a little flower in his lapel. He had never done that before. He really was a dreamy man."

"Thank you, Miss Judd," Delaney said, tipping his homburg.

When he came outside, he found the day transformed. A thick cloud cover was churning over Manhattan, the wind had taken on a raw edge, the light seemed sourish and menacing. The gloom fitting his mood exactly.

He was disgusted with himself, for he had been trying to bend the facts to fit a theory instead of devising a theory that fit all the facts. That kind of thinking had been the downfall of a lot of wild-assed detectives.

It was those two sets of footprints soaked into the Ellerbees' carpet that had seduced him. That and the gap in the victim's time schedule. It seemed to add up to *two* late patients on the murder night. But though Carol Judd said it was possible, there wasn't a shred of evidence to substantiate it.

Still, he told himself stubbornly, it was crucial to identify Ellerbee's late visitor or visitors. One of them had been the last person to see the victim alive and was a prime suspect.

Plodding uptown, he remembered what he had said to Monica about assembling a jigsaw puzzle. He had told her that he had found some straight-edged pieces and was putting together the frame. Then all he needed to do was fill in the interior pieces of the picture.

Now he recalled that some puzzles were not pictures at all. They were rectangles of solid color: yellow, blue, or blood red. There was no pattern, no clues of shape or form. And they were devilishly hard to complete.

When he entered the brownstone, he heard the phone ringing and rushed down the hallway to the kitchen. But Monica was there and had already picked up.

"Who?" she said. "Just a minute, please." She covered the mouthpiece with her palm and turned to her husband. "Timothy Hogan," she reported. "Do you know him?"

"Hogan? Yes, he's one of the new men. I'll talk to him."

She handed him the phone.

"I couldn't get ahold of Jason or Boone," Hogan whined, "so that's why I'm calling. I'm at St. Vincent's Hospital."

"What happened?"

"I started checking out that Joan Yesell. She didn't report to work today. Okay? So I go down to her place in Chelsea. She ain't home, and her mother ain't home. So I start talking to the neighbors. Okay? This Joan Yesell, she tried to do the Dutch yesterday afternoon, but blew it. Just nicked her left wrist with a kitchen knife. A lot of blood, but she's okay. They kept her here overnight, under observation. Her mother is signing her out right now. You want I should question them?"

"No," Delaney said promptly, "don't do that. Let them go home. You can catch up with them tomorrow. Do you know what time yesterday she cut herself?"

"They brought her into St. Vincent's Emergency about four-thirty, so I guess she sliced herself around four o'clock. Okay?"

"Thank you, Hogan. You did exactly right to call me. Pack it in for the day."

He hung up and turned to Monica. He told her what had happened.

"The poor woman," she said somberly.

"If she tried suicide yesterday at four o'clock, it couldn't have been more than an hour after Boone and I had questioned her. I hope to God we didn't trigger it."

"How did she seem when you left?"

"Well, she's a mousy little thing and suffers from depression. She was very quiet and withdrawn. Dominated by her mother. But she sure didn't seem suicidal. I wonder if it was anything we said."

"I doubt that. Don't worry about it, Edward."

"This morning I was happy that things were beginning to happen, that we were *making* them happen. But I didn't figure on anything like this."

"It's not your fault," she assured him. "She's tried before, hasn't she?"

"Three times."

"Well, there you are. Don't blame yourself."

"Son of a bitch," he said bitterly. "I just don't get it. We talk to her, very politely, no arguments, we leave, and she tries to kill herself."

"Edward, maybe it was just talking about the murder that pushed her over the edge. If she's depressed to start with, reminding her of the death of someone who was trying to help her might have made her decide life wasn't worth living."

"Yes," he said gratefully, "it could have been that. I'm going to have a slug of rye. Would you like one?"

"I'll have a white wine. We're having linguine with clam sauce tonight. I added a can of minced clams and a dozen fresh cherrystones."

"Very good," he said approvingly. "In that case, I'll have a white wine, too. By the way, Chief Suarez is stopping by later. I don't know what time, but he'll call first. I'd like you to meet him; I think you'll like him."

After dinner, Delaney went into the study to write out a report on Carol Judd. Suarez called around eight o'clock and said he was on his way uptown. But it was almost nine before he arrived. Delaney took him into the living room and introduced him to Monica.

"What can I get you, Chief?" he asked. "You look like you could use a transfusion."

Suarez smiled wanly. "Yes, it has been that kind of a day. Would a very, very dry gin martini on the rocks be possible?"

"Of course. Monica, would you like anything?"

"A small Cointreau would be nice."

Delaney went into the kitchen and made the drinks. He put them on a tray along with a brandy for himself.

"Delightful," Chief Suarez said, when he tasted his. "Best martini I've ever had."

"As I told you," Delaney said, shrugging away the compliment, "I have no good news for you, but I wanted you to know what we've been doing."

Rapidly, concisely, he summarized the progress of his investigation to date. He omitted nothing he thought important, except the lifting of the ball peen hammer from Ronald Bellsey's Cadillac. He expressed no great optimism, but pointed out there was still a lot of work to be done, particularly on those vague alibis of the six patients.

Monica and the Chief listened intently, fascinated by his recital. When he finished, Suarez said, "I do not believe things are as gloomy as you seem to suggest, Mr. Delaney. You have uncovered several promising leads—more, certainly, than we have found. I commend you for persuading Doctor Diane Ellerbee to furnish a list of violence-prone patients. But you should know, that lady and the victim's father continue to bring pressure on the Department, demanding a quick solution."

"That's Thorsen's problem," Delaney said shortly.

"True," Suarez said, "and he handles it by making it *my* problem." He glanced around the living room. "Mrs. Delaney, you have a lovely home. So warm and cheerful."

"Thank you," she said. "I hope you and your wife will visit us. A social visit—no talk of murder."

"Rosa would like that," he said. "Thank you very much."

He sat a moment in silence, staring into his glass. His long face seemed drawn, olive skin sallow with fatigue, the tic at the left of his mouth more pronounced.

"You know," he said with his shy, rueful smile, "since the death of Doctor Ellerbee, there have been perhaps fifty homicides in the city. Many of those, of course, were solved immediately. But our solution rate on the others is not what it should be; I am aware of that and it troubles me. I will not speak to you of our manpower needs, Mr. Delaney; I know you had the same problem when you were in the Department. I mentioned all this merely to tell you how grateful I am for your assistance. I wish I could devote more time to the Ellerbee murder, but I cannot. So I am depending on you."

"I warned you from the start," Delaney said. "No guarantees."

"Naturally. I realize that. But your participation lifts part of my burden and gives me confidence that, during this difficult time, I badly need. Mrs. Delaney, do you have faith in your husband?"

"Absolutely," she said.

"And do you think he will find Ellerbee's killer?"

"Of course he will. Once Edward sets his mind on something, it's practically done. He's a very tenacious man."

"Hey," Delaney said, laughing, "what's this—the two of you ganging up on me?"

"Tenacious," Chief Suarez repeated, staring at the other man. "Yes, I think you are right. I am not a betting man, but if I was, I would bet on you, Mr. Delaney. I have a good feeling that you will succeed. Now I have a favor I would like to ask of you."

"What's that?"

"I would like it if we could call each other by our Christian names."

"Of course, Michael."

"Thank you, Edward."

"And I'm Monica," she said loudly.

They all laughed, and Delaney went into the kitchen for another round of drinks.

After the Chief had left, Delaney came back into the living room and sprawled into his chair.

"What do you think of him?" he asked.

"A very nice man," Monica said. "Very polite and soft-spoken. But he looks headed for a burnout. Do you think he's tough enough for the job?"

"It'll make him or break him," Delaney said roughly. "Headquarters is a bullring. Turn your back for a second and you get gored. Monica, when I was telling him what we're doing in the Ellerbee case, was there anything special that caught your attention? Something that sounded false? Or something we should have done that we haven't?"

"No," she said slowly, "nothing in particular. It sounded awfully complicated, Edward. All those people . . ."

"It *is* complicated," he said, rubbing his forehead wearily. "In the first stages of any investigation, you expect to be overwhelmed by all the bits and pieces that come flooding in. Facts and rumors and guesses. Then, after a while, if you're lucky, they all fall into a pattern, and you know more or less what happened. But I admit this case has me all bollixed up. I've been trying to keep on top of it with reports and files and time schedules, but it keeps spreading out in more directions. It's so complex that I'm afraid I may be missing something that's right under my nose. Maybe I'm getting too old for this business."

"You're not getting older," she said loyally, "you're getting better."

"Keep telling me that," he said.

# 15.

During the next two days, the disorder in the Ellerbee case that had troubled Edward X. Delaney showed signs of lessening.

"It's still confusion," he told Sergeant Boone, "but it's becoming *organized* confusion."

Driving his little task force with stern directives, he was able to move them around so each had the chance to eyeball several patients. By Wednesday night, Delaney, Boone, and Jason were able to achieve optimum pairings of detective and subject. They went like this:

Benjamin Calazo—Isaac Kane.

Robert Keisman—Harold Gerber.

Ross Konigsbacher—L. Vincent Symington.

Helen K. Venable—Joan Yesell.

Timothy Hogan—Ronald J. Bellsey.

Brian Estrella—Sylvia Mae Otherton.

"If it doesn't work out," Delaney told his people, "we'll switch you around until we start getting results."

Brian Estrella, the pipe-smoker, hoped he wouldn't be switched from Sylvia Mae Otherton. The woman fascinated him, and he thought he could do some good there.

On the morning he started out to meet her for the first time, his horoscope in the *Daily News* read: "Expect a profitable surprise." And as if that wasn't encouraging enough, his wife, Meg, called from the nursing home to report she was feeling better, her hair was beginning to grow back in, and she would be home soon.

Which was, Estrella knew, a lie—but a brave, happy lie all the same.

Sergeant Boone had warned him what to expect, but still it was something of a shock to walk into that dim, overheated apartment and confront someone who looked like all she'd need would be a broomstick to soar over the rooftops.

She was wearing a voluminous white garment which could have been a bedsheet except that it was inset with triangles of white lace. It hung quite low, almost to the floor, but not low enough to hide Otherton's bare feet. They were short and puffy, the toenails painted black.

Boone had mentioned the woman's jewelry and perfume, the wildly decorated room and burning incense. It was all there, but what surprised Detective Estrella was Otherton's patience. After all, this was the third time she had been braced by the cops on the Ellerbee kill, and he expected her to be hostile and indignant.

But she led him into her apartment without demur and answered his questions freely without once reminding him that she had replied to the same queries twice before. He appreciated that, and decided to try an absolutely honest approach to see if that might tempt her into additional disclosures.

"You see, ma'am," he said, "we're most concerned about your whereabouts the night of the crime. You've told us you were here alone. That may be true, but we'd feel a lot better if we could confirm it. Did you go out at all that night?"

"Oh, no," she said in a low voice. "I very rarely go out. That's part of my problem."

"And you say you had no visitors, saw no one, made and received no phone calls?"

She shrugged helplessly. "No, I'm afraid not."

"I wish you'd think hard and carefully about that night, Miss Otherton, and see if you can remember anything that will help confirm what you've told us."

"I'll try," she said. "Really I will."

Estrella looked at that face marred with clown's makeup and suddenly realized that with the chalky mask removed, and the long, unkempt hair brushed, she would be reasonably comely—maybe not pretty but pleasant enough.

To his horror, he found himself blurting all that out, and more, telling this strange woman how she might improve her appearance, her dress, not so much to impress others but for the sake of her own self-esteem.

"You mustn't stay locked up in here," he said earnestly. "You must try to get out into the world."

She stared at him, and her eyes slowly filled, tears began to drip down her fleshy cheeks. He was distressed, thinking he had insulted her. But . . .

"Thank you," she said in a choky voice. "It's kind of you to be concerned. To show an interest. Most people laugh at me. Doctor Simon never did. That's why I loved him so much. I know I am not living a normal life, but with Doctor Simon's help I was trying to come out of it. Now, with him gone, I don't know what I'm going to do."

Then she told Detective Estrella about her childhood rape and her aversion to bearded men—things he already knew. She said her life was a sad tangle, and she was close to giving up hope of "ever getting my head together."

Estrella told her how important it was to think positively, and then told her of his wife's terminal illness and how courageously she was dealing with that.

"Your mental attitude," he said, "is even more important than the way you look. But I think in your case, those things are connected. And if you start by improving your appearance, your state of mind will improve too, and the way you live."

She brought them little glasses of dry sherry, and they began to converse in an animated fashion, discovering they had a common interest in astrology, lecithin, numerology, and UFOs. He asked if he might smoke a pipe, and she said yes, she had always admired men who smoked pipes.

After a while, Estrella was enjoying their conversation so much—he hadn't had a long talk with a woman in months; his visits to Meg were severely limited—that he felt guilty because he had forgotten the reason he was there.

"I hope, Miss Otherton—" he started, but she interrupted.

"Sylvia," she said.

"Sylvia," he repeated. "That's a lovely name. It means 'forest maiden.' Did you know that? My first name is Brian, which means 'strong and powerful,' and you can see how silly that is! But what I was going to say, Sylvia, is that I hope if you can think of anything you feel might help us find Doctor Ellerbee's killer, you'll give me a call. I'll leave you my card."

She stared at him a long moment. "I know how to find out who did it," she said intensely.

He felt a surge of excitement. "How?" he said hoarsely.

She rose, went into the bedroom, came back carrying a Ouija board and planchette.

"Do you believe?" she asked him.

"It can't do any harm," he said, shrugging.

"You *must* believe," she said, "if the spiritualistic messages are to come through."

"I believe," he said hastily. "I really do."

She put the board on the round cocktail table, and they pulled their armchairs close, leaning forward. She put her fingertips lightly on the planchette and closed her eyes.

"Now ask the question," she said in a hollow voice.

"Who killed Doctor Ellerbee?" Detective Estrella said.

"No, no," she said. "The questions must be directed to those who have passed over."

"Doctor Ellerbee," Estrella said, happy that Edward X. Delaney wasn't there to see what he was doing, "who killed you?"

They waited in silence. The planchette did not move.

"Who crushed your skull, Doctor Ellerbee?" the detective asked in a quiet voice.

He watched, fascinated, as the planchette under Sylvia Mae Otherton's fingertips began to move slowly. Not smoothly, but in little jerks. It took a long time, but the pointer moved from letter to letter and spelled out B-L-I-N-D: blind. Then it stopped.

Otherton opened her eyes. "What did it say?" she asked eagerly.

"Blind," Estrella said. "It spelled out 'blind.' "

"What do you suppose that means?"

"I don't know."

"It couldn't have been a blind man who did it, could it?"

"I doubt that very much."

"We could try again," she said hopefully.

"I've got to go," he told her. "Maybe next time."

"You'll come back?"

"Of course. But there are some things I have to check out first."

Before he left he got from her the names of the few friends who called her occasionally, and the list of neighborhood stores that delivered her groceries and drugs.

"Thank you for your help, Sylvia," he said.

She went up on her toes to kiss his cheek. "Thank you, Brian," she said breathlessly.

Going down in the elevator, he debated with himself whether or not to include the Ouija board episode in his report. He finally decided to put it in. Hadn't Delaney said he wanted *everything?*

And *everything* was exactly what Delaney was getting in the daily reports. He was satisfied; better too much than not enough. Most of the stuff was boilerplate, but there were some significant revelations:

—Benjamin Calazo reported that Isaac Kane said he had left the Community Center at 9:00 P.M. on the night of the crime, but Kane admitted he hadn't returned home right away. He was unable or unwilling to account for the intervening time.

—L. Vincent Symington, according to Ross Konigsbacher, had a sheet. A few years previously he had been arrested in a raid on a gay after-hours joint on 18th Street. There was no record of the disposition of the case.

—Timothy Hogan spent some time shmoozing with workers at Ronald J. Bellsey's wholesale meat market, and had learned that six months ago Bellsey and a butcher had a bloody fight with meat hooks that resulted in serious injuries to the butcher. He had sued, but the case was settled out of court.

—Joan Yesell, Helen K. Venable wrote, had injured herself more seriously in her suicide attempt than first thought. Tendons in her wrist had been cut, and Yesell was not expected to return to work for at least a month.

—Detective Robert Keisman reported that Harold Gerber's sheet listed several arrests for assaults, refusing to obey the lawful order of a police officer, and committing a public nuisance. Because of Gerber's war record, all charges were eventually dropped. But, Keisman noted, Gerber had received a less than honorable discharge from the army due to several offenses, including slugging an officer.

—Finally, Brian Estrella wrote about his meeting with Sylvia Mae Otherton, briefly mentioning the incident involving the Ouija board. Edward X. Delaney told Monica about that, thinking she'd be amused. But that most rational of women didn't laugh.

All in all, Delaney was gratified. He had the feeling that the investigation was beginning to lurch forward. It was not unlike an archeological dig, with each layer scraped away bringing him closer to the truth.

Detective Ross (Kraut) Konigsbacher thought he already knew the truth about L. Vincent Symington: The guy was a screaming faggot. It wasn't only that arrest on his record, it was the way he dressed, the way he walked, even the way he handled a cigarette.

Every dick had a different way of working, and Konigsbacher liked to circle his prey, learn all he could about him, study his lifestyle. Then, when he felt he knew his target from A to Z, he'd go for the face-to-face and shatter the guy with what he had learned about him.

The Kraut talked to Symington's neighbors, the super of his townhouse, owners of stores where he shopped. Konigsbacher even got in to interview the personnel manager of the investment counseling firm where Symington worked.

Using a phony business card, Konigsbacher said he was running a credit check on Symington in connection with a loan application for a cooperative apartment. The manager gave Symington a glowing reference, but the Kraut discounted that because he thought the personnel guy was a fruitcake, too.

Outside of business hours, L. Vincent Symington liked to prowl. He dined at a different restaurant almost every night, sometimes alone, sometimes with another man, never with a broad.

After dinner, he'd go bar-hopping. But invariably, around midnight, he'd end up in a place on Lexington Avenue near 40th Street, the Dorian Gray. From the outside it didn't have much flash; the façade was distressed pine paneling with one small window that revealed a dim interior with lighted candles on the tables and a piano at the rear. It was usually crowded.

On the third night Konigsbacher tailed Symington to the Dorian Gray, waited about five minutes, then went inside. It turned out to be the most elegant gay bar the Kraut had ever seen—and he had seen a lot of them, from the Village to Harlem.

This joint was as hushed as a church, with everyone speaking in whispers and even the laughter muted. The black woman at the piano played low-keyed Cole Porter, and the bartender—who looked like a young Tyrone Power—seemed never to clink a bottle or glass.

The Kraut stood a moment at the entrance until his eyes became accustomed to the dimness. There were maybe two or three women in the place, but all the other patrons were men in their thirties and forties. Practically all of them wore conservative, vested suits. They looked like bankers or stockbrokers, maybe even morticians.

Most of the guys at the small tables were in pairs; the singles were at the bar. Konigsbacher spotted his victim sitting alone near the far end. There was an empty barstool next to him. The Kraut sauntered down and swung aboard. The bartender was there immediately.

"Good evening, sir," he said. "What may I bring you?"

The Kraut would have liked a belt of Jack Daniel's with a beer chaser, but when he looked around he saw all the other customers at the bar were having stemmed drinks or sipping little glasses of liqueur.

"Vodka martini straight up with a twist, please," he said, surprised to find himself whispering.

"Very good, sir."

While he waited for his drink, he glanced at the tinted mirror behind the bar and locked stares with L. Vincent Symington. They both looked away.

He drank half his martini, slowly, then pulled a pack of Kents and a disposable lighter from his jacket pocket. The beautiful bartender was there immediately with a small crystal ashtray. The Kraut lighted his cigarette, then left the pack and lighter on the bar in front of him.

A few moments later Symington took a silver case from his inside pocket, snapped it open, selected a long, cork-tipped cigarette.

"I beg your pardon," he said to Konigsbacher in a fluty voice. "I seem to have forgotten my lighter. May I borrow yours?"

It was like a dance, and the Kraut knew the steps.

"Of course," he said, flicked the lighter, and held it for the other man. Symington grasped his hand lightly as if to steady the flame. He took a deep drag of his cigarette and seemed to swallow the smoke.

"Thank you," he said. "Dreadful habit, isn't it?"

"Sex, you mean?" Konigsbacher said, and they both laughed.

Ten minutes later they were seated at a small table against the wall, talking earnestly. They leaned forward, their heads almost touching. Beneath the table, their knees pressed.

"I can tell, Ross," Symington said, "that you take *very* good care of yourself."

"I try to, Vince," the Kraut said. "I work out with weights every morning."

"I really should do that."

He hesitated, then asked, "Are you married, Ross?"

"My wife is; I'm not."

Symington leaned back and clasped his hands together. "Love it," he said. "Just *love* it! My wife is; I'm not. I'll have to remember that."

"How about you, Vince?"

"No. Not now. I was once. But she walked out on me. Taking, I might add, our joint bank account, our poodle, and my personal collection of ancient Roman coins."

"So you're divorced?"

"Not legally, as far as I know."

"You really should be, Vince. You might want to remarry someday."

"I doubt that," Symington said. "I doubt that very much."

"It's a sad, sad, sad, sad world," the Kraut said mournfully, "and we must grab every pleasure we can."

"Truer words were never spoken," the other man agreed, snapped his fingers at the pretty waiter, and ordered another round of drinks.

"Vince," Konigsbacher said, "I have a feeling we can be good friends. I hope so, because I don't have many."

"Oh, my God," Symington said, running his palm over his bald pate. "You, too? I can't *tell* you how lonely I am."

"But there's something you should know about me," the Kraut went on, figuring it was time to get down to business. "I'm under analysis."

"Well, for heaven's sake, *that's* no crime. I was in analysis for years."

"*Was?* You're not now?"

"No," Symington said sorrowfully. "My shrink was killed."

"Killed? That's dreadful. An accident?"

The other man leaned forward again and lowered his voice. "He was murdered."

"Murdered? My God!"

"Maybe you read about it. Doctor Simon Ellerbee, on the Upper East Side."

"Who did it—do they know?"

"No, but I keep getting visits from the police. They have to talk to all his patients, you know."

"What a drag. You don't know anything about it—do you?"

"Well, I have my ideas, but I'm not telling the cops, of course. Hear no evil, see no evil, speak no evil."

"That's smart, Vince. Just try to stay out of it."

"Oh, I will. I have my own problems."

"What kind of a man was he—your shrink?"

"Well, you know what they're like; they can be just *nasty* at times."

"How true. Do you think he was killed by one of his patients?"

Symington swiveled his head to look carefully over both shoulders, as if suspecting someone might be listening. Then he leaned even closer and spoke in a conspiratorial whisper.

"About six months ago—it was on a Friday night—I was crossing First Avenue. I had just had dinner at Lucky Pierre's. That's a marvelous restaurant—really the yummiest escargots in New York. Anyway, it was about nine o'clock, and I was crossing First Avenue, and there, stopped for a light, was Doctor Ellerbee. I saw him plain as day, but he didn't see me. He was driving his new green Jaguar. Then the light changed and he headed uptown. Now I ask you, what does that suggest?"

Konigsbacher was bewildered. "That he had been somewhere?"

"Somewhere with *someone*. And obviously not his wife; she was nowhere to be seen; he was alone in the car."

"I don't know, Vince," the Kraut said doubtfully. "He could have been anywhere. Seeing a patient, for instance, or at a hospital. Anything."

"Well," Symington said, sitting back and smirking with satisfaction, "that's not the *only* thing. I could tell the cops but won't. Let them do their own dirty work."

"Very wise. You keep out of it."

"Oh, I intend to. I don't want to get involved."

Konigsbacher peered at his watch. "Oh dear," he said, "it's later than I thought. I'll have to split."

"Must you, Ross?"

"I'm afraid so, Vince," the Kraut said, having decided to play this fish slowly. "Thank you for a lovely evening. I really enjoyed it."

"It *was* fun, wasn't it? Do you think you might drop in here again?"

"I think I might. Like tomorrow night."

They both laughed, beamed at each other, shook hands lingeringly. Konigsbacher departed, leaving the other man to pick up the tab. Fuck him.

Driving home to Riverdale, the Kraut went over the night's conversation. Not much, but a hint of goodies to come. He'd put it all in his report and let Delaney sort it out.

Edward X. Delaney read the report with something less than admiration. He knew what the Kraut was doing and didn't like it. But after thinking it over, he decided to let the detective run and see what he turned up. Delaney wasn't about to indulge in a soggy philosophical debate over whether or not the end justified the means. He had more immediate concerns.

The techs reported on the ball peen hammer lifted from the trunk of Ronald Bellsey's Cadillac. Negative. Not only no bloodstains, but no indications, even, that the damned thing had been recently used. Sergeant Boone did another lock-picking job and slipped it back into the trunk.

The problem of the late patient continued to nag Delaney. He kept thinking he had solved it, only to find he had uncovered a bigger mystery.

Going through Simon Ellerbee's appointment book for the umpteenth time, he noted that occasionally late patients were scheduled—6:00, 7:00, 8:00, and even 9:00 P.M. He attempted to see if there was any pattern, if certain patients habitually made late appointments.

He then reasoned that late patients who were *not* scheduled in the appointment book—the ones who made panicky phone calls—would certainly be noted in Dr. Ellerbee's billing ledger. Hadn't Carol Judd said that the doctor would leave a note on her desk the next morning, telling her to bill so-and-so for an evening session?

It made sense, but he could find no billing ledger, or anything that resembled it, among the records sent over by Suarez's investigative team. He and Boone spent a frustrating afternoon on the phone, trying to locate it.

Dr. Diane Ellerbee said yes, her husband had kept such a financial journal, with each session noted: name of patient, date, and time. She assumed the police had taken it when they gathered up the rest of Simon's records.

Carol Judd also said yes, there had been such a billing ledger. She kept it in the top drawer of her desk in the outer office, and used it to send out invoices and statements to patients.

Dr. Diane, when he called back, agreed to make a search for the journal, and then phoned to say she could not find it in the receptionist's desk, her husband's office, or anywhere else.

Boone talked to the Crime Scene Unit men and the detective who had taken all the files from the victim's office. None of them could recall seeing anything resembling a billing ledger.

"All right," Delaney said, "so it is missing. Did the killer grab it? Probably. Why? Because it would show how often he or she had been a late patient."

"I don't get it," Boone said.

"Sure you do. We add up the number of sessions for one particular patient in one month, as noted in the appointment book. Then we compare that to the patient's total billing for the month. If the bill is higher than it should be by, say, a hundred bucks, we can figure that the patient had one unscheduled session."

"Now I get it," Boone said. "But it's all smoke if we can't find the damned ledger."

Delaney learned more about the business practices of psychiatrists from Monica who, as promised, had talked to her friends who were in analysis.

"They said their doctors generally sent monthly bills," she reported. "Sometimes it gets complicated when the patient has medical insurance that includes psychotherapy. And some companies have health plans for their employees that pay all or part of psychological counseling fees."

"What does the shrink do if the patient can't or won't pay?"

"Gets rid of them," Monica said. "The theory is that if you pay for therapy, it'll seem more valuable to you. If you get it for nothing, that's what you'll think it's worth. Some shrinks will carry patients for a while if they're having temporary money problems. And some shrinks will adjust their fees or accept stretched-out payments. But no psychiatrist is going to work for free, except for charity. Which reminds me, buster—how much are you getting for all the hours you're putting in on the Ellerbee case?"

"Bupkes is what I'm getting," Delaney said.

Thanksgiving Day arrived at just the right time to provide a much needed respite from records, reports, and unanswered questions.

The roast goose, with wild rice and brandied apples, was pronounced a success. Rebecca Boone had brought a rum cake for dessert, soaked with liquor. She had even prepared a little one, without rum, for her husband.

They carried dessert and coffee into the living room, and lounged in soft chairs with plates of cake on their laps and didn't even mention the Ellerbee case—for at least three minutes.

"You'll laugh at me," Rebecca said, "but I think a total stranger did it."

"Brilliant," her husband said. "The doctor wouldn't buzz the downstairs door for a stranger, and there were no signs of forced entry. So how did the stranger get in?"

"That's easy. He waited in the shadows, maybe behind a parked car, and when the late patient arrived, the killer rushed right in after him, threatening him with the hammer or a gun or knife. And that's why," she finished triumphantly, "there were two sets of footprints on the carpeting."

"It's possible," Delaney admitted. "Anything's possible. But why would a stranger want to kill Doctor Ellerbee? There were no drugs on the premises, and nothing was missing—except that damned billing ledger. I can't believe Ellerbee was murdered for that."

"The killer was in love with Diane Ellerbee," Monica said flatly, "and wanted the husband out of the way so he could marry the widow."

"That's sufficient motive," Delaney acknowledged, "if we could find the tiniest scrap of evidence that Doctor Diane had been playing around —which we can't."

"Maybe she wasn't playing around," Monica said. "Maybe the killer had a crazy passion for her that she wasn't even aware of."

"Why *do* people murder?" Rebecca asked.

Delaney shrugged. "A lot of reasons. Greed, fear, anger, jealousy— the list goes on and on. Sometimes the motive is so trivial that you can't believe anyone would kill because of it."

"I had a case once," Sergeant Boone said, "where a guy stabbed his neighbor to death because the man's dog barked too much. And another where a guy shot his wife because she burned a steak while she was broiling it."

"Did you ever have a case," Monica asked, "where a wife killed her husband because he ate sandwiches while leaning over the kitchen sink?"

The Boones laughed. Even Delaney managed a weak grin.

"What do you think the motive was in the Ellerbee case?" Rebecca asked.

"Nothing trivial," Delaney said, "that's for sure. Something deep and complex. What do you think it was, Sergeant?"

"I don't know," Boone said. "But I doubt if it was money."

"Then it must have been love," his wife said promptly. "I'm sure it had something to do with love."

She was a short, plump, jolly woman with a fine complexion and long black hair falling loosely about her shoulders. Her eyes were soft, and there was a cherub's innocence in her expression. She was wearing a tailored flannel suit, but nothing could conceal her robust grace.

Delaney was aware that she treated him with a deferential awe, and it embarrassed him. Monica addressed Boone familiarly as Abner or Ab, but Rebecca wouldn't dare address Delaney as Edward. And since Mr. Delaney was absurdly formal, she simply used no name or title at all.

"Why do you think love was the motive, Rebecca?" he asked her.

"I just feel it."

The Sergeant burst out laughing. "There's hard evidence for you, sir," he said. "Let's take that to the DA tomorrow."

Later that night, when they were preparing for bed, he said to Monica, "Do you agree with Rebecca—that love was the motive for Ellerbee's murder?"

"I certainly think it was involved," she said. "If it wasn't money, it had to be love."

"I wish I could be as sure of anything," he said grouchily, "as you are of everything."

"You asked me, so I told you."

"If you women are right," he said, "maybe we should forget about checking out violence-prone patients and concentrate on love-prone patients."

"Are there such animals?" she asked. "Love-prone people?"

"Of course there are. Men who go from woman to woman, needing love to give their life meaning. And women who fall in love at the drop of a hat—or a pair of pants."

"You're a very vulgar man," she said.

"That's true," he agreed. "Has Rebecca put on weight?"

"Maybe a pound or two."

"She's not pregnant, is she?"

"Of course not. Why do you ask that?"

"I don't know . . . there was a kind of glow about her tonight. I just thought . . ."

"If she were pregnant, she'd have told me."

"I guess. If they are going to have children, they better get cracking —if you'll excuse another vulgarism. Neither of them is getting any younger."

He was sitting on the edge of his bed, dangling one of his shoes. Monica came over, plumped down on his lap, put a warm arm about his neck.

"I wish you and I had children, Edward."

"We do. I think of your girls as mine. And I know you think of my kids as yours."

"It's not the same," she said. "You know that. I mean a child who's truly ours."

"It's a little late for that," he said. "Isn't it?"

"I suppose so," she said sadly. "I'm just dreaming."

"Besides," he added, "would you want the father of your child to be a man who eats sandwiches leaning over the kitchen sink?"

"I apologize," she said, laughing. "I shouldn't have mentioned that in front of company, but I couldn't resist it."

Before she released him, she put her face close to his, stared into his eyes, said, "Do you love me, Edward?"

"I love you. I don't want to think how empty and useless my life would be without you."

She kissed the tip of his nose, and he asked, "What brought that on?"

"All the talk tonight about love and murder," she said. "It bothered me. I just wanted to make sure the two don't necessarily go together."

"They don't," he said slowly. "Not necessarily."

# 16.

No one knew how or where the expression started, but that year everyone in the Department was using "rappaport." Street cops would say, "I get good rappaport on my beat." Detectives would say of a particular snitch, "I got a good rappaport with that guy."

Actually, when you analyzed it, it was a useful portmanteau word. Not only did you have rapport with someone, but you could rap with them. It fit the bill.

Detective Robert Keisman figured to establish a rappaport with Harold Gerber, the Vietnam vet. The black cop, skinny as a pencil and graceful as a fencer, knew what it was like to feel anger eating at your gut like an ulcer; he thought he and Gerber would have a lot in common . . .

. . . Until he met Gerber, and saw how he lived.

"This guy is a real bonzo," he told Jason.

But still, intent on establishing a rappaport, Keisman costumed himself in a manner he thought wouldn't offend the misanthropic vet: worn jeans, old combat boots, a scruffy leather jacket with greasy buckskin fringe, and a crazy cap with limp earflaps.

He didn't mislead Gerber; he told him he was an NYPD dick assigned to the Ellerbee case. And in their first face-to-face, he asked the vet the same questions Delaney and Boone had asked, and got the same answers. But the Spoiler acted like he didn't give a shit whether Gerber was telling the truth or not.

"I'm just putting in my time, man," he told the vet. "They're never going to find out who offed Ellerbee, so why should I bust my hump?"

Still, every day or so Keisman would put away his elegant Giorgio

Armani blazer and Ferragamo slacks. Then, dressed like a Greenwich
Village floater, he'd go visit Gerber.

"Come on, man," he'd say, "let's get out of this latrine and get us a
couple of brews."

The two of them would slouch off to some saloon where they'd drink
and talk the day away. Keisman never brought up the subject of Ellerbee's murder, but if Gerber wanted to talk about it, the Spoiler listened sympathetically and kept it going with casual questions.

"I'm nowhere yet," he reported to Jason Two, "but the guy is beginning to open up. I may get something if my liver holds out."

One afternoon he and Gerber were in a real dump on Hudson Street
when suddenly the vet said to Keisman, "You're a cop—you ever ice a
guy?"

"Once," the Spoiler said. "This junkie was coming at me with a shiv,
and I put two in his lungs. I got a commendation for that."

Which was a lie, of course. Keisman had been on the Force for ten
years and had never fired his service revolver off the range.

"Once?" Harold Gerber jeered. "Amateur night. I wasted so many in
Nam I lost count. After a while it didn't mean a thing."

"Bullshit," the Spoiler said. "I don't care how many you kill, it still
gets to you."

"Now that *is* bullshit," the vet said. "I'm telling you, man, you never
give it a second thought. See that guy over there—the fat slob at the bar
trying to make out with the sad old whore? I never saw him in my life.
But if I was carrying a piece and felt like it, I could walk up to him,
plink his eyes out, and never lose a night's sleep."

"You're crapping me."

"I swear," Gerber said, holding up a palm. "That's the way I feel—or
don't feel."

"Shit, man, you're a walking time bomb."

"That's right. Doc Ellerbee was trying to grow me a conscience
again, but it was heavy going."

"Too bad he was dusted," Keisman said. "Maybe he could have
helped you."

"Maybe," Gerber said. "Maybe not."

He went over to the bar and brought back another pitcher of beer.
"You pack a gun?"

"Sure," Keisman said. "Regulations."

"Lend it to me for a minute," Harold Gerber said. "I'll put that
shithead out of his misery."

"You crazy, man?" the Spoiler said, definitely nervous. "I don't give a fuck what you do, but I lend you my iron and it's my ass."

"Slob," Gerber muttered, glaring at the man at the bar. "If you won't lend me, maybe I'll just go over and kick the shit out of him."

"Come on," Keisman said. "I'm on duty; I'm not even supposed to be drinking, especially with a pistol like you."

"Well . . ." the vet said grudgingly, "if it wasn't for that, I'd put the bastard away. It wouldn't mean a thing to me. If I was alone, I'd just ace him, come back to the table, work on my beer, and wait for the blues to come get me."

"I believe you would."

"You bet your ass I would. It wouldn't be the first time. What if I told you I put Doc Ellerbee down—would you believe me?"

"Did you?"

"If I told you I did, would you believe me?"

"Sure, I'd believe you. Did you do it?"

"I did it," Harold Gerber said. "He was a nosy fucker."

Detective Robert Keisman reported this conversation to Jason, and the two of them decided they better bring it to Delaney in person.

It hadn't been a good day for Delaney. Too many phone calls; too many people leaning on him.

It started right after breakfast when he went into the study to read the morning *Times.* There was a front-page article, with runover, about the declining solution rate for homicides in the New York area. It wasn't cheerful reading.

The lead-in was about the murder of Dr. Simon Ellerbee, and how, after weeks of intensive investigation, the police were no closer to a solution than they had been the day the body was found. Delaney was halfway through the article when the phone rang. "Thorsen," he said aloud and picked up.

"Edward X. Delaney here," he said.

"Edward, this is Ivar. Did you see that thing in the *Times?*"

"Reading it now."

"Son of a bitch!" the Deputy said bitterly. "That's all we need. Did you come to that paragraph about Suarez?"

"Not yet."

"Well, it said that he's Acting Chief of Detectives, and implied that the outcome of the Ellerbee case will probably have a crucial effect on his permanent appointment."

"That's true enough, isn't it? Ivar, what's all the foofaraw about the

Ellerbee case? Suarez must have at least a dozen other recent unsolved homicides in his caseload."

"Come on, Edward, you know the answer to that: Ellerbee was *someone*. The moneyed East Side people couldn't care less if some hophead gets knocked off in the South Bronx. But Ellerbee was one of their own kind: an educated professional, wealthy, with a good address. So the powers that be figure if it could happen to him, it could happen to them, and they're running scared. I've already had four phone calls on that *Times* article this morning. That kind of publicity the Department doesn't need."

"Tell me about it."

"Any progress, Edward?"

"No," Delaney said shortly. "A lot of bits and pieces, but nothing earthshaking."

"I don't want to pressure you, but—"

"But you are."

"I just want to make certain you're aware of the time element involved. If this thing isn't cleared up by the first of the year, we might as well forget about it."

"Forget about trying to find Ellerbee's killer?"

"Now you really are acting like Iron Balls. You know what I mean. The Ellerbee file will remain open, of course, but we'll have to pull manpower. And Suarez goes back to his precincts—if he's lucky."

"I get the picture."

"Oh, by the way," the Admiral said breezily, "you may be getting calls from the Ellerbees—the widow and the father. To get them off my back, I suggested that you represent our best chance of solving the case."

"Thank you very much, Ivar. I really appreciate your kind cooperation."

"I thought you would," the Deputy said, laughing. "I'll keep in touch, Edward."

"Please," Delaney said, "don't bother."

The two Ellerbees called all right. Both were in a surly mood to start with, and even surlier when they hung up.

Delaney would give them no comfort whatsoever. He said several leads were being followed, but no one had been identified as a definite suspect, and a great deal of work remained to be done.

"When do you think you'll have some good news?" Henry Ellerbee demanded.

"I have no idea," Delaney said.

"When do you think you'll find the killer?" Dr. Diane Ellerbee said sharply.

"I have no idea," Delaney said.

The three phone calls irritated him so much that he was tempted to seek the solace of a good sandwich—but he resisted. Instead, he went to his files, driving himself to read through the records one more time.

The purpose here was to immerse himself in the minutiae of the case. At this stage he could not allow himself to judge some details significant and some meaningless. All had value: from the hammer blows to Ellerbee's eyes to Sylvia Mae Otherton's use of a Ouija board.

Now there was a curious coincidence, he suddenly realized. The victim had been deliberately blinded, and the Ouija planchette had spelled out "blind." What did that mean—if anything? He began to feel that he was sinking deeper into the irrational world of Ellerbee's patients.

Hundreds of facts, rumors, and guesses had been accumulated, with more coming in every day. What detection came down to, in a case of this nature, was a matter of choice. Selection: that was the detective's secret—and the poet's.

He was bleary-eyed when Jason and Keisman arrived, providing a welcome break.

Delaney listened carefully as the Spoiler gave a complete accounting of his most recent conversation with Harold Gerber.

When the black detective finished, Delaney stared at him thoughtfully.

"What's your take?" Delaney finally asked. "You think he was telling the truth or was it just drunken bragging?"

"Sir, I can't give you a definite answer, but I think it's a big possible. That guy is bonkers."

"So far we've had at least ten fake confessions on the Ellerbee homicide. Suarez's men have checked them all out. Zero, zip, zilch. Just crazies and people wanting publicity. But we've got to take this one seriously."

"Pull him in?" Jason suggested.

"No," Delaney said. "If he turns out to be clean, that will be the end of Keisman's contact with him. He'll know who spilled the confession."

"You can say that again," the Spoiler agreed. "And I really don't enjoy the idea of that whacko being sore at me."

"Then you'll have to check out his confession yourself. Find out what time he got there. Did he have an appointment? Was he the late patient?

How did he get up to Ellerbee's office: subway, bus, taxi? He knows the victim was killed with a ball peen hammer because Boone and I asked him if he owned one and he said no. So ask him where he got the hammer, and check it out. Then ask him what he did with the hammer after he killed Ellerbee, and check *that* out. Ask him how many times he hit the victim and how Ellerbee fell. Facedown or up? Finally, ask him if he did anything else to the corpse. That business of the two hammer blows to the eyes was never released to the media; only the killer would know about it. I could be wrong, but I think Gerber is just blowing smoke. He may have thought about chilling Ellerbee, maybe dreamed about it, but I don't think he did it. He's so fucked-up that he'd admit kidnapping Judge Crater if it occurred to him."

"I feel sorry for the guy," Jason said.

"Sure," Delaney said, "but don't feel *too* sorry. Remember, he could be our pigeon. But what interests me even more than the confession was what he wanted to do to the fat guy at the bar. Keisman, you think he meant it?"

"Absolutely," the Spoiler said immediately. "I'm convinced of that. If I hadn't calmed him down and got him talking about other things, he'd have jumped the guy."

"Well, he's done it before," Delaney said. "The man is a walking disaster. Jason, I think you better work on this, too. Check out that confession both ways from the middle. Keisman, were you able to find out where Gerber was drinking the night of the murder?"

"Negative, sir. I talked to three or four bartenders who know him— they all say he's strictly bad news—but none of them can remember whether or not he came in that Friday night. After all, it was weeks ago."

Delaney nodded, looking down at his clasped hands. He was quiet a long moment, then he spoke in a low voice without raising his eyes.

"Do me a favor, Jason. There's got to be a counseling service for Vietnam veterans somewhere in town. A therapy clinic maybe, or just a place where he can go and talk with other vets. See if you can get some help for him, will you? I hate to see that guy go down the drain. Even if he didn't zap Ellerbee, he's heading for bad trouble."

"Yes, sir," Jason Two said. "I'll try."

After they left, Delaney went back to the study and added a report on Harold Gerber's confession to his file. Another fact or fantasy to be considered. He thought it was fantasy, not because Gerber wasn't capable of murder but because Delaney just couldn't believe the Ellerbee case would break that easily and that simply.

Maybe, he admitted ruefully, he didn't want it to. It would be as disappointing as a game called off because of rain. If he was absolutely honest, he'd concede he was enjoying the investigation. Which proved there was life in the old dog yet.

Another person who was enjoying the search for Simon Ellerbee's killer was Detective Helen K. Venable. For the first time in her career she was on her own, not saddled with a male partner who insisted on giving her unwanted and unneeded advice or asked her raunchy questions about her sex life.

Also, she felt a strong affinity for Joan Yesell. Venable was younger than the Yesell woman, but she too had a bitch of a mother, lacked a special man in her life, and sometimes felt so lonely she could cry—but not try to slash her wrists; things never got that bad.

She had talked to Joan twice, and thought they hit it off well, even though that bulldog mother was present at both meetings and kept interrupting. Venable asked the same questions that Delaney and Boone had asked, and got the same answers. She also asked a few extras.

"Joan," she said, "did you ever meet Simon Ellerbee's wife, Diane?"

"I met her once," Yesell said nervously. "While I was waiting for my appointment."

"I hear she's stunning. Is she?"

"Oh, yes! She's beautiful."

"In a hard sort of way," Mrs. Blanche Yesell said.

"Oh?" the detective said, turning to the mother. "Then you've met her, too?"

"Well . . . no," Mrs. Yesell said, flustered. "But from what my Joan says . . ."

"I've never seen Diane," Venable said to the daughter. "Can you describe her?"

"Tall," Joan Yesell said, "slender and very elegant. A natural blonde. She was wearing her hair up when I met her. She looked like a queen—just lovely."

"Humph," Mrs. Yesell said. "She's not so much."

Following orders, Venable included this little byplay in her report to Boone, although she didn't think it meant a thing. Neither did the Sergeant, who initialed the report and forwarded it to Delaney, who made no judgment but filed the report away.

On the Friday night following Thanksgiving, restless in her Flatbush apartment and bored with her mother's chittering about the latest scandal in the *National Enquirer,* Helen decided to drive over to Chelsea and have another talk with Joan Yesell.

She phoned first, but the line was busy and she didn't bother calling again. She got into her little Honda and headed for New York—which was what most Brooklynites called Manhattan. She had nothing special in mind to ask Joan Yesell; it was just a fishing expedition. And also, she was lonely.

Helen was happy to find Mrs. Yesell out. Joan seemed delighted to see the detective. She made them a pot of tea and brought out a plate of powdered doughnuts. They were comfortable with each other and chatted easily about what they had eaten for Thanksgiving dinner. Then Helen asked, "How's the wrist coming along?"

"Better, thank you," Joan said. "I'm getting strength back in my fingers. I exercise by squeezing a rubber ball. The doctor said he'll take the bandage off next week, but he wants me to wear an elastic strap for a while."

"The next time you feel like doing something like that, will you call me first?"

"All right," Joan said faintly.

"Promise?"

"I promise."

Then the talk got around to tyrannical mothers, and they traded anecdotes, each trying to outdo the other with tales of outrageous maternal despotism.

"I've got to get my own place," Helen said, "or I'm going to go right up the wall. The only trouble is, I can't afford it. You know what rents are like today."

"I'd love to get out, too," Joan said forlornly. Then she suddenly brightened. "Listen, I make a good salary. Do you think we might take a place together?"

"That's an idea . . ." the detective said cautiously. She liked Joan and thought they would get along, but even if she were ruled out as a suspect it was possible her problems would be too severe for Helen to live with.

Still, they talked for a while about where they'd like to live (Manhattan), the kind of place they'd need (preferably a two-bedroom apartment), and how much rent they could afford.

"I'll need a desk," Venable said. "For my typewriter and reports."

"I'll want at least one cat," Joan said.

"I have some furniture. My bed is mine."

"I don't own any of these things," Joan said, looking around at the overstuffed apartment. "And even if I did, I wouldn't want any of it for my own place. Our own place. I hate all this; it's so suffocating. You should see the Ellerbees' home; it's beautiful!"

"His office, too?"

"Well, that was very—you know, sort of empty. I mean, it was all right, but very white and efficient. Almost cold."

"Was he like that?"

"Oh, no. Doctor Simon was a very warm man. Very human."

"Which reminds me," Helen said, "if you and I ever do get an apartment together, what about men? Would you object if I brought a man home—for the night?"

Yesell hesitated. "Not if we had separate bedrooms. Do you do that often?"

"Bring a guy home to my place? Are you kidding? If I did that, my mother would have one of her famous nosebleeds. No, the only times I've been with men have been at their place, in cars, and once at a motel."

Joan said nothing, but lowered her eyes. She touched the bandage on her left wrist lightly. The two, like enough to pass as sisters, sat in silence awhile, the detective staring at the bowed head of the other woman.

"Joan," she said gently, "you're not a virgin, are you?"

"Oh, no," Yesell said quickly. "I've been with a man."

"A man? One man?"

"No. More than one."

"But it never lasted?"

Joan shook her head.

"No," Helen said, "it never does—the bastards!" Then, because she could see that Joan was depressed by this kind of talk, she changed the subject. "I wish I had your figure. But I've got a weight problem and these doughnuts aren't helping."

They talked about diets and aerobic dancing and jogging for a while and then got into clothes and how difficult it was to find anything nice at a decent price. After about an hour, the doughnut plate being empty, the detective rose to leave.

"Take care of yourself, kiddo," she said, leaning forward to kiss Joan's cheek. "I expect I'll be around again—it's my job—but don't be bashful about calling me if you're feeling blue. Maybe we could have a pizza together or take in a movie or something."

"I'd like that," Joan said gratefully. "Thank you for dropping by, Helen."

At the door, the detective, tugging her knitted cap down around her ears, said, "Where's Mama tonight—sowing some wild oats?"

"Oh, no," Joan said, laughing, "nothing like that. She's at her bridge club. They're neighborhood women, and they get together every Friday night without fail. It usually breaks up around eleven, eleven-thirty."

"I wish my old lady would get out of the house occasionally," Helen grumbled. "One night without her is like a weekend in the country."

She was halfway down the stairs when it hit her, and she started trembling. She didn't stop shaking until she got into the Honda, locked the doors, and took a deep breath. She sat there in the darkness, gripping the wheel, thinking of the implications of what she had just heard.

She knew Joan Yesell's alibi: She had come home from work at about 6:00 on the Friday night Simon Ellerbee was killed, and had never left the house. Her mother had said yes, that was true.

But now here was mommy dearest out to play bridge every Friday night and not returning until 11:00 or 11:30. That would give Joan plenty of time to get up to East 84th Street and get home again before her mother returned.

And why was Mrs. Blanche Yesell lying? Because she was trying to protect "my Joan."

Wait a minute, Detective Venable warned herself. If Mama's bridge club was like most of them, they'd rotated meeting places, with each player acting as hostess in turn. Maybe on the murder night they all met and played bridge in the Yesells' apartment.

But if that was so, why hadn't Joan or her mother mentioned it? It would have given them three more witnesses to Joan's presence that night.

No, Mrs. Blanche Yesell had gone elsewhere for her weekly bridge game.

But what if there was no game that night? It was raining so hard, maybe they decided to call it off, and Mrs. Yesell really was at home, playing two-handed bridge with her daughter.

Helen leaned forward, resting her forehead on the rim of the steering wheel, trying to figure out what to do next. First of all, she wasn't about to throw poor Joan to the wolves. Not yet. Second of all, she wasn't about to turn over a juicy lead like this to one of the men and let him grab the glory.

It had happened to her too many times in the past. She'd uncover something hot in an investigation and they'd take the follow-up away from her, saying in the kindliest way imaginable, "Helen, that's nice going, but we'll want a guy with more experience to handle it."

Bull*shit!* It was all hers, and this time she was going to track it down herself. Wasn't that what a detective was supposed to do?

She decided not to submit a report to Boone on the night's conversation with Joan Yesell or even mention the mother's Friday-night bridge club and how it was possible she was lying in confirming her daughter's alibi. When Detective Venable checked it all out, *then* she'd report it. Until that time, all those more experienced guys could go screw.

That same evening, one of those more experienced guys, Edward X. Delaney, was in a mellow mood. His irritation of the afternoon had disappeared with a dinner of pot roast, potato pancakes, and buttered carrots—all sluiced down his gullet with two bottles of dark Löwenbräu.

Monica leaned forward to pat his vested stomach. "You ate everything on your plate except the flowers," she said. "Feeling better?"

"A lot better," he affirmed. "Let's just leave everything for now and have our coffee in the living room."

"There's nothing to leave. We went through everything like a plague of locusts."

"I remember my mother used to say a good digestion is a blessing from heaven. Was she ever right."

In the living room, Monica said, "You don't talk much about your mother."

"Well, she died when I was five; I told you that. So my memories are rather dim. I have some old snaps of her in the attic. I'll dig them out one of these days. A lovely woman; you'll see."

"What did she die of, Edward?"

"In childbirth. So did the baby. My brother."

"Was he baptized?"

"Of course. Terence. Terry."

"What was your father's first name?"

"Marion—believe it or not. He never remarried. So you and I are both only children."

"But we have each other."

"Thank God for that."

"Edward, why don't you go to church anymore?"

"Monica, why don't you go to the synagogue anymore?"

They both smiled.

"A fine couple of heathens we are," he said.

"Not so," she said. "I believe in God—don't you?"

"Of course," he said. "Sometimes I think He'd like to be Deputy Commissioner Thorsen."

"You nut," she said, laughing. "Want to watch the news on TV?"

"No, thanks. I think I'll spend a nice relaxed evening for a change. I need a—"

The phone rang.

He got heavily to his feet. "There goes my nice relaxed evening," he said. "Bet on it. I'll take it in the study."

It was Dr. Diane Ellerbee.

"Mr. Delaney," she said, "I want to apologize for the way I spoke to you this morning. I realize you're volunteering your time, and I'm afraid I was rather hard on you."

"Not at all. I know how concerned you are. Sometimes it's tough to be patient in a situation like this."

"I'm driving up to Brewster tonight," she said. "To spend the weekend. There's something I'd like to tell you that may or may not help your investigation. Would it be possible for me to stop by your home for a few minutes?"

"Of course. We've finished dinner, so come whenever you like."

"Thank you," she said. "I'll be there shortly."

He went back into the living room and reported the conversation to Monica.

"Oh, lord," she said. "We've got to get the kitchen cleaned up. Are there fresh towels in the hall bathroom? Do I have time to change?"

"To what?" he said. "You look fine just the way you are. And yes, there are fresh towels in the bathroom. Take it easy, babe; this isn't a visit from the Queen of England."

But by the time Dr. Diane arrived, the kitchen was cleaned up, the living room straightened, and they were sitting stiffly, determined not to be awed by the visitor—and not quite succeeding.

Diane Ellerbee was graciousness personified. She complimented them on their charming home, unerringly selected the finest piece in the living room to admire—a small Duncan Phyfe desk—and assured Delaney that the vodka gimlet he mixed for her was the best she had ever tasted.

In fact, she played the grande dame so broadly that he made a cop's instant judgment: The woman was nervous and wanted something. Having concluded that, he relaxed and watched her with a faint smile as she chatted with Monica.

She was wearing a sweater and skirt of mushroom-colored wool, with high boots of buttery leather. No jewelry, other than a plain wedding band, and very little makeup. Her flaxen hair was down, and her classic features seemed softened, more vulnerable.

"Mr. Delaney," she said, turning to him, "was that list of patients I gave you any help?"

"A great deal. They are all being investigated."

"I hope you didn't tell them I gave you their names?"

"Of course not. We merely said we're questioning all your husband's patients—which is true—and they accepted that."

"I'm glad to hear it. I still don't feel right about picking out those six, but I wanted to help any way I could. Do you think one of them could have done it?"

"I think possibly they are all capable of murder. But then, a lot of so-called normal people are, too."

"I really don't know exactly how you go about investigating people," she said with a confused little laugh. "Question them, I suppose."

"Oh, yes. And their families, friends, neighbors, employers, and so forth. We go back to them several times, asking the same questions over and over, trying to spot discrepancies."

"Sounds like a boring job."

"No," he said, "it isn't."

"Edward has the patience of a saint," Monica said.

"And the luck of the devil," he added. "I hope."

The doctor laughed politely. "Does luck really have much to do with catching a criminal?"

"Sometimes," he said, nodding. "Usually it's a matter of knocking on enough doors. But sometimes chance and accident take a hand, and you get a break you didn't expect. The criminal can't control luck, can he?"

"But doesn't it work the other way, too? I mean, doesn't luck sometimes favor the criminal?"

"Occasionally," he agreed. "But it would be a very stupid criminal who depended on it. 'The best laid schemes . . .' and so on and so on." He turned to Monica. "Who said that?" he asked her, smiling.

"Shakespeare?" she ventured.

"Robert Burns," he said. "Shakespeare didn't say *everything.*" He turned to Diane Ellerbee. "Now it's your chance. Who wrote, 'O what a tangled web we weave, when first we practise to deceive!'?"

"That *was* Shakespeare," she said.

"Sir Walter Scott," he said, still smiling. "Did you say you had something to tell me, doctor?"

"Oh, you'll probably think it's silly," she said, "but it's been bothering me, so I thought I'd tell you anyway. The first time you and Sergeant Boone came to see me, you asked a lot of questions, and I answered them to the best of my ability. After you left, I tried to remember everything I had said, to make sure I hadn't unintentionally led you astray."

She paused.

"And?" he said.

"Well, it probably means nothing, but you asked if I had noticed any change in Simon over the last six months or year, and I said no. But then after thinking it over, I realized there had been a change. Perhaps it was so gradual that I really wasn't aware of it."

"But now you feel there was a change?" Delaney asked.

"Yes, I do. Thinking over this past year, I realize Simon had become —well, distant and preoccupied is the only way I can describe it. He had been very concerned about his patients, and I suppose at the time I thought it was just overwork that was bothering him. But yes, there was a change in him. I don't imagine it means anything, but it disturbed me that I hadn't given you a strictly accurate answer, so I thought I better tell you."

"I'm glad you did," Delaney said gravely. "Like you, I don't know if it means anything or not, but every little bit helps."

"Well!" Diane Ellerbee said, smiling brightly. "Now I do feel better, getting that off my conscience."

She drained her gimlet, set the glass aside, and rose. They stood up. She offered her hand to Monica.

"Thank you so much for letting me barge in," she said. "You have a lovely, lovely home. I wish the two of you would come up to Brewster soon and see our place. It's not at its best in winter, but Simon and I worked so hard to make it something special, I'd like to have you see it. Could you do that?"

"We'd be delighted," Monica said promptly. "Thank you."

"Let's wait for a weekend when no blizzards are predicted," Diane Ellerbee said, laughing. "The first good Saturday—all right?"

"We don't have a car," Delaney said. "Would you object if Sergeant Boone and his wife drove us up?"

"Object? I'd love it! I have a marvelous cook, and Simon and I laid down some good wines. I enjoy having company, and frankly, it's lonely up there now. So let's all plan on getting together."

"Whenever you say," Monica said. "I'm sorry you have to leave so soon. Drive carefully."

"I always do," Dr. Ellerbee said lightly. "Good night, all."

Delaney locked and bolted the front door behind her.

"What an intelligent woman!" Monica said when he came back to the living room. "Isn't she, Edward?"

"She is that."

"You'd like to see her Brewster home, wouldn't you?"

"Very much. The Boones will drive us up. We'll make a day of it."

"What she said about her husband changing—does that mean anything?"

"I have no idea."

"She really is beautiful, isn't she?"

"So beautiful," he said solemnly, "that she scares me."

"Thanks a lot, buster," she said. "I obviously don't scare you."

"Obviously," he said, and headed toward the study door.

"Hey," Monica said, "I thought you weren't going to work tonight."

"Just for a while," he said, frowning. "Some things I want to check."

# *17.*

Detective Benjamin Calazo was a month away from retirement and dreading it. He came from a family of policemen. His father had been a cop, his younger brother was a cop, and two uncles had been cops. The NYPD wasn't just a job, it was a *life*.

Calazo didn't fish, play golf, or collect stamps. He had no hobbies at all, and no real interests outside the Department. What the hell was he going to do—move the wife to a mobile home in Lakeland, Florida, and play shuffleboard for the rest of his days?

The Ellerbee case seemed like a good way to cap his career. He had worked with Sergeant Boone before, and knew he was an okay guy. Also, Boone's father had been a street cop killed in the line of duty. Calazo had gone to the funeral, and you didn't forget things like that.

The detective had asked to be assigned to Isaac Kane for the reason he stated: His nephew was retarded, and he thought he knew something about handling handicapped kids. Calazo had three married daughters, and sometimes he wondered if they weren't retarded when he was forced to have dinner with his sons-in-law—a trio of losers, Benny thought; not a cop in the lot.

His first meeting with Isaac Kane went reasonably well. Calazo sat with him for almost three hours at the Community Center, admiring the kid's pastel landscapes and talking easily about this and that.

Every once in a while Calazo would spring a question about Dr. Simon Ellerbee. Isaac showed no hesitation in answering, and the subject didn't seem to upset him. He told the detective pretty much what he had told Delaney and Boone—which didn't amount to a great deal.

The boy didn't display any confusion until Calazo asked him about his activities on the night of the murder.

"It was a Friday, Isaac," Calazo said. "What did you do on that night?"

"I was here until the Center closed. Ask Mrs. Freylinghausen; she'll tell you."

"Okay, I'll ask her. And after the Center closed, what did you do then?"

"I went home."

"Uh-huh. You live right around the corner, don't you, Isaac? So I guess you got there around nine-five or so. Is that correct?"

Kane didn't look at the detective, but concentrated on adding foliage to a tree in his landscape.

"Well, uh, it was probably later. I walked around awhile."

"That was a very rainy night, Isaac. A bad storm. You didn't walk about in that, did you?"

"I don't remember!" Kane said, breaking one of his chalks and flinging it away angrily. "I don't know why you're asking me all these questions, and I'm not going to answer any more. You're just—" He began to stutter unintelligibly.

"All right," Benny said mildly, "you don't have to answer any more questions. I just thought you'd want to help us find out who killed Doctor Simon."

Kane was silent.

"Hey," the detective said, "I'm getting hungry. How about you? There's a fast-food joint on the corner. How's about I pick up a couple of burgers and coffee for us and bring them back here?"

"Okay," Isaac Kane said.

Calazo brought the food and they had lunch together. An old lady wheeled up her chair and stared at the detective with ravenous eyes. He gave her his slice of dill pickle. He didn't mention Ellerbee again, but got Kane talking about his pastels and why he did only landscapes.

"They're pretty landscapes," Isaac explained. "Not like around here. Everything is clean and peaceful."

"Sure it is," the detective said. "But I notice you don't put in any people."

"No," Kane said, shaking his head. "No people. Those places belong to me."

Calazo checked with Mrs. Freylinghausen. She confirmed that Isaac Kane came in every day and stayed until the Community Center closed at nine o'clock. The detective thanked her and walked around the corner to Kane's home, timing himself. Even at a slow stroll it took less than two minutes.

Kane lived with his mother in the basement apartment of a dilapidated brownstone on West 78th Street. It was next to an ugly furniture warehouse with rusty steel doors for trucks and sooty windows on the upper floors. Both buildings were marred with graffiti and had black plastic bags of garbage stacked in front. Some of the bags had burst or had been slashed open.

Benjamin Calazo could understand why Isaac Kane wanted to draw only pretty places, clean and peaceful.

He walked cautiously down three crumbling steps to a littered doorway. The name over the bell was barely legible. He rang, and waited. Nothing. Rang again—a good long one this time. A tattered lace curtain was yanked aside from a streaky window; a gargoyle glared at him.

Calazo held his ID close to the window. The woman tried to focus, then she disappeared. He waited hopefully. In a moment he heard the sounds of locks opening, a chain lifted. The door opened.

"Mrs. Kane?" he asked.

"Yeah," she said in a whiskey-blurred voice. "What the hell do you want?"

A boozer, he thought immediately. That's all I need.

"Detective Benjamin Calazo, NYPD," he said. "I'd like to talk to you about your son."

"He ain't here."

"I know he's not here," Calazo said patiently. "I just left him at the Center. I want to talk to you *about* him."

"What's he done now?" she demanded.

"Nothing, as far as I know."

"He's not right in the head. He's not responsible for anything."

"Look," the detective said. "Be nice. Don't keep me standing out here in the cold. How's about letting me in for a few questions? It won't take long."

She stood aside grudgingly. He stepped in, closed the door, took off his hat. The place smelled like a subway urinal—only the piss was eighty proof. The half-empty whiskey bottle was on the floor, a stack of paper cups beside it.

She saw him looking. "I got a cold," she said. "I been sick."

"Yeah."

She tried a smile. Her face looked like a punched pillow. "Want a belt?" she asked.

"No, thanks. But you go ahead."

She sat on the lumpy couch, poured herself a drink, slugged it down. She crumpled the cup in her fist, threw it negligently toward a splintered wicker wastebasket. Bull's-eye.

"Nice shot," Calazo said.

"I've had a lot of practice," she said, showing a mouthful of tarnished teeth.

"Is Mr. Kane around?" the detective asked. "Your husband?"

"Yeah, he's around. Around the world. Probably in Hong Kong by now, the son of a bitch. Good riddance."

"Then you and your son live alone?"

"So what?"

"You on welfare?"

"Financial assistance," she said haughtily. "We're entitled. I'm disabled and Isaac can't hold a job. You an investigator?"

"Not for welfare," Calazo said. "Your son goes to the Community Center every day?"

"I guess so."

"Don't you know?"

"He's of age; he can go anywhere he likes."

"What time does he leave for the Center?"

"I don't know; I sleep late. When I wake up, he's gone. What the hell is all this about?"

"You're not asleep when he gets home from the Center, are you? What time does he get here?"

She peered at him through narrowed eyes, and he knew she was calculating what lies she could get away with. Not that there was any need to lie, but this woman would never tell the truth to anyone in authority if she could help it.

She stalled for time by taking another shot of the booze, crumpling the paper cup, tossing it toward the wastebasket. This time it fell short.

"No," she said finally, "I'm not asleep in the evening. He gets home at different times."

"Like what?"

"After nine o'clock."

"How much after nine?"

"Different times."

"Now I'll tell you what this is about," the old gumshoe said tonelessly. "This is about a murder, and if you keep jerking me around, I'm going to run your ass down to the drunk tank so fast your feet won't touch the ground. You can dry out with all those swell people in there until you decide to answer my questions straight. Is that what you want?"

Her face twisted, and she began to cry. "You got no right to talk to me like that."

"I'll talk to you any goddamned way I please," Calazo said coldly. "You don't mean shit to me."

He swooped suddenly, grabbed her bottle of whiskey, headed for the stained sink in a kitchenette so malodorous he almost gagged.

She came to her feet with a howl. "What are you doing?" she screamed.

"I'm going to dump your booze," he said. "Then go through this swamp and break every fucking jug I can find."

"Please," she said, "don't do—I can't—the check isn't due for—I'm an old woman. What do you want to hurt an old woman for?"

"You're an old drunk," he said. "An old smelly drunk. No wonder your son gets out of the house every day." He held the whiskey bottle over the sink. "What time does he get home at night?"

"At nine. A few minutes after nine."

"Every night?"

"Yes, every night."

He tilted the bottle, spilled a few drops.

She wailed. "Except on Fridays," she said in a rush. "He's late on Fridays. Then he comes home at ten, ten-thirty—like that."

"Why is he late on Fridays? Where does he go?"

"I don't know. I swear to God I don't."

"Haven't you asked him?"

"I have, honest to God I have, but he won't tell me."

He stared at her a long time, then handed her the whiskey bottle. She took it with trembling claws, hugged it to her, cradling it like an infant.

"Thank you for your cooperation, Mrs. Kane," Detective Calazo said.

Outside, he walked over to Broadway, breathing deeply, trying to get rid of the stench of that shithouse. It wasn't the worst stink he had ever smelled in his years on the Force, but it was bad enough.

He found a sidewalk telephone kiosk that worked and called his wife.

"I'm coming home for dinner, hon," he reported, "but I'll have to go out again for a while. You want me to pick up anything?"

"We're having knockwurst," she said. "There's a little mustard left, but maybe you better get a new jar. The hot stuff you like."

"Okay," he said cheerfully. "See you soon."

That night, warmed by a good solid meal (knockwurst, baked beans, sauerkraut), Calazo was back at 79th Street and Broadway by 8:30. He drove around, looking for a parking space, and ended up pulling into the driveway of the warehouse next to the Kanes' brownstone, ignoring a big sign: NO PARKING OR STANDING AT ANY TIME.

He locked up carefully and walked back to the Community Center, taking up his station across the street. He trudged up and down to keep his feet from getting numb, but never took his eyes off the lighted windows of the Center for more than a few seconds.

The Medical Examiner had said that Simon Ellerbee had died at 9:00 P.M. But that was an estimate; it could be off by a half-hour either way. Maybe more.

So if Isaac Kane had left the Community Center at nine o'clock on that Friday night, he could have made it across town to East 84th Street, bashed in Ellerbee's skull, and been home by 10:00, 10:30. Easily. Benny Calazo didn't think the boy did it, but he *could* have.

The lights in the Center began to darken. Calazo leaned against a mailbox, chewing on a cold cigar, and waited. A lot of people came out, one on crutches, two using walkers. Then Isaac appeared.

The detective crossed the street and tailed him. It didn't take long. Isaac went directly home. Calazo got into his parked car and watched. He sat there until 10:30, freezing his buns. Then he drove home.

That was on a Wednesday night. The detective spent Thursday morning and afternoon checking out Kane at the clinic where he had met with Dr. Ellerbee. They wouldn't show him Kane's file, but Calazo talked to several people who knew him.

They confirmed that Isaac was usually a quiet, peaceable kid, but had occasional fits of uncontrollable violence during which he physically attacked doctors and nurses. Once he had to be forcibly sedated.

On Thursday night, Calazo went through the same drill again: tailing Kane home from the Community Center, then waiting to see if he came out of the brownstone again. Nothing.

He took up his post a little earlier on Friday evening, figuring if anything was going to happen, it would be on that night.

Isaac Kane left the Center a few minutes before nine o'clock. Calazo got a good look at him from across the street. He was all dolled-up, with a tweed cap, clean parka, denim jeans. He was carrying a package under his arm. It looked like one of his pastels wrapped in brown paper.

He turned in the opposite direction, away from his home, and Calazo went after him. He tailed Kane uptown on Broadway to 83rd Street, and west toward the river. Isaac crossed West End Avenue, then went into a neat brownstone halfway down the block.

The detective slowed his pace, then sauntered by the brownstone, noting the address. Kane was not in the vestibule or lobby. Calazo took up his patrol across the street, lighting a cigar, and walking heavily up and down to keep the circulation going. He wondered how many miles he had plodded like this in his lifetime as a cop. Well, in another month it would be all over.

Kane came out of the brownstone about 10:15. He was no longer carrying the package. Calazo tailed him back to his 78th Street home. When Isaac was inside, the detective went home, too.

He was out early the next morning and parked near the neat brownstone on West 83rd Street a few minutes before 8:00 A.M. He figured that most people would be home at that hour on a Saturday. He went into the vestibule and examined the bell plate. There were twelve apartments.

He began ringing, starting at the top and working his way down. Every time the squawk box clicked on and someone said, "Who is it?", Calazo would say, "I'd like to talk to you about Isaac Kane." He got answers like "Who?" "Never heard of him." "Get lost." "You have the wrong apartment." And a lot of disconnects.

Finally he pushed the 4-B bell. A woman's voice asked, "Who is it?", the detective said, "I'd like to talk to you about Isaac Kane," and the woman replied anxiously, "Has anything happened to him?" Bingo. The names opposite the bell were Mr. & Mrs. Judson Beele and Evelyn Packard.

"This is Detective Benjamin Calazo of the New York Police Department," he said slowly and distinctly. "It is important that I speak to you concerning Isaac Kane. Will you let me come up, please? I will show you my identification."

There was a long silence. Calazo waited patiently. He was good at that. Then the door lock buzzed, he pushed his way in, and clumped up the stairs to the fourth floor.

There was a man standing in the hallway outside apartment 4-B. He was wearing a flannel bathrobe and carpet slippers. A Caspar Milquetoast with rimless glasses, a fringe of fluff around his pale scalp, and some hair on his upper lip that yearned to be a mustache and didn't quite make it. Calazo thought a strong wind would blow the guy away.

He proffered his ID and the man examined the wallet carefully before he handed it back.

"I'm Judson Beele," he said nervously. "What's this all about? You mentioned Isaac Kane to my wife."

"Could I come in for a few minutes?" the detective asked pleasantly. "It shouldn't take long."

There were two women in the warm, comfortable living room. Both were in bathrobes and slippers. A hatchet-faced blonde, smoking a cigarette in a long holder, was standing. The other, younger, with softer features, was in a wheelchair. There was an afghan across her lap, concealing her legs.

Beele made the introductions. The blonde was his wife, Teresa. The girl in the wheelchair was his wife's sister, Evelyn Packard. Calazo bowed to both women, smiling. Like most veteran detectives, he knew when to play Mr. Nasty and when to play Mr. Nice. He reckoned niceness would do for this household. That wife looked like she had a spine.

"I want to apologize for disturbing you at this hour," he said smoothly. "But it's a matter of some importance concerning Isaac Kane."

"Is Isaac all right?" a jittery Evelyn Packard said. "He hasn't been in an accident, has he?"

"Oh, no," Calazo said, "nothing like that. He's fine, as far as I know. Could I sit down for a few minutes?"

"Of course," the wife said. "Let me have your hat and coat. We were just having coffee. Would you care for a cup?"

"That would be fine. Black, please."

"Judson," she said, "bring the coffee."

Calazo made a few comments about the weather and what an attractive home they had. Meanwhile he was taking them in, trying to figure the tensions there, and also eyeballing the apartment. The first things he noted were five of Isaac's pastels on the walls. Someone had done a nice job framing them.

"Good coffee," he said. "Thank you. Well, about Isaac Kane . . . I notice you have some of his drawings here. Pretty things, aren't they?"

"They're beautiful!" Evelyn burst out. "Isaac is a genius."

Her sister laughed lightly. "Picasso he ain't, dear," she advised. "They're really quite commercial. But remarkable, I admit, considering his—his background."

"I've been thinking of buying one of his things," the detective said.

"Would you mind if I asked how much you paid for these? Without the frames."

"Oh, we didn't buy them," Teresa Beele said. "They were gifts to Evelyn. Isaac is madly in love with her."

"Teresa!" her sister said, blushing. "You know that's not so."

"It is so. I see how he looks at you."

"Isaac is a lonely boy," Judson Beele said in a troubled voice. "I don't think he has many friends. Evelyn is . . ." He didn't finish.

Calazo turned to the young woman in the wheelchair. "How did you meet him, Miss Packard?"

"At the Center. Teresa took me there once, and I never want to go again; it's so depressing. But I met Isaac, and he asked if he could come visit me."

"A perfect match," her sister murmured, fitting another cigarette into the long holder.

Bitch, Calazo thought. "And how long have you known him, Miss Packard?"

"Oh, it's been about six months now. Hasn't it, Judson?"

"About," her brother-in-law said, nodding. Then to Calazo: "Can you tell us what this is all about?"

"In a minute," the detective said. "Does he come to visit you every Friday night, Miss Packard?"

"He comes a-courting," Teresa said blithely, and Calazo realized he could learn to hate that woman with very little effort.

"Yes," the girl in the wheelchair said, lifting her chin. "He visits on Friday night."

"*Every* Friday night? Hasn't he ever missed? Come to see you some other night?"

She shook her head. "No. Always on Friday night." She looked at the other two. "Isn't that right?"

They agreed. Isaac Kane visited only on Friday nights. Every Friday night. For almost six months.

"You're always here when he comes?" Calazo asked the Beeles. "You're never out—to a movie or somewhere else?"

"We're here," the wife said grimly. "I wouldn't leave Evelyn alone with that person. Considering his mental condition, I think it best that we be present."

"Teresa!" her sister said angrily. "Isaac has always been perfectly well behaved."

"Still, you never know with people like that."

"Look," Calazo said. "There was a very minor robbery in the brownstone where Kane lives. It doesn't amount to much, but it's my job to check the whereabouts of everyone in the building at the time it happened. It was four weeks ago, at about nine-thirty on a Friday night."

"He was here," Evelyn said, promptly and firmly. "He couldn't have done it because he was here. Besides, Isaac wouldn't do anything like that."

"All of you would swear that he was here?" the detective said, looking from one to another.

They nodded.

It wasn't complete. It wasn't absolutely perfect. But it never was. There were always possibilities: forgetfulness, deliberate lying, unknown motives. But it would take a hundred years to track down everything, and even then there might be blanks, questions, doubts.

Calazo couldn't recall ever clearing a case where every goddamned thing was tied up neatly. You went so far and then decided on the preponderance of evidence and your own instinct. There came a time when more investigation and more and more was just gunning an engine with no forward motion: a waste of time.

"I think Isaac Kane is clean," he declared, standing up.

"Of course he is," Evelyn Packard said stoutly. "He's a dear, sweet boy. He'd never do anything bad."

"Sure," her sister said skeptically.

Her husband blinked behind his rimless glasses.

"How did you connect Isaac with us?" Teresa Beele asked.

"I followed him to this building last night," he told her. "Then, this morning, I rang every bell until I found someone who knew him."

"My," she said mockingly, "aren't you the smart one."

"Sometimes," he said, staring at her coldly.

"Judson," she said, "bring the policeman his hat and coat."

Calazo drove home and spent Saturday afternoon working on a report for Boone. He wrote that in his opinion Isaac Kane could be cleared, and further investigation was unwarranted.

When he had finished, he read over what he had written and reflected idly on the relationship between Teresa and Judson Beele, and between Evelyn Packard and Isaac Kane, and between Teresa and her sister, and between Evelyn and her brother-in-law.

"You know, hon," he said to his wife, "life really is a fucking soap opera."

"I wish you wouldn't use words like that," she said.

"Soap opera?" he asked innocently. "What's wrong with soap opera?"

"Oh, you," she said.

He laughed and goosed her. "What's for dinner?" he said.

Calazo wasn't the only one thinking about Saturday night dinner. Detective Timothy (Big Tim) Hogan was beginning to wonder if he would ever eat again.

It had been a long day. Hogan was parked outside Ronald J. Bellsey's high-rise by 8:00 A.M., and sat there for almost an hour. Just when he thought it might be safe to make a quick run for a coffee and Danish, he saw Bellsey's white Cadillac come out of the underground garage.

The subject was alone in the car, and Hogan tailed him over to the wholesale meat market on West 18th Street. Bellsey parked and went inside. Hogan had no idea how long he'd be there, but figured this would be a good chance to brace Bellsey's wife without her husband being present.

Hogan was not a great brain and he knew it. So he always did his best to go by the book, thinking that would keep him out of trouble. It hadn't, but none of his stupidities had been serious enough to get him broken back to the ranks—so far.

It wasn't strictly true that Big Tim was stupid, but he was unimaginative and not strong at initiating new avenues of investigation. Another problem was that he didn't *look* like a detective, being short, dumpy, and bald, with a whiny voice. His third wife called him Dick Tracy, which Hogan didn't think was funny at all.

As soon as Bellsey was safely inside his place of business, the detective drove back to the high-rise to put the arm on the wife. As long as he was deserting the subject, he could have stopped for breakfast right then, but it didn't occur to him. Hogan found it difficult to keep two ideas in his head at the same time.

Mrs. Lorna Bellsey let him into her apartment without too much of a hassle. She was so flustered that she didn't even ask to see his ID. Hogan planned to lean on her hard. He didn't even take his hat off, fearing his nude pate wouldn't enhance the image of the hard-boiled detective.

She was a wisp of a woman with thinning gray hair and defeated eyes. She was wearing something shapeless with long sleeves and a high neck that effectively hid her body. Hogan wondered what she was like in bed, and guessed she'd be similar to his second wife who, during sex, would say things like, "The ceiling needs painting."

"Look, Mrs. Bellsey," he started, scowling at the timid woman, "you know why I'm here. Your husband is involved in the murder of Doctor Ellerbee, and we don't believe he was home that night like he says."

"He was," she said nervously, "he really was. I was here with him."

"From when to when?"

"All evening. All night."

"And he never went out?"

"No," she said, lowering her eyes. "Never. He was here all the time."

"Did he tell you to say that?"

"No, it's the truth."

"Did he say if you didn't back him up, he'd belt you around?"

"No," she said, finally showing a small flash of spirit, "it's not like that at all."

"You say. We're checking all your husband's hangouts—those bars he goes to where he beats up strangers. If we find out that he wasn't here that night, do you know what we'll do to you for lying?"

She was silent, clasping her hands tightly, knuckles whitening.

"Come on, Mrs. Bellsey," Hogan said in a loud, hectoring voice, "make it easy on yourself. He went out that night, didn't he?"

"I don't know," she said in a low, quavery voice.

"What do you mean you don't know?"

She didn't answer.

"Do I have to take you in?" he demanded. "Arrest you as an accessory? March you through the lobby in handcuffs? Put you in a filthy cell with whores and dope fiends? Come on, what do you mean you don't know if he went out?"

"I had a headache," she said faintly. "A migraine. I went to bed early."

"How early?"

"About eight-thirty I think it was."

"On the night Ellerbee was killed?"

"Yes."

"Your husband was here then?"

"Yes."

"You went into the bedroom?"

"Yes."

"Did you close the door?"

"Yes. He was watching television."

"Did you sleep?"

"Well, I took my medicine. It makes me very drowsy."

"So you slept?"

"Sort of."

"What time did you get up?"

"I got up around eleven to go to the bathroom." She wouldn't look at him when she said that.

"At eleven," Hogan repeated. "Was your husband here then?"

"Yes, he was," she said defiantly. "I saw him."

"But you didn't see him from eight-thirty to eleven?"

She began to cry, small tears sliding down her cheeks.

"Don't yell at me," she said, choking. "Please."

"Answer my question. Otherwise I'll take you downtown."

"No!" she screamed at him. "I didn't see him from eight-thirty to eleven."

Got him! Detective Timothy Hogan thought with savage satisfaction.

He drove back to 18th Street, delighted with his coup and hoping he hadn't lost Bellsey to mar the triumph. But the white Cadillac was still outside the meat market. Hogan parked nearby where he could watch the door. He urinated into an empty milk carton he always brought along on stakeouts for emergencies.

He sat there all day, getting hungrier and hungrier, and cursing his failure to buy a sandwich, candy bar, coffee—anything. He went through almost a pack of cigarettes, but the son of a bitch still didn't come out.

"What the hell is he *doing* in there?" the detective said aloud. And having said it, began to dream of what the market contained: steaks, chops, ground meat, chickens. It made him faint to think about it, he was so ravenous.

He dozed off a couple of times, but when he jerked awake, the Cadillac was still there. Hogan stuck it out, trying to keep himself alert by recalling the interrogation of Mrs. Lorna Bellsey and planning how he would word it in his report: play down the threats, play up the sublety of his questions.

It was almost 8:45 P.M.—the streetlights on—when Bellsey came out of the meat market with two other guys. They stood joking, laughing, pushing each other. Hogan wondered if they had been boozing.

Finally they separated. Bellsey got in his car and took off. Hogan followed him up Eighth Avenue, sticking close in the heavy traffic, not wanting to lose him after sitting for so many hours and nearly dying of hunger.

Bellsey hung a left on 53rd Street and headed for the river through a darkened factory and warehouse district. Where the *hell* is he going? Hogan puzzled, and dropped back a half-block as traffic thinned. The Cadillac turned onto Eleventh Avenue and went two blocks, slowing. Then Bellsey found a parking slot and pulled in.

Beautiful, Hogan thought. It was a great neighborhood—if your life insurance was paid up.

He cruised along slowly and saw the subject go into a tavern. The street lighting wasn't the brightest, but Hogan could make out the name of the place: TAIL OF THE WHALE. Charming. Why didn't they call it Moby's Dick and be done with it?

He parked and walked back. The windows were steamed up, and he couldn't see inside, but it looked like a seamen's bar, a boilermaker joint, and if you asked for an extra-dry martini with two olives, they'd look at you with loathing and throw your ass out on the street.

He couldn't make up his mind whether to go in, wait in his car for Bellsey to come out, or just scratch the day and go home. What decided him was a big sign over the door: FRANKS, BURGERS, CHILI DOGS, HOT SANDWICHES. He went in.

It was about what he figured: a real bucket of blood. White tiled walls slick with grease. An old-fashioned mahogany bar on one side, tables and booths on the other. A TV set suspended from the tin ceiling on chains. Lighted jukebox and cigarette machine. In the back, a grill and steam table presided over by a fat black who was dripping sweat onto the sausages.

Hogan saw Bellsey at the bar, talking to two other guys. It looked like they were all working on doubles. The detective slid into an empty booth across the room and started on a new pack of cigarettes. He looked around.

A good crowd for so early in the evening; by midnight it would probably be jammed. Bellsey was the best-dressed man in the joint. Most of the others looked like cruds: construction workers in hard hats, seamen with stocking caps, a sprinkling of derelicts. There was one bum facedown on a table, sleeping off a drunk.

Hogan couldn't figure why a moneyed guy like Bellsey would patronize a grungy joint like this—until he saw that the wall behind the bar was covered with framed and autographed photos of boxers: dead ones, old ones, new ones—all in trunks, gloved, posed in attitudes of ferocious attack.

Big Tim remembered that Jason had said Bellsey was an ex-pug, so he probably dropped in here to gas about fights and fighters. The guys he was talking to, and the bartender, had all the stigmata: hunched shoulders, bent noses, cauliflower ears. They looked like they could chew up Timothy Hogan and spit him over the left-field fence.

"Yeah?"

He looked up, startled. A waitress was slouched by his booth. She was an old dame with lumpy legs encased in thick elastic stockings. There was a heavy wen on her chin with two wiry black hairs sticking out.

"What kind of bottled beer you got?" he asked her.

"Bud, Miller, Heineken."

"I'll have a Bud and a burger."

"Okay."

"Make the burger rare."

"Lotsa luck," she said dourly and shuffled away.

He had two hamburgers—so bad that he would have walked out after the first bite if he hadn't been so hungry. Even the dill pickle was lousy. How in hell could a cook spoil a pickle?

He saw that Bellsey was alone now, talking to the bartender. Hogan carried his second bottle of beer and glass over to the bar and took a nearby stool. The two men were arguing about who had the better right hook, Dempsey or Louis.

Hogan took a swallow of beer. "What about Marciano?" he said loudly.

Bellsey turned slowly to look at him. "Who the fuck asked you?" he demanded.

"I was just—" the detective started.

"Just butt out," the other man advised. "This is a private conversation."

If Timothy Hogan had had any sense, he'd have stopped right there, finished his beer, paid his bill, and left. He could see his first guess had been right: Bellsey *had* been boozing that afternoon, maybe all day, and was carrying a load.

He wasn't swaying or slurring his speech or anything like that, but his eyes were shrunken and bloodshot, and he was leaning forward with a truculent chin thrust out. He looked ready and eager to climb into a ring and go ten.

"What the hell you staring at?" Bellsey said to him. "You piece of shit."

Hogan reached casually inside his jacket to touch his holster. He knew it was there, but he wanted to make sure.

"Take it easy," he said to Bellsey. "I don't like talk like that."

"Well, fuck you, fatso," Bellsey said. "You don't like it, wheel your ass somewhere else."

"Hey, Ron," the bartender said in a raspy voice, "cool it. More trouble I don't need."

By this time the bar had quieted. Everyone seemed to have his head down, staring into his drink. But they were all listening.

"No trouble, Eddie," Bellsey said. "Not from this little shithead."

"Mister," the bartender said to Hogan, "do me a favor: Finish your beer, pay up, and try another joint. Please."

It gave the detective an out, and finally he had enough sense to take it. He finished his beer, put a bill on the bar.

"What kind of a place you running here?" he said aggrievedly and stalked toward the door.

"Asshole!" Bellsey yelled after him.

Hogan walked toward his car, thinking the subject was a real psycho and an odds-on favorite for having bashed Ellerbee's skull. He was so intent on planning what he was going to put in his report to Jason T. Jason that he didn't hear the soft footfalls behind him.

The first punch was to his kidneys and felt like someone had swung a sledgehammer. He went stumbling forward, mouth open, gasping for air. He tried to grab at a trash can for support, but a left hook crunched into his ribs just below the heart, and he went down into the gutter, fumbling at his holster.

Heavy shoes were thudding into his gut, his head, and he tried to cover his eyes with folded arms. It went on and on, and he vomited up the beer and burgers. Just before he lost consciousness he was certain he was gone, and wondered why he was dying in a street like this, his vital report unwritten.

A different report from Roosevelt Hospital went up and down the chain of police command, and eventually a blue working the case called Jason. He, in turn, alerted Boone. By midnight, the two of them were at Roosevelt, talking to doctors and guys from Midtown North, trying to collect as much information as they could before taking it to Edward X. Delaney.

They woke him up a little after 5:00 A.M. Sunday morning and related what had happened. He told them to come over as soon as possible. He said he'd have coffee for them.

"What is it, Edward?" Monica said drowsily from her bed.

"Tell you later," he said. "Boone and Jason are coming over for a few minutes. You go back to sleep."

When they arrived, he took them into the kitchen. He was wearing his old flannel bathrobe with the frayed cord. His short hair spiked up like a cactus.

He had used the six-cup percolator and put a tray of frozen blueberry muffins in the oven. They sat around the kitchen table, sipping the steamy black coffee and munching on muffins while Sergeant Boone reported what had happened.

A squad car on patrol had spotted Detective Timothy Hogan lying semiconscious in the gutter and had called for an ambulance. It wasn't until they got him to Roosevelt Emergency that they found his ID and knew that one of New York's Finest had been assaulted.

"He had his ID?" Delaney said sharply.

"Yes, sir," Boone said. "And his gun."

"And his wallet," Jason added. "Nothing missing. It wasn't one of your ordinary, everyday muggings."

"But he's going to be all right?"

"Oh, hell, yes," Boone said. "Cracked ribs, bruised kidneys, a gorgeous shiner, and assorted cuts and abrasions. He looks like he's been through a meat grinder—stomped up something fierce."

"I think his pride was hurt more than anything else," Jason offered.

"It should be," Delaney said grumpily. "Letting himself be jumped like that. You talked to him?"

"For a while," Boone said. "They got him shot full of painkillers so he wasn't too coherent."

He told Delaney what they had been able to drag out of a groggy Timothy Hogan:

How he had made Mrs. Lorna Bellsey admit she was asleep and could not swear that her husband was home from eight-thirty to eleven o'clock on the murder night.

How he had followed Bellsey up to the Tail of the Whale on Eleventh Avenue and gotten into a hassle with him at the bar.

How he was unexpectedly attacked while he was returning to his car.

"He swears it was Ronald Bellsey," Boone said.

"He saw him?" Delaney demanded. "He can positively identify him?"

"Well . . . no," Boone said regretfully. "He didn't get a look at the perp, and apparently no words were spoken."

"Jesus Christ!" Delaney said disgustedly. "Can you think of any mistakes Hogan *didn't* make? Did the investigating officers go back to the bar—what's its name?"

"Tail of the Whale. Yes, sir, they covered that bar and four others in the area. No one saw anything, no one heard anything, no one knows Ronald J. Bellsey or anyone resembling him. And no one admits seeing Tim Hogan either. It's a blank."

"You want us to pull Bellsey in, sir?" Jason Two asked. "For questioning?"

"What the hell for?" Delaney said irritably. "He'll just deny, deny, deny. And even if we get the bartender and customers to admit there was a squabble in the Tail of the Whale, that's no evidence that Bellsey put the boots to Hogan. I'm going to call Suarez in a couple of hours and ask him to put a lid on this thing. We'll go at Bellsey from a different angle."

Sergeant Boone took folded papers from his inside jacket pocket and handed them to Delaney. "Benny Calazo stopped by my place last night and dropped off this report. He says that in his opinion, Isaac Kane is clean."

"You trust his opinion?" Delaney said sharply.

"Absolutely, sir. If Calazo says the kid is clean, then he is. Ben has been around a long time and doesn't goof. I was thinking . . . Hogan's going to be on sick leave for at least a month. How about putting Calazo onto Bellsey? If anyone can put the skids under that bastard, Ben will do it."

"Fine with me," Delaney said. "Brief him on Bellsey and tell him for God's sake not to turn his back on the guy. Jason, you're still working with Keisman on Harold Gerber's confession?"

"Yes, sir. Nothing new to report."

"Keep at it. There's one blueberry muffin left; who wants it?"

"I'll take it," Jason Two said promptly. "I could OD on those little beauties."

After they were gone, Delaney sat at the kitchen table and finished his lukewarm coffee, too keyed-up to go back to bed. He reflected on the latest developments and decided he had very little sympathy for Detective Timothy Hogan. You paid for your stupidity in this world one way or another.

He rinsed out the cups and saucers, set them in the rack to dry, cleaned up the kitchen. He took Calazo's report on Isaac into the study and put on his glasses. He read slowly and with enjoyment. Calazo had a pungent style of writing that avoided the usual Department gibberish.

When he finished, Delaney put the report aside and lighted a cigar. He pondered not so much the facts Calazo had recounted but what he had implied.

The detective (covering his ass) had said there was a possibility he was wrong, but he believed Isaac Kane innocent of the murder of Dr. Simon Ellerbee. He was saying, in effect, that there were no perfect solutions, only judgments.

Edward X. Delaney knew that mindset well; it was his own. In the detection of crime, nothing cohered. It was an open-ended pursuit with definite answers left to faith. There was a religious element to detection: Rational investigation went only so far. Then came the giant step to belief for which there was no proof.

Which meant, of course, that the detective had to live with doubt and anxiety. If you couldn't do that, Delaney thought—not for the first time —you really should be in another line of business.

# 18.

Detective Helen Venable was having a particularly severe attack of doubt and anxiety. She was uncertain of her own ability to establish the truth or falsity of Joan Yesell's alleged alibi without seeking the advice of her more experienced male colleagues.

She was nervous about her failure to report Mrs. Blanche Yesell's possible absence from her apartment on the murder night. She was worried that there were inquiries she should be making that she was not. And she fretted that an entire week had to pass before she could confirm or deny the existence of the stupid bridge club.

But her strongest doubt was a growing disbelief in Joan's guilt. That soft, feeling, quiet woman, so overwhelmed by the hard, brutal, raucous world of Manhattan, was incapable of crushing the skull of a man she professed to admire. Or so Detective Venable thought.

She met with Joan every day, spoke to her frequently on the phone, went out with her Monday night for a spaghetti dinner and to a movie on Thursday afternoon. The closer their relationship became, the more Helen was convinced of the woman's innocence.

Joan was almost physically sickened by the filth and ugliness of city streets. She was horrified and depressed by violence in any form. She could not endure the thought of cruelty to animals. The sight of a dead sparrow made her weep. She never objected to Helen's squad room profanity, but the detective could see her wince.

"Kiddo," Venable told her, "you're too good for this world. Angels finish last."

"I don't think I'm an angel," Joan said slowly. "Far from it. I do awful, stupid things, like everyone else. Sometimes I get so furious with Mama that I could scream. You think I'm goody-goody, but I'm not."

"Compared to me," Helen said, "you're a saint."

Frequently, during that week, the detective brought the talk around to Dr. Simon Ellerbee. Joan seemed willing, almost eager, to speak of him.

"He meant so much to me," she said. "He was the only therapist I ever went to, and I knew right from the start that he would help me. I could see he'd never be shocked or offended by anything I'd tell him. He'd just listen in that nice, sympathetic way of his. I'd never hold back from him because I knew I could trust him. I think he was the first man —the first person—I really and truly trusted. We were so close. I had the feeling that things that hurt me hurt him, too. I suppose psychiatrists are like that to all their patients, but Doctor Simon made me feel like someone special."

"Sounds like quite a guy," Venable said.

"Oh, he was. I'm going to tell you something, but you must promise never to tell anyone. Promise?"

"Of course."

"Well, sometimes I used to daydream about Doctor Simon's wife dying. Like in a plane crash—you know? Quick and painless. Then he and I would get married. I imagined what it would be like seeing him every day, living with him, spending the rest of my life with him."

"Sounds to me like you were in love with him, honey."

"I suppose I was," Yesell said sorrowfully. "I guess all his patients were. You call me a saint; he was the real saint."

Another time she herself brought up the subject of the murder:

"Are the police getting anywhere?" she asked Venable. "On who killed Doctor Simon?"

"It's slow going," the detective admitted. "No good leads that I know of, but a lot of people are working on it. We'll get the perp."

"Perp?"

"Perpetrator. The one who did it."

"Oh. Well, I hope you do. It was an awful, awful thing."

They talked about the apartment they might one day share. They talked about their mothers, about clothes, and foods they liked or hated. They recalled incidents from their girlhood, giggled about boys they had known, traded opinions on TV stars and novelists.

It was not a rare occurrence, this closeness between detective and suspect. For did they not need each other? Even a murderer might find the obsession of his pursuer as important to himself as it was to the hunter. It gave meaning to their existence.

"Gotta work late on Friday night, dear," Venable told her target. "Reports and shit like that. I'll call you on Saturday and maybe we can have dinner or something."

"I'd like that," Joan said with her timid smile. "I really look forward to seeing you and talking to you on the phone."

"Me, too," Helen said, troubled because she was telling the truth.

On Friday night at seven o'clock, Helen was slouched down in her Honda, parked two doors away from the Yesells' brownstone. She could watch the entrance in her rearview mirror, and kept herself alert with a little transistor radio turned to a hard-rock station.

She sat there for more than an hour, never taking her eyes from the doorway. It was almost 8:15 when Blanche Yesell came out, bundled up in a bulky fur coat that looked like a bearskin. There was no mistaking her; she was hatless and that beehive hairdo seemed to soar higher than ever.

Venable slid from the car and followed at a distance. It didn't last long; Mrs. Yesell scurried westward and darted into a brownstone one door from the corner. The detective quickened her pace, but by the time she got there, the subject had disappeared from vestibule and lobby, with no indication of which apartment she had entered.

Helen stood on the sidewalk, staring up, flummoxed. If Calazo had been faced with the problem, he probably would have rung every bell in the joint, demanding, "Is Mrs. Blanche Yesell there?" And within an hour, he'd have statements from the other bridge club members and know if Mrs. Yesell was or was not at home on the murder night and could or could not testify as to her daughter's presence.

But such direct action did not occur to Helen. She pondered how she might identify and question the bridge club members without alerting the Yesells that Joan's alibi was being investigated.

She went back to the Honda and sat there a long time, feeling angry and ineffective because she couldn't think of a clever scam. Finally, taking a deep breath, she decided she better write a complete report on Mrs. Yesell's Friday night bridge club and dump the whole thing in Sergeant Boone's lap.

It was a personal failure, she acknowledged, and it infuriated her. But the fear of committing a world-class boo-boo and being bounced down to uniformed duty again was enough to convince her to go by the book. It turned out to be a smart decision.

If Helen was suffering from doubts, Detective Ross Konigsbacher was inflated with confidence, convinced he was on a roll. On the same night Helen was brooding unhappily in her Honda, the Kraut was rubbing knees with L. Vincent Symington at a small table at the Dorian Gray.

Symington had insisted on ordering a bottle of Frascati, served in a silver ice bucket. The detective had made no objections, knowing that Symington would pick up the tab. That was one thing you could say for the creep: There were no moths in his wallet.

"A dreadful day," he told Konigsbacher. "Simply *dreadful.* This is a nice little wine, isn't it? One crisis after another. I'm on Wall Street, you know—I don't think I told you that—and today the market simply collapsed. What do you do, Ross?"

"Import-export," he said glibly, having prepared for the question. "Plastic and leather findings. Very dull."

"I can imagine. Are you in the market at all?"

"I'm afraid not."

"Well, if you ever decide to take a flier, talk to me first; I may be able to put you into something sweet."

"I'll do that. But my wife has been nagging me about a new fur coat, so I won't be able to take a flier in stocks or anything else for a while."

"What a shame," Symington said. "Women can be *such* bitches, can't they? Are you still working out, Ross?"

"Every morning with the weights."

"Oh, my!" the other man said, laughing brightly. "You're getting me all excited. And what does your *wife* do while you're exercising in the morning?"

"She snores."

"Now that *is* dull. Here, let me fill your glass. This goes down easily, doesn't it?"

"Like some people I know," the Kraut said, and they both shook with silent laughter.

"Vince, have you had any more visits from the cops—about the murder of your shrink?"

"Not a word. But I'm sure they're investigating me from A to Z. Let them; I have nothing to hide."

"I hope you have a good alibi for the time it happened."

"I certainly do," Symington said virtuously. "I was at a very posh affair at the Hilton. My company was giving a birthday dinner for the founder. A dozen people saw me there."

"Come on, Vince," Konigsbacher said, smiling. "Don't tell me you were there all night. I know how boring those things can be. Didn't you sneak out for a teensy-weensy drink somewhere else?"

"Oh, Ross," the other man said admiringly, "you *are* clever. Of course I split for a while. Simply couldn't endure all that business chit-chat. I found the grungiest, most vulgar bar in the city over near Eighth Avenue. It's called Stallions. How does that grab you? Rough trade? You wouldn't believe! I just sat in a corner, sipped my Perrier, and took it all in. What a spectacle! You and I must drop by there some night just for laughs. I've never seen so much black leather in my *life!*"

"Meet anyone interesting?" the detective asked casually.

"Well, if you must know . . ." Symington said coyly, twirling his wineglass by the stem, "there was one boy . . . I bought him a drink—he was having banana brandy; can you imagine!—and we talked awhile. His name was Nick. He was one of those dese, dem, and dose boys, and said he wanted to be an actor. 'Hamlet?' I asked, but it went right over his head! I spent a fun hour there, and then I went back to the party at the Hilton. I'm sure not a soul noticed I had been gone."

"Oh, Vince," the Kraut said seriously, "I hope you weren't gone during the time your psychiatrist was killed. The cops aren't dummies, you know. They're liable to find out you left the party and come around to question you again."

"You think so?" the other man said, beginning to worry. "Well, as a matter of fact, I *was* away from the Hilton from about nine to ten o'clock or so, but I can't believe the cops could discover that."

"They might," Detective Konigsbacher said darkly. "They have their ways."

"Oh, God!" Symington said despairingly. "What do you think I should do? Maybe I'll look up those two cops who came to question me and tell them about it. That would prove I have nothing to hide, wouldn't it?"

"Don't do that," the Kraut said swiftly. "Don't volunteer anything. Just play it cool. And if they dump on you for not telling them about being away from the party, tell them you forgot. After all, that boy—what was his name?"

"Nick."

"Nick can back up your story."

"If they can ever find him," the other man said dolefully. "You know what those kids are like—here today, gone tomorrow."

"Well, don't worry about it," Konigsbacher advised. "As long as you're innocent, you have nothing to fear. You *are* innocent, aren't you, Vince?"

"Pure as the driven snow," Symington said solemnly, and both men laughed immoderately.

"Ross, have you had dinner yet?"

"As a matter of fact, I haven't. You?"

"No, and I'm famished. I know absolutely the *chicest* French bistro in town; their bouillabaisse is divine. Would you care to try it? My treat, of course."

"Sounds like fun," Konigsbacher said. "It's got to be better than my wife's cooking. She can't boil water without burning it."

"Ross, you're a scream!"

Symington paid the bill and they left for the chicest French bistro in town. The detective told himself he was living high off the hog and plotted how he might make this cushy duty last. Incomplete reports to Sergeant Boone and Delaney would help.

Delaney himself was sinking in a swamp of incomplete data. He couldn't get a handle on the alibis of Otherton, Bellsey, Yesell, or Symington, and Harold Gerber's confession was still neither verified nor refuted. Other than eliminating Kane as a suspect, little hard progress had been made.

What Delaney found most bothersome about this puzzle wasn't the factual alibis but the enigmas that showed no signs of yielding to investigation. In his dogged, methodical way, he made a list of what he considered the key mysteries that seemed to defy solution:

*Major riddles:*

    1. Who was the late patient Dr. Ellerbee was expecting on the night he was killed?

    2. Why were there two sets of wet footprints on the townhouse carpeting?

    3. What was the meaning of the hammer blows to the victim's eyes after he was dead?

    4. Who stole the billing ledger—and for what reason?

    5. What was the cause of Ellerbee's change of personality during the past year?

*Minor riddles:*

    1. Did L. Vincent Symington's sighting of Dr. Ellerbee driving alone on a Friday night have any significance?

2. Why did Joan Yesell attempt suicide immediately after she was questioned about the case?

3. What was the real purpose of Dr. Diane Ellerbee's visit to the Delaney's home—and her unexpected friendliness?

He hunched over his desk, studying the list with the feeling—a hope, really—that finding the answer to one riddle would serve as a key, and all the others would then give up their secrets in a natural progression, the entire case suddenly revealed as a rational and believable chain of events. It existed, he was convinced, and remained hidden only because he hadn't the wit to see it.

He was rereading his list of conundrums when the phone rang.

"Edward X. Delaney here."

"This is Detective Charles Parnell, Mr. Delaney. How are you, sir?"

"Fine, thank you. And you?"

"Having fun," Daddy Warbucks said, laughing. "I'm ass-deep in numbers, trying to put away a guy who was running a Ponzi scam in Brooklyn. Took his relatives, friends, and neighbors for about a hundred big ones. Interesting case. I'll have to tell you about it someday. But the reason I called . . . I promised you I'd follow up on Simon Ellerbee's will. It's been filed for probate, and I can give you the scoop."

"Excellent," Delaney said. "Wait a minute until I get pen and paper . . . Okay, what have you got?"

"Everything goes to his wife, Diane, except for some specific bequests. Twenty thousand to his alma mater, ten to his father, five to Doctor Samuelson, one thousand to his receptionist, Carol Judd, and small sums to the super of the townhouse, the Polish couple who work for the Ellerbees up in Brewster, and a few others. That's about it. Nothing that might be the motive for murder that I can see."

"Doesn't sound like it," Delaney said slowly. "The widow's got plenty of her own. I can't see her chilling him for a little more."

"I agree," Parnell said. "The only thing interesting in the will is that Ellerbee specifically cancels all debts owed to him by his patients. Apparently some of the screwballs were strictly slow-pay, if not deadbeats. Well, Ellerbee's will wipes the slate clean. That was decent of him."

"Yes," Delaney said thoughtfully, "decent. And a little unusual, wouldn't you say?"

"Oh, I don't know," Daddy Warbucks said. "Everyone says he was a great guy. Always helping people. This sounds right in character."

"Uh-huh," Delaney said. "Well, thank you very much. You've been a big help, and I'll make sure Chief Suarez knows about it."

"It couldn't hurt," Detective Parnell said.

After Delaney hung up, he stared at the notes he had jotted down. He pondered a long while. Then, sighing, he reached for his "agony list" of unsolved puzzles. He added a fourth item under *Minor riddles:* Why did Dr. Ellerbee cancel his patients' debts?

And, having done that, he tramped gloomily into the kitchen, hoping to find the makings of a prodigious sandwich that might relieve his depression.

Detective Brian Estrella was also thinking of food. Since his wife, Meg, had been in the hospital and nursing home, he had been baching it and hating every minute. He was unused to solitude, and a real klutz when it came to cooking and household chores.

He had what he considered a brainstorm: He called Sylvia Mae Otherton on Friday night and suggested, with some diffidence, that they have dinner together. He would find a Chinese take-out joint and buy enough food for both of them. All Sylvia would have to supply would be hot tea. She thought it was a marvelous idea.

Estrella bought egg rolls, barbecued ribs, noodles, wonton soup, shrimp in lobster sauce, fried rice, sweet-and-sour pork, fortune cookies, and pistachio ice cream. Everything was packed in neat cardboard containers, and they even put in plastic forks and spoons, paper napkins.

It was like a picnic, with all the opened containers on the cocktail table along with cups of hot tea Sylvia provided. They agreed it was just the kind of spicy, aromatic food to have on a cold winter night with a hard wind rattling the windows and flurries of snow glistening in the streetlight.

The detective didn't neglect to compliment Sylvia on how attractive she looked, and indeed she had done much to improve her appearance. Her hair was washed and coiffed in a loose, fluffy cut. The excess makeup was gone, and the garish costume replaced by a simple shirtwaist.

More important, her manner had undergone a transformation. She seemed at once confident and relaxed. She smiled and laughed frequently, and told Estrella she had gone out that afternoon and spent two hours shopping, going from store to store—something she hadn't done since Dr. Ellerbee died.

"That's wonderful," the detective said. "See, you *can* do it. You should try to get out of the house every day, even if it's only for a few minutes."

"I intend to," Otherton said firmly. "I'm going to take charge of my life. And I owe it all to you."

"Me? What did I do?"

"You cared. You have no idea how important that was to me."

They finished everything and cleared away the empty containers. Then Sylvia asked about Estrella's wife, and he told her the doctors didn't hold out much hope, but Meg was in good spirits and spoke optimistically of coming home soon.

"I think she knows she's not going to do that," the detective said in a low voice, "but she tries to keep cheerful so *I* don't get depressed."

"She sounds like a wonderful woman, Brian."

"Yes. She is."

Then, before he knew it, he was telling Sylvia all about Meg, their life together, the child they had lost (leukemia), and how sometimes Estrella wondered how he was going to get through the rest of his life without his wife.

He poured it all out, realizing now how lonely he had been and how he had been hoping to tell someone how he felt. It was a kind of tribute to Meg: public acknowledgment of the happiness she had given him.

Sylvia listened intently, only asking sympathetic questions, until Estrella was done. They were sitting close together on the couch and, halfway through his recital, she took his hand and held it tightly.

She wasn't coming on to him; he knew that. Just offering the comfort of her physical presence, and he was grateful. When he had finished, he raised her hand and lightly kissed her fingertips.

"Well . . ." he said, "that's the sad story of my life. Forgive me for making you listen to all this. I know you have your own problems."

"I only wish I could help you," she said sorrowfully. "You've helped me so much. Now let's have an after-dinner drink."

She rose to bring the decanter from an ornate Korean cupboard.

"Oh," she said, "pardon me a moment; I have to make a short phone call."

The reproduction of a fin de siècle French phone was on a small, marble-topped Victorian stand. She dialed a three-digit number.

"Charles?" she said. "This is Sylvia Mae Otherton. How are you tonight? . . . Good . . . Fine, thank you . . . Anything for me today? . . . Thank you, Charles. Good night."

She came back to Estrella with the sherry.

"No mail today," she said lightly. "Not even a bill."

He stared at her. Then he glanced at his wristwatch. Fourteen minutes after nine. He put his pipe aside.

"Sylvia," he said in a strained voice, "was that the guy at the lobby desk you were talking to?"

"Yes, that was Charles. He works nights. I called to ask if there's any mail in my box. It saves me a trip downstairs. My agoraphobia again!"

"You call him every night to check on your mail?"

"Yes. Why do you ask?"

"You always call about this time?"

"Usually. But why—"

She stopped, her eyes widened, her mouth fell open. One hand flew to cover it.

"Oh, God!" she gasped.

"You told us you hadn't made any phone calls that night."

"I forgot!" she wailed. "It's a regular habit, a routine, and I forgot. Oh, Brian, I'm so sorry. But I'm sure I called Charles that night."

"I'll be right back," Estrella said. "Keep your fingers crossed."

He went down to the lobby, identified himself, and talked to Charles for almost five minutes. The clerk swore that Sylvia Otherton called about her mail between 9:00 and 9:30 every weekday evening.

"A lot of the tenants do that," he said. "Especially the older ones. Saves them a trip downstairs. And I don't mind. Things are slow around here at night, and it gives me someone to talk to, something to do."

"Does Otherton ever miss calling you?"

"Not that I remember. Every night during the week, like clockwork."

"Between, say, nine and nine-thirty?"

"That's right."

"Do you remember her calling on a Friday night four weeks ago—the night of that terrific rainstorm?"

"I can't remember that particular night. All I know is that she hasn't missed a night since I been working here, and that's almost three years now."

"Thank you, Charles."

Upstairs again, Estrella said, "Sylvia, as far as I'm concerned, you're cleared—and that's what I'm going to put in my report."

He thought that would please her, but instead she looked like she was about to cry.

"Does that mean I won't be seeing you anymore?"

He touched her shoulder. "No," he said gently, "it doesn't mean that."

"Good," she said happily. "Brian, would you like to try the Ouija board again? Maybe it will help you find out who did it."

"Sure," he said, "let's try."

They sat as they had before, the board between them on the cocktail table. Sylvia put her fingers lightly on the planchette and closed her eyes.

"Doctor Ellerbee," Detective Brian Estrella said in a hollow voice, "was the person who killed you a stranger?"

The planchette did not move.

Estrella repeated his question.

The planchette jerked wildly. It spelled out KGXFTD, then stopped.

"Doctor Ellerbee," the detective tried once more, "was the person who killed you a stranger?"

The planchette moved slowly. It pointed to N and then to I. NI. Then it stopped.

"Sylvia," Brian said softly, "I don't think we're getting anywhere. It spelled out NI. That doesn't mean anything."

She opened her eyes. "Maybe he's just not getting through to me tonight. His spirit may be busy with another medium."

"That could be it," Estrella acknowledged.

"But we'll try again, won't we, Brian?" she asked anxiously.

"Absolutely," he said.


On Saturday afternoon, Delaney, Boone, and Jason held a council of war. They shuffled through all the reports that had come in during the week and discussed reassignments.

"Estrella says Otherton is clean," Delaney said. "You willing to accept that?"

"I am, sir," Jason said promptly. "He did a thorough job on her—checked all her friends and neighborhood stores. It was just by luck that he got onto the phone call to the lobby clerk. I think she's clean."

"Boone?"

"I'll go along with Jase, sir."

"What's this Ouija board nonsense in his report? It's the second time he's mentioned that. Is the man a flake?"

"No, sir," Jason Two said. "He's a steady, serious kind of guy. But his wife is very sick, and maybe he's got that on his mind."

"Oh," Delaney said. "I didn't know that and I'm sorry to hear it. Does he want a leave of absence?"

"No, he says he wants to keep on working."

"Probably the best thing," Delaney said. "All right, let's clear Otherton. She may be a nut case, but I can't see her as a killer. Now about this report from Detective Venable . . . That *is* interesting. Sounds to me like Mrs. Yesell has been leading us up the garden path."

"Her story sure needs work," Sergeant Boone said. "If Otherton is cleared, how about switching Estrella to Joan Yesell? He can work with Helen on finding the members of Mrs. Yesell's bridge club."

"Yes," Delaney said, "let's do that. Boone, you're working with Calazo on Ronald J. Bellsey?"

"Every chance I get."

"And, Jason—you and Keisman are covering Harold Gerber?"

"That's right, sir. Nothing new to report."

"And Konigsbacher has nothing new to report on Symington. But I've got something new that may interest you."

He told them about Detective Parnell's report—that Dr. Simon Ellerbee's will had specifically canceled all his patients' outstanding bills.

"Now what the hell do you suppose that means?" he asked the two officers.

They both shook their heads.

"Beats me," Boone said.

"Probably nothing," Jason said.

"Probably," Delaney said, sighing. "We've sure got a lot of probabilities in this case and damned little we can sink our teeth in. Well, what can I tell you except to keep plugging and pray for a break."

After they left, he returned to the study to paw through the scattered reports again. He was in a sour, dispirited mood. "Keep plugging." That was stupid, unnecessary advice to give his aides. They were experienced police officers and knew that plugging was the name of the game.

What always bemused Delaney in cases like this was the contrast between the grand passion that incited the murder of a human being and the pedestrian efforts of the police to solve it.

In a crazy kind of way, it was like solving the mystery of a Rembrandt by analyzing pigments, brushstrokes, and the quality of the canvas, and then saying, "There! Your mystery's explained." It wasn't, of course. Mystery was mystery. It defied rational explication.

Even if the Ellerbee homicide was closed, Delaney suspected the solution would merely be a resolution of the facts. The enigma of human behavior would remain hidden.

# 19.

Two weeks before Christmas, and the city had never been more enchanting. The "city" being Manhattan, and more particularly midtown Manhattan, with streets glowing with lights and tinsel. Amplified carols rang out everywhere, along with the jingle of bells and cash registers. The annual shopping frenzy was in full swing, stores mobbed, the spending fever an epidemic. "Take my money, miss—*please!*"

But downtown, on Seventh Avenue South, there were no lights, no tinsel, no carols. Just some foul remains of the last snowfall, clotted with garbage and dog droppings. Harold Gerber's tenement showed no festive trappings. Paint peeled, plaster fell away, the bare, lathed walls oozed a glutinous slime that smelled of suppuration.

"O little town of Bethlehem," Detective Robert Keisman sang.

"How about 'Come, All Ye Faithful'?" Jason suggested.

The two detectives were lounging around Gerber's ruinous pad, working on a six-pack of Schaefer. The two black officers were wearing drifter duds, and all three men were bundled in down jackets, with caps and gloves. It was damp, and cold enough to see their breath.

"Let's go through it once more," Jason Two said.

"Ahh, Jesus," Gerber said, "do we have to?"

"Sure we have to," Keisman said lazily. "You're aching to get your ass locked up, aren't you? Spend a nice warm holiday in durance vile—right? You say you snuffed Doc Ellerbee. Well, yeah, that may be so, but on the other hand you may just be jerking us around."

"See, Harold," Jason said, "we run you in, and it turns out you're just a bullshit artist wasting everyone's time—well, that don't look so good on our records."

"Shit," Gerber said, "you write out any kind of a confession you like —put anything in it you want—and I'll sign it."

"Nah," the Spoiler said, "that's not how it's done, Harold. You got to tell us in your own words. You say you took a cab over to Ellerbee's townhouse on that night?"

Gerber: "That's right."

Jason: "What kind of cab? Yellow, Checker, gypsy?"

Gerber: "I don't remember."

Keisman: "How long did it take you to get there?"

Gerber: "Maybe twenty minutes."

Jason: "Where did the cabby drop you?"

Gerber: "Right in front of Ellerbee's office."

Keisman: "How did you get in?"

Gerber: "Rang the bell. When he answered, I told him I was in a bad way and had to see him. He let me in."

Jason: "You were carrying the hammer?"

Gerber: "Sure. I carried it with me for the express purpose of killing Ellerbee. It was a premeditated murder."

Keisman: "Uh-huh. Now tell us again where you got the hammer."

Gerber: "I boosted it from that hardware store near Sheridan Square."

Jason: "Just put it under your jacket and walked out?"

Gerber: "That's right."

Keisman: "We checked with them. They lose a lot to shoplifters, but no ball peen hammers."

Gerber: "They don't know their ass from their elbow."

Jason: "All right, now you're inside Ellerbee's townhouse, carrying a hammer. What did you do next?"

Gerber: "Walked upstairs."

Keisman: "You were wearing your boots?"

Gerber: "Sure, I was wearing boots. It was a fucking wet night."

Jason: "You see anyone else in the townhouse?"

Gerber: "No. Just Ellerbee. He let me into his office."

Keisman: "He was alone?"

Gerber: "Yeah, he was alone."

Jason: "Did you talk to him?"

Gerber: "I said hello. He started to say, 'What are you doing—' and then I hit him."

Keisman: "He was facing you when you hit him?"

Gerber: "That's right."

Jason: "How many times did you hit him?"

Gerber: "Two or three. I forget."

Keisman: "Where did you hit him? His brow, top of his head, temples—where?"

Gerber: "Like on the hairline. Not on top of his head. High up on the forehead."

Jason: "He went down?"

Gerber: "That's right."

Keisman: "On his back?"

Gerber: "Yeah, on his back."

Jason: "Then what did you do?"

Gerber: "I saw he was dead, so I—"

Keisman: "You didn't hit him again when he was down?"

Gerber: "What the hell for? The guy was fucking dead. I've seen enough stiffs to know that. So I got out of there, walked over to York, and got a cab going south."

Jason: "And what did you do with the hammer?"

Gerber: "Like I told you—I pushed it in a trash can on Eighth Street."

Keisman: "Why did you kill him, Harold?"

Gerber: "Jesus, how many times do I have to tell you? He was a nosy fucker. After a while he knew too much about me. Hey, let's have another brew; I'm thirsty."

The three sat there in silence, the two officers staring at the other man's wild, flaming eyes. As usual, Gerber needed a shave, and uncombed hair still spiked out from under his black beret.

"You going to take me in?" he asked finally.

"We'll think about it," Jason Two said.

"I did it. That's God's own truth. I'm guilty as hell."

They didn't reply.

"Hey, you guys?" Gerber said brightly, straightening up. "I'm moving. A city marshal showed up with an eviction notice. I've got to vacate the premises, as they say."

"Yeah?" the Spoiler said. "Where you moving to?"

"Who the hell knows? I've got to look around. I want another place as swell as this one."

"Need any help moving?" Jason offered.

"Moving *what?*" Harold Gerber said with a ferocious grin. "I can carry all my stuff in a shopping bag. I'm going to leave a lot of shit right here. You guys want any books? I've got a pile of paperbacks over there under the sink. Some hot stuff. You're welcome to any or all."

"Yeah?" Jason said. "Let's take a look. Maybe there's something my wife would like. She's always got her nose in a book."

He squatted down at the sink, began to inspect the jumble of books. He pulled out a thick one.

"What's this?" he said. "A Bible?"

"Oh, that . . ." Gerber said casually. "I fished it out of a garbage can. I flipped through it. A million laughs."

Jason inspected the book.

"Douay Version," he read aloud. "That's a Catholic Bible, isn't it? You a Catholic, Harold?"

"I was. Once. What are you?"

"Baptist. Mind if I take this along?" Jason Two asked, holding up the Bible.

"Be my guest," Gerber said. "Read the whole thing. I won't tell you how it comes out."

They sat around awhile longer before the two officers left, promising Gerber they'd tell him the next day whether or not they would arrest him.

They sat in Jason's car, the heater on, trying to get warm.

"He's full of crap," Keisman said. "A complete whacko."

"Oh, yeah," Jason agreed. "Doesn't even know how Ellerbee died."

"Why do you figure he wants to get busted?"

"I don't know for sure. Something to do with guilt, I suppose. What happened in Vietnam . . . It's too deep for me."

"What's with the Bible?" the Spoiler asked, jerking a thumb at the book. "Why did you glom on to that?"

"Look at it," Jason Two said, ruffling the pages. "It's full of dog-ears. Someone's been doing some heavy reading. And I don't believe he found it in a garbage can. *Nobody* throws out a Bible."

"Jase, that's the Baptist in you talking."

"Maybe. But he says he used to be a Catholic, and this is a Catholic edition. Funny a backslid Catholic should find a Catholic Bible in a garbage can."

" 'God moves in a mysterious way His wonders to perform.' "

"Hey," Jason said admiringly, "there's more to you than Gucci after all, isn't there?"

"I was brought up right," Keisman said. "Didn't go bad until—oh, maybe the age of six or so."

"Well . . ." Jason T. Jason said, staring down at the book in his hands, "it may be nothing, but what say we give it the old college try?"

The Spoiler groaned. "You mean check every Catholic church in the city?"

"I don't think we'll have to do that. Just the ones in Greenwich Village. I'm hoping that poor son of a bitch was praying in some church on that Friday night."

"Man, you really dig the long shots, don't you?"

Because of previous arrests, there was a photo of Harold Gerber in his NYPD file, and Jason cajoled a police photographer into making two copies, one for himself, one for Keisman.

At the same time, Detective Calazo was having more serious photo problems. Apparently there was no shot of Ronald Bellsey in the files. Calazo could have requested that a police photographer take a tele-photo of Bellsey without the subject's knowledge—but that meant making out a requisition and then waiting.

The old, white-haired gumshoe had been around a long time, and knew a lot of ways to skin a cat in what he sometimes called the "Dick Biz." He looked up the name and address of a trade magazine, *The Wholesale Butcher,* and visited their editorial offices on West 14th Street.

Sure enough, they had a photograph of Ronald J. Bellsey in their files. Calazo flashed his potsy and borrowed the shot, promising to return it. He didn't bother asking them not to tell Bellsey about his visit. Let them tell the fink; it would do him good to sweat a little.

Then Benny, with the aid of Sergeant Boone, when he could spare the time, tailed the subject for almost a week. He discovered that Bellsey had three bars he favored: the Tail of the Whale on Eleventh Avenue, a tavern on Seventh Avenue near Madison Square Garden, and another on 52nd Street, just east of Broadway.

He also discovered that Bellsey got his ashes hauled two afternoons a week by a Chinese hooker working out of a fleabag hotel on West 23rd Street. She had a sheet a yard long, all arrests for loitering, solicitation, and prostitution. She was getting a little frazzled around the edges now, and Calazo figured she'd be lucky to get twenty bucks a pop.

He didn't move on her—just made sure he put her name (Betty Lee), address, room, and phone number in his report to Boone. Then he turned his attention to those three hangouts Bellsey frequented.

All three were patronized by boxers, trainers, managers, agents, bookies, and hangers-on in the fight racket. And all three had walls covered with photos and paintings of dead and living pugs, along with such memorabilia as bloodied gloves, trunks, shoes, and robes.

Calazo then checked the records at Midtown North and Midtown South to see how many times the cops had been called to the three joints, and for what reasons. This would have been an endless task, but Benny had friends in every precinct in Manhattan, so, with a little help, the job took only two days.

After winnowing out incidents of public drunkenness, free-for-all donnybrooks, robberies, attempted rape, and one case of indecent exposure, Calazo was left with four unsolved cases of assault that pretty much followed the pattern of the attack on Detective Timothy Hogan.

In all four episodes, a badly beaten man had been found on the sidewalk, in an alley, or in the gutter near one of the three bars. None of the victims could positively identify his assailant, but all four had been drinking in one of Bellsey's favorite hangouts.

Showing the borrowed photo to owners, waiters, bartenders, and regular customers, Calazo learned a lot about Bellsey—none of it good. The detective was convinced the subject had been responsible for the four unsolved assaults, plus the attack on Tim Hogan. But he doubted if there would ever be enough evidence to arrest, let alone indict and convict.

His main problem, he knew, was to determine if Bellsey was really at home on the night Ellerbee was killed. Mrs. Lorna Bellsey had told Hogan that she hadn't actually seen her husband from eight-thirty to eleven o'clock. But that didn't necessarily mean he wasn't there.

In addition to solving that puzzle, Calazo was determined to do something about Hogan's beating. Big Tim was *estupido,* but still he was a cop, and that meant something to Benjamin Calazo.

Also, he hated guys like Ronald J. Bellsey who thought they could muscle their way through life and never pay any dues. So, in his direct way, Calazo began to plot how he might solve his problems and, at the same time, cut Bellsey off at the knees.

The fact that he would be retired, an ex-cop, in another three weeks, was also a factor. He would end his career gloriously by teaching a crud a lesson, avenging a fellow officer and, with luck, discovering who hammered in Dr. Ellerbee's skull.

That would be something to remember when he was playing shuffleboard in Florida.

If Edward Delaney had known what Calazo was planning, he'd have understood how the detective felt and sympathized. But that wouldn't have prevented him from yanking Calazo off the case. Personal hatreds had a way of fogging a man's judgment, and the downfall of Ronald Bellsey was small potatoes compared to finding Ellerbee's killer.

At the moment, Delaney had concerns of his own. Chief Suarez called and, in almost despairing tones, asked if there had been any progress. Delaney told him there had been a few minor developments, no breakthroughs, and suggested the two of them get together and review the entire investigation. They agreed to meet at Delaney's home at nine o'clock on Wednesday night.

"I wish Mrs. Suarez could come with you," Delaney said. "I know my wife would like to meet her."

"That is most kind of you, sir," Suarez said. "I shall certainly ask her, and if we are able to arrange for the children, I am sure she will be delighted to visit your charming home."

Delaney repeated this conversation to Monica. "The guy talks like a grandee," he said. "He must drive those micks at headquarters right up the wall."

"Well, we got an invitation, too," Monica said. "Diane Ellerbee called and asked if we'd like to come up to her Brewster place with the Boones this Saturday. I told her I'd check with you first, then call her back. I spoke to Rebecca and she said she and Abner would love to go. Shall I tell Diane it's okay for Saturday?"

"Oh-ho," he said. "Now it's 'Diane,' is it? What happened to 'Doctor Ellerbee'?"

"I have a lot in common with her," Monica said loftily, "and it's silly not to be on a first-name basis."

"Oh? What do you have in common with her?"

"She's a very intelligent woman."

"You win," he said, laughing. "Sure, call and tell her we'll be there on Saturday. Is she going to feed us?"

"Of course. She said she's thinking about a buffet dinner for early evening."

"A buffet," he said grumpily. "That's as bad as a cafeteria."

Promptly at nine o'clock on Wednesday evening, Michael and Rosa Suarez arrived at the brownstone, both wearing what Delaney later described as Sunday-go-to-meeting clothes. Introductions were made and the two couples settled down in the big living room, close to the fireplace, where a modest blaze warmed and mesmerized.

They talked of the current cold snap, of the problems of raising children, of the high cost of ground beef. Mrs. Suarez spoke little, at first, but Delaney had prepared hot rum toddies (with lemon and nutmeg), and after two small cups of that, Rosa's shyness thawed and she began to sparkle.

Monica brought out a plate of her special Christmas treats: pitted dates stuffed with almond paste, covered with a flaky pastry crust and then rolled in shredded coconut before baking. Rosa tried one, rolled her eyes ecstatically.

"Please," she begged, "the recipe!"

Monica laughed and held out her hand. "Come into the kitchen with me, Rosa. We'll trade secrets and let these two grouches talk business."

Delaney took Suarez into the study and provided cigars.

"First of all," the Chief said, "I must tell you that I have been forced to cut the number of men assigned to the Ellerbee homicide. We were getting no results, *nada,* and the murder was a month ago. More than a month. Since then there have been many, many things that demand attention. What I wish to say is that you and the people assigned to you are now our only hope. You understand why it was necessary to pull men off this case?"

"Sure," Delaney said genially. "What are you averaging—four or five homicides a day? I know you have a full plate and can't give any one case the coverage it needs. Believe me, Chief, it's always been that way. The problem comes with the territory."

"On the phone you spoke of some developments. But nothing important?"

"No," Delaney said, "not yet."

He then told Suarez how Isaac Kane and Sylvia Mae Otherton had been eliminated as suspects.

"That leaves us with four possibly violent patients, one of whom has confessed. I don't think that confession is worth a tinker's dam—but still, it's got to be checked out. The alibis of the other three are being investigated. At the moment, I'd say that Joan Yesell is the most interesting. It seems likely her mother lied when she told us Joan was home at the time of the killing. I've got two people working on that."

"So you *are* making progress."

"I don't know if you can call it progress," Delaney said cautiously.

"But we are eliminating the possibles and getting down to the probables. Yes, I guess that's progress."

Suarez was silent, puffing on a cigar. Then he said, "But what if—"

Delaney held up a palm to stop him. "What if! Chief, the what-ifs can kill you if you let them. I think we've cleared Kane and Otherton. I believe it on the basis of good detective work and a little bit of luck. But what if Kane offed Ellerbee, and then cabbed back to the Beeles' apartment on West Eighty-third Street? They might remember him being there on the murder night, but couldn't swear to the time he arrived. And what if Otherton called the lobby clerk from *outside* on the night of the murder? What if she clubbed Ellerbee and then used his office phone to call the clerk just to set up an alibi? All I'm saying is that you can drown yourself in what-ifs. A detective has got to be imaginative, but if you let yourself get *too* imaginative, you're lost."

Michael Ramon Suarez gave him a wan smile. "That is very true— and a lesson I am still learning. It is a danger to assume that all criminals are possessed of super intelligence. Most of them are quite stupid."

"Exactly," Delaney agreed. "But some of them are also quite shrewd. After all, it's their ass that's on the line. What I believe is that all detectives have to walk a very thin line between the cold, hard facts and the what-ifs. Sometimes you have to go on a wing and a prayer."

"But in spite of all this, Edward, you are still confident the Ellerbee case can be cleared?"

"If I didn't believe that, I'd have told you and Thorsen and cleared out. I have a sense the pace is quickening. We've already eliminated two possible suspects. I think we're going to eliminate more."

Suarez sighed. "And what if you eliminate all six suspects? Where do you go from there?"

Delaney smiled grimly. "There you go with a what-if again. If all six are cleared, I can't tell you what I'll do next. *Someone* killed Ellerbee; we know that. If all six patients are eliminated, then we'll look around for other directions to take."

The other man looked at him curiously. "You do not give up easily, do you?"

"No, I do not. From all accounts, Doctor Ellerbee was a decent man living a good, worthwhile life. I don't like the idea of someone chilling him and walking away scot-free."

"Time," the Chief said, groaning. "How much time can we give this thing?"

"As long as it takes," Delaney said stonily. "I worked a murder-rape for almost two years and finally got the perp. I know your career depends on this being cleared up as soon as possible. But I've got to tell you now that if it isn't, and the detectives you've given me are withdrawn, I'll keep working it myself."

"Forever?"

"No, not forever. I may be an obstinate son of a bitch, but I'm not a romantic. At least I don't think I am. The time may come when I'll have to admit defeat. I've done that before; it won't kill me. Shall we see what the ladies are up to?"

The ladies were back in the living room, sitting close together on the couch and obviously enjoying each other's company.

"We must do this again," Monica said. "Our children will be home for Christmas, but perhaps after the holidays . . ."

"Then you must visit our home," Chief Suarez said. "For dinner. Rosa makes a paella that is a hint of what heaven must be like."

"I have a feeling," Delaney said, "that this friendship is going to prove fattening. Tell me, how did you two meet?"

"Rosa's parents owned a bodega in East Harlem," Suarez said. "It was ripped off, and I was a detective third at the time and sent to investigate. The first thing I said to her was, 'I shall marry you.' Is that not so, Rosa?"

She nodded happily. "And you?" she asked Monica.

"My first husband was murdered. Edward had charge of the case, and that's how we met."

Rosa was shocked. "And did"—she faltered—"was the killer caught?"

"Oh, yes," Monica said. "Edward never gives up. He is a very stubborn man."

"That is what I believe also," Suarez said. "It is very encouraging."

"Chief," Delaney said, "if the Ellerbee killing isn't cleared, and you don't get permanent appointment, I suppose you'll be returned to precinct duty. Can you take that?"

Suarez shrugged, spreading his hands helplessly. "It would be a disappointment. I would not be honest if I said I did not care. I could endure it, but still it would be a defeat. I think I would be more sorry for Thorsen than for myself. He has worked very hard to bring minorities into appointive ranks. My failure would be his failure as well."

"Don't worry too much about Ivar," Delaney advised. "He'll land on his feet. He's learned how to survive in the political jungle. Something I never did. But you're a young man with your career ahead of you. Do you have any contacts with the Hispanic political structure in the city?"

"I know some of the people, of course," Suarez said cautiously. "But I am not close to them, no."

"Get close to them," Delaney urged. "They have a lot of clout now, and are going to have more as voting patterns change. Let them know you're around. Invite them to your home for dinner. All politicians like the personal touch. That's their business. If Rosa's paella is as good as you say, you may have a secret weapon there."

Her hands flew to her face to hide her blush, and she giggled.

"I'm serious about this," Delaney continued. "You're getting up in ranks where you'll have to pay as much attention to politics as you do to police work. Think of it as another part of your job. I wasn't able to hack it, but don't make my mistakes. This is a big, brawling, confused city, and politics is the glue that holds it together. I admit that sometimes the glue smells like something the cat dragged in—but can you think of a better, more human system? I can't. I'm willing to see us go blundering along, making horrendous mistakes. It can be discouraging, but it's a hell of a lot better than a storm trooper shouting, 'You *vill* obey orders!' So get into politics, Chief. Or at least touch bases with the heavies. It could do you a lot of good."

"Yes," Suarez said thoughtfully, "I think you are correct. I have been so busy with the nuts and bolts of my job that I have neglected the personal relations that might have made my job easier. Thank you for your advice, Edward."

"Don't just thank me—*do* it!"

Later that night, preparing for bed, Delaney said, "Nice, nice people."

"Aren't they," Monica agreed. "That Rosa is a doll. Were you really serious about him cultivating the politicos?"

"Absolutely. If he wants to protect his ass. Thorsen can do just so much. But Suarez would be wise to build up some political muscle with the power brokers."

"Well, if he's going to do that, I better take Rosa in hand. She dresses like a frump. She's really a very attractive woman and could do a lot more with herself than she does."

"You mean," he said solemnly, "you want to convert her into a sex object?"

"And you can go to hell," his wife said, but Delaney was still pursuing Suarez's career.

"I don't know the man too well," Delaney said. "A couple of meetings, a couple of phone calls . . . But I have the feeling his strong suit is administration. I really don't think he's got the basic drive to be a good detective. He's a little too cool, too detached. There's no obsession there."

"Is that what a good detective needs—an obsession?"

"You better believe it. Abner Boone has it and I'm betting Jason has it, too."

"Do you have it?"

"I suppose," he said shortly. He turned to stare at her. "You're a beautiful woman. Did I ever tell you that?"

"Not recently."

"Well, I'm telling you now."

"And what, pray, is the reason for this sudden romantic frenzy?"

"I thought you might be properly appreciative," he said, winking at her.

"I am," she said, crooking a finger at him.

# 20.

Detectives Helen Venable and Brian Estrella had never worked together before, but they found to their pleased surprise that they made a good team. He thought her a bright, vigorous woman willing to take on her share of the donkeywork. She thought him a bit stodgy, but smart and understanding. Best of all, he didn't pull any of that macho bullshit she was used to from other cops.

She told him everything she had learned about Joan Yesell, and especially the business of Mrs. Blanche Yesell and her Friday night bridge club.

"The old bitch was lying to us," she said bitterly.

"Maybe and maybe not," Estrella said. "There was a bad storm that night; the bridge game could have been called off. In that case she was probably home like she says. What's your take on Joan?"

"I can't believe she's the perp. I swear to God, Brian, she wouldn't hurt a fly."

"But she'll hurt herself. She's suicidal, isn't she?"

"Suicidal, yes; homicidal, no."

He went through the slow routine of packing his pipe, tamping down the tobacco, lighting up, puffing. "Helen, sounds to me like you've already made up your mind about this woman. You like her?"

"Very much. We're even talking about sharing an apartment."

"Take it easy," he advised. "Wait'll we clear her first."

"Brian, she's such a little mouse. She hasn't got a mean bone in her body. I tell you she's just incapable of snuffing Ellerbee—or anyone else. She cries when she sees a stray dog."

"Uh-huh," he said. "The meanest killer I ever scragged raised gerbils."

"You want to talk to Joan and see for yourself?"

"Not yet," he said. "You keep up the buddy-buddy routine with her, but don't tell her I'm working with you."

Without making it obvious, he spent all week double-checking Venable's investigation—and couldn't fault it. He talked to doctors at St. Vincent's, with fellow employees at Yesell's law office, with neighbors, storekeepers, even the postman who delivered mail to the Yesells' brownstone.

Everything he heard substantiated what Helen had told him: Joan Yesell was a timid, withdrawn woman. The only gossip Estrella picked up was that Blanche Yesell was a real battle-ax who treated her daughter like a cretin without the brains or will to make her own decisions.

On Friday night the two detectives were slouched in Venable's Honda parked a few doors down from the Yesells' home.

"With my luck," Helen said gloomily, "Mama Blanche will have the bridge club meeting at her apartment tonight."

"Doesn't make any difference," Estrella said. "If she does, you and I will tail two of the women after the game breaks up. Brace them, get their names and addresses, and we'll take it from there. But if Mrs. Yesell comes out—"

And, while he was talking, she did come out. She turned eastward and crossed the street.

"That's her," Venable said tensely.

"Okay," Estrella said, "you go after her and get the number of the building she goes into. I'm going to make a phone call. Meet you back here."

Helen took off after the scurrying Mrs. Yesell. Brian headed for Eighth Avenue and used a wall phone in an all-night deli. He called the Yesells' apartment.

A faint voice, "Hello?"

"Mrs. Blanche Yesell, please," Estrella said.

"She's not here right now. Who's calling?"

"This is Detective Brian Estrella of the New York Police Department. To whom am I speaking?"

"This is Joan Yesell, Mrs. Blanche Yesell's daughter."

"Miss Yesell, it is important that I contact your mother tonight. There's a document we'd like her to sign. It's just routine, but we do have to go by the rules and regulations, you know."

"A document? About Doctor Ellerbee's death?"

"Yes. Just her statement that she was home with you on that night. Could you tell me where I might reach her?"

"She's at her bridge club."

"Could you give me the phone number so I can contact her?"

"Well, she's at Mrs. Ferguson's tonight."

"Do you have the phone number?" he persisted.

She hesitated a moment, then gave him the number. Using a ballpoint pen, he jotted it down on the back of his hand.

"Thank you very much, Miss Yesell."

A few minutes later he was back at the Honda. Helen was waiting for him.

"I got the address," Venable said.

"And I got the name and phone number. We're in business."

The next morning Delaney felt equally optimistic as he and Monica set out with the Boones for Diane Ellerbee's country home. "Looks like a splendid day," Delaney gloated.

And so it was. A blue sky shimmered like a butterfly's wing. The sun was a hot plate and there, to the east, one could see a faint smudge of white moon. The sharp air bit like ether, and the whole world seemed scrubbed and polished.

Traffic was heavy, but they made surprisingly good time, stopping only once at a Brewster gas station to ask directions, use the rest rooms, and buy five gallons of gas in gratitude.

They drove slowly along a country road, commenting on the mailboxes: a windmill, a miniature house, a model plane.

"Very cutesy," Delaney said. "What's the Ellerbees' going to be—a little black leather couch with a red flag?"

But the mailbox marked ELLERBEE was the plain aluminum variety. It was at the entrance to a narrow side road that curved through a stand of skeleton trees up to the house and outbuildings. The gentle rise was not high enough to be called a hill, but sufficiently elevated to provide a pleasant view of the rolling countryside.

Boone drove onto the graveled apron outside the three-car garage. Parked outside was a dusty Volkswagen and the Ellerbees' Jeep station wagon. The garage door was up, and they could see Dr. Simon's bottle-green XJ6 Jaguar sedan and Dr. Diane's silver and black 1971 Mercedes-Benz.

"I've got to get a look at that Mercedes," Delaney said. "It's a beauty."

He and Boone went into the garage while their wives slowly strolled up to the main house along a curving pathway of slate flagstones.

Delaney and Boone spent a few minutes admiring the handsome cars in the garage.

"I'll take the Jag," Boone said, then laughed. "Can you imagine me driving up to Midtown North in that buggy? They'd know I was in the bag for sure."

"Mmm," Delaney said. "I wonder why she hasn't sold it. Who needs a Jaguar *and* a Mercedes?"

"Maybe she can't find a buyer," the Sergeant said. "About all I can afford is that old Beetle parked outside. Who do you suppose owns it?"

They walked up to the main house. The door was open, and on the small stoop, awaiting them, was Dr. Julius Samuelson.

"Now you know who owns the Beetle," Delaney said, sotto voce.

Inside, there was warmth, fragrance from scented pressed logs blazing in a fireplace, and redolent cooking odors.

"Ahh," Delaney said, sniffing appreciatively, "garlic. I love it."

"You better," Dr. Diane said, laughing. "That's Beef Bourguignonne bubbling away, and my cook has a heavy hand with the garlic. But there's fresh parsley in the salad, and that should help. Now let's all have a drink before I give you the grand tour." She gestured toward a marble-topped sideboard laden with bottles and decanters.

The spacious living room had exposed oak ceiling beams and a fieldstone fireplace. Floors were random-width pine planking. French doors at the rear opened onto a tiled patio and the swimming pool, now emptied and covered.

The master bedroom on the ground floor and the guest bedrooms on the second had individual fireplaces and private baths. The modern kitchen was fitted with butcherblock counters and track lighting. There was a small attached greenhouse.

The dining room was dominated by an impressive ten-foot table topped with a single plank of teak that looked thick enough to stop a cannonball.

There was no disguising the loving care (and money) that had gone into that home. Later, Delaney remarked to Monica that there wasn't a single piece of furniture, painting, rug, or bibelot that he didn't covet for his own.

But finally, what impressed the guests the most was the informal comfort: warm colors, glowing wood, gleaming brass and copper. It was easy to understand how such a place could serve as sanctuary from the steel and concrete city.

Looking around, Delaney could appreciate Dr. Diane's fury at her husband's murder and her desire for vengeance. For he knew that possessions charm most when shared with others, and thought it possible that since Dr. Simon's death, all those lovely things had begun to pall. Now they were just *things* to Diane Ellerbee.

The women bundled up to stroll across the patio and inspect the design of the formal English garden. Dr. Samuelson stayed close to the living room fire, but Delaney and Boone took a turn around the grounds, admiring the view and imagining what a gem this place would be in spring and summer.

They wandered down behind the main house, beyond the swimming pool and garden. Hands in their pockets, shoulders hunched, they tramped to a copse of bony trees. And there they saw the stream, looking black and cold, with a lacework of ice building out from both banks.

"Fish?" Abner Boone said. "D'you suppose?"

"Could be," Delaney said. "Depends on where it comes from. And where it ends up. I wonder if they swim in it in the summer."

He pried a small stone loose from the hard earth and tossed it into the water. But they could not judge its depth.

Back in the house, everyone had another drink and clustered around the fireplace. It was early afternoon, but already the day had grayed, the sun had lost its brilliance.

"I'm going to put out some hors d'oeuvres," Diane said. "Marta and Jan worked all morning on the food, but I let them go home. We can serve ourselves, can't we?"

"Of course," Delaney said with heavy good humor. "We're all housebroken. What can I do to help?"

"Not a thing," she said. "Just eat. Julie, give me a hand in the kitchen."

He followed her obediently.

There was a feast of appetizers: boiled shrimp, chunks of kielbasa, olives stuffed with peppers, sweet gherkins, smoked salmon and sturgeon, thick slices of sharp cheddar and Stilton, four different kinds of crackers and biscuits, chicken livers in a wine sauce, paper-thin slices of prosciutto, and brisling sardines in olive oil.

"Here goes my diet," Rebecca Boone said, sighing.

"Just remember to leave room for dinner," Diane said, laughing.

"Edward will do his share," Monica Delaney said. "He could live on food like this."

"Live and thrive," her husband agreed happily, sampling everything. "This salmon makes me believe in God."

Finally they were surfeited and sat back with glazed eyes, holding up hands in surrender.

"Julie," Diane Ellerbee said crisply, "let's clean up."

But Delaney was on his feet before Samuelson could struggle out of his armchair.

"It's my turn," he said to Samuelson. "You just sit there and relax. I'm good at this; Monica trained me."

So he and Diane cleaned up the living room, Delaney demonstrating his proficiency as a waiter with four or five plates laid along a steady, outthrust arm.

In the kitchen, he admired her efficiency. All the leftovers went into separate airtight containers. Plates and cutlery were rinsed in a trice and stacked in the dishwasher. She worked with quick grace, not a wasted movement.

She was wearing black cashmere—sweater and skirt—and her flaxen hair was coiled high and held in place with an exotic tortoiseshell comb. He saw her in profile and once again marveled at the classic perfection of her beauty: something chiseled—the stone cut away to reveal the image.

"Well!" she said brightly, looking at her aseptic, organized kitchen. "I think that does it. Thank you for your help. Shall we join the others?"

"A moment," he said, holding out a hand to stop her. "I think you deserve a report on what we've been doing."

She stared, the hostess's mask dropping, features hardening: the vengeful widow once again.

"Yes," she said. "Thank you. I was hoping you'd volunteer."

They sat close together on high stools at the butcherblock counter. They could hear soft conversation and laughter from the living room. But the kitchen provided a sense of secret intimacy as he told her what they'd learned.

"In my judgment," he concluded, "Kane and Otherton are clean. That leaves four of the patients you gave us. Their alibis are still being checked. It's a long, laborious process, and we are still left with the mysterious second set of footprints."

"What do you mean?" Diane said.

"There were apparently two visitors to your husband's office that night. At the same or different times? We don't know. Yet. Now I have a question for you: Were you surprised that your husband canceled all his patients' outstanding bills?"

She peered at him in the gloom, wide-eyed, her mouth open. "Oh," she said. "How did you find out about that?"

"Doctor Ellerbee," he said patiently, "this is a criminal investigation. Everything is important until proved otherwise. Naturally we were interested in the probate of your husband's will, hoping it might give us a lead. Were you surprised that he forgave his patients' debts?"

"No, I wasn't surprised. He was a very generous man. It was entirely in character for him to do something like that."

"Then you were aware of what was in his will before he died?"

"Of course. Just as he was aware of what was in my will. We had no secrets from each other."

"You and your late husband had the same attorney, did you?"

"No," she said, "as a matter of fact we didn't. Simon used an old college friend of his—a man I couldn't stand. I have my own attorney."

"Well, it isn't important," Delaney said, waving it away. "About those four patients we haven't yet cleared—did you ever meet them personally?"

"I met several of my husband's patients," she said. "Usually briefly, and by accident. Is there one in particular you want to know about?"

"Joan Yesell."

"The suicidal woman? Yes, I met her once. Why do you ask?"

"It's possible that she's given us a fake alibi. What was your take on her?"

"I only met her for a moment—hardly long enough to form an opinion. But I thought her a rather plain, unattractive woman. Not much spark to her. But as I say, it was just a brief meeting. My husband introduced her and that was that. And now I think we should join the others."

But before they went into the living room, she put a hand lightly on his arm.

"Thank you for keeping me informed, Mr. Delaney," she said huskily. "I know you're working very hard on this, and I appreciate it."

He nodded and held open the swinging kitchen door for her. She passed close to him and he caught her scent: something strong and musky that stirred him.

They came into the living room, where the other four sat logy with food and drink.

"Doctor Ellerbee," Delaney said, hoping to stir his friends. "Doctor Samuelson . . . did it ever occur to you that the roles of the detective and the psychiatrist are very similar? We both use the same investigative techniques: endless interrogation, the slow amassing of what may or may not be consequential clues, the piecing together of a puzzle until it forms a recognizable pattern. Psychiatrists are really detectives—are they not?"

Dr. Julius K. Samuelson straightened up, suddenly alert and interested.

"The techniques may be similar," he said in his high-pitched voice, "but the basic motives are antipodal. The detective is conducting a criminal investigation. He seeks to assign blame. But blame is not in the psychiatrist's lexicon. The patient cannot be punished for what he has become. He is usually a victim, not a criminal."

"You mean," Delaney said, deliberately provoking, "he is without guilt? What about a psychopath who kills? Is he totally guiltless?"

"I think," Diane said in assertive tones, "that what Julie is suggesting is that the act of murder is in itself prima facie evidence of mental or emotional instability."

"Oh-ho," Delaney said. "The poor lads and lasses who kill—all sick are they? To be treated rather than punished. And what of the man who molests children? Just a little ill, but blameless?"

"And what about the guy who kills for profit?" Sergeant Boone said hotly. "We see it all the time: Some innocent slugged down for a few bucks. Is the killer to go free because society hasn't provided him with a guaranteed income? You think a total welfare state will eliminate murder for profit? No way! People will continue to kill for money. Not because they're sick, but because they're greedy. Capital punishment is the best treatment."

"I don't believe in the death penalty," Rebecca Boone said stoutly.

"I agree," Diane said. "Execution is not the answer. Statistics prove it doesn't act as a deterrent."

"It sure as hell deters the guy who gets chopped," Delaney said. "He's not going to get paroled, go out, and kill again. The trouble with you psychiatrists is that you're as bad as priests: You think everyone can be redeemed. Tell them, Sergeant."

"Some people are born rotten and stay rotten the rest of their lives,"

Boone said. "Ask any cop. The cruds of this world are beyond redemption."

"Right!" Delaney said savagely. He turned to the two doctors. "What you won't admit is that some people are so morally corrupt that they cannot be helped. They accept evil as a way of life. They love it! They enjoy it! And the world is better off without them."

"What about someone who kills in passion?" Monica asked. "A sudden, uncontrollable passion."

"Temporary insanity?" Boone said. "Is that what you're pleading? It just won't wash. We're supposed to be *Homo sapiens*—wise, intelligent animals with a civilized rein on our primitive instincts. A crime of passion is a *crime*—period. And the reasons should have no effect on the verdict."

Then they all began to argue: blame, guilt, capital punishment, parole, the conflict between law and justice. Delaney sat back happily and listened to the brouhaha he had started. A good house party. Finally . . .

"Did you ever notice," he said, "that when a killer is nabbed bloody-handed, the defense attorney always goes for the insanity plea and hires a battery of 'friendly' psychiatrists?"

"And meanwhile," Boone added, "the accused announces to the world that he's become a born-again Christian and wants only to renounce his wicked ways and live a saintly life."

"You're too ready to find excuses for your patients," Delaney said to the two psychiatrists. "Won't you admit the existence of evil in the world? Would you say Hitler was evil or just mentally ill?"

"Both," Dr. Samuelson said. "His illness took the form of evil. But if it had been caught in time it could have been treated."

"Sure it could," Delaney said grimly. "A bullet to the brain would have been very effective."

The argument flared again and gradually centered on the problem of the "normal" person living a law-abiding existence who suddenly commits a totally inexplicable heinous crime.

"I had a case like that once," Delaney said. "A dentist in the Bronx . . . Apparently under no great emotional stress or business pressures. A quiet guy. A good citizen. But he started sniping at people from the roof of his apartment house. Killed two, wounded five. No one could explain why. I think he's still in the acorn academy. But I never thought he was insane. You'll laugh when I tell you what I think his motive was. I think he was just bored. His life was empty, lacked excitement. So he started popping people with his hunting rifle. It gave a kick to his existence."

"A very penetrating analysis," Samuelson said admiringly. "We call it anomie: a state of disorientation and isolation."

"But no excuse for killing," Delaney said. "There's never an excuse for that. He was an intelligent man; he knew what he was doing was wrong."

"Perhaps he couldn't help himself," Diane Ellerbee said. "That does happen, you know."

"No excuse," Delaney repeated stubbornly. "We all may have homicidal urges at some time in our lives, but we control them. If there is no self-discipline, then we're back in the jungle. Self-discipline is what civilization is all about."

Diane smiled faintly. "I'm afraid we're not all as strong as you."

"Strong? I'm a pussycat. Right, Monica?"

"I refuse to answer," she said, "on the grounds that I might incriminate myself."

Diane laughed and got up to prepare dinner. The women set out plates, glasses, thick pink napkins, and cutlery on linen place mats.

The Beef Bourguignonne was in two cast-iron Dutch ovens that had to be handled with thick asbestos mitts. Delaney and Boone carried the pots into the dining room and set them on trivets. Samuelson handled the salad bowl and baskets of hot, crusty French bread. Then Diane Ellerbee put out a '78 California cabernet sauvignon.

"That's beautiful," Delaney said, examining the label.

"The last of the last case," their hostess said sadly. "Simon and I loved it so much. We kept it for special occasions. Mr. Delaney, would you uncork the bottles?"

"My pleasure," he said. "All of them?"

"All," she said firmly. "Once you taste it, you'll know why."

They had plenty of room at the long table. The hostess sat at the head and filled plates with the stew, and small wooden bowls with the salad.

"It's heaven," Monica said. "Diane, you'll never make me believe this is stew meat."

"As a matter of fact, it's sirloin. Please, when you're ready for seconds, help yourself; I'm too busy eating."

They were all busy eating, but not too busy to keep the talk flowing. Abner Boone was seated next to Monica, and Rebecca was paired with Dr. Samuelson. Delaney sat on the right of the hostess.

"I hope," he said, leaning toward her, "you weren't upset by the conversation before dinner. All that talk about crime and punishment."

"I wasn't upset at all," she assured him. "I found it fascinating. So many viewpoints . . ."

"I was a little hard on psychiatrists," he admitted. "I'm really not that hostile toward your profession. I was just—"

"I know what you were just," she interrupted. "You were trying to get an argument started to wake everyone up. You succeeded brilliantly, and I'm grateful for it."

"That's me," he said with a wry smile. "The life of the party. One thing you said surprised me."

"Oh? What was that?"

"Your objection to capital punishment. After what you've been through, I'd have thought you'd be in favor of the death penalty."

"No," she said shortly, "I'm not. I want Simon's murderer caught and punished. To the limit of the law. But I don't believe in an eye for an eye or a life for a life."

He was saved from replying by Dr. Samuelson, who raised a hand and called in a squeaky voice, "A question!" They all quieted and turned to him. "Will anyone object if I sop up my gravy with chunks of this marvelous bread?"

There were no objections.

As the hostess had predicted, the wine went swiftly, and the stew and salad were almost totally consumed. Later, when the table was cleared, the women went into the kitchen, shooing the men back to the living room. The room had become chilly, and Samuelson added two more pressed logs to the fireplace.

"There's central heating, of course," he told the others, "but Diane prefers to keep the thermostat low and use the fireplaces."

"Can't blame her for that," Abner Boone said. "Saves on fuel, and an open fire is something special. But shouldn't she have a screen?"

"I think there's one around," Samuelson said vaguely, "but she doesn't use it."

They sat staring into the rejuvenated blaze.

"I was afraid we might have upset Doctor Ellerbee," Delaney said to Samuelson, "with all our talk about murders. But she says no."

"Diane is a very strong woman," Samuelson said. "She has made a very swift recovery from the trauma of Simon's death. Only occasionally now do I see how it has affected her. Suddenly she is sad, or sits in silence, staring at nothing. It is to be expected. It was a terrible shock, but she is coping."

"I suppose her work helps," Boone said.

"Oh, yes. Dealing with other people's problems is excellent therapy for your own. I speak from personal experience. Not a total cure, you understand, but a help. Tell me, Mr. Delaney, you are making progress in the investigation?"

"Some," he said cautiously. "As Doctor Ellerbee probably told you, we're still working on the alibis. I haven't yet thanked you for getting her to cooperate."

Samuelson held up a hand. "I was happy to assist. And do you think any of the patients she named might have been capable of the murder?"

"Too early to tell. We've eliminated two of them. But there's one, a woman, who claims an alibi that doesn't seem to hold up."

"Oh? Did Diane give you any background on her?"

"Suffers from depression. And she has attempted suicide several times. Once since we started questioning her."

"Well . . ." the psychiatrist said doubtfully, "she may be the one you seek, but I find it hard to believe. I can't recall a case when a suicidal type turned to homicide. I am not saying it could not happen, you understand, but the potential suicide and the potential murderer have little in common. Still, human behavior is endlessly different, so do not let my comments influence your investigation."

"Oh, they won't," Delaney said cheerfully. "We'll keep plugging."

The women came in, and the men rose. They talked for a while, and then, catching Monica's look, Delaney suggested it might be time for them to depart, not knowing what traffic would be like on Saturday night. The hostess protested—but not too strongly.

They thanked Dr. Ellerbee for her hospitality, the wonderful food, and complimented her again on her beautiful home.

"Do plan to come back," she urged them. "In the spring or summer when the trees are out and the garden is planted. I think you'll like it."

"I know we shall," Monica said. She and Rebecca embraced their hostess and they were on their way.

On the drive back to Manhattan, Delaney said, "Do you suppose Samuelson is staying for the weekend?"

"You dirty old man," Monica said. "What if he does?"

"She's got three servants," Abner Boone said. "The Polack couple and him."

"Oh, you picked up on that, did you?" Delaney said. "You're right. 'Julie, mix the drinks. Julie, get the coffee.' He hops."

"I think he's in love with her," Rebecca said.

"Well, why not?" Monica said. "A widow and a widower. With so much in common. I think it's nice they have each other."

"He's too old for her," the Sergeant said.

"You think so?" Delaney said. "I think she's older than all of us. Good Lord, that's a grand home!"

"A little *too* beautiful," Rebecca said. "Like a stage set. Did you notice how she kept emptying the ashtrays?"

"If it's full ashtrays you want," Delaney said, "how about stopping at our place for a nightcap?"

# 21.

Detective Ross Konigsbacher had to admit he was enjoying the best duty in fourteen years with the Department. This faggot he was assigned to, L. Vincent Symington, was turning out to be not such a bad guy after all.

He seemed to have all the money in the world, and wasn't shy about spreading it around. He picked up all the tabs for dinners and drinks, and insisted on taking cabs wherever they went—even if it was only a five-block trip. He was a manic tipper, and he had already started buying gifts for the Kraut.

It began with a bottle of Frangelico that Vince wanted him to taste. Then Ross got an identification bracelet of heavy silver links, a cashmere pullover, a Countess Mara tie, a lizard skin belt, a foulard ascot. Every time they met, Symington had a present for him.

Ross had been invited to Vincent's apartment twice, and thought it the greatest pad he had ever seen. On one of those visits, Symington had prepared dinner for them—filet mignon that had to be the best steak Konigsbacher ever tasted.

Meanwhile, the Kraut was submitting bullshit reports to Sergeant Boone, wanting this assignment to go on forever. But Boone couldn't be scammed that easily, and recently he had been pressuring Konigsbacher to show some results: Either confirm Symington's alibi or reject it. So, sighing, Ross did some work.

The first time he went into Stallions, he bellied up to the bar, ordered a beer, and looked around. Symington had been right: He had never seen so much black leather in his life. All the weirdos were trying to look like members of motorcycle gangs. Their costumes creaked when they moved, and they even had zippers on their cuffs.

"Nick been around?" he asked the hennaed bartender casually.

"Nick who, darling? I know three Nicks."

"The kid who wants to be an actor."

"Oh, *him.* He's in and out of here all the time."

"I'm casting for a commercial and might have a bit for him. If you see him, tell him, will you?"

"How can he get in touch with you, sweet?"

"My name is Ross," Konigsbacher said. "I'll be around."

The bartender nodded. No last names, no addresses, no phone numbers.

The Kraut spent more time at Stallions than he did at home. He slowly sipped beers in the late afternoons and early evenings before his dinner dates with Symington. He began to like the place. You could get high just by breathing deeply, and if the Kraut wanted to set a record for drug busts, he could have made a career out of this one joint.

It took him five days. He was sitting at a small corner table, working on a brew, when a kid came over from the bar and lounged in front of him. He had a 1950 duck's-ass haircut with enough grease to lubricate the *QE2.* He was wearing tight stone-washed jeans, a T-shirt with the sleeves cut off, and a wide leather bracelet with steel studs.

"You Ross?" he asked lazily, eyes half-closed, doing an early Marlon Brando.

"Yeah," the Kraut said, touching a knuckle to his blond mustache. "You Nick?"

"I could be. Sidney pointed you out. Something about a commercial bit."

"Pull up a chair. Want a beer? Or would you prefer a banana brandy?"

Then the kid's eyes opened wide. "How'd you know what I drink?"

"A fegela told me. You know what a fegela is? A little bird. Now sit down."

Nick hesitated a moment, then pulled up a chair.

"You don't look like a film producer to me," he said.

"I'm not," Konigsbacher said. "I'm a cop." Then, when Nick started to rise, the Kraut clamped onto his wrist and pulled him down again. "Be nice," he said. "You're carrying a switchblade on your hip. It shows. I could run you in on a concealed weapons charge. It probably wouldn't stick, but it would be a pain in the ass for you and maybe a night in the slammer where the boogies will ream you. Is that what you want?"

The kid had moxie; he didn't cave.

"Let's see your ID," he said coldly.

Konigsbacher showed it to him, down low, so no one else in the bar would notice.

"Okay," Nick said, "so you're a cop. What do you want?"

Symington was also right about the accent; it came out "waddya wan'?"

"Just the answers to a few questions. Won't take long. Do you remember a Friday night early in November? There was a hell of a rainstorm. You were in here that night."

"You asking me or telling me?"

"I'm asking. A rainy Friday night early in November. A guy came in, sat with you, bought you a few banana brandies. This was about nine, ten o'clock. Around there."

"Yeah? What'd he look like?"

Konigsbacher described L. Vincent Symington: balding, flabby face, little eyes. A guy running to suet, probably wearing a bracelet of chunky gold links.

"What's he done?" Nick asked.

"Do you remember a guy like that?" Ross asked patiently.

"I don't know," the kid said, shrugging. "I meet a lot of guys."

The Kraut leaned forward, smiling. "Now I tell you what, sonny," he said in a low, confidential voice, "you keep smart-assing me, I'm going to put the cuffs on you and frog-march you out of here. But I won't take you to the station house. I'll take you into the nearest alley and kick your balls so hard that you'll be singing soprano for the rest of your life. You don't believe it? Just try me."

"Yeah, I met a guy like that," Nick said sullenly. "A fat old fart. He bought me some drinks."

"What was his name?"

"I don't remember."

"Try," Ross urged. "Remember what I said about the alley, and try real hard."

"Victor," the kid said.

"Try again."

"Vince. Something like that."

Konigsbacher patted his cheek. "Good boy," he said.

As far as the Kraut was concerned, that was enough to clear L. Vincent Symington. He had never believed in the poof's guilt in the first

place. Vince could never kill anyone with a hammer. A knife maybe—a
woman's weapon. But not a hammer.

So, Konigsbacher thought sadly, that was the end of that. He'd submit a report to Boone and they'd shift him to some shit assignment. No
more cashmere sweaters and free dinners and lazy evenings sitting
around Symington's swell apartment, soaking up his booze and trading
dirty jokes.

But maybe, the Kraut thought suddenly, just maybe there was a way
he could juggle it. He would clear Symington—he owed the guy that—
but it didn't mean the gravy train had to come to a screaming halt.
Confident again, he headed for dinner at the Dorian Gray, wondering
what Vince would bring him tonight.


Robert Keisman and Jason thought Harold Gerber might be a
whacko, but he was innocent of the murder of Dr. Simon Ellerbee.
Gerber's confession was what Keisman called a "blivet"—four pounds
of shit in a two-pound bag.

The Vietnam vet just didn't know enough of the unpublished details
to fake a convincing confession. But Delaney wanted the guy's innocence proved out one way or another, and that's what the two cops set
out to do.

The Catholic Bible was a flimsy lead. They had no gut reaction one
way or the other. The only reason they worked at it was that they had
nothing else. It was just something to do.

They started with the Manhattan Yellow Pages and found the section
for Churches—Roman Catholic. There were 103 listings, some of them
with odd names like Most Precious Blood Church and Our Lady of
Perpetual Help. The thought of visiting 103 churches was daunting, but
when they picked out the ones in the Greenwich Village area, the job
didn't seem so enormous.

The Spoiler took the churches to the east of Sixth Avenue and Jason
Two took those to the west. Carrying their photos of Harold Gerber,
they set out to talk to priests, rectors, janitors, and anyone else who
might have seen Gerber on the night Ellerbee was murdered.

It was the dullest of donkeywork: pounding the pavements, showing
their ID, displaying Gerber's photograph, and asking the same questions over and over: "Do you know this man? Have you ever seen him?
Has he been in your church? Does the name Harold Gerber mean
anything to you?"

Sometimes the church would be locked, no one around, and Keisman and Jason would have to go back two or three times before they could find someone to question. They worked eight-hour days and met after five o'clock to have a couple of beers with Harold Gerber. They never told him what they were doing, and he always asked complainingly, "When are you guys going to arrest me?"

"Soon, Harold," they'd tell him. "Soon."

They kept at it for four days, and were beginning to think they were drilling a dry hole. But then the Spoiler got a break. He was talking to a man who worked in an elegant little church on 11th Street off Fifth Avenue. The old man seemed to be a kind of handyman who polished pews and made sure the electric candles were working—jobs like that.

He examined Keisman's ID, then stared at the photo of Harold Gerber.

"What's he wanted for?" he asked in a creaky voice.

"He's not wanted for anything," the Spoiler lied smoothly. "We're just trying to find him. He's in the Missing Persons file. His parents are anxious. You can understand that, can't you?"

"Oh, sure," the gaffer said, still staring at Gerber's photo. "I've got a son of my own; I know how they'd feel. What does this kid do?"

"Do?"

"His job. What does he work at?"

"I don't think he works at anything. He's on disability. A Vietnam vet. A little mixed up in the head."

"That I can understand. A Vietnam veteran you say?"

"Uh-huh."

"And he's a Catlick?"

"That's right."

"Well," the handyman said, sighing. "I'll tell you. There's a priest—well, he's not really a priest. I don't mean he's unfrocked or anything like that. But he's kind of wild, and he's got no parish of his own. They more or less let him do his thing, if you catch my drift."

Keisman nodded, waiting patiently.

"Well, this priest," the janitor went on, enjoying his long story more than the Spoiler was, "Father Gautier, or Grollier, some name like that —he opened a home for Vietnam vets. Gives them a sandwich, a place to flop, or just come in out of the cold. I'm not knocking him, y'understand; he's doing good. But he's running a kind of scruffy joint. It's not a regular church."

"Where does he get the money?" the detective asked. "For the sandwiches, the beds, or whatever? The Church finance him?"

"You kidding? He does it all on his own. He gets donations from here, there, everywhere. Somehow he keeps going."

"That's interesting," Keisman said. "Where's his place located?"

"I don't know," the old guy said. "Somewhere south of Houston Street, I think. But I don't know the address."

"Thank you very much," the Spoiler said.

He told Jason about the priest, and they agreed it was the best lead— the *only* lead—they had uncovered so far. So they started making phone calls.

They phoned the Archdiocese of New York, the Catholic Press Association, Catholic Charities, the American Legion, asking if anyone knew the address of a Catholic priest who was running a shelter for Vietnam vets somewhere around Houston Street in Manhattan. No one could help them.

Then they called the Catholic War Veterans and got it: Father Frank Gautier, in a storefront church on Mott Street, a block south of Houston.

"Little Italy," Jason said. "I used to pound a beat down there."

"Wherever," Keisman said. "Let's go."

They found the place after asking four residents of the neighborhood. It looked like a Mafia social club, the plate-glass window painted an opaque green, and no name or signs showing. The door was unlocked and they pushed in. There was a big front room that looked like it might have been a butcher shop at one time: tiled walls, a stained plank floor, tin ceiling.

But it was warm enough. Almost too warm. There were about a dozen guys, maybe half of them blacks, sitting around on rickety chairs, reading paperbacks, playing cards, dozing, or just counting the walls. They all looked like derelicts, with unlaced boots, worn jeans, ragged jackets. One was in drag, with a blond wig and a feathered boa.

No one looked up when the two officers came in. Keisman stood close to a man holding a month-old copy of *The Wall Street Journal.*

"Father Gautier around?" he asked pleasantly.

The man looked up, slowly examined both of them, then turned to a back room.

"Hey, pop!" he roared. "Two new fish for you!"

The man who came waddling out of the back room was shaped like a ripe pear. He was wearing a long-sleeved black blouse with a white, somewhat soiled clerical collar. His blue Levi's were cinched with a cowboy belt and ornate silver buckle. He was bearded and had a thick mop of pepper-and-salt hair.

"Father Gautier?" Jason asked.

"Guilty," the priest said in a hoarse voice. "Who you?"

They showed him their IDs.

"Oh, God," he said, sighing, "now what? Who did what to whom?"

"No one we know of," Keisman said. He held out the photo of Harold Gerber. "You know this man?"

Gautier looked at the photograph, then raised his eyes to the officers. "You got any money?" he demanded.

They were startled.

"Money!" the priest repeated impatiently. "Dough. Bucks. You want information? No pay, no say. Believe me, it's for a good cause. You'll get your reward in heaven—or wherever."

Sheepishly Jason and Keisman pulled out their wallets. They each proffered a five. Gautier grabbed the bills eagerly.

"You, Izzy!" he yelled at one of the lounging blacks. "Take this to Vic's and get us a ham. Tell him it's for us, and if it has as much fat on it as the last one, we'll come over there and trash his place. Bone in."

"Yassa, massa," the black said, touching a finger to his forehead.

"You two come with me," the Father said, and led the way into the back room. He took them into a cluttered office hardly larger than a walk-in closet. He closed the door, turned to face them.

"Yeah, I know him," he said. "Harold Gerber. What's he done?"

"Nothing we know for sure," the Spoiler said. "We're just trying to establish his whereabouts on a certain Friday night."

"He was here," Gautier said promptly.

"Hey," Jason said, "wait a minute. We haven't told you *which* Friday night."

The priest shook his head. "Doesn't make any difference. Harold is here *every* Friday night. Has been for more than a year now."

The two officers looked at each other, then back to the priest.

"Why Friday nights?" Keisman asked.

Gautier stared at him fixedly. "Because I hear confessions on Friday nights."

"You trying to tell us," Jason said, "that Gerber has been confessing to you every Friday night for more than a year?"

"I'm not *trying* to tell you, I *am* telling you. Every Friday night. Take it or leave it. If you don't believe me, I'll put on a damned cassock, go into a court of law, and swear by Almighty God I'm telling the truth."

"I don't think that'll be necessary, Father," Keisman said. "What time does he usually get here?"

"Around nine o'clock. I hear confessions from eight to ten. Then he usually sits around awhile, bullshitting with the boys. If he can spare it, he leaves a couple of bucks."

"No disrespect to you, Father," Jason said, "but the guy was going to a psychiatrist."

"I know he was. I'm the one who convinced him to get professional help."

"So if he was going to a shrink, what did he need you for?"

"He was brought up a Catholic," Frank Gautier said. "You don't shake it easily."

"You think he was making progress?" the Spoiler asked.

The priest got angry. "Are you making progress? Am I making progress? What's this making progress shit? We're all just trying to survive, aren't we?"

"I guess we are at that," Jason said softly. "Thank you for your time, Father. I think we got what we came for."

At the door, Keisman turned back. "Who does the cooking around here?" he asked.

"I do," the priest said. "Why do you think I'm so fat? I sample."

Jason Two smiled and raised a pink palm. "Peace be unto you, brother," he said.

"And peace be unto you," Gautier said seriously. "Thanks for the ham. You saved us from another night of peanut butter sandwiches."

Outside, walking back to the car, Jason Two said, "Nice guy. You think he's lying? Protecting one of his boys?"

"I doubt he *can* lie," Keisman said. "I think that Gerber is doing exactly what Gautier said—confessing his sins every Friday night."

"Crazy world," Jason said.

"And getting crazier every day. Will you do the report for Delaney?"

"Sure. Tonight. What do you want to do right now?"

"Let's go back and have a beer or two with Gerber. That poor slob."

Detective Benjamin Calazo sat lumpishly in the rancid lobby of the fleabag hotel on West 23rd Street, waiting for Betty Lee, the Chinese hooker, to return from her daily visit to her mother. Mama-san lived down on Pell Street and looked to be a hundred years old at least.

Calazo had been tailing Betty for four days and thought he had her time-habit pattern down pat. Left the hotel around 9:00 A.M., had coffee and a buttered bagel at a local deli, then cabbed down to Chinatown. Spent the morning with Mama, sometimes bringing her flowers or a Peking duck. A good daughter.

Then back to the hotel by noon. The first john would arrive soon after—probably a guy on his lunch hour. Then there would be a steady parade until three or four o'clock, when business would slack off and Betty would go out to dinner. Things picked up again after five o'clock and continued good until two in the morning.

Betty wasn't pounding the pavements as far as Calazo could tell. She had a regular clientele, mostly older guys with potbellies and cigars. There were also a few furtive young kids who rushed in and out, looking around nervously like they expected to get busted at any minute.

Betty Lee herself was far from what Benny Calazo envisioned as the ideal whore. She was dumpy and looked like she bought her clothes in a thrift shop. But she must have had something on the ball to attract all those johns. Maybe, Calazo mused idly, she did cute things with chopsticks—it was possible.

She came into the hotel lobby. Benny folded his *Post,* heaved himself to his feet, and followed her into the cage elevator. They started up. He knew her room was 8-D.

"Good morning," he said to her pleasantly.

She gave him a faint smile but said nothing.

When she got off on the eighth floor, he followed her down the hall to her door. She whirled and confronted him.

"Get lost," she said sharply.

He showed her his shield and ID.

"Oh, shit," she said wearily. "Again? Okay. How much?"

"I don't want any grease, Betty."

"A nice blowjob?" she said hopefully.

He laughed. "Just a few minutes of your time."

"I got a client in fifteen minutes."

"Let him wait. We going to discuss your business in the hall or are you going to invite me in?"

Her little apartment was surprisingly neat, clean, tidy. Everything dusted, everything polished. There was a small refrigerator, waist-high, and a framed photograph of John F. Kennedy over the bed. Calazo couldn't figure that.

"You like a beer?" she asked him.

"That would be fine," he said gratefully. "Thank you."

She got him a cold Bud, one of the tall ones. He sat there in his

overcoat and old fedora, so worn that there was a hole in the front at
the triangular crease.

"Betty," he said, "you got a nice thing going here. You take care of
the locals?"

"Of course," she said, astonished that he would ask such a question.
"And the prick behind the lobby desk. And the alkie manager. How
else could I operate?"

"Yeah," he said, "it figures. I've been checking you the last three or
four days. Regulars mostly, aren't they?"

"Mostly. Some walk-in trade. Friends of friends."

"Sure, I understand. You got a regular named Ronald Bellsey?"

"I don't ask last names."

"All right, let's concentrate on Ronald. Comes in two afternoons a
week. A chunky guy, an ex-pug."

"Maybe," she said cautiously.

"What kind of a guy is he?"

"He's a pig!" she burst out.

"Sure he is," Calazo said cheerfully. "Likes to hurt you, doesn't he?"

"How did you know that?"

"That's the kind of guy he is. I want to take him, Betty. With your
help."

"Take him? You mean arrest him?"

"No."

"Kill him?"

"No. Just teach him to straighten up and fly right."

"You want to do that here?"

"That's right."

"He'll kill me," she said. "You take him here and you *don't* kill him,
he'll come back and kill *me.*"

"I don't think so," Detective Calazo said. "I think that after I get
through with him, he'll stay as far away from you as he can get. So
you'll lose one customer—big deal."

"I don't like it," she said.

"Betty, I don't see where you have any choice. I don't want to close
you down, I really don't, though I could do it. All I want to do is
punish this scumbag. If he does come back, you can always tell him the
cops made you do it."

She thought about it a long time. She went to the small refrigerator
and poured herself a glass of sweet wine. Calazo waited patiently.

"If he gets too heavy," Betty Lee said finally, "I could always go to Baltimore for a while. I got a sister down there. She's in the game, too."

"Sure you could," the detective said, "but believe me, he's not going to come on heavy. Not after I get through with him."

She took a deep breath. "How do you want to handle it?" she asked him.

He told her. She listened carefully.

"It should work," she said. "Give it to him good."

Detectives Venable and Estrella walked in on Mrs. Gladys Ferguson without calling first. They didn't want her phoning Mrs. Yesell and saying something like: "Blanche, two police officers are coming to ask me about you and our bridge club. What on earth is going on?"

Mrs. Ferguson turned out to be a tall, dignified lady who had to be pushing eighty. She walked with a cane, and one of her shoes had a built-up sole, about three inches thick. She was polite enough to the two cops after they identified themselves, but cool and aloof.

"Ma'am," Estrella started, "we'd like to ask you a few questions in connection with a criminal investigation we're conducting. Your answers could be very important. I'm sure you'll want to cooperate."

"What kind of a criminal investigation?" she asked. "Into what? I've had nothing to do with any crime."

"I'm sure you haven't," Detective Estrella said. "This involves the whereabouts of witnesses on a night a crime was committed."

She stared at him. "And that's all you're going to tell me?"

"I'm afraid it is."

"Will I be called to testify?" she said sharply. "At a trial?"

"Oh, no," Detective Helen Venable said hastily. "It's really not a sworn statement we want from you or anything like that. Just information."

"Very well then. What is it you wish to know?"

"Mrs. Ferguson," Estrella said, "are you a member of a bridge club that meets on Friday nights?"

Her composure was tried, but it held. "What on earth," she said in magisterial tones, "does my bridge club have to do with any criminal activity?"

"Ma'am," Helen said, beginning to get teed off, "if you keep asking *us* questions, we're going to be here all day. It'll be a lot easier for all of us if you just answer our questions. Are you a member of a bridge club that meets on Friday nights?"

"I am."

Estrella: *"Every* Friday night?"

"That is correct."

Venable: "How long has this club been meeting?"

"Almost five years now. We started with two tables. But members died or moved away. Now we're down to one."

Estrella: "And you've never missed a single Friday night in those five years?"

"Never. We're very proud of that."

Venable: "Have all the current members of the club been together for five years?"

"No. There have been several changes. But the four of us have been playing together for—oh, I'd say about two years."

Estrella: "I presume you rotate as hostesses. The game is held at a different home each Friday?"

"That is correct. I wish you would tell me exactly what you're trying to get at."

Estrella: "Do you recall a Friday night early in November this year? There was a tremendous rainstorm—one of the worst we've ever had."

"There's nothing wrong with my memory, young man. I remember that night very well."

Venable: "In spite of the dreadful weather, your bridge club met?"

"You're not listening to me, young lady. I *told* you we have not missed a single Friday night in almost five years."

Estrella: "And at whose home was the game that particular night?"

"Right here. That is one of the reasons I remember it so clearly. It was supposed to be held at the home of another member. But the weather was so miserable, I called the others and asked if they'd mind coming to me." She tapped her built-up shoe with her cane. "Because of this, I don't navigate too well in foul weather. The other members kindly agreed to come here. It wasn't a great imposition; they all live within two blocks."

Venable: "At whose home was the game originally scheduled?"

"Mrs. Blanche Yesell."

Venable: "But she came here instead?"

"Must I repeat everything twice?" Mrs. Gladys Ferguson said testily. "Yes, she came here instead, as did the others."

Estrella: "We just want to make certain we understand your answers completely, Mrs. Ferguson. What time do you ladies usually meet?"

"The game starts at eight-thirty, promptly. The members usually arrive a little before that. We end at ten-thirty, exactly. Then the hostess serves tea and coffee with cookies or a cake. Everyone usually departs around eleven o'clock."

Detective Venable took out her notebook. "We already know that you and Mrs. Blanche Yesell are two of the members. Could you give us the names and addresses of the other two?"

"Is that absolutely necessary?"

Estrella: "Yes, it is. You'll be assisting in the investigation of a violent crime."

"That's hard to believe—the Four Musketeers involved in a violent crime. That's what we call ourselves: the Four Musketeers."

Venable: "The names and addresses, please."

The detectives spent the next two days questioning the other two members of the club. They were both elderly widows of obvious probity. They corroborated everything that Mrs. Gladys Ferguson had stated.

"Well," Estrella said, staring at his opened notebook, "unless the Four Musketeers are the greatest criminal minds since the James Gang, it looks like Mrs. Yesell is lying in her teeth. She wasn't home that night, and her daughter is still on the hook."

"Son of a bitch!" Helen Venable said bitterly. "I still can't believe Joan was the murderer. Brian, she's just not the type."

"What type is that?" he asked mildly. "She's human, isn't she? So she's capable."

"But *why?* She keeps saying how much she admired the doctor."

"Who knows why?" he said, shrugging. "We'll let Delaney figure that out. Let's go up to Midtown North and borrow a typewriter. We'll work on the report together. I'd like to get it to Sergeant Boone tonight. I have a heavy date with a Ouija board."

"And I was going to share an apartment with her," Venable mourned.

"Count yourself lucky," Estrella advised. "You could have picked Jack the Ripper."

# 22.

"I hope you have some good news for me," First Deputy Commissioner Ivar Thorsen said. "I sure could use some."

The Admiral was slumped in a leather club chair in the study, gripping a beaker of Glenfiddich and water, staring into it as if it might contain the answers to all his questions.

"Ivar, you look like you've been through a meat grinder," Delaney said from behind his cluttered desk.

"Something like that," Thorsen said wearily. "A tough day. But they're all tough. If you can't stand the heat, get out of the kitchen. Isn't that what they say?"

"That's what they say," Delaney agreed. "Only you happen to like the kitchen."

"I suppose so," the Deputy said, sighing. "Otherwise why would I be doing it? When I leave here, I've got to get over to the Waldorf—a testimonial party for a retiring Assistant DA. Then back downtown for a meeting with the Commish and a couple of guys from the Mayor's office. We're getting a budget bump, thank God, and the problem is how to spend it."

"That's easy. More street cops."

"Sure, but who gets the jobs—and where? Every borough is screaming for more."

"You'll work it out."

"I suppose so—eventually. But to get back to my original question—any good news?"

"Well . . ." Delaney said, "there have been developments. Whether they're good or not, I don't know. So far we've eliminated four of the patients: Kane, Otherton, Gerber, and Symington. Some good detective work there—and some luck. Anyway their alibis have been proved out —to my satisfaction at least."

"But you've still got two suspects?"

"Two *possible* suspects. One is Ronald Bellsey, a nasty brute of a man. Detective Calazo is working on him. In his last report, Calazo says he hoped to have definite word on Bellsey within a few days. Calazo is an old cop, very thorough, very experienced. I trust him.

"The other possible suspect, more interesting, is Joan Yesell, suicidal and suffering from depression. Her mother claims she was home at the time of the murder. Detectives Venable and Estrella have definitely proved the mother is lying. She was somewhere else and can't possibly alibi her daughter."

"You're going to pick them up?"

"Mother and daughter? No, not yet. I've switched everyone except Calazo to round-the-clock surveillance of the daughter. Meanwhile we're digging into her background and trying to trace her movements on the day of the murder."

"Why do you think the mother lied?"

"Obviously to protect the daughter. So she must have some guilty knowledge. But it doesn't necessarily have anything to do with Ellerbee's death. Joan Yesell could have been shacked up with a boyfriend, and the mother is lying to protect her reputation—or the boyfriend's."

Thorsen took a gulp of his drink and regarded the other man closely.

"Yes, that's possible. But you have that look about you, Edward—the end-of-the-trail look, a kind of suppressed excitement. You really think this Joan Yesell is involved, don't you?"

"I don't want to get your hopes up too high, but yes, there's something that's not kosher there. I've spent all afternoon digging through the files, pulling out every mention of the woman. Some of the stuff that seems innocent on first reading takes on a new meaning when you think of her as a killer. For instance, right after Boone and I questioned her for the first time, she attempted suicide. That could be interpreted as guilt."

"What would be her motive?"

"Ivar, we're dealing with emotionally disturbed people here, and ordinary motives don't necessarily hold. Maybe the doctor uncovered something in Yesell's past so painful that she couldn't face it and couldn't endure the thought of Ellerbee knowing it. So she offed him."

"That's possible, I suppose. Sooner or later you're going to have to confront her, aren't you?"

"No doubt about that," Delaney said grimly. "And the mother, too. But I want to do my homework first—learn all I can about Joan and her movements on the murder night. Maybe she really was with a boyfriend. If so, we'll find out."

"Meanwhile," Deputy Thorsen said, "the clock is running out. Ten days to the end of the year, Edward. That's when the PC selects his Chief of Detectives."

Delaney took a packet of cigars from his desk drawer, held it out to the Admiral. But the Deputy shook his head. Delaney lighted up, using a gold Dunhill cutter his first wife had given him as a birthday present twenty years ago.

"At least," he said, puffing, "this investigation has taken the heat off the Department. Right? You're not getting pressure from the victim's widow and father anymore, are you? And I haven't seen anything on the case in the papers for two weeks."

"I'd like to see something in the papers," Thorsen said. "A headline like: COPS SOLVE ELLERBEE MURDER. That would be a big help to Suarez."

"How's he doing? I haven't spoken to him for a while. Maybe I'll give him a call tonight."

"He's a better administrator than he is a detective. But I suppose you saw that, Edward."

"Well, we've still got ten days. For what it's worth, I believe we'll clear it before the end of the year, or the thing will just drag on and on with decreasing hopes for a solution."

"Don't say that," the Deputy said, groaning. "Don't even suggest it. Well, thank you for your hospitality; I've got to start running again."

"Before you go, Ivar, tell me something—how are your relations with the DA's office?"

"The Department's relations or mine, personally?"

"Yours, personally."

"Pretty good. They owe me some favors. Why do you ask?"

"I have a feeling that if we can pin the killing on Ronald Bellsey or Joan Yesell, there's not going to be much hard evidence. All circumstantial. Would the DA take the case, knowing the chances of a conviction would be iffy?"

"Now you're opening a whole new can of worms," Thorsen said cautiously. "Ordinarily I'd say no. But this homicide attracted so much attention that they might be willing to take a chance just for the publicity. They're as eager for good media coverage as we are."

Delaney nodded. "Well, you might sound them out. Just to get their reaction."

Thorsen stared at the other man fixedly. "Edward, you think this Joan Yesell could be it?"

"At the moment," Delaney said, "she and Ronald Bellsey are all we've got. Light a candle, Ivar."

"One candle? I'll set fire to the whole church."

After the Deputy departed, Delaney returned to his study and called Suarez. But the Chief wasn't home. Delaney chatted a few minutes with Rosa, wishing her a Merry Christmas, and asked her to tell her husband that he had called—nothing important.

Then he went back to the stack of reports on Ronald Bellsey. According to Calazo, the subject was a prime suspect in four brutal beatings in the vicinity of Bellsey's hangouts.

Add to that Delaney's personal reactions to the man, and you had a picture of a thug who got his jollies by pounding on weaker men, including Detective Timothy Hogan. There was little doubt that Bellsey was a sadistic psychopath. The question remained: Was he a homicidal psychopath?

Uncertainties gnawed. Would a loco who derived pleasure from punishing another human being with his fists and boots resort to hammer blows to kill? If Ellerbee had been beaten and kicked to death, Delaney would have been surer that Bellsey was the killer.

He groaned aloud, realizing what he was doing: applying logic to a guy who acted irrationally. You couldn't do that; you had to adopt the subject's own illogic. Once Delaney did that, he could admit that Bellsey might use a ball peen hammer, an icepick, or kill with a bulldozer if the madness was on him.

Joan Yesell might be suicidal and depressed, but she didn't seem to share Bellsey's mania for wild violence. But who knew what passions were cloaked by that timid, subdued persona she presented to the world? Outside: Mary Poppins; inside: Lizzie Borden.

Between the two of them, Delaney leaned toward Yesell as the more likely suspect, but only because her alibi had been broken.

He knew full well how thin all this was. If he wanted to be absolutely honest, he'd have to admit he was no closer to clearing the Ellerbee homicide than he had been on the evening of Thorsen's first visit.

He looked at his littered desk, at the open file cabinet overflowing with reports, notes, interrogations: all those muddled lives. All that confusion of wants, fears, frustrations, hates.

He thrust his hands deep into his pockets and went lumbering into the living room where Monica sat reading the latest Germaine Greer book.

"What's wrong, Edward?" she asked, peering over her glasses and catching his mood.

"We're all such shitheads!" he burst out. "Every one of us gouging our way through life fighting and scrambling. Not one single, solitary soul knowing what the fuck is going on."

"Edward, why are you so upset? Because life is disordered and chaotic?"

"I suppose so," he muttered.

"Well, that's your job, isn't it? Making sense of things. Finding the logic, the sequence, the connecting links?"

"I suppose so," he repeated. "To make sense out of the senseless. Up at Diane Ellerbee's place, I said detectives are a lot like psychiatrists—and so we are. But psychiatrists have dear old Doctor Freud and a lot of clinical research to help them. Detectives have percentages and experience—and that's about it. And detectives have to analyze a dozen people in a single case. Like this Ellerbee thing . . . I feel like giving up and telling Ivar I just can't hack it."

"No," she said, "I don't think you'll do that. You have too much pride. I can't believe you're going to give up."

"Nah," he said, kicking at the carpet. "I'm not going to do that. It's just that someone—the murderer—is playing with me, jerking me around, and I can't stand that. It infuriates me that I can't identify the killer. It offends my sense of decency."

"And of order," she added.

"That, too," he agreed. He laughed shortly. "Goddamn it, I don't know what to do next!"

"Why don't you have a sandwich," she suggested.

"Good idea," he said.

On that same evening, Detective Ross Konigsbacher was lounging on Symington's long sectional couch. He was dragging on one of Vince's homemade cigarettes and sipping Asti Spumante.

"No one drinks champagne anymore," Symington had said. "Asti Spumante is *in.*"

So the Kraut was feeling like a jet-setter, with his pot and *in* drink.

He was also feeling virtuous because he had filed a report clearing Vincent of any complicity in the murder of Dr. Simon Ellerbee. That had been his official duty. And, as he had anticipated, he had been rewarded by being shifted to a shit detail—spending eight hours that day sitting in a car outside the Yesells' home waiting for Joan to come out. She hadn't.

"A great meal, Vince," he said dreamily. "I really enjoyed it."

"I thought you'd like the place," Symington said. "Wasn't that smoked goose breast *divine?*"

When they had returned to the apartment after dinner, Vince had changed into a peach-colored velour jumpsuit with a wide zipper from gullet to crotch.

"And that silk underwear," Konigsbacher remembered. "Thank you *so* much. You've been so good to me, Vince. I want you to know I appreciate it."

Symington waved a hand. "That's what friends are for. We *are* friends, aren't we?"

"Sure we are," the Kraut said. And because he felt himself hazing from the grass and all the booze they'd had that night, he figured he better make his pitch while he was still conscious.

"Vince," he said, "I've got a confession to make to you. I know you're going to *hate* me for it, but I've got to do it."

"I won't hate you," Symington said, "no matter what it is."

"You better hear me first. Vince, I'm a cop, a detective assigned to check you out on the Ellerbee kill. Here—here's my ID."

He fished out his wallet. Symington looked at the shield and card.

"Oh, Ross," he said in a choked voice, "how *could* you?"

"It was my *job,*" the Kraut said earnestly. "To get close to you and learn your movements the night of the murder. I admit that when I started, I really thought of you as a suspect. But as I got to know you, Vince, I realized that you're completely incapable of a vicious act of violence like that."

"Thank you, Ross," Symington said in a low voice.

"But," Konigsbacher said, taking a deep breath, "you stated you had left the party at the Hilton about the time Ellerbee was killed."

"Only for a little while," Symington said nervously. "Just to get a breath of air. I told you where I went, Ross."

"I know, I know," the detective said, patting one of Vince's pudgy hands. "But you can see how it complicates things."

Symington nodded dumbly.

"It was a serious problem for me, Vince. I knew you were innocent. My problem was whether or not to report that you had left the Hilton. I worried about it a long time, and you know what I finally decided? Not to mention it at all. I just don't think it's important. I just stated that you were at the Hilton all evening and couldn't possibly be involved. You're cleared, Vince, completely cleared."

"Thank you, Ross," Symington said in a strangled voice. "Thank you, thank you. How can I ever thank you enough?"

"We'll think of something, won't we?" the Kraut said.

Two days before Christmas, Edward Delaney, wearing hard homburg and lumpy overcoat, trudged through a mild fall of snow to buy a Scotch pine for the holidays. When he saw the prices, he almost settled for something skinnier and scrawnier.

But, what the hell, Christmas only comes once a year, so he bought the fat, bushy tree he wanted and lugged it home, dragged it into the living room, and got to work. He went up to the attic and brought down the old-fashioned cast-iron Christmas tree stand with four screw clamps, and boxes and boxes of ornaments, some of them of pre-World War II vintage. He also carried down strings of lights, shirt cardboards wound with tinsel, and packages of aluminum foil icicles, carefully saved from more Christmases than he cared to remember.

He was trying a string of lights when Monica came bustling in, wearing her sheared beaver, burdened with two big shopping bags of store-wrapped Christmas gifts. Her cheeks were aglow with the cold and the excitement of spending money. She stopped in the doorway and stared at the tree, wide-eyed.

"Happy Chanukah," he said, grinning.

"And a Merry Christmas to you, darling. Oh, Edward, it's a marvelous tree!"

"Isn't it," he said. "I'm not going to tell you how much it cost or it would spoil your pleasure."

"I don't care what it cost; I love it. Let me take off my coat and put these things away, and we'll decorate it together. What a tree! Edward, the fragrance fills the whole room."

Turning the radio to WQXR and listening to Vivaldi, they spent two hours decorating their wonderful tree. First the strings of lights, then the garlands of tinsel, then the individual ornaments, then the foil icicles. And finally Delaney cautiously climbed the rickety ladder to put the fragile glass star on the top.

He descended, turned on the lights, and they stood back to observe the effect.

"Oh, God," Monica said, "it's so beautiful I want to cry. Isn't it beautiful, Edward?"

"Gorgeous," he said, touching her cheek. "I hope the girls like it. When are they coming?"

Detective Benjamin Calazo was not a cop who had just fallen off the turnip truck. He had been around a long time. He had been wounded twice, and had once booted a drug dealer into the East River and let the guy swallow some shit before hauling him out.

Benny knew that some of the younger men in the NYPD regarded him with amused contempt because of his white hair and shambling gait. But that was all right; when he was their age he treated his elders the same way. Until he learned how much the gaffers could teach him.

Calazo was a good cop, serious about his job. He had witnessed a lot of crap, on the streets and in the Department, but he had never lost his Academy enthusiasm. He still believed what he was doing was important. The Sanitation guys, for instance—a lousy job but absolutely essential if the public didn't want to drown in garbage. The same way with cops; it had to be done.

Most of the time Calazo went by the book. But like all experienced cops, he knew that sometimes you had to throw the book out the window. The bad guys didn't follow any rules, and if you went up against them with strict adherence to regulations, you were liable to get your ass chopped off.

This Ronald Bellsey was a case in point. The detective knew that Bellsey was guilty of the attacks near his hangouts, plus the stomping of Detective Tim Hogan. Calazo also knew there was no way Bellsey could be racked up legally for his crimes. Not enough evidence to make a case.

So the choice was between letting Bellsey waltz away free or becoming prosecutor, judge, and jury himself. The fact that Bellsey had been going to a shrink to cure his violent behavior didn't cut any ice with Calazo and he went about planning the destruction of Ronald Bellsey without a qualm. The fact that Calazo was completely fearless helped. If a guy like Bellsey could cow him, then his whole life had been a scam.

When headquarters had been in that old building on Centre Street, there had been a number of nearby shops catering to the special needs of cops: gunsmiths, tailors, guys who made shoulder holsters that didn't chafe, and such esoterica as ankle holsters, knife sheaths, brass knuckles, and the like.

There was one place that made the best saps in the world, any length and weight you wanted, rigid or pliable. Sixteen years ago Calazo had bought a beauty: eight inches long with a wrist thong. Made of supple calfskin and filled with birdshot, it was double-stitched, and in all the years he had used it, it had never popped a stitch. And it had done rough duty.

When he prepared to confront Ronald Bellsey, that beautiful sap was the first thing that went into Calazo's little gym bag. He also packed handcuffs, a steel come-along, and two thick rolls of wide electrician's tape. He had his .38 Special in a hip holster. He didn't think he'd need anything else.

It was a Thursday afternoon, and Bellsey always got it off at three. Calazo arrived at Betty Lee's fleabag hotel at 2:45 and called upstairs from the lobby to make sure the coast was clear. She gave him the okay.

"You got it straight?" he asked her, taking off his fedora and overcoat. "He knocks, you let him in, and I take over from there. Then you get lost. Don't come back for an hour at least. Two would be better. He'll be gone by then."

"You're sure this will go okay?" she said nervously.

"Like silk," Calazo said. "Not to worry. You're out of it."

Bellsey was a few minutes late, but the detective didn't sweat it. When the knock came, Calazo nodded at Betty Lee, then stepped to the side of the door.

"Who is it?" she called.

"Ronald."

She opened the door. He came in. Hatless, thank God. The detective took one step forward and laid the sap behind Bellsey's left ear. It was a practiced blow, not hard enough to break the skin, but strong enough to put Bellsey facedown on the carpet.

"Thank you, Betty," Calazo said. "Out you go."

She grabbed up her coat and scampered away. Ben locked and chained the door behind her. He patted Bellsey down but found no weapons. The only thing he took was Ronald's handkerchief, somewhat soiled—which was okay with Calazo.

It took a lot of lifting, pulling, hauling, but finally the detective pulled Bellsey up into a ratty armchair. He wound tape around his torso to keep him upright. He taped his ankles to the legs of the chair. Then he taped his forearms tightly to the arms. Bellsey would only be able to move his hands.

Finally, Calazo stuffed Bellsey's handkerchief into the man's mouth. He watched closely to make certain his color wasn't changing. Then, when he was satisfied Bellsey was breathing through his nose, he went into the bathroom, got a glass of water, brought it back, and threw it into Bellsey's face.

It took about three minutes and another glass of water before Ronald roused. He looked around him dazedly with glazed eyes.

"Good morning, glory," Detective Calazo said cheerily. "Got a little headache, have you?"

He felt around on Bellsey's scalp and found the welt behind the left ear. Bellsey winced when he touched it.

"No blood," Calazo said, displaying his fingertips. "See?"

Bellsey was choking on the handkerchief, trying to spit it out.

"We got some ground rules here," the detective said. "The gag comes out if you promise not to scream. One scream and the gag goes back in. No one's going to notice one scream in a joint like this. Got it? You want the gag out?"

Bellsey nodded. Calazo pulled out the handkerchief. Bellsey licked his gums and lips, then looked down at his taped arms. He flapped his hands a few times. He tested the tape around his chest, then his legs. He looked up at Calazo standing over him, softly smacking his sap into the palm of one hand.

"Who the fuck're you?" Bellsey demanded hoarsely.

"The Scarlet Pimpernel," Calazo said. "Didn't you recognize me?"

"How much you want?"

"Not much," the detective said. "Just a little information."

Bellsey strained against his bonds. Then, when he realized that was futile, he began to rock back and forth on the chair.

"Stop that," Calazo said.

"Fuck you," Bellsey said, gasping.

The detective brought the sap thudding down on the back of the man's right hand. Bellsey opened his mouth to shriek, and Calazo jammed the wadded handkerchief back in his mouth.

"No screams," he said coldly. "Remember our agreement? Gonna keep quiet?"

Bellsey sat a moment, breathing deeply. Finally he nodded. Calazo pulled out the gag.

"You better kill me," Bellsey said. "Because if you don't, when I get loose I'm going to kill you."

"Nah," Ben Calazo said, "I don't think so. Because I'm going to hurt you—I mean *really* hurt you, just like you've hurt so many other people. And you're never going to be the same again. After you get hurt bad, your whole life changes, believe me."

Something in Bellsey's eyes altered. Doubt, fear—whatever—shallowed their depths.

"Why do you want to hurt me?"

"That's easy. I don't like you."

"What'd I ever do to you?"

"What'd those four guys you stomped ever do to *you?*"

"What four guys?"

Calazo brought the sap down again on the back of Bellsey's left hand. The man's head jerked back, his eyes closed, his mouth opened wide. But he didn't scream.

"The hand . . ." Calazo said. "A lot of little chicken bones in there. Mess up your hands and you're in deep trouble. Even after lots of operations they never do work right again. Now tell me about the four guys."

"What four—" Bellsey started, but when he saw his captor raise the sap again, he said hastily, "All right, all right! I got into some hassles. Street fights—you know? They were fair fights."

"Sure they were," Calazo said. "Like that detective you took outside the Tail of the Whale. A kidney punch from behind. Then you gave him the boot. That was fair."

Bellsey stared at him. "Jesus Christ," he gasped, "you're a cop!"

Calazo brought the bludgeon down on the back of Bellsey's right hand: a swift, hard blow. They both heard something snap. Bellsey's eyes glazed over.

"You did it—right?" the detective said. "The four guys near your hangouts and the cop outside the Tail of the Whale. All your work—correct?"

Ronald Bellsey nodded slowly, looking down at his reddened hands.

"Sure you did," Calazo said genially. "A tough guy like you, it had to be. It's fun slugging people, isn't it? I'm having fun."

"Let me go," Bellsey begged. "I admitted it, didn't I? Let me loose."

"Oh, we got a way to go yet, Ronald," Calazo said cheerfully. "You're not hurting enough."

"God a'mighty, what more do you want? I swear, I get out of here, I'm going to cut off your schlong and shove it down your throat."

Calazo brought the sap down again on the back of Bellsey's right hand. The man passed out, and the detective brought more water to throw in his face.

"Keep it up, sonny boy," he said when Bellsey was conscious again. "I'd just as soon pound your hands to mush. You're not going to do much fighting with broken hands, are you? Maybe they'll fit you with a couple of hooks."

"You're a cop," Bellsey said aggrievedly. "You can't do this."

"But I *am* doing it—right? Get a good look at me so you can pick me out of a lineup. The trouble with you tough guys is that you never figure to meet anyone tougher. Well, Ronald, you've just met one. Before I'm through with you, you're going to be crying and pissing your pants. Meanwhile, let's get to the sixty-four-dollar question: Where were you the night your shrink was killed?"

"Oh, my God, is that what this is all about? I was home all night. I already told the cops that. My wife was there. She says the same thing."

"What'd you do at home all night? Read the Bible, do crossword puzzles, count the walls?"

"I watched television."

"Yeah? What did you watch?"

"That's easy. We got cable, and I remember from nine to eleven there was a special on Home Box: *Fifty Years of Great Fights, 1930–1980.* It was films from all the big fights, mostly heavyweights. I watched that."

Calazo looked at him thoughtfully. "I saw that show that night. Good stuff. But you could have chilled your shrink and checked *TV Guide* just to give yourself an alibi."

"You fucker," Bellsey said in a croaky voice, "I really did—"

But Calazo snapped the sap down on the back of Bellsey's left hand, and the bound man writhed with pain. Tears came to his eyes.

"See," the detective said, "you're crying already. Don't call me names, Ronald; it's a nasty habit."

Calazo stood there, staring steadily down at his captive. Bellsey's hands had ballooned into puffs of raw meat. They lay limply on the arms of the chair, already beginning to show ruptured blood vessels and discolored skin.

"I wish I didn't believe you," Calazo said. "I really wish I thought you were lying so I could keep it up for a while. I hate to say it, but I think you're telling the truth."

"I am, I am! What reason would I have to kill Ellerbee? The guy was my *doctor,* for Christ's sake!"

"Uh-huh. But you hurt five other guys for no reason, didn't you? Well, before I walk off into the sunset, let me tell you a couple of things. Betty Lee had nothing to do with this. I told her if she didn't, she'd be in the clink. You understand that?"

Bellsey nodded frantically.

"If I find out you've been leaning on her," Calazo continued, "I'm going to come looking for you. And then it won't be only your hands; it'll be your thick skull. You got that?"

Bellsey nodded again, wearily this time.

"And if you want to come looking for *me,* I'll make it easy for you: The name is Detective Benjamin Calazo, and Midtown North will tell you where to find me. Just you and me, one on one. I'll blow your fucking head off and wait right there for them to come and take me away. Do you believe that?"

Ronald Bellsey looked up at him fearfully. "You're crazy," he said in a faltering voice.

"That's me," Calazo said. "Nutty as a fruitcake."

With two swift, crushing blows, he slammed the sap against Bellsey's hands with all his strength. There was a sound like a wooden strawberry box crumpling. Bellsey's eyes rolled up into his skull and he passed out again. The stench of urine filled the air. The front of Bellsey's pants stained dark.

Detective Calazo packed his little gym bag. He put in the sap, the rolls of remaining tape. Then he stripped the tape from Bellsey's unconscious body, wadded it up, and put that in the bag, too. He donned fedora and overcoat. He looked around, inspecting. He remembered the glass he had used to throw water in Bellsey's face, and took that.

He opened the hallway door, wiped off the knob with Bellsey's handkerchief, and threw it back onto the slack body. He rode down in the elevator, walked casually through the lobby. The guy behind the desk didn't even look up.

Calazo called the hotel from two blocks away.

"There's a sick man in room eight-D," he reported to the clerk. "I think he's passed out. Maybe you better call for an ambulance."

Then he drove home, thinking of how he would word his report to Sergeant Boone, stating that, in his opinion, Ronald J. Bellsey was innocent of the murder of Dr. Simon Ellerbee.

The girls arrived at the Delaney brownstone on the afternoon of Christmas Eve: Mary and Sylvia, two bouncy young women showing promise of becoming as buxom as their mother. The first thing they did was to squeal with delight at the sight of the Christmas tree.

Sylvia: "Fan-tastic!"

Mary: "Incredibobble!"

The second thing they did was to announce they would not be home for Christmas Eve dinner. They had dates that evening with two great boys.

"What boys?" Monica demanded sternly. "Where did you meet them?"

Mother and daughters all began talking at once, gesturing wildly. Delaney looked on genially.

It became apparent that on the train down from Boston, Mary and Sylvia had met two *nice* boys, seniors at Brown. They both lived in Manhattan, and had invited the girls to the Plaza for dinner and then on to St. Patrick's Cathedral for Handel's *Messiah* and midnight mass.

"But you don't even know them," Monica wailed. "You pick up two strangers on the train, and now you're going out with them? Edward, tell them they can't go. Those men may be monsters."

"Oh, I don't know . . ." he said easily. "Any guys who want to go to St. Pat's for midnight mass can't be all bad. Are they supposed to pick you up here?"

"At eight o'clock," Sylvia said excitedly. "Peter—he's my date—said he thought he could borrow his father's car."

"And Jeffrey is mine," Mary said. "Really, Mother, they're absolutely respectable, very well behaved. Aren't they, Syl?"

"Perfect gentlemen," her sister vowed. "They hold doors open for you and everything."

"Tell you what," Delaney said, "when they arrive, ask them in for a drink. They're old enough to drink, aren't they?"

"Oh, Dad," Mary said. "They're *seniors.*"

"All right, then ask them in when they come for you. Your mother and I will take a look. If we approve, off you go. If they turn out to be a couple of slavering beasts, the whole thing is off."

"They're not slavering beasts!" Sylvia objected. "As a matter of fact, they're rather shy. Mary and I had to do most of the talking—didn't we, Mare?"

"And they're going to wear dinner jackets," her sister said, giggling.

"So we're going to get all dressed up. Come on, Syl, we've got to get unpacked and dressed."

"Oh, sure," Delaney said solemnly. "Go your selfish, carefree way. Your mother and I have been waiting months to see you, but that's all right. Go to the Plaza and have your partridge under glass and your Dom Perignon. Your mother and I will have our hot dogs and beans and beer; we don't mind. Don't even think about *us.*"

The two girls looked at him, stricken. But when they realized he was teasing, flew at him, smothering him with kisses.

He helped them upstairs with their luggage, then came down to find Monica in the kitchen, sliding a veal casserole into the oven.

"What do you think?" she asked anxiously.

He shrugged. "We'll take a look at these 'perfect gentlemen' and see. At least they're picking up the girls at their home; that's a good sign."

Just then they heard chimes from the front door.

"Now who the hell can that be?" Delaney said. "Don't tell me Peter and Jeffrey have turned up three hours early."

But when he looked through the judas, he saw a uniformed delivery-man holding an enormous basket of flowers, the blooms lightly swathed in tissue paper. Delaney opened the door.

"Mr. and Mrs. Delaney?"

"Yes."

"Happy Holiday to you, sir."

"Thank you, and the same to you."

He signed for the flowers, handed over a dollar tip, and brought the basket back to the kitchen.

"Look at this," he said to Monica.

"My God, it's enormous! Is it for the girls?"

"No, the deliveryman said Mr. and Mrs. Delaney."

Monica pulled the tissue away carefully, revealing a splendid arrangement of carnations, white tea roses, lilacs, and mums, artfully interspersed with maidenhair fern.

"It's gorgeous!" Monica burst out.

"Very nice. Where the hell did they get lilac this time of year? Open the card."

Monica tore it open and read aloud: " 'Happy Holidays to Monica and Edward Delaney from Diane Ellerbee.' Oh, Edward, wasn't that sweet of her?"

"Thoughtful," he said. "She must have spent a fortune on that."

"Would you like a carnation for your buttonhole?" Monica asked mischievously.

He laughed. "Have you ever seen me wear a flower?"

"Never. Not even at our wedding."

"What would you think if I suddenly showed up with a rose in my lapel?"

"I'd suspect you had fallen in love with another woman!"

They had a leisurely dinner at the kitchen table: veal casserole, three-bean salad, and a small bottle of California chablis that wasn't quite as dry as the TV commercials claimed. They talked about how well the girls looked and what time they should be home from their date.

"Make it two o'clock," Delaney said. "I forget how long midnight mass lasts, but they'll want to stop off somewhere for a nightcap."

"Two in the morning?" Monica said dubiously. "When I was their age I had to be home by ten in the evening."

"And that was only a few years ago," he said innocently.

"You!" she said, slapping his shoulder lightly. "I better go upstairs and see how they're coming along."

"Go ahead," he said. "I'll clean up in here."

After he had set the kitchen to rights, he inspected his liquor supply, wondering what he might offer the girls' gentlemen callers.

They'd know about martinis, he suspected, and daiquiris, margaritas, and black russians. He thought of the cocktails that had been popular when he was their age: whiskey sours, manhattans, old-fashioneds, and fizzes, smashes, and flips.

He suddenly decided to give them a taste of the old days, and stirred up a big pitcher of bronx cocktails, taking little sips until he had the mixture of gin, sweet and dry vermouth, and orange juice just right. Then he put the pitcher in the fridge to chill.

He went into the living room and plugged in the Christmas lights. He sat solidly in his favorite chair, stared at the beautiful tree, and brooded about Calazo's report exonerating Ronald Bellsey. How could the detective be so *sure?*

He had the feeling that Calazo's judgment had resulted from more than a friendly dialogue between cop and subject. But whatever it was, the report had to be accepted. They had taken the investigation of Bellsey's alibi as far as it could go. Which left Joan Yesell . . .

When he heard the door chimes, he glanced at the mantel clock and saw it was a few minutes after eight. At least they were prompt. He lumbered into the hallway to let them in, shouting upstairs, "Your perfect gentlemen are here!"

God, they were so young! But street cops now seemed young to Delaney. And what was worse, the nation had elected presidents who were younger than he.

The boys certainly were presentable in their dinner jackets. He didn't particularly care for ruffled shirts and butterfly bow ties—but different times, different fashions. What worried him most was that he couldn't tell one from the other, they were so alike. He addressed both as "young man."

"A drink while we're waiting?" he suggested.

"Don't go to any trouble, sir," one of them said.

"We have a reservation at nine, sir," the other one said.

"Plenty of time," Delaney assured them. "It's already mixed."

He brought in the pitcher of bronx cocktails and poured.

"Merry Christmas," he said.

"Happy Holidays," they said in unison, tried their drinks, then looked at each other.

"A screwdriver," one of them said. "Sort of."

"But there's vermouth in it," the other one said. "Right, sir?"

"Right."

"Whatever it is, it's special. I'd just as soon forget about the Plaza and stay right here."

"A bronx cocktail," Delaney said. "Before your time. Gin, sweet and dry vermouth, and orange juice."

"I'm going to sell it in mason jars," one of them said. "My fortune is made."

Delaney liked them. He didn't think they were especially handsome —go try to figure out what women saw in men—but they were alert, witty, respectful. And they didn't scorn small talk, so the conversation went smoothly.

Monica came down first, and both youths rose to their feet: another plus. Delaney poured her a cocktail and listened, as, within five minutes, she learned their ages, where they lived in Manhattan, what their fathers did for a living, what their ambitions were, and at what hour they intended to return her treasures, safe, sound, and untouched by human hands.

When Mary and Sylvia entered, they seemed so lovely to Delaney that his eyes smarted. He poured them each a half-cocktail, and a few minutes later said, "I guess you better get going. You don't want to keep the Plaza waiting. And remember, two o'clock is curfew time. Five minutes after that and we call the FBI. Okay?"

The girls gave him a quick kiss and then they were gone.

"Please, God," Monica said, "let it be a wonderful night for them."

"It will be," Delaney said, closing, locking, and chaining the door. "Nice boys."

"Peter's going on to medical school," Monica reported as they returned to the living room, "and Jeffrey wants to be an architect."

"I heard," Delaney said, "and I was disappointed. No cops."

The cocktail pitcher was still half-full, and he got ice cubes from the kitchen and poured them each a bronx on the rocks.

"Should we put the presents under the tree tonight or wait for tomorrow morning?" he asked.

"Let's wait. Edward, you go to bed whenever you like. I'll wait up for them."

"I was sure you would," he said, smiling. "And I plan to keep you company."

He sat relaxed in the high wing chair covered with bottle-green leather, worn to a gloss. Monica wandered over to Diane Ellerbee's basket of flowers placed on their Duncan Phyfe desk. She made small adjustments in the arrangement.

"It really is gorgeous, Edward."

"Yes—" he started, then stopped. He rose slowly to his feet. "What did you say?" he asked in a strangled voice.

Monica turned to stare at him. "I said it was gorgeous. Edward, what on earth is the matter?"

"No, no," he said impatiently. "I mean when the flowers first arrived and I brought them into the kichen. What did you say then?"

"Edward, what *is* this?"

"What did you say then?" he shouted at her. *"Tell me!"*

"I said they were beautiful and wondered if they were for the girls. You said no, they were for us."

"And what else?"

"I asked if you wanted a buttonhole. You said you didn't."

"Right!" he said triumphantly. "I asked if you had ever seen me wear a flower. You said no, not even at our wedding. Then I asked what you'd think if I showed up wearing a rose in my lapel. And what did you say then?"

"I said I'd suspect you had fallen in love with another woman."

He smacked his forehead with an open palm. "Idiot!" he howled. "I've been a goddamned *idiot!*"

He went rushing into the study and slammed the door. Monica looked on in astonishment. After a few minutes she settled down to watch a Christmas Eve program on television.

She resisted the temptation to look in at him for almost an hour, then, maddened by curiosity, she opened the study door just a few inches and peeked inside. He was standing at the file cabinet, his back to her, flinging reports left and right. She decided not to interrupt.

An hour later, figuring this nonsense had gone on long enough, she marched resolutely into the study and confronted him. He was slumped wearily in his swivel chair behind the desk, wearing his horn-rimmed specs. He was holding a sheet of paper, staring at it.

"Edward," she said severely, "you've got to tell me what's going on."

"I've got it," he said, looking up at her wonderingly. "The man was in love."

# 23.

It was supposed to be a festive day. They all came downstairs in pajamas, bathrobes, and slippers and opened the tenderly wrapped packages stacked under the tree. "Oh, you shouldn't have done it!" . . . "Just what I wanted!"

Delaney had given Monica a handsome choker of cultured pearls which she immediately put on.

Then they all sat around the kitchen table for a big breakfast: juice, eggs, ham, hashed-brown potatoes, buttermilk biscuits, lots of coffee, glazed doughnuts, and more coffee.

Delaney moved through all this jollity with a glassy smile, his thoughts far away. At 10:00 A.M. he ducked into his study to call Carol Judd, Simon Ellerbee's receptionist. No answer. He called every hour on the hour. Still no answer. Where the devil *was* the woman? He sighed. Spending Christmas Day with the boyfriend, he supposed. She was entitled.

There were calls to the girls from Peter and Jeffrey. That took an hour—at least. And then all the Delaneys sallied forth for a stroll down Fifth Avenue. They admired Christmas decorations, the tree at Rockefeller Center, and ended up having lunch at Rumpelmayer's.

They walked home up Madison Avenue, the girls stopping every minute to Ooh and Ahh at the windows of the new boutiques. Back in the brownstone, Delaney got on the phone again to Carol Judd. Still no answer.

They spent a pleasant afternoon hearing about the girls' lives at school, but although Delaney listened, he was in a fever of impatience and hoped it didn't show.

After dinner he dived back into his study and continued to call Carol

Judd, without success. Trying to control his anger, he went to the files and pulled out certain notes that now had a significance he hadn't recognized before.

Finally, at 10:00 P.M., he reached her.

"Edward X. Delaney here. I spoke to you a few weeks ago in connection with the police investigation into the death of Doctor Simon Ellerbee."

"Oh, yes. Merry Christmas, Mr. Delaney."

"Thank you. And a Happy Holiday to you."

He was forcing himself to slow down, play it cool. He didn't want to alert this young woman.

"Miss Judd, a few questions have come up that I think only you can answer. I was wondering if you'd be kind enough to give me a few minutes of your time."

"Well, I can't right now."

That probably meant the boyfriend was there.

"At your convenience," Delaney said.

"Umm . . . well, I'm working now."

"Glad to hear it," he said. "With another psychiatrist?"

"No, I'm with a dentist on West Fifty-seventh Street."

"I'll bet I know the building," he said. "Corner of Sixth Avenue?"

"That's right," she said. "Don't tell me your dentist is there?"

"No," he said, "but my podiatrist is. I have great teeth but flat feet. Miss Judd, you've been so cooperative that I'd like to take you to lunch. Do you get an hour?"

"Early. At twelve o'clock."

"There's a fine restaurant on Seventh Avenue just south of Fifty-seventh. The English Pub. Do you know it?"

"I've seen it but I've never been in."

"Good food, generous drinks. Could you meet me there for lunch tomorrow at, say, twelve-fifteen?"

"Sure," she said cheerfully. "Sounds like fun."

He was at the English Pub promptly at noon on December 26th. He took a table for two, sitting where he could watch the door. Carol Judd came in at 12:20 and stood looking around. He rose, waved at her. She came over laughing. He held the chair for her.

"Hey," she said, looking around at the restaurant, "this is keen."

He hadn't heard anyone use the word "keen" in twenty years, and he smiled.

"Nice place," he said. "There's been a restaurant here as long as I can remember. It used to be called the Studio, I think. Would you like a drink?"

"What're you having?"

"Vodka gimlet."

"I think I'd like a strawberry daiquiri. Okay?"

She was wearing a denim smock that hid her limber body. But her blond curls were still frizzy, and her manner as perky as before. She chatted easily about her new job and the funny things that happen in a dentist's office.

"Maybe we better order," he suggested, handing her a menu. "We can talk while we eat."

"Sure," she said. "What're you having?"

"I'm going for the club sandwich," he said. "I'm a sandwich freak. You have whatever looks good to you."

"Cheeseburger," she said, "with a lot of fries. And another strawberry daiquiri. Hey, you know what happened? Doc Simon left me a thousand dollars in his will!"

"I heard that," Delaney said. "Very nice of him."

"He was a sweetheart," Carol Judd said. "Just a sweetheart. I don't have the check yet, but I got a letter from the lawyers. When the money comes, me and my boyfriend are going to take a great weekend in Bermuda or the Bahamas or someplace like that. I mean it's found money—right?"

"Right," Delaney said. "Enjoy it."

"How you coming on the investigation? You find the guy who did it yet?"

"Not yet. But I think we're making progress."

Their food was served. She doused her cheeseburger and French fries with ketchup. Delaney slathered his wedges of club sandwich with mayonnaise.

"Carol," he said casually, "you told me you did the billing for Doctor Ellerbee. Is that correct?"

"Sure. I mailed out all the bills."

"How did you keep track of who owed what?"

"In a ledger. I logged in every patient's visit. We billed monthly."

"Uh-huh. Did you know the billing ledger is missing?"

She had her mouth open to take a bite of cheeseburger, but stopped. "You're kidding," she said. "First I heard of it. Who would want that?"

"The killer," Delaney said. "Maybe. Where did you keep it?"

"In the top drawer of my desk."

"Everyone knew that? I mean patients and other people coming in and out of the office?"

"I suppose so. I didn't try to keep it hidden or anything like that. No point, was there?"

"I guess not. Carol, the last time I spoke to you, we talked about Doctor Simon's change of mood in the last year. You said he was up and down, happy one day, depressed the next."

"That's right. He became, you know, changeable."

"And also," Delaney said cheerfully, "you mentioned that he wore a flower in his buttonhole."

"Well, it really wasn't in his buttonhole because he didn't have one on his suit. But it was pinned to his lapel, yes."

"And it was the first time you had seen him wear a flower?"

"That's right. I kidded him about it, and we laughed. He was happy that day."

"Thank you," Delaney said gratefully. "Now let's get back to that billing ledger for a minute. Were there patients who didn't pay or were slow on their payments?"

"Oh, sure. I guess every doctor has his share of slow payers and out-and-out deadbeats."

"And how did Doctor Ellerbee handle them?"

"I'd mail out second and third notices. You know—very polite reminders. We had a form letter for it."

"And what if they didn't pay up, even after the notices? What happened then? Did he drop them?"

"He never did," she said, laughing and wiping ketchup from her lips with her napkin. "He was really such a sweet, easygoing guy. He'd say, 'Well, maybe they're a little strapped,' and he'd keep treating them. A soft touch."

"Sounds like it," Delaney said. He had finished his club sandwich and the little container of cole slaw. Now he sat back, took a deep breath, and said, "Do you remember the name of the patient who owed Doctor Ellerbee the most money?"

"Sure," Carol Judd said promptly, popping the last French fry into her mouth with her fingers. "Joan Yesell. She owed almost ten thousand dollars."

"Joan Yesell?" he repeated, not letting his exultation show. "Ten thousand dollars?"

"About."

"That was more than any other patient owed?"

"A *lot* more."

"Did you send her second and third notices?"

"At first I did, but then the doctor told me to stop dunning her. He said she probably couldn't afford it. So he just carried her."

"Thank you," Delaney said. "Thank you very much. Now, how about some dessert?"

"Well . . ." Carol Judd said. "Maybe."

He plodded home on a steely-gray afternoon, smoking a Cuesta-Rey 95 and thinking he owned the world. Well, he didn't have it *all*, but he had most of it. Enough that made sense. The problem was: Where did he go from here?

The brownstone was silent and empty. The women, he supposed, were out exchanging Christmas gifts. He went into the study and got on the horn. It took almost an hour to locate Boone and Jason and summon them to a meeting at nine o'clock that night. He was ruthless about it: *Be here.*

But when they arrived and he had them seated, the study door closed against the chatter of the women in the living room, he wondered how he might communicate his own certainty. He knew it might sound thin, but to him it was sturdy enough to run on.

"Listen," he began. "I'm convinced Simon Ellerbee was in love, or having an affair, or both, with Joan Yesell. Four women, including his wife, said that his personality changed recently. But they don't agree on *how* it changed. He was up, he was down, he was this, he was that: a good picture of a guy so mixed up he couldn't see straight. Also, Ellerbee was carrying Yesell on the books. She owed him about ten grand and he was making no effort to collect. I got that from Carol Judd, his receptionist, just this afternoon."

The two officers were leaning forward, listening intently. He saw he would have no problem convincing them; they *wanted* to believe.

"That would explain his will," Boone said slowly. "Canceling his patients' debts. He put that in for Yesell's benefit. Right, sir?"

"Right. She owed much more than any other patient. Also, I went through his appointment book again. She's down as a late patient eleven times this year, always on Friday nights. But the interesting thing is that notation of those Friday night visits stopped in April. Only I don't think the sessions stopped. I believe they went on, but he didn't write them down in his book."

"You think he was screwing her?" Jason asked.

"Had to be," Delaney said. "A healthy, good-looking guy like that. They weren't playing tiddledywinks up in his office."

"Doctor Diane and Samuelson swear he was faithful," Boone pointed out.

"Maybe they didn't know," Delaney said. "Or maybe they were lying to protect his reputation. At the moment it's not important. What is important is that Yesell was meeting him late in his office on Friday nights while his wife was heading up to Brewster. I'll bet my left nut that's what was happening. Also I dug out a report from Konigsbacher that states Symington saw Ellerbee driving uptown alone on First Avenue at about nine o'clock on a Friday night. I figure he had just dropped off Yesell at her brownstone and was heading up to Brewster."

"The Yesell dame has no car," Jason said, nodding. "So she probably took a cab or bus to Ellerbee's office. Then he drove her home. That listens."

"Another thing," Boone said. "Right after we questioned her the first time, she tried to slit her wrists. That could mean guilty knowledge."

"And how about Mama lying to give her an alibi," Jason added. "I think we got enough right there."

They looked at each other, smiling grimly as they realized they had no hard evidence at all.

"We're going to have to brace her," Delaney said. "Sooner or later. Her and her mother, too. Really lean on them. But there are a few things I'd like to learn first. If she killed Ellerbee, what was the motive? Maybe he had promised to divorce his wife and marry her and then reneged or kept stalling. That's one possibility. Another is that he knocked her up."

"Jesus Christ," the Sergeant said. *"Her?"*

"It's possible," Delaney argued. "That woman detective, Helen Venable, she's close to Yesell, isn't she? See if she can find out if Yesell is pregnant or if she had an abortion. And while Venable is doing that, Jason, you find out who her personal physician is, and see what he can tell you. Probably not a goddamned thing, but *try*. Meanwhile, Boone, you get a man to St. Vincent's Emergency and wherever else she was taken after those suicide attempts. Try to get a look at the records and talk to the doctors and nurses. See if anyone noted pregnancy on her chart."

"A long shot," Boone said dubiously.

"Sure it is, but it's got to be done. Also, cover all the hardware stores in her neighborhood and in the area where she works. See if any clerk remembers selling a ball peen hammer to a woman answering her description."

"You really think she chilled Ellerbee, sir?" Jason asked curiously.

"I really think she was there that night and knows more than she's telling us. Anyway, see what you can find out, and tomorrow night let's all three of us confront her. Maybe we'll take Detective Venable along so Yesell won't be so frightened. But I want to wring that young lady dry."

"We could take her in," Boone suggested.

"For what?" Delaney demanded. "Unless we can tie her to the purchase of a hammer, we've got zilch. Our only hope is to break her down. I don't like doing it—she seems like a mousy little thing—but we can't let that influence us. I busted a woman once who stood four-nine and weighed about ninety pounds, soaking wet. She bashed in her boyfriend's skull with a brick while he was sleeping. Sometimes the mousy little things can surprise you. Well, Sergeant," Delaney concluded, looking directly at Boone. "What do you think?"

"As Jason said, it listens," Boone said cautiously. "I mean it all comes together and makes sense. So Joan Yesell and Ellerbee were making nice-nice. The only thing that sticks me is *why?* The doc had the most beautiful wife in the world—wealthy and smart, too. Why in God's name would he risk all that for a fling with someone like Yesell? Compared to Diane, she's a shadow."

"Right," Delaney said, nodding. "I've been thinking about that. I don't want to get too heavy, but here's how I figure it. We know Diane was Ellerbee's student. He sees this absolutely beautiful girl who doesn't want to be anything but beautiful . . . a princess. So he decides to convince her to use her brain. She follows his advice and goes on to make a great career. Sergeant, remember Samuelson talking about the Pygmalion-Galatea syndrome? That's what it was. Now, years later, Ellerbee meets Joan Yesell. He sees something there, too, and tries to bring it out. You know what his problem was? He had to *improve* his women. There are guys like that. They can't love a woman for what she is. They have to remake her to conform to some vision of their own. Does any of that make sense?"

"I've got a brother-in-law like that," Jason said. "Always nudging my sister to do this, do that, wear this, wear that. He just won't let her *be.* I give them another year or two. Then they'll split."

"That's it exactly," Delaney said gratefully. "And I think that was part of the attraction Ellerbee felt for Joan Yesell. He wanted to *create* her. Another thing—everyone kept telling Ellerbee how lucky he was. Remember? Man, are you ever lucky being married to a real goddess with all those bucks! Now I ask you: How long could *you* take that? Wouldn't it begin to wear after a while? Isn't it possible you'd prefer a plain little shadow who thinks you're God Almighty? Or maybe Ellerbee was just bored. Or Yesell was the greatest lay since Cleopatra—or at least better than Diane. In any case there are enough reasons to account for Ellerbee's infidelity. The poor guy," Delaney added, shaking his head. "He needed professional help."

# 24.

They all worked as fast as they could, but it was no good. By the evening of December 27th, Delaney had learned little more.

Helen Venable said she'd swear on a stack of Bibles yea high that Joan Yesell was not pregnant and never had been—but she couldn't prove it one way or the other. Jason had no luck with Yesell's physician. The doctor wouldn't talk and ordered the cop out of his office. Boone's men got nothing from St. Vincent's or the other emergency rooms that had handled Yesell's suicide attempts.

The canvassing of hardware stores yielded no better results. No one remembered selling a ball peen hammer to anyone resembling Joan Yesell. The super at her brownstone was questioned, but he didn't even know what a ball peen was, let alone own one. So that was that.

"All right," Delaney said, sighing, "let's go talk to the lady. The funny thing is, about a week ago, I suggested to Deputy Thorsen that maybe Mama Yesell had lied to cover up her daughter's affair with a boyfriend. That was on the mark, but who the hell could have guessed the boyfriend was the victim?"

They drove downtown in Jason's car and met Venable in front of Joan's brownstone.

"You going to take her in?" Helen demanded.

"Let's wait and see," Delaney said. "We've got no warrant, and right now we can't show probable cause. If she confesses—that's something else again. She's home?"

"She and Blanche both."

"Fine. You buzz her on the intercom and talk. Then we'll all go up."

When they marched into that overstuffed apartment, the two plump cats looked up at them sleepily but didn't bother rising. Blanche Yesell's reaction was more electric.

"What is the meaning of this intrusion?" she said sharply, her bee-hive hairdo bobbing with fury. "Haven't we suffered enough? This is harassment, pure and simple, and I assure you the police department will be hearing from my lawyer."

Delaney decided to set the tone of the interrogation right then and there.

"Madam," he thundered, "you lied to us. Do you wish to be arrested for obstruction of justice? If not, just sit down and keep your mouth shut!"

It stunned her into silence. Mother and daughter sat down abruptly on the ornate settee. After a few seconds they clasped hands and looked fearfully up at the four cops.

"You," Delaney said harshly, addressing Mrs. Blanche Yesell. "You said you were here with your daughter on the night Doctor Ellerbee was killed. A deliberate falsehood. Do you wish to revise your statement now, madam?"

"Well, uh . . ." she said, "I might have stepped out for a few minutes."

"A few minutes," he repeated scornfully, then turned to the three officers. "Did you hear that? A few minutes! Isn't that beautiful?" He turned back to the mother. "More like three hours and probably four. And we have the statements of your bridge club members to prove it. Three respectable women testifying to your perjury. Do you dare deny it?"

He had her intimidated, but she wasn't willing to give up yet.

"My Joan is innocent!" she cried in an anguished voice.

"Is she?" Delaney said contemptuously. "Is she really? And that's why you found it necessary to lie to us, was it?" He moved to confront the daughter, whose face had become ashen. "And now you, Miss Yesell. Were you aware that in his will Doctor Ellerbee canceled his patients' outstanding bills?"

The unexpected question startled her. She shook her head dumbly.

"How much did you owe him?" he said sternly.

"I don't remember," she faltered, "exactly."

"Sergeant Boone," Delaney said, "how much did Joan Yesell owe Doctor Ellerbee?"

"About ten thousand dollars," Boone said promptly.

"Ten thousand dollars," Delaney repeated, glaring at the young woman. "Much, much more than any other patient. And Doctor Ellerbee was making no effort to collect this debt. Why do you suppose that was, Miss Yesell?"

"He was a very kind man," her mother said in a low voice. "And we didn't have—"

"You had enough," Delaney interrupted roughly. "Your daughter had a good-paying job. You had enough to pay him if you had wanted to or he had dunned you for it. Boone, how do you see it?"

"I figure their affair started about a year ago," the Sergeant said glibly. "Then, around April, it got really serious. That was when he stopped noting her late Friday night visits in his appointment book."

"Friday nights," Delaney said, nodding. "Every Friday night he could make it. His wife would take off for Brewster, and you," he said, staring at the mother, "you would take off for your bridge game. A sweet setup. Did he promise to divorce his wife and marry you?" he shouted at Joan Yesell.

She began weeping, burying her face in her palms. Detective Venable took one step toward her, then stopped. She knew better than to interfere.

"We know, Joan," Delaney said, suddenly gentle. "We know all about your affair with Doctor Simon. Did he tell you he loved you?"

Her bowed head moved up and down.

"Sure he did," Delaney said in a soft voice. "Said he was going to divorce his wife and marry you. But he kept stalling, didn't he? So you . . . Jason, where do you suppose she got the hammer?"

"That's easy," the officer said. "Buy one in any hardware store in town. Then throw it in a trash can when you're finished with it."

*"No, no, no!"* Joan Yesell screamed, raising a tear-streaked face. "It wasn't like that at all."

"You stop this!" Mrs. Blanche Yesell said indignantly. "You stop it this instant. You're upsetting my Joan."

"No, madam, I will not stop," Delaney said stonily. "Your Joan was having an affair with a married man who was found murdered. We're going to get the truth if it takes all night." He whirled on the daughter. "You were there, weren't you? The night he was killed?"

She nodded, tears starting up again.

"What time did you get there?"

"A little before nine o'clock."

"Why so late?"

"It was raining so hard I couldn't get a cab. They were all on radio call. So I had to take a bus."

"What bus?"

"Across town to First Avenue. Then up First."

"Did you call Ellerbee to tell him you'd be late?"

"Yes."

"What did he say?"

"He said he'd wait."

"You got up to East Eighty-fourth Street and got off the bus. You walked over to his office?"

"Yes."

"What were you wearing?"

"A raincoat."

"Boots?"

"Yes, I was wearing rubber boots. And I had an umbrella."

"All right, now you're at the townhouse. Then what?"

"The downstairs door was open."

"Which door? Outer? Inner?"

"Both. The outer door is always open. But this time the inner door was open, too."

"How far? Wide open? A few inches?"

"A few inches."

"Then what did you do?"

"Before I went in, I rang his bell. He always told his late patients to give three short rings. So that's what I did. But he didn't buzz back."

"And you went in anyway? Through the opened door?"

"Yes."

"Did you see tracks on the carpet? Wet footprints?"

"I didn't notice."

"Then what?"

"I went upstairs, calling his name. No one answered."

"And when you got to his office?"

Her head sank down again. She shuddered. Her mother slid an arm around her shoulders.

"Then what?" Delaney insisted. "When you got to his office?"

"I found him. He was dead."

"Where was he?"

"In the outer office. Where the receptionist sat."

"What was his position?"

"I beg your pardon?" she said.

"Was he in a chair, lying on the floor, or what?"

"Don't you *know?*" Blanche Yesell said.

"Shut up!" Delaney snarled at her.

"He was on the floor," Joan said, trembling. "Face up. All bloody."

"What did you do then?"

"I screamed."

"And then?"

"I turned and ran."

"Did you touch anything in the room?"

"No."

"Did you bend over him, feel for his pulse?"

"No, no, no!"

"Then how did you know he was dead?"

"I just knew it. His eyes were all . . ."

"Why didn't you call the police?" Sergeant Boone asked.

"I don't know. I panicked. I wanted to get out of there."

"Where's the book?" Delaney said.

"What book?"

"The billing ledger. That you took from the top drawer of the receptionist's desk."

"I didn't! I swear I didn't! I didn't touch a thing."

"What did you do then?"

"I ran out of the office, down the stairs, out of the building."

"Did you see anyone in the townhouse?"

"No."

"Hear anything—like someone might be in one of the other offices?"

"No."

"Smell anything—any unusual odors?"

"No."

"Then what?"

"I ran over to York Avenue. It was still raining. I finally got a cab and came home."

"What kind of a cab?" Jason asked. "What color?"

"One of the big ones with those fold-up seats."

"A Checker?"

"Yes, a Checker cab."

"What time did you get home?" Delaney asked.

"A little before ten o'clock. I think."

"And you, madam," Delaney said, turning to Mrs. Yesell. "When did you get home? Let's have the truth this time."

She lifted her wattled chin. "About eleven-fifteen."

"And your daughter told you what had happened?"

"Yes. My Joan was crying. Almost hysterical. I thought I'd have to call a doctor for her."

"Did you?"

"No. I gave her some aspirin and a nice cup of hot tea."

"And then you concocted the fake alibi to lead us astray."

"I didn't think we should get involved. Joan had nothing to do with the death of that man."

Delaney groaned and looked at the officers with a hopeless shrug. "She didn't think they should get involved. How do you like that?" He turned ba k to Joan Yesell. "All right," he said, "let's go through it again."

This time he was even more demanding, pressing her ferociously for details. Were there other passengers on the buses she took uptown on the murder night? Could she describe the drivers? Did she see anyone when she walked over to the townhouse from First Avenue? What time had she called Ellerbee to tell him she would be delayed? Could she describe the driver of the cab she took home?

Then: When, precisely, had her affair with Ellerbee started? (In March.) How often did they meet? (As often as they could—two or three times a month.) Did he say he wanted to divorce his wife and marry her? (Yes.) When did he first speak about getting a divorce? (About three months ago.) Did he give her money? (No, but he gave her gifts.) Like what? (Jewelry, occasionally. A silk scarf. Things like that.)

Did Mrs. Yesell know of her daughter's liaison? (Yes.) Did you object, madam? (Uh . . . not exactly.) Did Ellerbee say his wife was aware of his infidelity? (He didn't say.) But he did say he was going to ask her for a divorce? (Yes.) But you don't know if he ever did? (No.)

During the whole interrogation, Delaney was at his ruthless best, alternately threatening and conciliatory, roaring and then speaking in the gentlest of tones. He would bully both women to tears, then slack off to give them time to recover. When Joan came close to hysteria, he would switch to the mother, keeping them both off-balance with unexpected questions.

Finally, when it had gone on more than two hours, and neither Delaney nor the three officers had sat down or removed their coats, he said suddenly: "All right, that's enough for now. Keep yourself available, Miss Yesell. There will be more questions. Don't even think of leaving town; you'll be watched."

He began to lead the procession from the apartment.

Detective Venable said hesitantly, "May I stay awhile?"

Delaney looked at her thoughtfully for a moment. "Yes," he said, "you do that. Have a nice cup of tea."

Jason drove them uptown. Boone and Delaney sat in the back seat.

"That place smelled of cats," the Sergeant said. "I don't care how often you change the litter box; you got cats, your apartment is going to smell of cats."

They discussed how they were going to check the buses and cab Joan Yesell claimed to have taken on the murder night. Probably an impossible task, involving bus schedules, drivers' time cards, and taxi trip-sheets, but it had to be done.

"You men write up reports on tonight's questioning," Delaney ordered. "I'll do the same. Between the three of us, we should be able to recall everything."

They pulled up in front of Delaney's brownstone, but he made no movement to get out.

"All right," he said, "let's take a vote. Jason, was she telling the truth?"

"I think she's clean, sir," the officer said. "Mostly because I can't see her having the muscle or the guts to pound in the skull of a guy she loved."

"Sergeant?"

"I think she was telling the truth. The second go-around was a replay of the first. Either she's one hell of an actress or she's telling it like it was."

"Yes," Delaney said morosely, "I'm afraid both of you are right."

"And besides," Boone added, "when we were up in Brewster, Samuelson said he doubted if a suicidal type would go for homicide."

Delaney slowly stiffened. He turned to stare at the Sergeant.

"Lordy, lordy," he said with a wobbly smile. "I do believe you just uttered the magic words."

He got out of the car without further comment and trudged up the steps to the front door. He put his homburg and overcoat in the hall closet, then went into the living room. The girls were at the theater with Peter and Jeffrey, but Monica was home, simultaneously watching television and meticulously checking her Christmas card list against those they had received in return. He stooped to kiss her cheek.

"How did it go?" she asked him.

"Okay," he said. "Tell you about it later. I've got a call to make and then some things to look up. I never get to see you anymore," he complained.

"And whose fault is that?" she demanded.

It took him almost thirty minutes to locate Dr. Murray Walden, including a call to Deputy Thorsen to get the police psychiatrist's unlisted number. He finally tracked down Walden at a big dinner-dance at the Americana. The doctor had to be paged.

"This better be important, Delaney," the psychiatrist said. "You dragged me away from the best tango New York has seen since Valentino."

"It is important. One question, but it's crucial. And I'd like a yes or no answer."

"That I can't guarantee. I told you, in my business nothing is definite."

"You guys are as bad as lawyers. All right, I'll try anyway. We've got a subject with a history of suicide attempts. Four, to be exact. Is such a person capable of homicide?"

Silence.

"Hello?" Delaney said. "Walden? Are you there?"

"Yes, but let me get this straight. Is a suicidal type capable of homicide? Is that your question? The answer is yes. Under certain circumstances, anyone is capable of murder. But if you're asking me if it's probable, the answer is no. In fact, I've never heard of a suicidal type turning to homicide. That's not to say it's not possible."

"Thank you very much, doctor," Delaney said. "Go back to your tango."

He spent another half-hour pulling certain reports and notes from the file cabinet. He laid all the documents on his desk, edges aligned and touching. He stared down at them with grim satisfaction, noting how they resembled pieces of that jigsaw puzzle, finally coming together and fitting.

He opened the door to the living room.

"Monica," he called, "could you come in for a while?"

She looked up. "Oh-ho. Feeling guilty for neglecting me, are you?"

"Sure I am," he said, smiling. "Also, I want your take on something."

She came into the study and took the club chair facing his desk.

"My," she said, "you look solemn."

"Do I? Serious maybe, not solemn. Listen, this may take some time."

He hunched forward, forearms on his desk and told Monica of the night's events.

"What do you think?" he asked after he had related Joan Yesell's story.

"The poor girl," Monica said slowly. "Were you hard on her, Edward?"

"As hard as I had to be. Does it sound to you like she's telling the truth?"

"I can believe it. A vulnerable woman like that. Not getting any younger. A good-looking man telling her that he loves her. Edward, it was a *romance,* like she's watched on TV. Maybe her last chance to have a close relationship with a man. And sex. If he didn't offer to divorce his wife and marry her, I don't think she would have insisted or even objected. Just being with him was so important to her."

"That's the way I see it," he said, nodding. "And you've got to remember he was her *doctor,* giving her sympathy and understanding and confidence. A real father figure."

"Transference," Monica said. "That's what they call it."

"Whatever," Delaney said. "Anyway, I think she's innocent of the murder, and so do Boone and Jason. So that puts us back to square one —right? And we've still got the problem of the other set of footprints. But then, just before I got out of the car, Boone said something that triggered a memory. He reminded me that when we were up in Brewster, Samuelson had said that he didn't think a suicidal personality was capable of homicide."

"I don't remember him saying that."

"You were in the kitchen cleaning up when we were talking about it. Boone's mentioning it reminded me of something. That call I made was to Doctor Murray Walden, the Department's psychiatrist, a very brainy guy. He substantiated Samuelson's comment: that it was extremely unlikely a potential suicide would turn to homicide."

"Edward, why is that so important? It's added evidence that Joan Yesell is innocent, isn't it?"

"It's more than that. Because when the Sergeant mentioned it, I remembered the meeting I had with Diane Ellerbee when she gave me the names of six of her husband's patients—all presumably capable of murder. She said she was including Joan Yesell because suicide, when tried so often, often develops into homicidal mania. Just to check my memory, I dug out my notes on that conversation. And here it is." He held up a sheet of paper. "That's what she said. Now Diane is an

experienced psychologist. Why should she say something like that when
Samuelson and Walden say it's a crock of shit?"

He looked at Monica steadily, seeing how her face tightened as she
began to understand the full import of what he had just told her.

"Edward, are you suggesting . . ."

"I'm not suggesting anything; I'm stating it flatly with no doubts
whatsoever: Diane Ellerbee knocked off her husband."

"But you don't—"

"Wait a minute," he interrupted, holding up a palm. "Before you tell
me I'm nuts, let me give you some background on this. Let's start with
my own stupidity in not seeing it sooner. About seventy-five percent of
all murders are committed by the spouse, relatives, or friends of the
victim. I've known that since the day I got my gold shield. But I forgot
the percentages in this case. Why? Probably because Diane Ellerbee was
so beautiful, so intelligent. She overwhelmed me. And, like an idiot, it
never occurred to me to think of her as a vicious, cold-blooded killer."

"But she couldn't—"

"Hold on," he interrupted again. "Let me finish. Neglecting the percentages wasn't the worst of my stupidities; I neglected the obvious.
Which, in this case, was her statement that she left Manhattan that
night about six-thirty and got up to Brewster around eight. Who says
so? She says so. Where's the proof? There is no proof. And like the
moron I am, I never even doubted her story, didn't try to prove it out
one way or the other."

"That doesn't mean she's guilty."

"No? Here's the scenario as I see it:

"Simon Ellerbee really has a thing for this Joan Yesell. And he's
straight; he's not scamming her. So he tells his wife he wants a divorce.
I figure that happened maybe three weeks, a month before he was
killed. Or maybe she found out about Yesell herself—who knows? But
the idea of divorce really shakes her. He's dumping the golden goddess
for a wimp? She starts plotting.

"So on the murder night, as usual, she tells him she'll drive up to
Brewster early, and he can follow after he gets rid of his late patient
who, Diane knows, is probably Yesell. Diane gets her car out of the
garage, but she never leaves Manhattan. Maybe she drives around, but I
have a feeling she parks somewhere on East Eighty-fourth, where she
can see the door of the townhouse, and just sits and waits.

"Yesell is late that night and doesn't show. But I figure Diane is in
such a state that it doesn't matter. I think she intended to kill the two of

them—I really do. She wants to waltz in on them while they're in each other's arms. Then she'll bash in their skulls with her trusty little hammer. Where she got the ball peen, I don't know yet, but I'll find out.

"Anyway, she's got herself psyched up for murder, and when Yesell hasn't shown up by, say, eight-thirty, Diane says to herself, the hell with it, I'm going to kill the man who betrayed me. Gets out of the car, plods through the rain, goes up to her husband's office, and kills him. The fatal blows landed high on his head, but from the back. So he had turned away from her, not expecting death. Afterwards she rolls him over, hammers out his eyes.

"Monica, let me get you a drink; you look a little pale."

He went into the kitchen, brought back a bottle of Frascati and two glasses. Then he sat down again, and poured the wine.

"Was I too graphic? I'm sorry. But do you see any holes in the story? It hangs together, doesn't it? Makes a crazy kind of logic?"

"I suppose," Monica said hesitantly. "But *why*, Edward? Was it just the woman scorned?"

"That was part of it, sure, but there was more to it than that. I completely misjudged that woman. I thought her cold, always in control, always thinking before she acted. But now I believe that behind that façade is a very passionate woman."

There were other things Delaney wanted to tell his wife. Why Diane Ellerbee had crushed her husband's eyes, for instance. But he thought Monica, now looking forlorn and shaken, had heard enough gore and violence for one night.

"Let's go watch some TV comedy," he suggested. "Or just sit and talk. We haven't had an evening together in a long time."

She smiled wanly. "No, we haven't. What are you going to do now, Edward? Arrest her?"

He shook his head. "I don't have enough for that yet. Everything I told you is just supposition. We'll have to try and come up with hard evidence. Maybe we will, maybe we won't. But I can tell you one thing: That bloody lady is not going to walk away from this whistling a merry tune."

# 25.

Early on the morning of December 28th, a Saturday, Delaney called Boone and Jason and asked both men to come to the brownstone at 11:00 A.M. By the time they had arrived, he had assembled more reports, notes, and data he felt clearly pointed to the guilt of Dr. Diane Ellerbee.

He sat them down and went through his presentation again, much as he had related it to Monica the night before.

"As I see it," he finished, "there's no way we're going to prove or disprove she went up to Brewster that night at the time she claimed. Unless an eyewitness comes forward—which is about as likely as a blizzard in July. But let's assume she had the opportunity to waste him. That leaves motive and method."

"Seems to me you've got the motive, sir," Boone said. "A wife being dumped for another woman. I've handled a dozen homicides like that."

"Sure you have," Delaney said. "Happens all the time. But I think there was more to it than that. This gets a little heavy, but bear with me. Here we have a beautiful young woman who's enjoying all the perks that beautiful young women enjoy. Then she becomes Ellerbee's student. He sees her potential and tells her that if she doesn't use her brain, she's nothing but a statue. Get it? He's saying that her looks don't mean damn-all; it's just a lucky accident of birth. He's not impressed by her beauty, he tells her, but he's impressed by her brain and convinces her that she's got to use it if she wants a fulfilling life. Okay so far?"

"He's trying to improve her," Jason Two said. "Like we talked about before."

"Right! He's telling her that beauty is only skin deep. She goes along

with that, makes a happy marriage and a successful career. Then, suddenly, she finds out he's got eyes for another woman. Get that—he's got
*eyes* for another woman."

The Sergeant said, "So you think that's why she put his eyes out?"

"Had to be," Delaney said definitely. "Not only was he being unfaith-
ful to her, but he was going back on everything he had told her. So,
after he was dead, she blinded him. Now you'll never find anyone more
beautiful than me, you son of a bitch—that's what she was saying."

"Hey," Jason said, "that's one crazy lady."

"Maybe she was when she did it," Delaney admitted, "but after it
was done she covered up like an Einstein and diddled us with no trouble
at all. I mean she was *thinking* every step of the way, acting like the
outraged widow seeking justice and making a great show of cooperating
with us any way she could. No dummy she."

"We're never going to hang it on her," Boone said. "What have we
got?"

"It's all circumstantial," Delaney said. "And thin at that. But we've
got to try to flesh it out. Here's what I want you men to do today . . .
You can divide it up any way you like. First, check out that Manhattan
garage where the Ellerbees kept their cars when they were in town.
Find out if the garage does any servicing or repairs. If so, did they lose a
ball peen hammer in the last three months? If that doesn't work, go up
to Brewster. They keep that Jeep station wagon up there; they must
have a local garage or gas station doing their servicing. Ask the same
question: Are you missing a ball peen hammer? I've got a couple of
things I want to check out. Let's all meet back here at, say, nine o'clock
tonight and compare notes. Boone, you look doubtful. Aren't you convinced she did it?"

"Oh, I'm convinced," the Sergeant said mournfully. "After listening
to Joan Yesell's story, Diane becomes the number one suspect. The only
thing that bothers me is that I think she's going to walk."

"Jason?"

"Yeah, I think the lady killed her husband. But like the Sergeant
says, pinning her is something else again."

"We'll see," Delaney said stolidly. "We'll see."

After they left, he went into the kitchen to fortify himself. The
women had gone shopping and then planned to catch the Christmas
show at Radio City Music Hall. So Delaney had the house to himself.
More important, he had the refrigerator to himself.

There was a marvelous loaf of marbled rye: half-rye, half-pumpernickel baked in a twist. With thick slices of smoked turkey, chips of kosher dill pickle, and a dousing of Tiger sauce, a great condiment he had discovered. At first taste it was sweet-and-sour. A moment later, sweat broke out on your scalp and steam came out of your ears.

He took that sandwich and a frosty bottle of Tuborg into the study and ate while he worked.

What was bothering him was this: In the first interview with Diane Ellerbee, she stated that she had noticed no recent change in her husband's behavior. Then, days later, she had come over to Delaney's brownstone and said yes, on second thought, she realized his manner had altered.

Now what in hell caused her to change her mind?

It took him almost a half-hour to find it, but find it he did. When he first phoned Carol Judd, he had suggested she call Diane Ellerbee to check him out. Carol had called, and met with him—at which time she had described the changes in Dr. Simon's personality; how he had started to wear a flower in his lapel.

Comparing the dates of his meeting with Judd and Diane's visit to the brownstone, Delaney guessed what had happened. But he had to confirm it. He dialed Carol Judd's number and, because he was a superstitious man, he told himself that if she was home, it would be a good omen and his theory would prove out.

She was home.

"Miss Judd?" he boomed. "Edward X. Delaney here."

"Oh, hi, Mr. Delaney. That was a nice lunch we had. When are we going to do it again?"

He laughed. "It looks like I owe you a lot of lunches. But meanwhile there's one little question you can answer for me. Remember when I first called you, I suggested you check with Diane Ellerbee to make sure I wasn't just a telephone freak."

"Sure, I remember that. I called and she said you were okay and I could talk to you."

"Uh-huh. Now for my question: Did she call you back later and ask you what questions I had asked?"

Silence for a second. Then: "Let's see . . . I think she called the next day. She was trying to find me a job, you know. We talked about that for a while and . . . Yes, you're right; she wanted to know what questions you had asked."

"And you told her," Delaney said, "that I had asked if you had noticed any change in her husband's personality. And you told her what you told me—right?"

"I really can't remember, but I suppose I did. Shouldn't I have?"

"Of course you should!" he said heartily. "Thank you for your help, Carol. And I was serious about having another lunch. May I call you?"

"Anytime," she said breezily.

He hung up, smiling coldly. That was some brainy lady. Not Carol Judd, but Diane Ellerbee. When she heard that he had asked if the victim's manner had changed, she realized he had probably asked the same question of Joan Yesell and Sylvia Mae Otherton and received similar answers.

But she, the wife, who should have been the most sensitive to her husband's moods, had said, oh, no, he hadn't changed. So, having lied and fearing that Delaney would pick up on it, she had hiked herself to the brownstone and confessed: Oops, I made a mistake; he had become moody in the past year.

Delaney could appreciate her thinking; she had made an error and was covering up. That was okay; her ass was on the line and she had to improvise to protect it. He could understand that. But as far as he was concerned, it was another indication of her guilt. Nothing that would condemn her in a court of law, but significant.

There was another question that had to be answered. He phoned Detective Charles (Daddy Warbucks) Parnell, and the wife said he was working at a Staten Island precinct and could probably be reached there. She gave Delaney the number, but when he called, they said Parnell had already left, heading for One Police Plaza.

Delaney finally tracked him down. After an exchange of pleasantries, he asked Parnell, "Do you know the attorney who wrote Simon Ellerbee's will and put it into probate?"

"Yeah, I know the guy. Not well, but I know him. What do you need?"

"Just the date when Ellerbee made out his will. That business of canceling his patients' outstanding bills—I'd like to find out when Ellerbee decided on that."

"I don't know if he'll tell me, but I'll try. On Saturdays he's usually playing squash at his club. I'll call him there and get back to you one way or another."

"Thank you," Delaney said gratefully. "I'll be here."

He went back to the kitchen for another Tuborg and brought it into the study, sipping thoughtfully out of the bottle. He returned to the matter of how Simon Ellerbee had changed in the last year of his life, after he had started his affair with Joan Yesell. He wondered why Simon's mentor, Dr. Samuelson, hadn't noticed any change in his closest friend's personality.

Delaney dug out the report on Samuelson and there it was:

Boone: "Did you notice any change in Simon Ellerbee in the last six months or a year?"

Samuelson: "No, no change."

Delaney stared at the written record of that exchange. Something wasn't kosher. For a brief moment he wondered if Samuelson had been an accessory to Diane Ellerbee's crime. He couldn't see it. Still . . .

He phoned Dr. Samuelson.

"Edward X. Delaney here," he said. "How are you today, sir?"

"Weary," Samuelson said. "Patients this morning. Saturday afternoons I reserve to get caught up on my reading. Professional journals. Very dull stuff."

"I can imagine," Delaney said. "Doctor, something important has come up concerning Simon Ellerbee's death, and I need your help. I was wondering if I could see you tomorrow morning. I know it'll be Sunday, but I hoped you'd still be willing to talk to me."

"Sure, why not?" Samuelson said. "What time?"

"Oh, say ten o'clock. All right?"

"In my office. I'll see you then."

Satisfied, Delaney hung up and swiveled back and forth in his chair, ruminating. He thought about the relationship between Samuelson and Diane Ellerbee, and remembered the way she had treated him when they were at Brewster. He also recalled Rebecca Boone's comment on the drive home.

"I think he's in love with her," Rebecca had said.

The anklebone was connected to the kneebone which was connected to the thighbone which was connected to the hipbone. Humming, Delaney went to his file cabinet and dug out the biographies.

He found what he was looking for in Jason's report on Samuelson. Some years ago, the doctor had a breakdown and was out of action for about six months. The dates were carefully noted. God bless Jason Two.

Next, Delaney looked up the date of Diane and Simon Ellerbees' marriage. Samuelson's crackup had occurred about two weeks later. Now that *was* interesting. Nothing you could take to the bank, but interesting. Another little piece falling into place.

He was still pondering the significance of the Ellerbee-Samuelson relationship when the phone rang. He picked it up, but before he had a chance to speak—

"Charles Parnell here," the detective said, laughing.

"Oh, yes. Thank you for calling back. How'd you make out?"

"Struck gold. The guy had won his squash match—against someone he's been trying to beat for years, so he was celebrating with dry martinis. Just high enough to talk more than he should have. Anyway, Ellerbee made out his will about five years ago. But the clause about his patients' outstanding bills was a codicil added three weeks before he died. Any help?"

"It's beautiful," Delaney said. "Thank you very much, and a Happy New Year to you and yours."

"Same to you, sir."

Another little piece of the puzzle: Ellerbee canceling Joan Yesell's bills just three weeks before he was wasted—about the time, Delaney figured, the victim told his wife he wanted a divorce. Was he just being generous to his new love or did he have a premonition of his death?

Simon: "Diane, I want a divorce."

Diane: "I'll kill you!"

Delaney could believe that imagined dialogue; the lady was capable of it. The lady was also capable of lying glibly when it was required. He had asked her if she was surprised by the clause in her husband's will about his patients' bills. No, she had said, she wasn't surprised, because she was aware of what was in his will. And that, Delaney figured, was world-class lying.

Thinking of what all this meant, he trundled into the kitchen and pulled a long white apron over his heavy, three-piece cheviot suit. The apron had KISS THE COOK printed on the front. Then he set to work preparing dinner for his family.

Since it was Saturday night, they would have hot dogs with toasted rolls, baked beans with a chunk of salt pork and an onion tossed in for flavor, and both hot and cold sauerkraut.

By nine o'clock the Delaneys' brownstone was jumping. Peter and Jeffrey had arrived, bringing along a new board game called "Love at First Sight," in which you threw dice to move from square one (Blind Date) to the winning square (Happy Marriage).

At about the same time the boys showed up, Boone and Jason arrived and were whisked into the study, the door firmly closed against the noisy gaiety in the living room.

" 'Tis the season to be jolly," Delaney said ruefully. "And they're doing it right here tonight. Before you tell me how you made out, let me fill you in on what I've been doing."

He told them why Diane had revised her statement about her husband's mood swings in the past year and the fact that Simon added the codicil to his will just three weeks before his death. He also discussed Dr. Samuelson's curious relationship with Diane.

"I called him," he said. "He agreed to see me tomorrow morning at ten. I think I'll lean on him."

"You want me to come along, sir?" Boone asked.

"No," Delaney said. "Thanks. But I think this better be a one-on-one. Also, he knows I have no official position; I'm just a friend of the family, so to speak. Maybe he'll be a little more open and spill. You've got to realize that everything I've told you won't make the DA lick his chops, but I think it's all evidence that we're heading in the right direction. Now let's hear what you dug up today. You both look like canary-eating cats, so I hope it's good news."

"The first thing we did," Boone said, "was to check the Manhattan garage where the Ellerbees kept their cars. It's just a parking garage, no servicing and no repairs. I don't think they even have a screwdriver in the place, let alone a ball peen hammer. So we drove up to Brewster. We went by the Ellerbee home. She had a crowd up there today, all women from what we could see. Maybe it's her garden club or something. Anyway, we stopped at a phone, and I called and got the houseman. I said I was from Al's Garage, soliciting business. He said, sorry, they dealt with May's Garage and Service Station, and were perfectly satisfied. I thanked him, and we went over to May's. It was that easy. Jase, you take it from there."

"We find the owner," Jason Two said, "a fat old tub named Ernest May. We flash our tin and ask him if he's lost a ball peen hammer in the last three months or so. His jaw dropped a mile, and he looks at us like we're from Mars or something. 'How the hell did you know that?' he says. Well, it comes out that, yeah, a ball peen hammer turned up missing about three months ago. It was the only ball peen in the joint, and he had to go out and buy a new one. He can't put an exact date on when he lost the hammer, but he figures it was early in October. Sergeant?"

"We asked him who had access to the tools in the garage," Boone said, "and he showed us around. Hell, *everyone* had access to the tools; they were laying all over the joint. It could have been one of his mechanics, a customer waiting to have a car serviced, or maybe just a sneak thief. I wish we could have brought you more, sir, but that's about it. At least we know there's a ball peen hammer missing from a Brewster garage."

Delaney pulled at his lower lip. "This Ernest May—he knows Diane Ellerbee?"

"Oh, hell, yes," the Sergeant said. "She's a good customer. Brings in all her cars to gas up. And for tune-ups. He put in new plugs in that Jeep station wagon not too long ago. The way he talked, she's at his place almost every weekend she's up there, for this or that."

Delaney nodded. "You know where the ball peen hammer is right now? Boone? One guess."

"At the bottom of that stream that runs through Ellerbee's property."

"Right," Delaney said decisively. "Under the ice. And getting silted over."

"A search warrant?" Jason suggested. "We could get some frogmen up there with grapples."

Delaney shook his head. "There's not a judge in the country who'd sign a warrant on the basis of what we've got. We can't tie her directly to boosting the hammer. We could scam it and send in frogmen claiming they were from some phony state environmental agency wanting to test the water or the streambed or some such shit. But even if they found the hammer, what good would it do us? Tainted evidence. And after being under running water for two months, would there be identifiable fingerprints or bloodstains? I doubt it."

"Goddamn it!" Boone burst out. "It's there, I know it is."

"You know it," Delaney said, "and I know it, and Jason knows it. So what? It's not going to put Diane in the slammer."

"What does that mean, sir?" Jason said anxiously. "We're not going to bust her?"

"No," Delaney said slowly, "it doesn't mean that. But right now we have nothing that would justify arrest, indictment, or conviction. There's got to be a way to destroy her, but at the moment I don't know what it is."

"You think if we brace her—" Boone said, "I mean really come on hard—she might crack?"

"And confess? Not that lady. You know what she'd say? 'I don't have to answer any of your questions.' And she'd be exactly right."

"Snookered," Jason Two said.

"No," Delaney said. "Not yet."

By midnight, the brownstone had emptied out: Boone and Jason gone, Peter and Jeffrey departed. The girls were up in their bedroom, doing their hair and giggling. Delaney made his nightly rounds, checking locks on doors and windows. Then, wearily, he dragged himself to the master bedroom, slumped on the edge of his bed, and tried to get up enough energy to undress.

Monica was at the vanity, brushing her hair. He watched her a long time in silence, the pleasure of that sight restoring his strength.

"You want to tell me about it?" she asked without turning around.

"Sure," he said, and related everything that had happened since he had first decided on Diane Ellerbee's guilt.

"You can't arrest her?" Monica said.

"Not on the basis of what we've got so far."

"But you're certain? Certain she did it?"

"I am. Aren't you?"

"I guess," she said, sighing. "But it's hard to admit it. I admired that woman."

"I did, too. I still admire her—but for different reasons. She thought this whole thing out very, very carefully. The only mistakes she's made so far are little ones—nothing that could bring an indictment."

"I must have missed something in her," Monica said. "Something that you saw and I didn't."

"It goes back to that conversation we had about beautiful women and how they think."

She put her brush aside and came over to him. She stood in front of him in a peach-colored nightgown and matching peignoir.

"Turn around," she said.

"What?"

"Sit sideways on the bed," she ordered. "Take off your tie and open your shirt and vest."

He obeyed, and she began to massage the meaty muscles of his neck and shoulders. Her strong fingers dug in, kneading and pinching.

"Oh, God," he said, groaning, "don't stop. What do you charge by the hour?"

"On the house," she said, her clever hands working. "Tell me—how do beautiful women think?"

"They can't face reality. Or at least not *our* reality. They live in a shimmering crystal globe. You know—those paperweights: a Swiss chalet scene. You turn them upside down and snow falls. It's a never-never land. Beautiful women live in it. Admiration from all sides. The love of wealthy men. They don't have to lift a finger, and their future is assured. All wants granted."

"You think Diane was like that?"

"Had to be. Beauty is a kind of genius; you can't deny it. You got it or you don't. Then along comes Simon Ellerbee, her teacher. He convinces her she's got a good brain too. Not only is she beautiful, but she's brainy. That crystal ball she lives in is now shinier and lovelier than ever."

"Then he asks for a divorce?"

"Right! Oh, hon, that feels so good. Up higher around my neck. Yes, her husband asks for a divorce. I'll bet my bottom dollar it was the first failure in her life. A defeat. We all learn to cope with defeats and disappointments. But not beautiful women; they're insulated in their crystal globes. It must have devastated her. The man who convinced her that she had a brain not only doesn't want her brain anymore, but doesn't want *her*. Can you imagine what that did to her ego?"

"I can imagine," Monica said sadly.

"When someone hurts you, you hurt back: that's human nature. But this was a cataclysmic hurt. And she responded in a cataclysmic way: murder. I told you that her reality was different from ours. When Simon asked for a divorce, he wasn't only destroying her, he was demolishing her world. And all for a little, plain, no-talent woman? If such things could happen, then Diane's reality had no substance. You can see that, can't you?"

"I told you," Monica said, "you see more than I do."

She moved away from him and began to turn down the blankets and sheet on her bed.

"Open the window tonight?" he asked her.

"Just a crack," she said. "It's supposed to be below freezing by morning."

He went in for a shower. Scrubbed his teeth, brushed his hair, climbed into his old-fashioned pajamas. When he came back into the bedroom, Monica was sitting up in her bed, back against the headboard.

"You don't like me much tonight, do you?" he said.

"It's not a question of liking you, Edward. But sometimes you scare me."

"Scare you? How so?"

"You know so much about Diane. It all sounds so logical, the way you dissect her. What do you think about *me?*"

He put a palm softly to her cheek. "That you're an absolutely magnificent woman, and I hate to imagine what my life would be without you. I love you, Monica. You believe that, don't you?"

"Yes. But there's a part of you I'll never understand. You can be so— so *strict* sometimes. Like God."

He smiled. "I'm not God. Not even close. Do you think Diane Ellerbee should get off scot-free?"

"Of course not."

"Of course not," he repeated. "So the problem now is how she can be made to pay for what she did."

"How are you going to do that, Edward?"

"I'm going to turn over her crystal globe," he said coldly, "and watch the snow come down."

He turned off the light and found his way to Monica's bed. She pulled the blankets up to their chins.

"Please don't tell me that I scare you," he begged. "That scares *me.*"

"You don't really scare me," she said. "It's just the way you become obsessed with a case."

"Obsessed? I guess so. Maybe that's the way you've got to be to get anything done. I just don't like the idea of someone getting away with murder. It offends me. Is that so awful?"

"Of course not. But sometimes you can be vindictive, Edward."

"Oh, yes," he readily agreed. "I plead guilty to that."

"Don't you sympathize with Diane at all?"

"Sure I do. She's human."

"Don't you feel sorry for her?"

"Of course."

"But you're going to destroy her?"

"Completely," he vowed. "But that's enough about Doctor Diane Ellerbee. What about us?"

"What about us?"

"Still friends?"

"Come closer," Monica said. "I'll show you."

"Oh, yes," he said, moving. "Thank you, friend."

# 26.

Delaney prepared carefully for his meeting with Dr. Julius K. Samuelson: went over once again the biography Jason had submitted, reviewed his report on the first interrogation, read his notes on Samuelson's comments and behavior during that visit to Brewster.

He had told Boone and Jason that he intended to lean on Dr. Samuelson. But in cops' lexicon, there are varieties of leaning, from brutal hectoring to the pretense of sorrowful sympathy. In this case, Delaney decided, tough intimidation would be counterproductive; he might achieve more with sweet reasonableness—an approach Delaney characterized as the "I need your help" style of interrogation.

He lumbered over to Samuelson's office at 79th Street and Madison Avenue. It was a harshly cold morning, the air still but the temperature in the teens. Delaney was thankful for his flannel muffler, vested suit, and balbriggan underwear. He thrust his gloved hands into his overcoat pockets, but he felt the cold in his feet, a numbing chill from the frozen pavement.

The doctor greeted him at the office door with a tentative smile. The little man was wearing his holey wool cardigan and worn carpet slippers. He seemed staggered by the weight of Delaney's overcoat, but he hung it away manfully and offered a cup of black coffee from a desk thermos. Delaney accepted gratefully.

"Doctor Samuelson," Delaney began, keeping his voice low-pitched and conversational, "thank you for giving me your valuable time. I wouldn't have bothered you, but some things have come up in the investigation of Simon Ellerbee's death that puzzle us, and I hoped you might be able to help."

The doctor made a gesture. "Whatever I can do," he said.

"First of all, we have discovered that for the past year or so, Doctor Simon had been having an affair with Joan Yesell, one of his patients."

Samuelson stared at him through the thick curved lens of his wire-rimmed glasses. "You are certain of this?"

"Absolutely, sir. Not only from a statement by the lady concerned, but from the testimony of corroborating witnesses. You were probably the Ellerbees' best friend, doctor—saw them frequently in town, visited their Brewster home on weekends—yet in our first meeting you stated that Doctor Simon was faithful to his wife, and theirs was a happy marriage. You had no inkling of Simon's infidelity?"

"Well—ah—I might have had a suspicion. But you cannot condemn a man because of suspicion, can you? Besides, poor Simon is dead, and what good would it do to tarnish his reputation? Is this important to your investigation?"

"Very important."

"You mean the patient involved, this Joan Yesell, may have killed him?"

"She is being watched."

Samuelson shook his head dolefully. "What a dreadful thing. And what a fool he was to get involved with a patient. Not only a horrendous breach of professional ethics, but a despicable insult to his wife. Do you think she was aware of his philandering?"

"She says no. Do you think she was?"

"Mr. Delaney, how can I possibly answer a question like that? I don't know what Diane thinks."

"Don't you, doctor? I noticed some unusual facts in your personal history. First, you were acquainted with both Ellerbees for some time prior to their marriage. Second, you suffered a breakdown two weeks after their marriage. Third, you continue to maintain a close relationship with Diane. I don't wish to embarrass you or cause you pain, but whatever you tell me will be of tremendous help in convicting Simon's killer. And will, of course, be held in strictest confidence. Doctor Samuelson, are you in love with Diane Ellerbee?"

The diminutive man looked like he had been struck a blow. His narrow shoulders sagged. The large head on a stalky neck fell to one side as if he hadn't the strength to support it. His grayish complexion took on an even unhealthier pallor.

"Is it that obvious?" he asked with a failed smile.

Delaney nodded.

"Well, then—yes, I love her. Have since the first time I met her. She was studying with Simon then. My wife had died years before that. I suppose I was a lonely widower. Still am, for that matter. I thought Diane was the most beautiful woman I had ever met. Had ever seen. Her beauty simply took my breath away."

"Yes, she's lovely."

"Every man who has met her feels the same way. I have always felt there is something unearthly about her beauty. She seems to be of a different race than human. There! You see the extent of my hopeless passion?"

That line was spoken with wry self-mockery.

"Why hopeless?" Delaney asked.

"Look at me," Samuelson said. "A shrimp of a man. Twenty years older than Diane. And not much to look at. Besides, there was Simon: a big, handsome, brilliant fellow closer to her own age. I could see the way she looked at him, and knew I had no chance. Is all this making me a prime suspect in the murder?"

"No," Delaney said, smiling, "it's not doing that."

"Well, I didn't do it, of course. I could never do anything like that. I abhor violence. Besides, I loved Simon almost as much as I did Diane—in a different way."

"You've spent a lot of time with her, doctor. Especially since her husband's death. Would you say she's a proud woman?"

"Proud? Not particularly. Confident, certainly."

"Very sure of herself?"

"Oh, yes."

"Obstinate?"

"She can be stubborn on occasion."

"What you're saying is that she likes her own way?"

Samuelson thought that over for a few seconds. "Yes," he said finally, "I think that's a fair assessment: She likes her own way. That's hardly a fault, Mr. Delaney."

"You're right, sir, it isn't; we all like to get our own way. Prior to Simon's death, did Diane give any indication at all that she was aware of her husband's unfaithfulness? Please think carefully before you answer, doctor; it's very important."

Samuelson poured them both more coffee, emptying the desk thermos. Then he sat back, patting the waves of his heavy russet hair. Delaney wondered again if it might be a rug.

"I honestly cannot give you a definite answer," the psychiatrist said. "Certain things, the way people talk and act, can seem perfectly normal, innocuous. Then someone like you comes along and asks, can you interpret that talk and those actions in this manner—is the person in question suspicious, jealous, paranoid, depressive, or whatever? And almost invariably the speech and actions can be so interpreted. Do you understand what I am saying, Mr. Delaney? Human emotions are extremely difficult to analyze. They can mean almost anything you want them to mean: open and above board or devious and contrived."

"I do understand that, doctor, and agree with you. But even with that disclaimer, can you state definitely that Diane was *not* aware of her husband's infidelity?"

"No, I cannot say that."

"Then, from your observations of her during the past year, can you say she *may* have been aware?"

"Possibly," Dr. Samuelson said cautiously.

Delaney sighed, knowing he was not going to get any more than that.

"Doctor, Diane strikes me as being a very controlled woman, always in command of herself. Do you agree?"

"Oh, yes."

"Did you ever see her when she was not in control?"

"Only once," Samuelson said with a rueful smile. "And then it was over such a stupid thing. It happened last year. I was out at their Brewster home for the weekend. It was in the fall, and quite cool. Simon liked to have dinner on the patio, and planned to grill steaks on the barbecue. Diane insisted it was too cold to eat out-of-doors, and wanted us to stay inside. A furious argument erupted. I stayed out of it, of course. They really went at it, hammer and tongs, and said a lot of things I'm sure they were sorry for later. Finally Diane grabbed the package of steaks—they were beautiful sirloins--ran out of the house, and threw them in the stream. That was the end of our steak dinner. But at least it had the effect of clearing the air, and after a while we were laughing about it. We opened two cans of tuna and had a salad and baked potatoes."

"Indoors?" Delaney said.

"Indoors," Samuelson said. "That was the only time I ever saw Diane lose her temper. But I admit her anger was frightening."

"I recall," Delaney said, "that when I was speaking to her of the possibility of patients assaulting their psychiatrists, I asked her if she had ever been attacked. She said most of her patients were children, but when they struck her, she hit back. Is this the usual treatment in situations like that?"

Dr. Samuelson shrugged. "It is not a technique that I myself would use, but whatever works . . . Psychotherapy is not an exact science."

"So I have learned. One final question, doctor—a very personal one: Have you asked Diane Ellerbee to marry you?"

Samuelson looked at him strangely. "I think you are in the wrong business, Mr. Delaney. Perhaps you should be sitting behind this desk."

"You haven't answered my question."

"The answer is yes, I asked Diane to marry me. She said no."

"A very independent woman," Delaney remarked.

Samuelson nodded.

Schlepping home in the cold, Delaney pondered the interview and what it had yielded. Not a hell of a lot. He liked that story about Diane throwing the sirloins in the stream. Last year, steaks; this year, a ball peen hammer.

The one question he hadn't been able to ask still gnawed at him: *Doctor Samuelson, do you think Diane Ellerbee murdered her husband?* Samuelson would have been outraged, and, considering his infatuation, would have been on the phone, warning her, the moment Delaney left his office. Better that Diane should believe herself unsuspected and safe. The shock would be that much greater.

He suddenly acknowledged they had all they were going to get. It was time for him to make his move. Not because of Thorsen's end-of-the-year deadline, although that was a consideration, but because the investigation had come up against a blank wall.

There was not going to be a sudden, neat denouement, the killer nabbed and proven guilty. He would have to settle for a half-loaf. But it would not be the first time that had happened to him, he reflected grimly, and he could live with it. *All* was best, but something was better than nothing.

He worked out the way he was going to handle it, manipulating people by appealing to their self-interest. It wouldn't be perfect justice —but when had justice ever been perfect?

He stopped at a couple of shops on the way home, and when he entered his empty brownstone—the women out shopping again, he supposed—he headed directly for the kitchen. There he made himself two toasted bagel sandwiches layered with cream cheese, sliced red onion, and capers. One sandwich got a thick slab of lox, the other smoked sturgeon.

He spent almost an hour on the phone, tracking down Thorsen and Suarez. He finally got everything coordinated, and both men promised to be at the brownstone at 9:30 P.M. Then he tried calling Dr. Diane Ellerbee at her office and at her Brewster home, but got no answer.

He worked all afternoon putting his files in order, holding out only those documents he might need. He then made notes of the presentation he intended to deliver to Thorsen and Suarez. He was confident he would succeed; he couldn't see that they had any choice but to go along with him.

He leaned back in his swivel chair, realizing it was all winding down. End of the trail. There was a certain satisfaction in that, and a certain sadness, too. It had been a nice chase, an excitement, but now it was done.

He reviewed the way he had handled it and couldn't see how he might have worked it differently with better results. If he had made any error, it was in looking for complexities in a homicide that was essentially simple: The Case of the Betrayed Wife. A detective couldn't go far wrong if he stuck to the obvious.

That night Delaney began by throwing them a curveball.

"Chief," he said to Suarez, "I want you to arrest Doctor Diane Ellerbee for the murder of her husband."

Thorsen was the first to recover. "My God, Edward," he said, "the last time we spoke, you said you thought it was the patient—what's her name?"

"Joan Yesell. No, she's clean. She was there on the night Ellerbee was killed, but she didn't do it."

"So it was the wife?" Suarez said wonderingly. "All the time it was the wife while we were chasing the patients?"

"That's right," Delaney said. "This is a long story, so bear with me."

He stood and began pacing back and forth behind his desk, occasionally glancing at the notes he had prepared.

He started with the affair between Simon and Joan Yesell, and how it had gone on for almost a year. Diane had probably been aware of it soon after it started, but it was only three weeks prior to his death that Simon had asked for a divorce.

"There's motive enough for you," Delaney said. "The scorned woman."

He analyzed the personality of Diane: a beautiful woman who had lived a fortunate and sheltered life and never suffered a disappointment. Then her husband says he wants to leave her for a Plain Jane and her whole world collapses.

He described Joan Yesell, a woman energized by love for the first time in her life. She would, Delaney said, have been willing to let the affair continue indefinitely, but he promised her marriage.

"So," Delaney said, "that's our triangle: three passionate and very flummoxed people."

Then Delaney reviewed the murder night, starting with the victim's announced intention of seeing a late patient: Diane's unproven statement that she had left Manhattan for Brewster; Joan Yesell's inability to get a cab, and her late arrival at the townhouse to find Dr. Simon dead.

"Diane had the motive," Delaney argued. "She had the opportunity, and here's how she got the means . . ."

He told them about the ball peen hammer stolen from the Brewster garage where the Ellerbees' cars were serviced. He described the stream running through the Ellerbees' property, and stated firmly that he believed the hammer had been thrown into that stream.

He began to pile on supporting evidence: the clause in Simon's will canceling his patients' outstanding bills, Joan Yesell's debt of nearly ten thousand dollars, Diane's erroneous statement that suicide-prone patients often become homicidal. . . .

"All right," Delaney said at last, "let's have your questions. I'm sure you've got them."

"In the absence of the billing ledger," Suarez said, "how do you know Joan Yesell would benefit from the doctor's canceling of patients' debts?"

Delaney explained that Simon's receptionist, Carol Judd, had provided that information.

Thorsen asked why Delaney was so certain of the intensity of the Ellerbee–Joan Yesell affair.

Delaney told them about the last interrogation of Yesell, her mother's attempt to alibi her, and Samuelson's acknowledgment that he had suspected for some time that Simon was involved with another woman. Delaney did not mention the flower that Simon wore in his lapel; he doubted they would consider that firm evidence of a romantic passion.

"Why would Ellerbee want to start an affair with such a dull woman," the Chief asked, "if his wife is as lovely as you say?"

Delaney repeated what he had told Boone and Jason—that Simon wanted to improve his women and had tired of being married to a paragon, with his friends constantly telling him how lucky he was.

"Maybe," Delaney added, "he wanted a relationship in which *he* was the paragon. It must be difficult being married to a work of art."

"Let's get back to that missing billing ledger," the Deputy said. "Who do you figure took it—Diane or Joan Yesell?"

"Diane," Delaney said promptly. "Look, Diane wants to implicate Yesell. That's why she gave us Joan's name in the first place. But at the same time, she doesn't want us to find out about Simon's affair. Diane is a very complex woman, torn between a need for vengeance and a need to protect her own self-esteem."

"Why did she put out his eyes?" Ivar asked—and with that question Delaney knew he had convinced them.

Again he repeated what he had told Boone and Jason—that Simon had persuaded Diane that her beauty meant little, but then had begun to look at another woman. She couldn't stand that.

There was silence.

"That's all?" Delaney said. "No more questions?"

Then, thinking it might be discreet to leave them alone for a few moments, he went into the kitchen and mixed himself a tall rye highball. He drank half of it off immediately, standing at the sink, then brought the remainder back into the study along with drinks for the others.

"All right," he said. "Did she or didn't she? Chief, what do you think?"

"I think she did it," Suarez said mournfully, his sad face sagging. "A beautiful woman like that—it is a true tragedy."

"Ivar?"

"Oh, she's guilty as hell," the Admiral said. "No doubt about it. But you know what you've got, Edward. Zero, zip, and zilch."

"Hard evidence, you mean?" Delaney said. "Of course I know that. And we're not going to get it. Continuing this investigation would be just spinning our wheels. But I want Diane Ellerbee charged for the murder of her husband."

"What good would that do?" Thorsen demanded, looking at him narrowly. "She'd be out in two hours, and that would be the end of that. And the DA will call us assholes for arresting her."

"I'll tell you what it'll do for *me*," Delaney said coldly. "It'll ruin her. The arrest will be headlined in every newspaper in town, and featured on every TV news program. She's going to walk anyway, isn't she? You know it and I know it. But we can drag her through the mud first. Even when she goes free, everyone will be saying, 'Where there's smoke, there's fire.' You think her reputation can take that? Or her career? I know we'll never get a conviction on what I've got—probably not even an indictment—but by God, we can make her suffer. That's what *I* want.

"As for you two, what you get out of his hyped-up circus is what *you* want: headlines of an important arrest, with statements by you, Chief, that you're convinced the Ellerbee homicide is cleared. Statements by you, Ivar, congratulating Suarez on his exceptional detective work in solving this extremely difficult case. Don't you think the PC is going to read the papers and watch TV?"

The two men turned and stared at each other.

"I do not know . . ." Suarez said hesitantly. "I am not sure . . . The law . . ."

Delaney whirled on him. "The law?" he said, snorting. "What the hell has the law got to do with this? We're talking about justice here. She's got to be made to pay. But this can't be decided on the basis of either law or justice. This is strictly a political decision."

"Welcome to the club," Thorsen said with a small smile. "But what if she sues for false arrest?"

"I wish she would," Delaney cried, "but she's too smart for that. Because that would bring her into a courtroom, and the carnival would continue. And the whole business of her late husband's affair would be dragged through the press. You think she'd enjoy that? Her lawyers won't let her sue the city after they look over what we've got. No way! They're going to tell her to forget it, lay low, and don't make waves."

"It's a gamble," the Deputy said thoughtfully. "Charging someone when we know we don't have an icicle's chance in hell of getting a conviction."

"I told you it was a political decision," Delaney said. "It's two days until the end of the year. You can still pull this out if you've got the balls for it."

"I do not like it," Suarez said. "It is somehow shameful. But still, the woman is guilty—no?"

"When would you want to do this?" Thorsen asked.

"Take her?" Delaney said. "Tomorrow night if I can set up a meet."

"Do you want the Chief and me there?"

"No, I don't think that would be wise. You keep your distance until it's done. But have your statements ready, and schedule a press conference. My God, Ivar, you know how to use the media; you've been doing it long enough. I'll take Boone and Jason. They've worked hard on this thing and should be in on the kill. And, by the way, Chief—I've got a list of people, including Boone and Jason, who deserve recognition for a hard job well done."

"Of course," Suarez said with a wave of his hand. "It is understood."

"Good. I'll hold you to that. Now let's get to the nitty-gritty and figure how this is going down."

# 27.

He finally got through to Diane Ellerbee late on Monday morning, December 30th.

"Edward X. Delaney here," he said briskly. "Doctor, there's been a major development in the investigation of your husband's death—something I think you should know about."

"You've found the killer?"

"I'd rather not talk about it on the phone. Could we meet sometime this evening?"

They finally agreed on 8:30 P.M., at the East 84th Street townhouse. Delaney hung up, satisfied, then immediately called Boone, asking him to pick him up at the brownstone at eight o'clock.

"And bring Jason with you," he told the Sergeant. "I'd like both of you to be in uniform."

"My God, sir, my blues need cleaning and pressing!"

"Try to get it done this afternoon. If you can't, wear them the way they are. Full equipment for both of you."

A short pause, then: "We're busting her?"

"Tell you tonight at eight," Delaney said, enjoying the suspense game as much as anyone.

He had promised his ladies a fine lunch, and put the Ellerbee case from his mind for a few hours while he acted the expansive host. He took them to Prunelle's on East 54th Street, where the women were suitably impressed with the Art Deco decor and burled maple walls.

"On the first day of the new year," Delaney vowed as they finished, "I am going to start my six thousand four hundred and fifty-eighth diet."

"Another of your one-day diets?" Monica said cruelly.

"You like me massive," he told her. "More of me to love."

"Hah!" she said.

Their luncheon took almost two hours, and after, the women declared their intention of checking out the post-Christmas sales in Fifth Avenue stores. Delaney left them outside the restaurant, determined to walk home and work off some of those calories.

The temperature hovered around the freezing mark, but it was a bright, pleasant day with a washed blue sky dotted with puffy clouds. He tramped north on Madison Avenue, marveling at the proliferation of art galleries, antique shops, and boutiques.

It was a long walk, almost thirty blocks, and he was happy to get in the warm brownstone, unlace his shoes, and treat himself to a cigar. He sat heavily in his swivel chair in the study and began plotting the confrontation with Diane Ellerbee.

He would dress somberly with white shirt and black tie. Something like a mortician, he thought, amused. The only prop he'd need, he decided, would be a clipboard holding a heavy sheaf of papers. It meant nothing, of course, but it would impress.

He was confident of his ability to wing it, adjusting his attitude and manner to counter her responses. Never for a moment did he expect her to admit anything; she would deny, deny, deny. But, being a civilian, he could badger her in ways a police officer on duty could not. He would not let her off the hook.

What he needed to do, he determined, was to rattle her from the start, knock her off balance, and keep her confused. She was an intelligent woman with an enormous ego. His best course would be to dent that self-esteem and then keep her disturbed and witless.

He wanted her to say to herself, "Can this be happening to *me?*"

So sure was he of her guilt that he designed her downfall coldly and without mercy. He never questioned his own motives. If Monica had said to him, "What right do you have to do this?" he would have looked at her in astonishment. For it wasn't *his* right; it was society's right—or perhaps God's.

Boone and Jason arrived promptly at eight o'clock, both in full uniform. He called them into the study for a few minutes to give them a quick rundown.

"We're going to take her tonight," he said. "Let me do the talking, but if you think I've missed something, don't be afraid to chime in. And don't be surprised to hear me state suppositions as facts; I want her to believe we've got a lot more than we actually have."

"One thing we haven't got is a warrant," Boone reminded him.

"True," Delaney said, "but we have probable cause. This is not a minor offense she's being charged with, and I think the courts will hold that a warrantless arrest was justified in this case by the gravity of the crime."

He didn't tell them that it was extremely unlikely the case would ever come to trial; they were smart cops and could figure that out for themselves.

"If this thing self-destructs," he told them, "neither of you will suffer. There will be no notations on your records that you participated. I have Deputy Thorsen's word on that. On the other hand, if it goes down as planned, Chief Suarez assures me you'll get something out of it. Any questions? No? Then let's get this show on the road."

They drove over to East 84th in Jason's car. When they stood in the lobby of the townhouse, Delaney was pleased with the way they looked: three big men with the physical presence to command respect. Or to intimidate.

He rang her bell. The intercom clicked on.

"Who is it?"

"Delaney," he said tensely.

"I'm in my office, Mr. Delaney. Please come up to the second floor."

The door lock buzzed. They pushed in and silently climbed the staircase. She was waiting in the hallway, and blinked when she saw the officers in uniform.

"Is this an official visit, Mr. Delaney?" she asked with a tight smile.

"You've already met Sergeant Boone," he said, ignoring her question. "This man is Officer Jason who, incidentally, was on the scene when the homicide was discovered. May we come in?"

She led the way into her office, and once again he admired her carriage: head held high, shoulders back, spine straight. But nothing was stiff; she moved with sinuous grace.

Her hair was up in a braided crown, her face free of makeup, that marvelous translucent complexion aglow. She was wearing an oversize block-check shirt in lavender and black, cinched at the waist with a man's necktie. And below, pants of purple suede, so snug that Delaney wondered if she had to grease her legs to get into them.

She sat regally behind her desk, hands held before her, fingertips touching to form a cage. Delaney pulled up an uncomfortable straight chair to face her directly. The two officers sat behind him in the cretonne-covered armchairs.

All three men had left their overcoats in the car, and Delaney's homburg as well. But he had instructed them to wear their caps and not to remove them indoors. Now they sat with peaks pulled low, as solid and motionless as stone monoliths.

"You say you have discovered something about my husband's death?" Dr. Ellerbee said, voice cool and formal.

With slow deliberation Delaney took a leather spectacle case from his inside jacket pocket, removed his reading glasses, donned the glasses, adjusting the bows carefully. He then looked down at the clipboard on his lap, made a show of flipping over a few pages.

He glanced sharply at the doctor. "Let's start from the beginning," he said in a hard, toneless voice. "For the past year your late husband was having an affair with one of his patients, Joan Yesell. Not only was this a violation of professional ethics, but it was also a betrayal of his marriage vows and a grievous insult to you personally."

He was watching her closely as he spoke, and saw no signs of surprise or horror. But those touching fingers clenched to form a ball of whitened knuckles, and the porcelain complexion blanched.

"You don't—" she began, her voice now dry and cracked.

"The evidence cannot be controverted," Delaney interrupted. He flipped through more pages on his clipboard. "We have the sworn statements of Miss Yesell, her mother, the testimony of an eyewitness who saw the doctor driving away after delivering Yesell to her home on a Friday night. And the clause canceling his patients' outstanding bills in your late husband's will was expressly designed to benefit Miss Yesell. Now do you wish to deny that Doctor Simon was carrying on an illicit relationship?"

"I was not aware of it," she said harshly.

"Ah, but you were. You are an intelligent, perceptive woman. We are certain you were aware of your husband's transgression."

Diane Ellerbee stood abruptly. "I think this meeting is at an end," she said. "Please leave before I—"

Delaney reached out to slap the top of her desk with an open palm. The sharp crack made her jump.

"Sit down, madam!" he thundered. "You are going nowhere without our permission."

She stared at him, blank-faced, and then slowly lowered herself back into her chair.

"Let's get on with it," Delaney said. "We don't want to waste too much time on a tawdry murder." That got to her, he could see, and he peered down at his clipboard, flipping pages with some satisfaction.

"Now then," he said, looking up at her again, "the evidence we have uncovered indicates that you became aware of your husband's affair sometime last year, probably soon after it started. This is supposition on my part, but I would guess you let it continue because you hoped it was just a passing fancy and would soon end."

"I don't have to answer any of your questions," she said.

Delaney showed his big yellow teeth in something approximating a smile. "But I haven't asked any questions, have I? Let me continue. About three weeks prior to his death, your husband came to you, confessed his love for Joan Yesell, and asked for a divorce. There went your hope that his adulterous relationship was a temporary infatuation. Worse, it was a tremendous blow to your self-esteem."

"You're a dreadful man," she whispered.

"That's true," he said, almost happily, "I am. Let me psychoanalyze *you*, doctor, for a few minutes. Turn the tables, so to speak. You are a beautiful and wealthy woman, and all your life you've lived in a cocoon, protected and sheltered from reality. What do you know about a waitress's aching feet or how hard the wife of a poor man works? It's all been peaches and cream, hasn't it? All those relatives dying and leaving you money. A successful career. And best of all, being worshiped by men. You could see it in their eyes and the way they acted. Every man you ever met wanted to jump on your bones."

"Stop it," she said. "Please stop it."

"Never a defeat," he continued relentlessly. "Never even a disappointment. But then your husband comes to you, says Bye-bye, kiddo, I want to leave you to marry another woman. And a quiet, timid, plain, rather dowdy woman at that. It was the worst thing that could possibly happen to you. Because you couldn't handle defeat. Didn't know how— you had no experience. So all you could feel was anger. Your husband's declaration of love for Yesell not only destroyed you, but it destroyed your world."

He paused a moment, expecting a reply. But when she said nothing, he flipped more pages on his clipboard, then looked up at her again.

"All right," he said, "so much for the psychoanalysis, doctor. No charge. But I think it gives us a motive a jury would believe. Now let's talk about the weapon—the ball peen hammer that crushed your husband's skull and put out his eyes. We spent a lot of time on that hammer, Doctor Ellerbee, and, lo and behold, we discovered a ball peen hammer was stolen sometime in October from May's Garage and Service Station in Brewster, where you take your cars. You could have lifted it. It's possible, isn't it? And where do you think that hammer is now? At the bottom of the brook that runs through your land. Which is why we're getting a warrant to drag the stream. And if we find it—what then? Fingerprints and bloodstains, I suppose. You'd be amazed at what the laboratory men can do these days."

She stirred restlessly, moving her body in the chair and turning her head back and forth. She reminded Delaney of one of the great cats he had seen behind bars in the Central Park Zoo—a cheetah, he recalled—whipping its head from side to side, pacing, endlessly pacing, plotting how to get out.

"Not much more now," he said stonily. "You couldn't handle your anger, so you got hold of the hammer and started planning. It had to be on a Friday night, because that's when Joan Yesell came up here, and she and your husband made love on his black leather couch. Right? So, on that stormy night, you didn't drive up early to Brewster at all, did you?"

"I did!" she cried. "I did!"

"Don't jerk me around," he said, tapping his clipboard. "We've got evidence here that you didn't. That instead you stayed in Manhattan, watched the townhouse, waiting for Joan Yesell to arrive. But she was late that night. Your anger was building, building . . . Finally you came in here and murdered your husband. And then smashed his eyes because he had the effrontery to look at another woman."

She stared at him with horrified wonder.

"Why are you doing this to me?" she asked. *"Why?"*

He stood suddenly and slammed a hard fist down on her desk top, a heavy blow that made everyone in the room jump. He leaned far over the desk.

"Why?" he said in a strangled voice, glaring at her. *"Why?* Because you visited my home, you were sweet to my wife, you invited us to your home and fed us. You actually sat down at table with us and acted the bountiful hostess. Then you sent us flowers. The beginning of your downfall—if only you could have known. But throughout you've played me for a fool—a *fool!* And that I can't take. You want to know why? That's why!"

He subsided into his chair, his fury ebbing. She looked at him, bewildered, not understanding. Boone and Jason understood but remained silent.

The silence grew. He gave her time, watching her face working. He guessed what was going through her mind. He could almost see her confidence slowly returning as she reviewed everything he had said. She straightened in her chair, raised a hand to make certain her braids were in place.

"You don't know that I stole a hammer from May's," she said finally, "and you certainly can't prove it."

"That's true," Delaney said, nodding.

"And you can't prove that I stayed in Manhattan that night."

He nodded again.

"You can't even prove I knew about my husband's sleazy little affair," she concluded triumphantly. "So you've got nothing."

He showed his teeth again. "We've got *you,* madam," he said.

She was shaken, expecting to hear a proven indictment. But this great, shaggy bear of a man sat silently, staring at her over his reading glasses.

"Stop calling me 'madam,' " she said petulantly. "If you don't wish to address me as 'Doctor,' then 'Mrs. Ellerbee' will do as well."

He leaned forward. "Why don't we cut out the shit," he said pleasantly, using the crude word deliberately to further unsettle her. "You're going to waltz away from this, smiling bravely. If you don't know it, your lawyers will."

"Well, then," she said, "this has all been an exercise in futility, hasn't it?"

"Not quite. If I had my druthers, you'd be behind bars for ten-to-twenty, eating off tin plates and afraid to pick up the soap in the shower. But if I can't have that, I'll settle for second best." He extended a big hand, fingers spread wide, then slowly clenched them into a rocky fist. "I'm going to crush you, *madam*—just like that."

She looked at him, then looked at the two uniformed officers sitting behind him. They returned her stare.

"Let me tell you what's going to happen to you," Delaney said, hunching forward to rest his clasped hands on the desk. "We're going to make what they call a media event out of this. We're going to arrest you, charging you with the premeditated murder of your husband, Simon Ellerbee. You'll be taken to the nearest precinct house, photographed, and fingerprinted. Then you'll be allowed a phone call to your attorney. While you're waiting for him, you'll be locked in a cage. Won't that be nice? Oh, you'll be out in a few hours, I'm sure—maybe a day at the most. Meanwhile we'll have alerted the newspapers and television stations. It's going to be a circus: *Wife accused in brutal slaying of husband.* The media will love it. Prominent East Side couple. Wealthy, well-known psychiatrists. And the other woman—a patient! Have you ever been photographed wearing a bikini? I'll bet the tabloids get hold of the photo and splash it all over their front pages."

"You wouldn't dare," she gasped, her face suddenly a death's-head.

"Oh, I'd dare a great deal more than that, *madam.* Leaks to the press about your husband's affair. Maybe Joan Yesell can sell her story and make a few bucks—she's entitled."

"I'll sue you!" she screamed. "I'll sue all of you!"

"Be my guest," he said with a frosty smile. "You sue, and you're going to be in the headlines a long time, lady. But meanwhile your career is down the drain. No more kiddie patients for you. And wherever you go, for the rest of your life, people will point a finger and whisper, 'That's the woman they said killed her husband.' You'll never outlive that."

"You're a brute," she shouted at him, quivering with anger. "A brute!"

"A brute, am I? And what do you call someone who hammers in the skull of another human being and then crushes his eyes? I'm a brute but you're not—is that the way your mind works? You didn't really think you were going to get off scot-free, did you? This is an imperfect, unfair world, I admit, but you sin and you pay the price, one way or another. It's payment time for you, doctor."

"I didn't do it!" she howled desperately. "I swear I didn't!"

"You did it," he said, looking at her steadily. "You know it, I know it, these officers know it, the Department knows it. And pretty soon the whole city will. You're going to be a nine-day wonder, Doctor Ellerbee. Maybe they'll even make up rhymes about you—like 'Lizzie Borden took an axe . . .' Won't it be great to be a superstar?"

She moved so swiftly they didn't have time to react. Instead of circling the desk, she launched herself over the top, claws out, going for Delaney's face. He jerked back, his chair went over with a crash, and he dragged her down atop him, hoping his glasses wouldn't break.

Boone and Jason Two pulled her off. She fought them frantically and they slammed her back into the chair behind the desk. Jason stood next to her, a meaty hand clamped on her shoulder.

Delaney climbed awkwardly to his feet. He set the chair upright, examined his reading glasses to make sure they weren't broken, and touched the stinging marks on his cheek. His fingers came away bloody. He pressed his handkerchief to the gouges.

"Anger," he said to the others, nodding. "Uncontrollable. The way she was when she killed her husband. Sergeant Boone, take a look out the window, see if the press is here."

Abner Boone looked down from the window fronting on East 84th Street.

"They're here," he reported. "A lot of guys with cameras and a TV crew."

"Right on schedule," Delaney said quietly. "I should tell you, Mrs. Ellerbee, that because this is a felony arrest, you will be handcuffed."

She sat, huddled and shrunken, head bowed, arms crossed over her breast, holding her elbows. She would not look at him.

"Do you understand what you did?" he asked gently, still pressing a handkerchief to his cheek. "You killed a human being. The man betrayed you, certainly. But was that sufficient reason to take a human life? Sergeant . . ."

Abner Boone stepped close to Diane.

"You have the right to remain silent . . ." he started.

Delaney sat while they took her away. He had no desire to watch from the window. But he saw the flash of photographer's lights and heard the uproar. Deputy Thorsen had delivered.

He waited until the noise and confusion had died away. He was out of it now; let Thorsen and Suarez carry the ball. His job was finished. He had done what they asked him to do, and if the result was less than perfect, they got what they wanted.

He gingerly touched the back of his head. It had smacked the floor when his chair went over, and he suspected he'd have a welt there. He was, he acknowledged, getting a bit long in the tooth for that kind of nonsense.

It wasn't so much that he was physically tired, but the evening had taken a lot out of him. He couldn't summon the energy to rise and tramp home to Monica and the girls. So he tucked his reading glasses away and just sat there, fingers laced across his vest, and brooded.

His first wife, Barbara, had once accused him of acting like God's surrogate on earth. He didn't think that was entirely fair. He had lost his hubris, he was convinced. What drove him now was more a sense of duty. But duty to *what* he could not have said.

Despite those things he had shouted about Diane Ellerbee playing him for a fool, he felt more pity for her than anger. He thought her life had been so structured, so neat and secure, that she had never learned to handle trouble.

But he could continue forever making up excuses. He was a cop, with a cop's bald way of thinking, and the naked fact was that she had killed and had to be punished for it.

He dragged himself to his feet, and, as if it were his own home, made the rounds of doors and windows in the deserted townhouse, making certain they were securely locked.

He stopped suddenly, wondering where the hell his overcoat and homburg were. Probably still in Jason's car, now parked outside the precinct house. But when he went down to the first floor, he found them waiting for him, neatly folded on a marble-topped lobby table. God bless . . .

He pounded home, head down, hands in pockets. He pondered how much to tell Monica of what had happened. Then he decided to tell her everything; he had to explain the jagged scrapes on his face. If it made him seem like a vindictive beast, so be it. He wasn't about to start lying to her now. Besides, she'd *know*.

He looked up suddenly, and beyond the city's glow saw the stars whirling their ascending courses. So small, he thought. All the poor, scrabbling people on earth caught up in a life we never made, breaking ourselves trying to manage.

Philosophers said you could laugh or you could weep. Delaney preferred to think there was a middle ground, an amused struggle in which you recognized the odds and knew you'd never beat them. Which was no reason to stop trying. Las Vegas did all right.

When he came to his brownstone, the lights were on, the Christmas wreath still on the door. And inside was the companionship of a loving woman, a tot of brandy, a good cigar. And later, a warm bed and blessed sleep.

"Thank you, God," he said aloud, and started up the steps.

# 28.

Delaney didn't want the girls to go out on New Year's Eve.

"It's amateur night," he told Monica. "People who haven't had a drink all year suddenly think they've got to get sloshed. Then they throw up on you or get in their cars and commit mayhem. The safest place for all of us is right here, with the door locked."

Wails and tears from Mary and Sylvia.

Finally a compromise was devised: They would have a New Year's Eve party at the brownstone, with Peter and Jeffrey invited. The rug would be rolled up and there would be dancing. Formal dress: The ladies would wear party gowns and the men dinner jackets.

"There I draw the line," Delaney protested. "My tux is in the attic, and probably mildewed. Even if I can find it, I probably won't be able to get into it; I've put on a few ounces, you know."

"No tux, no party," Monica said firmly. "And the girls go out."

So, grumbling, he trudged up to the attic and dug out his tuxedo from a grave of mothballs. It was rusty and wrinkled, but Monica sponged and brushed it. He could wear the jacket unbuttoned, and Monica assured him that with his black, pleated cummerbund in place, no one would know that the top button of his trousers was, by necessity, yawning.

Still grousing, he left the brownstone and marched out to purchase party supplies and food for a light midnight supper. He dragged along a wheeled shopping cart and thought he cut an undignified figure with his cart and black homburg. But he met no one he knew, so that was all right.

He returned home two hours later to find numerous messages waiting

for him. He went into the study to return the calls. He phoned Abner
Boone first.

"How did it go, Sergeant?" he asked.

"Just about the way you told her it would, sir. She's out now, back in
her townhouse."

"A lot of reporters?"

"*And* photographers *and* television crews. She cracked up."

"Cracked up? How do you mean?"

"A crying fit. Close to hysteria."

"Sorry to hear that. I thought she had more spine."

"Well, she just dissolved, and we had our hands full. Fortunately,
when her lawyer showed up, he brought along Doctor Samuelson, and
the doc gave her something that quieted her down. She didn't look so
beautiful when she left."

"No," Delaney said grimly, "and her husband didn't look so beautiful on the floor of his office. Thank you for all your help, Sergeant, and
please convey my thanks to Jason and all the others."

"I'll do that, sir, and a Happy New Year."

"Thank you. And to you and Rebecca. Give her our love."

"Will do. I hope we get a chance to work together again."

"I wouldn't be a bit surprised," Delaney said.

His next call was to First Deputy Commissioner Ivar Thorsen, who
sounded very ebullient and maybe a wee bit smashed.

"Everything's coming up roses, Edward," he reported exuberantly.
"We didn't make the first editions this morning, but we'll be in the
afternoon papers. Four TV news programs so far, and more to come.
The phone is ringing off the hook with calls from out-of-town papers
and news magazines. It looks like the press thinks we've solved the
case."

"That's what you wanted, isn't it?"

"Oh, hell, yes! The Commish is grinning like a Cheshire cat, and even
the Chief of Operations has congratulated Suarez. I think Riordan
knows he's lost. It looks good for Suarez to get the permanent appointment."

"Glad to hear it; I like the man. Ivar, Happy New Year to you and
yours."

"Same to you, Edward. Give Monica a kiss for me. You'll be getting
your case of Glenfiddich, but that doesn't begin to express my gratitude."

"All right then," Delaney said, "send two cases."

They hung up laughing.

On impulse, he phoned Dr. Samuelson. He was unable to reach him at his apartment or office. Thinking Samuelson might still be attending Diane Ellerbee, he called her number. He was prepared to hang up immediately if she answered, but he got a busy signal.

He phoned repeatedly for almost a half-hour, but couldn't get through. He thought perhaps Diane had taken the phone off the hook, or perhaps she was being bedeviled by calls from the media. But finally his call was answered.

"Yes? Who is this?"

He recognized the high-pitched, squeaky voice.

"Doctor Samuelson? Edward X. Delaney here."

"Ah."

"How is Doctor Ellerbee?"

"At the moment she is sleeping. I prescribed something. She is destroyed by this."

"I can imagine. Doctor, I have one question for you. You can answer or tell me to go to hell. Did you know, or guess, what she did?"

"Go to hell," the little man said and hung up.

The four Delaneys had an early pickup dinner, mostly leftovers, and then finished decorating the living room, rolled up the rug, and swept and waxed the bare floor. They prepared the midnight supper. Then they all went upstairs to dress.

"Shaving is murder," Delaney said to Monica in their bathroom. "She got me good."

"Want me to put on bandages or tape?"

"No, I'll leave them open to the air. I've been dabbing on hydrogen peroxide. They'll heal okay. Did you tell the girls what happened?"

"I just said you had assisted in the arrest of a mugger and had been attacked. They seemed satisfied with that."

"Good. When are the boys arriving?"

"They promised to be here by nine."

"What are you going to wear?"

"What would you like me to wear?" she asked coquettishly.

"The short black silk with no back and all the fringe," he said immediately. "It makes you look like a flapper from the twenties."

"So shall it be," she said, touching his cheek softly. "My poor wounded hero."

While they were dressing, she said, not looking at him, "You're absolutely certain she did it, Edward?"

"Absolutely. But you're not?"

"It's so hard to believe—that lovely, intelligent, talented woman."

"Loeb and Leopold were geniuses. There's no contradiction between intelligence and an urge to kill."

"Well, if she's guilty, as you say, I still don't understand why she's not going to be tried for it."

"The law," he said shortly. "We just don't have enough that'll stand up in court. But she'll pay."

"You think that's enough?" Monica said doubtfully.

"It's a compromise," he admitted. "I agree with you; a long prison term would have been more fitting. But since that was impossible, I went for what I could get. We all settle, don't we? One way or another. Who gets what they dream? We all go stumbling along, hoping for the best but knowing we're going to have to live with confusion, sometimes winning, sometimes cutting a deal, occasionally just being defeated. It's a mess, no doubt about it, but it's the price we pay for being alive. I like to think the pluses outnumber the minuses. They do tonight. You look beautiful!"

Peter and Jeffrey arrived promptly at nine o'clock, bringing along a bottle of Dom Perignon, which everyone agreed would not be opened until the stroke of midnight. Meanwhile, there were six bottles of Delaney's Korbel brut, and the party got off to a noisy, laughing start.

It took three glasses of champagne before Delaney finally broke down and consented to dance with his wife and stepdaughters. He shuffled cautiously around the floor with all the grace of a gorilla on stilts, and after one dance with each of the ladies was allowed (Allowed? Urged!) to retire to the sidelines where he stood beaming, watching the festivities and making certain glasses were filled.

At 11:30, dancing was temporarily halted while supper was served. There was caviar with chopped onions, grated hard-boiled eggs, sour cream, capers, melba toast, quarters of fresh lemon—all on artfully contrived beds of Bibb lettuce.

Monica and Delaney balanced their plates on their laps, but the young people insisted on sprawling on the floor. The television set was turned on so they could watch the mob scene in Times Square.

At about ten minutes to twelve the phone rang. Monica and Delaney looked at each other.

"Now who the hell can that be?" he growled, set his plate aside, and rose heavily to his feet. He went into the study and closed the door.

"Mr. Delaney, this is Detective Brian Estrella. Sorry to bother you at this hour, sir, but something came up I thought you should know about as soon as possible."

"Oh?" Delaney said. "What's that?"

"Well, right now I'm in Sylvia Otherton's apartment and we've been working on the Ouija board. You read about that in my previous reports, didn't you, sir?"

"Oh, yes," Delaney said, rolling his eyes upward. "I read about the Ouija board."

"Well, the first question we asked, weeks ago, was who killed him. And the board spelled out 'Blind.' B-L-I-N-D. Then, the second time, we asked if it was a stranger who killed him, and the board spelled out 'Ni,' N-I."

"Yes, I recall," Delaney said patiently. "Very interesting. But what does it mean?"

"Well, get this, sir . . ." Estrella said. "Tonight we asked the spirit of Simon Ellerbee whether it was a man or a woman who killed him, and the Ouija board spelled out 'Wiman.' W-I-M-A-N. Now that didn't make much sense at first. But then I realized this board has a slight glitch and is pointing to 'I' when it means 'O.' If you follow that, you'll see that the killer was blond, not blind. And the board meant to say 'No' instead of 'Ni' when we asked if the murderer was a stranger. And the final answer should have been 'Woman' instead of 'Wiman.' So as I see it, sir, the person we're looking for is a blond woman who was not a stranger to the victim."

"Thank you very much," Delaney said gravely.